Black Run

D. L. Marshall was born and raised in Halifax, West Yorkshire. Influenced by the dark industrial architecture, steep wooded valleys, and bleak Pennine moors, he writes thrillers tinged with horror, exploring the impact of geography and isolation. In 2016 he pitched at Bloody Scotland. In 2018 he won a Northern Writers' Award for his thriller novel *Anthrax Island*.

Also by D. L. Marshall

The John Tyler series

Anthrax Island
Black Run

BLACK RUN

D. L. MARSHALL

Don't go overboard

D. Marshall

1O CANELO

First published in the United Kingdom in 2021 by

Canelo
Unit 9, 5th Floor
Cargo Works, 1–2 Hatfields
London, SE1 9PG
United Kingdom

A CIP catalogue record for this book is available from the British Library.

Print ISBN 978 1 80032 277 6
Ebook ISBN 978 1 80032 276 9

Look for more great books at www.canelo.co

Printed and bound in Great Britain by Clays Ltd, Elcograf S.p.A.

For G and A

Chapter One

There was near silence as I switched off the ignition, just the ticking of the big V8 engine as it cooled, the soft patter of Atlantic sleet on the windscreen, and the muffled thuds coming from the boot.

'If you don't knock it off, I'll drive us into the sea.'

The thuds stopped.

I coughed, winced, angled up out of the seat and crept my fingers under my hoody. They came away wet so I already had my answer, but I held them up to the moonlight anyway. Sticky blood; the wound in my side was worse than I'd thought. I wiped my fingers on my jeans then drummed them on the worn-shiny steering wheel, scanning the dim road through the steam rising from the bonnet. My left hand flexed on the gear stick, clenching and unclenching my fingers, wincing with every click but refusing to let my damaged hand seize up. Not now, not when I still needed it. Not when I was so close to the end.

I should have been sat in a ride with dubious provenance, something still filled with someone else's CDs and sunglasses and sweet wrappers, the worn banknotes I'd handed over the only papers denoting ownership – at least until it was burned out. Unfortunately problems in the Alps meant I'd gone with plan B, hence sitting in my own Audi RS4 estate, albeit sporting false plates.

I looked at a scrunched-up cardboard tablet packet in the passenger footwell, a tear forced itself up into the corner of one eye. I blinked it back down, pushing the memories with it, down to join the others, at least until this was over.

Across the empty square, La Rochelle's Cathédrale Saint-Louis finished marking two a.m., its chimes rolling around the old buildings of the Place de Verdun. The Alps to the Atlantic coast in under eight hours, my hands buzzed, legs ached. I brushed hair from my clammy forehead, scratching at a tingling scar through my eyebrow. There was time enough to finish this before the meet. I closed my eyes, inhaled deeply, let the pattering sleet on the windscreen and distant gulls briefly carry me away.

The thudding in the boot started up again, but it was outdone by the sound of an approaching engine, I opened my eyes to see headlights shining on the wet cobbles and shops in front: a car approaching on the narrow road behind me. I slid down as it cruised past, leaning over into the passenger seat. When it turned at the end of the road I looked over the dash, catching police markings reflecting the dim streetlights. Thanks to my ageing Audi's unassuming appearance, its dull salesman road-furniture disguise, I hadn't warranted any attention.

I prayed the flashers didn't light up as I followed the cop's progress, watching as it crawled alongside the Place de Verdun. She didn't look back my way, I saw a ponytail flick as her attention was drawn to the far side of the square. I looked out of my side window, over the narrow road I'd parked on. Across the empty bike racks, the bony trees of the old town square webbed with twinkling Christmas lights, all the way to the cathedral.

Beneath its decorations a big black BMW had just been illuminated by the cop's headlights, the same big black BMW that'd been on my tail since I'd filled the car up outside Poitiers. I'd hit the outskirts of La Rochelle with the Beemer's headlights still in my rear-view mirror, so instead of heading straight to the port and my rendezvous I'd diverted here into the old town.

The police car slowed to inspect the BMW. A bored copper on night patrol wondering why a car full of people was parked up here, away from the bars and clubs – not that they were open at this time in December. I could picture her running the plates. She'd get fuck-all from them: they were Swiss and, like mine, probably false.

The police car moved on, darkness again beneath the cathedral. I ran a hand across my jaw, tracing the scars beneath the stubble, waiting for my eyes to readjust. Dim orange pinpricks moved inside the car, occasionally glowing brighter as the car's occupants dragged on their cigs.

In the cop's headlights I'd seen the BMW properly for the first time. Undoubtedly the same one that we'd seen in the ski resort, the stance fat, low, aggressive. Top-of-the-line M5. It had two extra cylinders and maybe a hundred more horsepower than my Audi, but the extra weight and all that power going to the rear wheels on these icy cobbles would make things interesting for them.

One cig winked out. Less than a minute later another fired out of a window to join hundreds more in the gutter. A silent signal: they were ready.

The G28 marksman rifle on the back seat was out of ammo, as was the MP5 submachine gun in the footwell. I hummed the Band Aid tune as I reached over into the glovebox, removed a Heckler & Koch VP70 pistol, slowly unscrewed the suppressor from the modified barrel, inserted a full magazine. I cocked it and stuck it between my thighs, handle upwards. Now I was ready, too.

The red digits on the dash winked to 02:03.

The BMW was illuminated a second time as another car approached, this time from behind. Blue flashing lights strobed the square: it was the same police car, she'd done a circuit around the block and returned, cruising to a halt a few metres off the Beemer's rear bumper. Obviously her plate check hadn't revealed anything but she'd decided to speak to them anyway. Good cop, big mistake; I could see what she couldn't. Multiple heads moving inside, arms reaching.

'Stay in the car,' I muttered. 'Drive away.'

She wouldn't. I flicked the window down and reached for my pistol.

Leaving the flashers on, the cop got out of her car, adjusted her hat, strode forward. Her bleeping and crackling radio cut through the icy air. The rear windows were down on the black car, shadows moving inside. Even at this distance I could see the fairy lights glinting off dark steel.

The crack of the gunshot echoed around the square. The cop dropped to the ground, the BMW's driver-side window exploded. I squeezed the trigger again, punching a hole somewhere in the car's bodywork. No more pissing around, time for the conclusion. As if to confirm their understanding of the new rules a flash replied, and chunks of pavement sprayed my car. The cop rolled away, scrabbling at her holster, then – realising she was in the middle of a gunfight – did the wise thing and crawled back to her car. A bullet punched through my rear door, another ricocheted off the bonnet.

Time to leave.

I twisted the key. The starter spun, the V8 caught. She roared angrily at being denied a rest. The BMW's headlights flared in response, cutting a path through the sleet. A burst of automatic gunfire tore up the night but missed me entirely as I floored the loud pedal. At the end of the street I turned left, along the main road.

Up into second, metallic snarls bouncing around the medieval walls. Too tight even for third gear, the revs screamed, past the ancient arcades that lined the streets of La Rochelle's old town. 450 horsepower and 0–60 in four seconds might be disgusting in a car with suit hangers in the back, but it meant I was out onto the wider road past the Natural History Museum, on to the next junction, before the lights appeared in my rear-view mirror.

They grew as I slammed the brakes – skidding to avoid a stupid cat – then took a right, accelerating hard again, into third gear. I hit eighty on the short stretch before nailing the clutch, toe on the brakes, side of my foot blipping the accelerator as I downshifted to turn again, heading right back into the old town.

My car was nimble and I had four-wheel drive on my side which meant the big BMW lost time on the corners, but its brute force caught up again on the straights. I backed off the accelerator and let it; losing them hadn't worked, it was time to end this.

We sped down the narrow street, the shopfronts flashing past getting shinier and more welcoming the closer we got to the centre. At an open corner with a memorial of some kind I turned right, clipping a Christmas tree and sending it spinning towards a terrified couple pressed hard into a doorway.

The Audi's V8 engine wailed, the Beemer's V10 roared, no doubt half the inhabitants of La Rochelle were out of bed and at their windows.

I braked, they tried to tap my bumper as I slowed to turn left, but too late as I was pulling away again. A fragment of limestone exploded from a column in front, bouncing over the bonnet and up the window as I sped past. Cracks of automatic gunfire chased me up the street and back out onto the square we'd started from, past the cop still ducking and shouting frantically into her radio, past the cathedral, onward towards the harbour.

At the next junction I was hard on the brakes, flicking off the lights, using every inch of road as I turned left down a side street then immediately right, losing some paint on a stone column as I turned *into* one of the arched pedestrian shopping arcades. I kept going straight, parallel to the street I'd been travelling on. The BMW howled onwards, they'd missed me turning.

I could see its lights flashing between archways in the side mirror, then it shot past on my right. It was a Euro-spec motor, steering wheel on the left, so the driver and I got a decent look at each other between blinking archways as they overtook me. Her hair flapped in the glassless door, jaw locked in determination. The expression turned to surprise as her brain finally caught up with her eyes, she tapped her brakes just as we hit the next junction, but it was too late. I shot out of the arcade half a second later, swinging back into the main road directly behind them.

Places switched, hunter hunted. I flicked my headlights back on as she accelerated, deep exhaust reverberating in the narrow street.

A flash from one of the rear windows, but the gunshots were drowned out by the enraged engines. The bullets went wide, ricocheting off columns and walls, punching through shop windows. I shifted into third and buried the accelerator, surging after the BMW. She was a good driver and had brute force on her side, but my little estate had a lot more going for it. I shunted the bumper, bouncing her tyre against the kerb. I ground the pedal again, switched my lights to full beam, forcing her onwards, forcing her to accelerate.

She was going far too fast to turn, and I knew a ninety-degree corner was inbound. I waited as long as I dared then stood on the brakes and let her find out the hard way.

Her brake lights flared, the briefest squeal of tyres on slick cobbles. A heartbeat later there was a crunch as the whole car lifted in front of me. She'd caught the rear side on a wall; she might have been a good driver but you can't fuck with physics. I flicked right, tyres protesting, Quattro four-wheel drive sorting out the corner for me and pouncing through the gap between the BMW's bonnet and a patisserie.

Another gunshot from behind, a flash in the rear-view mirror, their crash hadn't been the fatal blow I'd hoped for. The headlights lurched as they reversed then came after me again, *damn* she was good. At the end of the lane I turned towards the glowing lights of the old port, under the huge clock tower at the head of the marina, dripping with glimmering plastic icicles. The headlights in my mirror blazed again as the BMW limped to catch up. I turned away from the clock tower and accelerated hard down the harbour road. The lights strung between the trees reflected off shiny yachts on my left, in front the huge defensive tower at the mouth of the old harbour was growing rapidly. Next to it the gateway through the thick city walls looked far too narrow for a car. I glanced in the mirror: the BMW still hadn't made the turn at the head of the marina, by the clock tower behind me.

I yanked the wheel right, up a curb, brushing another Christmas tree, through the lowered bollards into a pedestrianised zone. Threading the car down a tight side street stacked with cafes I turned again, completing a loop, pointing back at the twinkling lights of the marina. Hard on the brakes, off with the headlights, I slid to a stop and wound down all the windows.

Sirens echoed around the old town, impossible to judge distance as they chased through the medieval streets. The boats in front lit up, now the BMW was tearing fearlessly down the harbour road, following the route I'd taken seconds before.

I floored the accelerator, my car leapt from the side alley as the Beemer flashed past, metres from my bumper. I caught up almost instantly, shunting their back end, smashing their rear lights, but the bigger car refused to be bullied. I pulled right and floored it again, going for the overtake. Engines screaming, we raced for the tower and that tiny gateway in the city walls that I knew was just wide enough for one car. She shunted me, my front wheels found grip and fought back. She pulled over to try to block me out, edging me further right, forcing me onwards, towards that thick wall and a very messy death.

One of the passengers leaned out of a rear window with a submachine gun. No seatbelt on and we were doing near eighty, which, if you ask me, is just asking for trouble on wet cobbles.

Keeping the wheel straight with one hand, I grabbed the pistol with my left and leaned over the passenger seat, squeezing the trigger three times, braking hard.

The BMW's rear right tyre disintegrated, flapping at the cobbles. The left maintained a decent grip, dragging the car round. The driver corrected, the car slewed the other way, heading straight for the cast iron bollards along the harbour wall. The heavy car oversteered again, the back end finally broke all pretence of traction, and began to slide. The driver did her best but as she turned into the skid the rear wheel tapped a bollard, and at that speed it's all that was required.

The car flipped onto its back in mid-air above the harbour, sailing upside down towards the sea but not managing to make it that far as it slammed into the super-structure of the last yacht in the row. Glass smashed, metal crunched, fibreglass splintered, the yacht tilted, grinding against the marina wall. I accelerated as the BMW slipped away in my rear-view mirror, dropping into the black.

Further behind, blue lights pulsed across the clock tower, sirens closing in. Keeping the speed up and the headlights off I screamed through the gateway in the town walls, into the car park overlooking the beach. Surprisingly, even at this time of year there were a few cars lined up in the bays. Further to the right the fairy-tale Tower of the Lantern was glowing blue as more police descended on the harbour.

I tucked into a spot between a Citroën and a Range Rover and turned the key, sliding down, still gripping my pistol. With my other hand I grabbed my phone from the door pocket, swiping to the fitness app. It showed a heightened heartbeat, a zigzag line panicking across the screen.

A distinctive French siren wailed past. They'd seal off the area soon. I dropped the phone and gun on the passenger seat, waited five seconds, turned the engine back on, reversing out of the space. Behind me flashing lights spilled through the city walls, the harbour aglow with the entire Commissariat de Police. I took the northern exit from the car park, keeping to the speed limit along the road that cut through the Parc Alcide d'Orbigny, heading west, hugging the coast all the way out to the industrial warehouses and boatyards of La Pallice.

At least the thudding from the boot had stopped.

Chapter Two

I'd left the Vieux Port de La Rochelle a couple of kilometres behind me, its marina, sirens, and blue flashing lights now hidden by the warehouses and repair yards of La Pallice. France's only Atlantic deepwater port is well used to noise throughout the night, difference here is the flashing lights strobing the buildings are orange, the sirens those of reversing trucks, the shouting from dock workers. Crashing containers loading and unloading, big diesels revving, trucks and container ships, arguments echoing around back alleys at all hours.

I turned away from the noisy waterfront, crawling alongside an enormous corrugated-metal warehouse for what seemed like miles, hands shaking on the steering wheel, an adrenaline comedown. When I finally reached the far end, I found a barrier straddling an entrance to an industrial estate. I pulled up to it slowly, watching a shadow detach itself from those of the warehouse. It pulled up a collar and swung open the gate. I rolled through and stopped, watching in my rear-view mirror as the man closed the gate behind me and secured it. I grabbed my pistol from the passenger seat, angling up to push it into the front of my jeans. My eyes were fixed on the mirror, on the man jogging to the car. I pulled my hoody down over the gun, pressed the central locking button, he pulled open the door and climbed into the passenger seat.

The glow from the interior light briefly lit up a wind-burnt face like an eroded headland, dark eyes and a darker expression. Long hair fell from beneath a flat cap, merging with a beard sprouting out from the upturned collar of a peacoat. The light dimmed, I shuffled in my seat again and pulled away, driving past derelict industrial buildings.

'Mornin' Blofeld, yer car break down or somethin'?' He pronounced it 'kaahh', thirty-odd years since he'd left Cape Cod and Miller's accent hadn't softened a cent.

I looked at the clock. I was three minutes late. 'Had to make sure I wasn't followed.'

'Lights off,' he grunted, gesturing to the right.

I switched them off and turned, following his waving hand as the buildings thinned, revealing a wide, open space. No street lighting here, the Moon the only navigation aid. It glowed off a monumental slab of windowless black concrete at the end of the loading area, a huge, evil-looking fortress of brutalism.

'Head for the far corner,' he pointed.

I followed his finger. He leaned over and flashed my headlights twice, in the shadows beneath the building a torch winked in response.

I kept the revs low, crawling across the tarmac. As we drew closer to the ominous structure I could make out an opening at the base, the only break in the feature-less monolith. Steel doors had been pulled aside for us, I pressed on through, driving straight into the old Nazi submarine pens.

The concrete wall was thicker than the length of my car and led down into a low tunnel. The doors were already closing behind, dim moonlight snuffed out. Down the short ramp, Miller gestured left along a wide passageway.

'Darker than a tomb in here, put your lights on. Side-lights only, mind. Don't want my crew blinded.'

I switched them back on, the dim beams illuminated green and black algae-crusted walls. Empty light fittings were rusted in place along the low ceiling, their trailing wires brushing the roof as we crept deeper into the darkness.

'There's no other boats?'

He shook his head. 'Place is off limits. Storage for the French Navy officially, but it's a deathtrap.'

'Reassuring.' Chunks of concrete were missing from the walls here and there, revealing corroded steel reinforcement bars, snapped and bent out like winter branches where trucks and forklifts had been careless in days gone by. Brown stains ran from the wounds, mixing with God-knows-what on the dank floor. Seaweed and decay hung in what was likely the original 1940s air, I could almost hear the klaxons, the angry shouting, smell the diesel and sweat, fear and fury. A broken, rotting, disused temple to Nazism was a fitting place to end this job.

The rumbling exhaust bounced between the walls in the enclosed space, rising and falling as we passed openings through to the deepwater sub pens themselves.

'You think you coulda picked a louder car?' He pointed over to the right. 'This one.'

I pulled through the opening into a soaring cathedral of concrete, edging along a narrow jetty with nothing but deep black sea on my right. A health and safety nightmare, there was barely enough room to drive on the greasy platform. As I crept along, my dim bulbs picked out rusting gantries hanging from the walls and discarded equipment dangling overhead, swinging into darkness.

A huge shadow loomed in front; the stern of a ship rising above the jetty, blocking the view out to the open sea. Sickly yellow work lamps lit the low deck and squat superstructure at the stern, oily davits holding a couple of dilapidated lifeboats that I prayed we wouldn't have to use. The light from the deck spots spilled across the grimy concrete quay, ending on a stack of rotting pallets blocking the way.

I stopped alongside the brown-stained steel plates of the hull, straining my eyes down the length of the small cargo ship. It was a relic itself, a perfect match for these sub pens. I killed the engine, what light there was on the dock died, just the anaemic work lamps and a few jerking torch beams as crew members moved around up on the stern. A shape stepped out from behind the crates in front, striding towards the car. Even in the flickering lights it was impossible to mistake the silhouette of his Kalashnikov rifle.

Chapter Three

With a beam of ten metres and just sixty metres length, the forward two thirds of it flat-decked with nothing but a couple of cranes jutting above the railings, the *Tiburon* was an ungainly workhorse. Captain Miller had described her as the *Millennium Falcon* of the Med which, now I saw her, I presumed to mean she was a pile of shit and often broke down. Miller had been adamant it was a compliment, something to do with her under-the-radar transport capabilities and impressive turn of speed when the mood took her.

Until proven otherwise I was sticking with my original presumption, though tentatively hoped the dilapidation was a façade. It was almost impossible to tell what colour she was supposed to be, not only because of the dim lights in the black sub pens, but also thanks to layers of multi-coloured paint in various stages of peeling from the hull and squat superstructure.

Patches around the hawseholes were scuffed down to the original colour of *fehgrau*, or squirrel grey, betraying the ship's true origins: the colour of the Volksmarine – the old East German Navy. Miller had told me she was an ex-light transport from the good old days of the Cold War, launched from the slipways of Rostock in the age of Ziggy Stardust.

A limp flag trailed threads down the stern, squares and stars of red, white and blue. Scabby white lettering across the rusty transom confirmed the *Tiburon* was registered in Panama, but I doubted she'd ever seen the place. To be honest, I wasn't convinced she'd make it halfway.

'Okay Blofeld, your henchmen are already aboard.' Captain Miller was reaching for the door handle. 'We cast off immediately.'

I climbed out, adjusting the pistol in my waistband, relieved to be able to stretch my legs. Wary of the menacing silhouette with the Kalashnikov I reached up, ran my fingers over the hull of Miller's ship, then looked at them, rubbing my fingers together. It was real rust all right. She certainly matched her captain, neither had aged particularly gracefully. Creaking and shifting in the light swell washing in from the harbour, she looked like she could tear a weld any minute.

'Don't you worry about her, she'll deliver,' said Miller, reading my mind. He gestured to the crew member, who stepped forward, brandishing his rifle, staring at me. 'It's cash up front.'

'That wasn't our agreement.'

'It's not that I don't trust you,' he said, throwing a thumb over his shoulder at his mate. 'It's my crew doesn't trust you.' The shadow behind him pointed the AK vaguely in my direction.

'Half now, as agreed.' I could feel my pistol beneath my T-shirt. 'Bank transfer when we dock.'

'I've known you too long, Blofeld. Trouble follows you around. What if you don't make it that far? What if you slip on the stairs or fall overboard? Anything can happen at sea, then what's in it for these hardworking sailors?'

'It's a dangerous business.' I patted the hull of the ship and wiped my hand on my jeans. 'I'll rest well knowing you're working so hard to keep me safe.'

I opened the rear door, moved my rifle out of the way. The AK twitched, I reached in and pulled out a backpack. I opened the flap at the top to show him the stacks of euro notes. 'Half now, as agreed,' I repeated.

Miller narrowed his eyes. He could never resist a punt, but he was right, he'd known me too long – too long to think I'd budge or be intimidated. It was all for show, he wanted to look like he'd at least tried.

He looked inside the bag then sighed. 'We're outta here in five. We discussed cargo?' He pointed at my car's boot.

I grabbed my Barbour motorbike jacket off the rear seat, swung the door shut, and blipped the key to lock it. 'Load the whole car.'

He frowned, removed a pack of Lucky Strikes from his grubby shirt pocket and fished in his combat pants for a light. One appeared by his face, held in the muscular arm of the crew member behind him, who looked from me to the car and lowered his AK-47.

'Hey Katanga,' said Miller, looking over his shoulder and taking a long drag. 'Load the car, he says.'

Katanga slung his rifle over his shoulder, took a cigarette from Miller, and laughed. 'Impossible.' He pronounced it the French way, sparking up his cig and pointed it at my car. 'Nic says the police are looking for a grey station wagon. Are those bullet holes?' He rolled his vowels round in a heavy francophone accent that I recognised from my time in the Congo.

Miller shook his head slowly. 'I don't wanna know.'

I sat the backpack of money on the car roof and pulled on my jacket, wincing as it brushed my ribs. 'Told you I'd be coming in hot. I had to make sure I wasn't followed.'

Miller looked at his mate. 'Fetch a gallon of fuel and a couple of flares.'

I shook my head. 'The car *is* the cargo, it comes with us.'

There was a scrape on the ground, I turned to see another big guy ambling up behind me, another rifle slung over a shoulder. The man who'd opened the sub-pen doors for us.

'Dusty Bin, how long's it been?'

He gave a slight nod of greeting. 'Never long enough.' Difficult to tell if he was joking, but I suspected not.

Miller shouted past me. 'Poubelle, tell this chowdahead why I don't want his car on my boat.'

He shone his torch over the Audi. 'Shame to burn it out.'

'That's gotta be a ten-ton crane,' I said, nodding towards the big crane at the bow of the *Tiburon*.

'Fifteen.' Poubelle clicked off his torch and cupped his hands against the windows, frowning at a sound from the boot.

'So the car's less than two tons.'

'It is,' he said, standing up straight, 'but the cargo hatches are only four metres square.'

Just over a week ago when we'd sat at the back of a dirty bar in Santander, Miller had told me his ship was big enough to carry anything I could bring by road. I reminded him of that.

'Fuckin' smartass,' he said.

'Okay, so it won't go in the hold. You'll have to strap it to the deck.'

Katanga laughed again.

'Fast passage to England,' Miller said. 'So we're running empty. Minimum ballast, nothing in the hold. Katanga, tell him what happens if you head out into the Bay of Biscay in winter with an empty hold and two tons strapped up on deck.'

Katanga grinned, flicking ash on the bonnet.

'Katanga,' I replied, grabbing the bag of cash off the roof, 'tell Captain Miller what happens when he slinks back to Marseille with no money to pay his creditors. Tell him specifically what'll happen to his kneecaps.'

'Storm's coming in.' He blew smoke and coughed, thumping his chest. 'Those euro notes ain't waterproof, they won't be worth shit if we capsize.'

'Then we're done.' I pulled out my car keys, turning to Poubelle. 'I'd get a job on another boat if I were you. The French Mediterranean fleet might be taking an interest in the *Tiburon*.'

Katanga stopped grinning. I yawned, reaching my arms out, my hoody riding up just enough to show the grip of the pistol in my jeans.

'I'm not getting on that deathtrap without my car,' I continued, pulling the bag of cash close to my chest and raising my voice. 'And if I don't get on board, none of you get paid.'

Miller glared. 'I let you off the full payment, but don't push your luck.' He held my eyes, we stared at each other for long seconds before he finally held his arms up in surrender. 'Seb!' he bellowed. 'Take on ballast.' He glared again, then shoved me out of the way. 'Poubelle, get the crane going!' He pointed at my car. 'You've got ten minutes to get this piece of shit lashed down.'

Chapter Four

Village of Château des Aigles, Haute Savoie, French Alps
Two weeks previously

A shadow fell over the table, blocking the last of the afternoon sun. The waitress deposited a glass of water and a hot chocolate with a smile, I returned it over the top of a dog-eared paperback, folded back on itself at the spine. My smile was entirely for her, not the mud in the cup – though unlike coffee it was at least mostly drinkable. Sadly there are very few places worth ordering tea outside the UK, probably the worst thing about being an international security contractor. I'd rank it higher than the incoming bullets.

She politely tried not to look at the ugly scar through my eyebrow and the myriad smaller wounds as she took away my plate, but her smile dropped as soon as she turned. The mirror on the wall had revealed her distaste at battle lines drawn too deeply to disappear after one afternoon in a cafe.

I put the book down, reached into my coat, pulled out a crumpled packet. The smudged label said Ciprofloxacin – a super-antibiotic used to treat anthrax exposure, among other things – but the packet was crammed with three other strips of tablets and capsules. I popped out a couple of each, lined them up on the table, then emptied a pack of the antibiotic granules into the water.

Outside the snow had started up again, great fat flakes that whirled and stuck to the full-length windows along one long side, slowly sliding down. I watched them racing. None made it very far thanks to the heat radiating from the huge Sixties-style fire, hanging from the ceiling like a prop from an Austin Powers film set. In the corner of my eye I saw the waitress start walking back towards me, I scooped up the pills and swallowed them with the bitter-tasting water, but she diverted to the fire to throw another log on. I pulled my eyes away from her and picked up the book.

My fingers ached from holding it at an odd angle, the result of a broken finger on my left hand a couple of weeks ago. I'd taken the splint off early but hoped it wouldn't impede anything when it was needed. I switched the book into my right hand, trusting my weakened left with a speculoos biscuit instead. It was dunked and inhaled in one, while I tried again to digest the paragraph.

The book was in its original language, and I'd lied to Holderness when I'd told him my French was up to scratch. I'd not spoken it in anger for a while, though thanks to the week or so I'd spent here it was slowly returning. I wished it'd hurry up. Like so many of the skills I'd acquired over the years, it was buried deep and, if prior form was anything to go by, would resurface too late to be of real advantage. Such was the nature of these rush jobs.

I turned the page and mouthed the words silently, one eye on the book and the other constantly monitoring my surroundings. The English couple one table over were looking at me, the man opened his mouth, I made a show of looking down.

'Maigret?' He'd decided to speak anyway, what sort of Englishman was this that couldn't pick up on the subtle gestures broadcasting that I wanted to be left alone?

I put the book down, looked up and sighed. '*Oui, j'adore les livres mystères.*' I love mystery books.

'Oh sorry, I thought you were English for some reason.'

I shrugged. '*Désolé monsieur, je regrette de ne parler anglais.*' I gave him a curt smile and lifted the book.

A group walked past the window. I didn't look up, instead watching the skewed reflections in the polished domed top of the fireplace: three distorted men walking along the snow-covered pavement in the direction of the village square. *Could be...* I turned casually, looking at the mirrored wall behind the counter. Twenty-somethings kitted out in snowboarding gear. Not interested.

One of my eyes went back to the book.

I'd finally finished the page, turning the book over when a burst of orange flashed past outside. A trio in fancy matching Moncler ski jackets, the straggly-haired guy in the middle flanked by two obvious skinhead toughs carrying skis over their shoulders.

I watched them cross the road, waiting until they'd passed the door, then gulped a mouthful of melted marsh-mallows off the top of the hot chocolate, stood, slid the book into my coat pocket.

Outside a fourth orange jacket walked past, his hat straining to cover his enormous head. The man-mountain always hung back to follow from a distance, but was impossible to miss in his matching jacket. I left a twenty-euro note on the table and a smile with the English couple, walking towards the doors, pulling on my coat.

The snow-lined street was darkening, flurries swirling in the cold wind. I tugged my hat lower and pushed through the doors, following the men towards the crowds of the village square. I flinched as a high-revving engine started up to cheers and rounds of applause ahead. Among the tourists, swirling like the snowflakes, the orange ski jackets were easy to see. Like ridiculous Bond-villain uniforms, they couldn't be more conspicuous if they tried. *Complacency.*

The complacency of money, of power, of big hard bastards with guns on either side of you. A complacency fostered by several years of pandering to right-wing populism, stoking up fear, resentment. A complacency born of believing themselves superior, that their view wasn't far off the majority view. I was here to teach them otherwise.

The jackets pushed their way through the crowds, leaving people tutting in their wake. The guy on the right didn't usually ski with them but was lugging a set of skis regardless: the target never carried his own. I thought that seemed pretty stupid, slowing your bodyguards down by making them carry your shit, but there was that complacency again.

In front of a huge Christmas tree on the far side of the square, a nutter was throwing a chainsaw up in the air to whoops of terror and delight from the crowd. Ice chips sprayed as he carved a block of ice into what I guessed by the ears would end up being Mickey Mouse, but at the moment looked uncannily like a giant cock and balls. Festive family fun.

The men took a right, behind the Christmas tree. I glanced across the square, at another big guy leaning on his skis outside a toy shop, eying the crowds. He saw me, picked up his skis, shuffling off, disappearing behind the tree in the same direction as the orange jackets.

Scanning the crowds, alert for any tails and satisfied there were none, I followed the men round the tree, past a huge pile of ice deposited by those clearing the square after each snowfall, children laughing and sliding down it on their backs and struggling to climb up again. The orange jackets had disappeared.

On the opposite side of the road the other skier broke into a jog. I did too, sticking to my side of the road, scanning the bobbing hats and jutting skis, looking for a glimpse of orange. Up ahead, the dark mountain blocked out the waking stars in the deep blue sky, substituting its own meandering chains of lights that marked the runs and roads. Another line of lights moved up and down: the bubble lift to the runs above. Restaurants and bars flanking the road nestled in the glow of the cable car station. The street was crowded, skiers coming down from the piste and mixing with people getting an early drink in before tea. The bright orange jackets threaded through them, heading for the cable cars.

Ski guy had seen them too, and sped up, overtaking them, pushing his way through the groups of people ahead of me. I picked up the pace.

They'd almost reached the bubble lift. The crowds were thinning, everyone else was making their way down the mountain as the temperature dropped in sync with the sun. I jostled between couples, wincing as pain erupted in my side, barely healed wounds slowing me as I rushed to get behind the group. Up ahead, the skier had made it through the turnstiles and was staring resolutely ahead, eyes on the glass windows of the cable cars rolling past, on the reflection of those orange jackets a few people behind him. They'd closed up now, all four men stood as a group, bodyguards scanning late skiers coming off the lifts as the guy in the middle of them eyed the woman in front.

The doors slid shut, a group was whisked up the mountain, another gondola came round. Everyone shuffled forward. I blipped my pass on the turnstile and followed.

Ski guy climbed in, propped his skis against the far window, and sat down. A family crowded in after him, laughing, kids elbowing each other to sit by the windows. The doors slid shut, the gondola carried on, the next came round.

The woman strode forward, expensive tight gear accentuating every curve. Like me, her lack of skis suggested that she was going up for a drink or to meet someone. The man looked her up and down and pushed into the gondola with her, her lip curled, she muttered something in German. His thugs stepped forward, I did too, shoving into the back of the huge guy. He turned and snarled.

I put my hand up. '*Désolé.*'

He jabbed me in the ribs with the back of the skis. 'Full.'

I put a hand over my body, curled my right into a fist. He didn't notice, swinging the skis round and storming into the gondola. They sat down, the doors slid shut with him scowling at me.

I waited for the next car, took a deep breath, then climbed into the swaying coffin. No one followed, the doors closed, taking me up the mountain alone.

I unzipped my jacket and sat down, examining a thick pink-and-red line snaking across my ribs. I ran my hand all the way around. No blood. It hadn't reopened the wound, but it hurt like hell. I clenched both fists again, allowed myself a few seconds to imagine beating his face flat. The temporary pain was worth it, because now I knew two things. I knew the big guy only spoke English and his native Serbian – or, at least, he didn't speak French. More importantly, I now knew he carried his pistol in a holster beneath his left armpit. Big gun too, wouldn't be surprised if he had a Desert Eagle in there, it'd be about the right size for those giant fists.

I zipped back up, propped my boots on the seat opposite, and sat back, eyes on the gondola in front rather than the pines a vomit-inducing distance below. After another minute, the gondola in front of us had almost reached the top. I pulled out a cheap phone and brought up a contact on speed dial.

'Yup,' a Scottish guy answered.

'They're in the car behind you.'

'Yeah I saw, what happened to you?'

'Altercation. I'm in the one behind them.'

'You'd better hurry.'

'Don't worry, she got in with them.'

'Alone? Is that wise…?'

'She can take care of herself.' I accidentally looked down at the trees below and felt my heart skip, I gripped the bar in one hand and closed my eyes, massaging my ribs. 'That big guy's as solid as the Terminator.'

'Branko, yeah. Mean-looking bastard.'

'He's mine.'

'He'd flatten you, Tyler. I was told you were once beaten up by a one-armed girl.'

'Sexist *and* ableist, nice.'

'Besides, I thought you said no killing?'

'Change of plan. *Some* killing.'

Chapter Five

Tiburon, **Commercial deepwater port of La Rochelle**

The whole ship shuddered as the big diesels started up, lights winked in the gloomy bridge. Miller was leaning on the railings outside on the bridge wing, firing off instructions to the crew prepping for sailing below. I looked through the windows at the deck stretching out in front, squinting into the darkness at a couple of crew still ratcheting straps across my car on the forward hold covers. Another man was busy in front of them securing the crane.

I pulled my phone from my pocket and pressed on the fitness app again. The heartbeat in my boot was steady.

'Drink?'

Miller let the door swing shut behind him and bent to a cupboard. He'd begrudge sharing his booze with me but couldn't deny his superstitions. I waited until he reappeared holding a bottle of something brown.

'I will if that's rum.'

'You're in luck, we're all outta Scotch.' He poured a generous measure in a dirty glass tumbler, passed it to me then grabbed a radio handset hanging from the ceiling. 'How's she lookin', chief?'

The speaker crackled static for a few seconds. 'She doesn't like the look of this weather,' came the reply, French-accented.

'They're marine diesels, for Christ's sake.' He covered the handset. 'Lazy bastard means *he* doesn't like the weather.'

'They're still bedding in, Skip. Now's not the time to be pushing them.' As with most of Miller's crew, his English was near flawless.

'Vincent, if we're not under way in thirty seconds you can stay in France and Seb will take over.'

The radio crackled and muttered in French. Miller flicked it off and collapsed into his chair. '*À la tienne.*'

'Cheers.' We clinked glasses, I avoided a chip in the rim and downed half. I eased off my Barbour motorcycle jacket and peeled off the hoody underneath, threw them on the chart table, and went back to the window to watch the loading. They'd strapped the car so tight it was pulled right down on its already lowered suspension, probably scratching the shit out of my paintwork. I sighed and shook my head.

'You've got some new ink.' Miller pointed at the thick black outlines snaking round my left arm.

I grunted in reply, rubbing the raised outline of a small island on the inside of my wrist. Next to it a fresh scar cut through an old tattoo of Libya, puckered skin red and raw even now, weeks later. I downed the rest of the rum to wash down memories of bitter antibiotics.

'You're bleeding, too,' he said, already refilling his glass.

I looked down at my T-shirt, ran my hand across my ribs. 'I'm always bleeding from somewhere.'

He grabbed the radio handset again. 'Doc to the bridge.'

'And I thought you didn't care.'

'Like you said, gotta keep you safe until you can make that bank transfer.'

I rubbed my fingers together, smearing blood. 'You always said you'd retire before you hit fifty. You're what, five years overdue?'

'Only three, but the money's too good; especially jobs like this. Who's paying the bills this time?'

'As far as you're concerned – me.' I leaned on the control console to look down on the figures on deck. 'How's the new mate?'

'Katanga, known the guy years. Got tired of running guns up the Niger.'

'Can he be trusted?'

'He knows the score.'

I narrowed my eyes.

'Yeah, all of it,' Miller continued. 'So when the time comes, you let him know.' He nodded at the window. 'So what's special about this car?'

I raised my brows in mock surprise. 'What's not special about it?'

'Cars ain't my thing, but I know it's not worth what you're paying. What's in the trunk?'

'I'm paying you not to ask those sorts of questions.' I watched a couple of the crew untie the bow lines, holding out the glass behind me, it clinked as Miller topped it up.

'Well you hired me, so obviously can't risk a ferry. It's illegal; all well and good, but I need to know if it's heavy? Corrosive? Fire hazard? Likely to blow a huge fuckin' hole through the hull and send us to the bottom?'

I took a sip of rum and rubbed my eyes. 'None of the above.'

The vibrations underfoot rose, the ship lurched. Miller stood, sliding the bottle into a bag hanging from the table and placing his glass on the console. He gave a signal out of the window, flicked a switch to douse the spotlights, then dimmed the bridge lights.

'Once more unto the breach,' he bellowed theatrically.

A speaker above the window crackled and started playing the opening to 'Kashmir' by Led Zeppelin.

'Cry God for fucking England.' I took another mouthful.

Miller pushed the throttle forward a touch, the big diesels joined the rolling drums and out-of-step guitar as he eased the wheel away from the quay. He tapped the floor with a grimy work boot, keeping the speed down as we moved towards the mouth of the sub pen, edging from under the concrete monolith and out into the basin. Sleet flecked the windows, leaving glistening trails down the glass.

The rum tasted good, warming my throat. We were finally under way, leaving my pursuers behind us, the last leg of my journey. For the first time in days I could stand still and breathe, possibly even get some sleep.

'How long you had this piece of shit, then?' I asked.

'The *Tiburon*?' He somehow patted the wheel in time with the guitar and kicked the floor in time with the drums, no mean feat. 'Coupla years. Some German yuppie had ideas about a floating strip club until he saw the cost of the refit. I got her real cheap.'

'No offence, but I can see why.'

Lights from warehouses and forklift trucks glittered on the basin's millpond surface, spotlights and amber flashers shimmering in the frigid air. At the far end, the lock gates were open ready for us. The high tide meant we could pass straight out, through the outer harbour and into the Atlantic; the time of our rendezvous and rapid departure was no accident or coincidence. No one gave us a second glance, or if they did, they didn't give two fucks about it.

I pressed against the port-side window to watch the lights of the incoming container ships. 'What was the name of your other boat?'

Miller gave a blast of the horn as we passed a trawler. 'When I pulled you out of Somalia? The *Aurora*.'

'That was it. Why the change?'

'Christ, that was three boats ago. Uh, she went down off Cyprus.'

'Don't tell me, running arms into Syria? No, wait, running people out of Syria?'

Miller smirked and swigged his drink. 'Why not both?'

A couple of miles beyond the breakwaters at the mouth of the harbour, the lights of the Île de Ré glimmered.

'*Aurora*,' I repeated. 'Yeah, she was much nicer.'

'Not a patch on *Tiburon*.'

'At least she was built during my lifetime.' I patted the cracked top of the console, a bank of lights and gauges winked out. 'Electrics worked, too, if I'm remembering right.'

Miller leaned over and banged a fist on the console angrily, the gauges sprang back to life. 'Converted trawlers have nowhere near the storage of this baby.'

'Can't get as much heroin in a fish hold, eh?'

Miller didn't answer; much like me, he got touchy when his morals were called into question. Out of the harbour mouth he steered a hard ninety degrees to starboard, bringing us under the long bridge connecting the port city to the upmarket island just offshore. It didn't look like we were going to make it, I instinctively ducked as we passed beneath it.

'How's Étienne?' I asked, still hunched over, looking up at the underside of the road bridge. 'I'll go down and see him later.'

Miller pushed the throttles and the ship surged forward. Credit where it's due, she'd some impressively smooth power delivery.

'Étienne's dead.' He stared into the rain ahead.

'Shit, I'm sorry.'

Miller grunted and grabbed the radio handset. 'Doc, bridge, now.'

'He was a good lad.'

Miller jerked a thumb at the rucksack of cash on the table. 'You're paying for his funeral.'

I thought about it for a second before the penny dropped. 'When?'

'Last week. Mugged outside a bar.'

'And you didn't think to tell me?'

He looked at me, all I could see were his eyes shining in the dim bridge lights. 'My crew's no concern of yours.'

'It is if you've got new hands since I hired you. Who's the replacement?'

'They're good men, I vouch for them all. It's the passengers that worry me.' He put a cigarette between his lips and muttered, 'You and your friends are the killers for hire.' He sparked it up and turned back to the sleet-crusted window.

I was about to press him further when the outside door swung inwards followed by Katanga. He slammed it behind him, peeling off a yellow slicker and hanging it on the door. With a wary glance at me he rubbed rain off his tight curls, grabbed a bottle from the fridge, and took a seat at the chart table.

'You got Blofeld's car secured good and tight?'

'Ain't going nowhere. That ghost's back with us though.'

Robert Plant's haunting wails crackled through the speaker in the ceiling.

Miller scowled. 'Next man to mention ghosts can repaint the hold.'

'I meant the car, Skip.' Katanga smiled at me. 'Makin' some strange noises. Mustn't like being shot, eh?'

Miller turned to me and frowned. I changed the subject. 'What's our course then?' I left the window to look over Katanga's shoulder.

He cracked the lid off his bottle of beer on the edge of the table and ran a finger over the map. 'North-west 30 clicks to clear the island. Open up the engines, steam due west to the shelf. Weather gets hairy out there.' He drained half the bottle in one go and wiped his mouth with the back of his hand. 'Then it's north for 350 clicks, takes us to about midday tomorrow.'

'Why not follow the coast?'

Miller cleared his throat. 'I'll chance heavy seas over coastal patrols, especially with you on board. Besides, see these waves?' he gestured out of the window. 'Wind's coming up from the south-west, we need to take these waves on an angle to the bow, can't take them on the beam.'

'Won't it add to the time?'

'Not much.' Katanga took another swig and unfolded the map some more. 'We kiss Ushant, landing in *La Manche* here at about seventeen-hundred hours,' he jabbed a grimy, chewed finger somewhere south of Cornwall, 'then an easy run to Poole.'

I nodded. A straight drive from there to RAF Boscombe Down.

The song finished, the speaker buzzed then went silent.

'Kat, take the wheel,' said Miller. 'I'm gonna see where the hell Doc is.'

He stood; Katanga eased himself into his place.

Miller grabbed the rucksack of money and paused at the door. 'Your friends below are getting pretty restless, ya know.'

'They're employees, technically. Do me a favour, could you send King up?'

He nodded and left, taking the internal stairs below rather than the treacherous route I'd taken to get to the bridge, via the outside stairways and slippery gangways.

'You mind if I use your table?'

Katanga looked back over his shoulder. 'Your charter, boss.'

I folded the chart and slipped my pistol out of the waist holster, laying it on the table.

'What was that about a ghost?'

Katanga looked back at me, shaking his head. 'Captain don't like to talk about the curse.'

'The captain's not here.'

'She doesn't like taking passengers.'

'The *Tiburon*?'

'Uh huh.' Katanga, who was leaning one arm across the wheel, turned in his seat, lit like a demon in the red lights of the dials. 'Bad things happen.'

I supressed a laugh.

'Why does the captain call you Blofeld?' he asked.

34

I pointed at the jagged scar bisecting my right eyebrow, the slight trace of it continuing just below my eye. 'He's a comedian.'

He nodded, smiling. 'I've heard a lot about you, Mr Tyler. Your appearance is exactly the way I imagined.'

'He said he'd filled you in?'

Katanga nodded. 'Yes indeed. He says having you on board is like picking a wasp out of a jam jar.' He laughed, grabbing the radio handset from above his head. 'Full ballast now, I think, Sébastien.'

'Aye,' the radio crackled back.

'I thought we were running light, for speed?'

'We didn't expect to be carrying a car on deck.' Katanga pointed ahead through the windows. 'We're heading towards the continental shelf, wind blows all the way from America. Cap'n told you about them waves.'

I looked at the flashing skies reflecting off white peaks. 'Looks like it's gonna get bumpy.'

He nodded. 'They'll be much worse when we clear the island. Storm's coming in, we don't take on more ballast, you see how bumpy it gets then.' He spoke into the handset again. 'And fill the aft peak tank, Sébastien.' He looked back at me. 'To offset the car, we set the stern lower in the water so the screws don't get lifted out on the back of a wave. We lose momentum, get spun full broadside to those waves, you'll know about it.'

He hung the handset above his head, a moment later a hum reverberated through the floor as the pumps started up, flooding the tanks at the keel with seawater.

I spent the next few minutes stripping my Heckler & Koch pistol down and reassembling it. Sliding the magazine out, I started to stand all the hollow points up in a row but stopped when the ship rolled, tipping them onto the floor. Katanga glanced round and chuckled as the boat slewed back, bullets rolling the other way across the metal floor. I sighed as I bent to pick them up, the boat rolling in deepening arcs as we moved into an ever-wider channel, heading for the open Atlantic.

Chapter Six

Château des Aigles
Thirteen days previously

I popped several pills and capsules from a packet, gulped them down, and tossed the box back in the glovebox. The woman in the passenger seat tutted. I ignored her and took a different coloured packet from the centre console, popped a tablet from its foil, and swallowed again. The woman in the passenger inhaled loudly.

I leaned over and pushed the second pack into the glovebox: she slammed it shut, almost catching my hand:

I looked at her. 'Ready?'

She glared back at me, swept her blonde hair from her face, and nodded. I turned off the ignition. As soon as the wipers stopped the windscreen was thick with snow. I opened the door and climbed out, swapping the heated bucket seat for a minus-five blizzard.

'Ay, stay there!' came a shout from the darkness, English for my benefit.

The Christmas Wonderland had been heaving when we'd driven up earlier, the huge tree at the back of the car park dripping with strings of twinkling lights. Now it was an impenetrable black mass, holding us in its menacing shadow. I pulled up my hood and held my hands out, squinting at the two cars pulled close beneath it.

Lights blazed on from one of them, I raised a hand to my eyes. When the spots had faded I kept my hand over my eyes and tried to look beyond the beam. An old Mercedes saloon, three men, a fourth standing next to a shiny Porsche hybrid SUV pulled in close to the pines at the edge.

One of the men broke away from the others and crunched through the snow.

'You are George Kaplan?' he asked, breath swirling with the flakes in the headlights.

I nodded. Not the most original of names but hey, I'm a sucker for the classics.

'You are late,' he said with a frown. 'This means I am already angry.'

Lowlife gobshite in a leather jacket and trackie pants, the right pocket clearly weighed down with something heavy. The guy wasn't a poker player, then.

'The car is ready,' he continued, stopping just short of my bonnet and making a grabbing motion with a fat hand. 'Show me the money.'

I opened the back door and picked a shopping bag off the back seat, holding it up. 'You put the plates on?'

'Cloned from same model of car in Nice, there will be no problems.' His fat hand was still beckoning at the air, after the money.

I tossed the bag back on the seat. 'We'll test drive it first.'

He frowned again, cocking his head on one side. 'You want a test drive, there is a Porsche dealership in Geneva.'

'Car's no good to me if the immobiliser kicks in as soon as we leave the *département*.'

'I tell you we disabled the tracker and immobiliser as discussed.' He rubbed his shaved head and glanced behind, the group of men shuffled forward nervously. 'You do not trust us?'

'I trust a gang of car thieves as much as you trust a couple who need a stolen car.' I gestured to the woman in the passenger seat, she opened the door and climbed out, leaning against the roof. I gave her a nod.

'I will take the Porsche for ten minutes,' she said in clipped, German-accented English. 'He will stay with the money.'

'This is not what we agreed.' Gobshite glanced behind again. 'This is not...'

'This is what is happening,' she said with a sigh. 'If you have a problem, we will take our money elsewhere.'

He held his hands up, walking backwards to his associates. They conferred for a moment. The woman reached into the passenger footwell and reappeared with a small rucksack.

The gobshite walked forward again, holding the keys out. She took them from him, flashing me a look. I started to walk forward with her but the man pulled his other hand from his pocket. A pistol glinted in the lights of the Mercedes.

'We will count the money now.' He waved the gun at my car.

I gave the woman a nod, she walked over to the Porsche, throwing her rucksack in and climbing after it. It started with a hum, shed the snow from its windscreen and pulled forward, almost silent but for the crunching, squeaking snow beneath its chunky BF Goodrich off-road tyres. Four-wheel drive and nearly 700 horsepower when required, but on electric mode it was quieter than a skateboard, perfect for what we had in mind. She pulled past us, red tail lights disappearing down the access road behind me.

We'd agreed she'd blast it for a couple of miles, get a feel for it and check the modifications had been made to her specs, before pulling into a layby we'd already scoped. There she'd use the tools in the rucksack to look over the electronics, check the bypass job on the alarm and immobiliser, the disabled tracker. Ten minutes was tight, but she was bloody good.

The gobshite motioned again towards my car, I grabbed the bag and carried it round, placing it on the bonnet.

He reached in greedily, thumbing wads of euro notes.

'It's all there.'

I was paying well for a hot Porsche but with the mods, the plates, the fact it was the range-topping Turbo S model, and of course the added short-notice tax, it was worth it. Besides, it's not like I was paying. He waved me away as he carried on counting. I took my keys from the ignition, pocketed them, strolling off to the side of the car park, out of the headlights, letting my eyes adjust so I could get a better look at the three men still huddled by the Merc.

'Hey!' shouted Gobshite.

I looked back at my car.

He grinned, gripping the bag of money tightly in his hammy fist. 'The price is another ten thousand.'

'I'm already paying too much.'

He shrugged and held up the bag. 'This is for the car. The extra is for the test drive.'

'I don't have any more.' I sighed, walking back towards him, arms out in a placatory fashion. I had plenty of cash for expenses but I wouldn't be handing over any more to this scumbag chancer.

He withdrew a pistol from his jacket. 'Let's check what you have…'

Too late, I'd closed the distance. Reaching behind my back, under my hoody, I pulled out my own pistol. The extra length of the suppressor swung down, breaking his wrist as I continued to close the gap between us. He howled, dropping his pistol into the snow. The other three were slow to react; by the time they had their own guns on me I had Gobshite in front of me, arms pinned, grinding the business end of that suppressor into his flabby neck.

He yelped, one of the men started walking forward, waving a gun stupidly, shouting French obscenities. The other two fanned out, sidestepping with their guns held firm, so maybe they weren't quite as dense. From the look of their stances, the way they moved and held their weapons, I guessed ex-military, whereas the vocal guy was a street thug.

'Please, I am just here to translate,' the man in my arms whimpered. 'You understand, he is the, the… *Je ne connais pas les mots.*'

I pressed the gun harder into his neck. 'Shut the fuck up.'

The other man was striding forward in the headlights now, big ugly head like a block of ice carved by that chainsaw sculptor from the village, and he had a pistol in each hand, waving them out wide thinking he was in a John Woo film. He started to count down loudly. The two ex-military types had me perfectly flanked from either side of the car park. Over a hundred-degree angle between the three of them, too spread out for me to pick off easily, plus the two flanking guys had taken cover now, one behind a plywood Father Christmas's sleigh and the other round a happy elf workshop.

'He will kill you, he doesn't care about me,' screamed Gobshite.

The man stopped, his count reached *un*, both pistols swung in my direction. I didn't see many options. His fingers were on the triggers, already squeezing, though two pistols meant the idiot wasn't really aiming either.

I let go of Gobshite, dropping down behind him as the first gun fired. He didn't get a chance to fire the second, my pistol snapped once, the man dropped. Two more gunshots rang out from either side of the car park, and the ex-military guys slumped in my peripheral vision.

Silence in the falling snow.

That the thug's bullet had missed me was no real surprise given his ridiculous gun discipline, but I was thankful it'd missed my car, too. I reached forward to pick up Gobshite's pistol then trudged through the snow to the thug's body, picking up his cheap Chinese Beretta copies from beside his ruined head, which sank deeper into the snow as the red mess melted down.

I turned to look back at Gobshite, still whimpering on the ground, clutching his wrist. He looked from one body to another. Over on the right, on the small hill overlooking the car park, a snowdrift shuddered. It grew, and the snow fell off to reveal a figure in arctic camo gear holding a stubby Ruger Ranch Rifle.

Another camo-clad figure walked out of the woods on the left holding my HKG28 marksman, all sprayed up in white and hung with torn strips of sheet. The two of them swept towards the car park, picking up the weapons then heading for the gang's Merc to check it out.

Snow crunched on the access road behind, the Porsche's headlights came round the corner. She slowed, pulling up alongside my Audi, winding the window down.

'You can't even do the simplest job, can you Tyler?' she said without a trace of a smile.

'How's the car?' I asked.

She gave me a nod and a chef's kiss, wound the window back up, started a three-point turn. The camo guys were crunching through the snow towards us, rifles slung over their shoulders.

The first guy pulled his hood down and opened the Porsche's boot. 'It's a real nice rifle,' he said with a Scottish accent, 'but I'll stick with my Ruger.' He unslung my HK and placed it in the boot.

The second guy pulled up his ski mask and shook his head. He was an Iraqi, but you wouldn't know it from his use of vernacular. 'Fucking amateurs. Always greedy.'

He placed the Ruger rifle in the boot and pressed the close button.

'Kill him,' said the woman, pointing behind me.

I looked round at Gobshite, still whimpering on his knees in the snow, shook my head, picked up the bag of cash. I took out one banded stack of twenties and put it in his shaking hand.

'Merry Christmas.'

Chapter Seven

Tiburon

King, my friend and colleague of years, arrived on the bridge before the doctor. Katanga turned to offer a grunted greeting then went back to a Game Boy; sounded like he was playing Mario one-handed while he steadied the wheel with the other.

King was tall, powerfully built, and looked like George Lazenby after he'd finished playing Bond and had gone all George Best. Spoke like Lazenby too, when he was acting Bond anyway, which I'd always thought was weird given King had grown up in a mining family in north Wales.

He'd looked the same for at least fifteen years, I felt like I was a portrait in his attic, suffering his ageing for him. The easy-going air only made it as far down as his powerful shoulders, the rest of him was all business: hard, muscular, and today clad in tactical black. Boots, combat trousers, a vest with more loops and clips than a fisherman, finished off with a holster strapped to his right thigh and a knife on the left.

'Smells of Acqua di Parma and blood in here,' he said. 'The inimitable John Tyler must be on board.'

'What's the fashion-conscious mercenary wearing this season, then?' I stood to shake King's hand and he pulled

44

me in, clapping me on the back. I winced. 'Always over-dressed.'

'And as usual, you're underdressed!' He moved back, gripping the chair, looked me up and down, putting his other hand on the table to steady himself. 'Jeez, you look like you haven't slept.'

'I haven't, been driving all night.'

'No, I meant *ever*. You've got red on you.'

Katanga turned from the wheel and eyed me suspiciously, pulling a pouch of tobacco from his pocket.

'Bullet got a bit close this time,' I said, sticking a finger through the hole in my T-shirt. 'It's been too long, King. Wish it was in different circumstances.'

His face darkened. 'When I asked you not to call me I meant it.'

'You still came.'

King steadied himself against the table and sighed deeply. 'I'm thinking it was a mistake. Although this gig's gonna be duller than Coldplay.'

'Give it chance,' I said, though I hoped he was right. 'You're looking greener than usual, you all right?'

'It's less swayey below deck.' He was trying to do that trick of looking at the horizon to ward off the sickness, but unfortunately in between the flashes of lightning there wasn't much of one to see. He gave up on his legs and collapsed into the chair opposite. 'Christ, you still haven't got a decent piece.' He reached and slid my gun across the table, ran a finger over the scuffed slide.

I took it back, snapping the magazine into place. 'All the best things come from the Seventies. What's with the Glock, you always swore by a Sig?'

'Only had it a few months, it's the new 47.' He leaned to one side, pulled it out and turned it over, proudly showing me the scars where he'd ground off the markings. 'You can't even buy them. Department of Homeland Security only.'

I took it, weighed it in my hands, held my Heckler & Koch up in the other. 'This was made in 1974, I've had it for twenty years, modified it myself. It's been on all seven continents, to both poles, Himalayas to the Sahara. I've never had a stoppage and usually hit my target.' I pushed it into my waist holster. 'Get back to me when your Glock's been tested that much.'

He snatched his gun back and pointed it at the blood-soaked hole in my shirt. 'You're not quick enough to be using a museum piece. Get with the times, retro isn't always better.'

'Films, TV, music, cars…'

'And Thatcher, right?' He grinned.

'Might be preferable to the current shitshow, you know.'

He arched an eyebrow. 'That shitshow, I assume, is paying our wages?'

'Touché.' I knocked back the last of the rum and refilled my glass from the bottle Miller had left swinging in the bag under the table. I offered it to King but he shook his head. 'So how are our two friends?' I asked.

'Martinez seems capable, doesn't talk a lot though. Not what I expected.'

'In what way?'

'Well, Yank for a start. She's more your type.'

'My type?'

'How's… What was her name? That German getaway driver…'

I cut him off with a glare.

46

'Well, Martinez is probably the best-looking person on this tub anyway.'

Katanga looked up from his Game Boy. 'I resent that, Mr King.'

King held his hands up in apology. 'Second best.' He moved a hand to his mouth, looked like he was going to throw up.

'And Fields?' I asked.

He shrugged, looked at the ceiling, closed his eyes, breathing deeply. 'Seems decent, been around the block, usual places, knows his shit. Scottish, and you can pick him out as an ex-Marine at a mile, but I won't hold either of those things against him. Where did you drag them up from?'

'Yellow Pages.'

'Well, they're asking questions. You're paying a shitload of money just for us to ride shotgun.'

'Like I said to Miller, they're also being paid not to ask questions.'

'You feel that?' asked Katanga.

King and I looked at each other and shrugged.

'Seb!' Katanga shouted into the radio. 'Seb, how is that aft tank?'

The radio crackled but no reply. Lightning flashed outside the windows, the wave crests were growing even as we watched.

'Seb,' Katanga repeated. 'Come in, Seb.'

'Problem?' I asked.

'Too much trim by stern,' he said. 'Far too much.'

'What does that mean?' asked King.

'In your terms, Mr King, it means we are sinking.'

He jumped up, looking around. I stood less quickly and more painfully.

Katanga laughed. 'We don't have to get in the lifeboats just yet.' He spoke into the handset again. 'Seb, what does the aft peak say?'

Still no response. Katanga flipped a switch on the radio and spoke into the handset again. 'Captain Miller to the bridge.' The speaker on the ceiling was silent. 'The electrics in this ship...' He shook his head and muttered something rapidly in French, I caught what I thought was 'curse'. Lightning flashed again, the ship shuddered with the impact of a bigger wave. 'Kat, what's happening?' I asked.

He hung the handset back up and turned. 'I asked Seb to fill the aft tank to set the stern low in the water, ready for this storm, but now it's too low.'

The radio crackled. 'What d'ya want, Kat?'

'Seb, what's the aft peak say?'

'Hang on, I've had my hands full with these engines.' There was a moment's silence and then, 'It's not filling. Valve must be faulty. I'll check it out in a bit.'

'She must be filling, we're down at the stern.'

'I'm telling you, ballast tank's empty.'

'Can you get back there and check?'

'In a word, no. Starboard engine's running cool, port side's doing the legwork. I told the captain...'

'Let me know how it goes.' Katanga hung the handset back above his head. He leaned over, opening a cupboard next to his leg, pulling out a torch and a walkie-talkie and handing them to King. 'I need you to go back there and check it out.'

King held the items up in his hands like they were alien devices. 'Back where, check what out?'

Katanga pulled out another walkie-talkie and switched it on. 'I'll guide you.'

'Why can't you go?'

Katanga pointed through the window at the lightning flashing off the black waves. 'You want to take the wheel?'

'Come on,' I grabbed King and opened the internal door. 'Where we going?'

'Sorry, Mr Tyler.' Katanga pointed at the door outside, onto the bridge wing. 'You'll need to take your coat.'

Chapter Eight

Tiburon

'It's there,' I yelled above the wind, pointing at a hatch in the middle of the deck under the lifeboat davits. Gone was the sleet, replaced by driving rain, mixing with the spray whipped by the howling gale from the top of the waves crashing up the hull.

We were on the dark stern, behind the superstructure, clinging to the railings as the ship heaved and fell in the face of the oncoming storm. Katanga had told us what to look for and put the work lights on for us, but they'd flickered and shut off after a few seconds, leaving me to sweep the rain-washed deck with the torch.

I gestured to King and ran, sliding to my knees and grabbing the latch. He stumbled after me, tripping over a rope and falling as a wave pitched the deck. I grabbed him, putting his hand on the big latch and twisting. It slid surprisingly easily. King swung the heavy hatch open as I shone the torch down into the darkness. The bright beam lit rungs descending to the level below, so rusted I was getting tetanus just looking at them. With a nod to King, I clamped the torch between my teeth and swung inside. It was a short climb, just a few metres until I touched the lower deck. I looked down at the flaking metal, gave it a tentative press with my toe, then stepped off the ladder.

Above me King climbed in, swung the cover closed and knocked the latch back on. The water stopped swilling in from the deck, but the reverberating waves increased in volume.

I shone the torch around the small space. The wall in front of us was curved, we were looking at the inside plates of the stern, with their corroded rivets and creaking welds.

Katanga had explained that we'd drop into an access area belowdecks for the bilges and steering gear. Beneath our feet the huge propshafts headed outside, their constant churning echoing in the claustrophobic space. I knocked a hand against one wall, it clanged hollow.

'We had to go outside to come back in again,' said King. 'Why?' I turned, he was pointing his own torch at a door in the bulkhead behind us. 'This must come out by the cabins.'

I grabbed the latch, it didn't budge. I leaned in close, the door had been crudely welded shut.

'Must be an old access.'

'Miller and his bloody deathtraps. Why couldn't we have taken a nice P&O, with a bar and a restaurant? And on that point, when are you gonna fill me in on what we're actually doing here? You said you needed me, all right, I'm here, but you sure as shit didn't get me onto this stinking tub for a babysitting job.'

'How do you figure that?'

He held my shoulders and looked into my eyes. 'Because you wouldn't do that to me.'

The walkie-talkie crackled on King's belt, Katanga's voice echoed in the darkness. 'Did you find the hatch yet?'

King let go of me and lifted the walkie-talkie. 'We're inside.' He shone the torch up at the dripping ceiling. 'It's snug.'

'It gets worse, Mr King. Do you see the hatch in the floor?'

I pointed the torch at a round hatch cover at the foot of the ladder.

'Down again?' asked King.

'Just you, there's no room to turn around at the bottom.'

I swung open the cover, the torch beam illuminated a narrow shaft straight down, not much wider than me, ending in a tank of water.

I looked up into King's face, he was grimacing.

'Fuck that, I can't go,' he said, shuffling back.

'I'm injured.'

'I've got my wings, I belong up there, in the open air.'

'Rock paper scissors?' I said, holding up my fist.

'Remember Misrata? I didn't make you go on the chopper, did I?'

I looked down at the rusty rungs welded into the side of the shaft, like a row of staples in a gangrenous wound dropping into darkness. 'Fuck's sake, we're even now.' I took off my jacket, threw it on the floor, and swung my feet down.

'Take this one, it's waterproof.' King was holding out his powerful Lenser torch.

I clamped it between my teeth, handed him mine, and started to climb. The pipe was so tight the sleeves of my T-shirt rode up, my shoulders scraping down either side as Katanga relayed instructions to King above me. Halfway down my shoes hit water, I kept going, into the freezing cold, like climbing down inside a half-submerged Pringles tube. I winced when it hit my crotch, then my shoes hit the bottom.

I switched on the torch. 'Okay, what am I looking for?' I shouted as the icy water rose and fell with the ship.

'He says open the hatch below you.'

'How can I do that, I'm stuck in a tube?'

There was a pause as he conferred with Katanga on the radio, then his silhouettë filled the dim circle of light above.

'He says you can scooch off the bottom and crawl.'

'Crawl?' I kicked my legs about, the tunnel did seem to open up, problem being it was three feet under water.

'He says when you've got the hatch open check the tank below for water.'

'I don't need to open the hatch for that, I'm up to my arse in it.'

Again a pause, and then, 'No, he says you're in the dry zone, the ballast tank is below you.'

'He's welcome to come and check.'

I stuck the torch back between my teeth then took a breath and pushed down, below the surface, walking my hands down the ladder. My legs disappeared back into a void until my belly brushed the deck. I opened my eyes, saltwater stung but in the light of the torch between my teeth I could see the outline of the hatch cover, bobbing up and down with the motion of the ship. I swung it fully open and pushed my head through, the torch beam didn't reach the bottom or sides in the murk.

My lungs began to protest, I pushed up and hit the underside of something. I put my hands up, feeling the ceiling above me, pulling myself forward until I found the ladder. My lungs screamed, I forced myself not to panic, pulling up hand over hand into the shaft, breaking the surface to take a deep breath.

'And?' shouted King.

I panted for a moment longer then shouted up. 'The whole thing's flooded. And it's getting deeper.' With my shoes planted firmly on the floor either side of the hatch, the water now reached my chest.

'Seb says the gauge is showing empty.'

'Again, he's welcome to come and bloody check.'

I screwed my eyes shut, took a breath, ducked under again, right down the ladder. I felt for the hatch beneath my feet, and climbed straight down into the ballast tank.

When I ran out of ladder I opened my eyes. The dirty water surged in the narrow space, slamming me against the baffles – internal walls designed to prevent the whole lot sloshing side to side in the tank and destabilising the ship. I looked up, the light above flashed as the hatch cover lifted and dropped with the motion of the water. The ship tilted, I grazed my arms bouncing between the baffles, something dug into my side. I shone the torch down and found a slender pipe attached to the inside of the tank, running up towards the ceiling. Next to it, the hatch cover had swung shut.

I pushed off the bottom and reached for it. Another wave hit, the water surged around the narrow steel canyon. I spun, sliding along one of the walls. I was disoriented, like being inside a sensory deprivation chamber. My lungs screamed at me to get out. I rolled over, shining the torch around, found the hatch a few metres away and swam for it. I grasped the handle and shoved, planting my feet on the rungs welded to the wall. The cover groaned open, I collided painfully with the side as I grabbed the ladder and hauled myself through.

This time I had to climb a couple of rungs to get to the surface, when I did my trainers were off the floor. Not sure if it was my imagination but the pipe seemed to be leaning slightly, the stern was slipping lower by the second.

'What are you *doing* down there?'

I breathed deeply for a few seconds. 'I couldn't give two shits what that gauge says, the tank filled ages ago.' I rubbed my stinging eyes. 'It's filling up the ship now, why aren't the bilge pumps kicking in?'

The bilge pumps should have been on auto, switching on when water washing around the lower spaces rose above a certain level.

'Mate, do I look like a sailor? Get back up here, let them fix it.'

'King, if we don't do something right now, we'll be on the bottom soon.'

I took a breath and climbed down the ladder, straight into the tank again. I pushed my hand against the wall, the other shining the torch across the flaking panels until I found the pipe I'd fallen against. I followed it down to the bottom of the tank, fingers closing around something squashy. I pulled it free and kicked upwards, hitting my head on a girder as the ship groaned and tilted.

I coughed, swallowing seawater, the ship rolled further, I tumbled. I dropped the torch, the beam spun away into the back of the tank, rolling under one of the gaps beneath the baffles. In its flickering light a shape floated through the opening, like oil. Black tendrils took shape, a shadow of a man drifting through the twisting compartment. An arm reached for my foot.

I screwed my eyes shut, kicked backwards, grabbing for the steel ribs of the ceiling. I opened my eyes, nothing in the narrow space but the rusty baffles either side, the murky churning water, the torchlight flashing under the gaps in the metal.

I spun round, lungs burning, muscles cramping. A dim flicker of light was just visible through the banging hatch cover above. I kicked out towards it.

My ears were ringing as I pulled myself towards the light. Finally I reached the hatch, thrusting myself up through it, fingers curling around the rungs of the ladder. I climbed up as quickly as I could, my sight dimming, muscles burning from lack of oxygen. I broke the surface, took a deep breath, and threw up into the water.

I was only half a metre below the upper hatch now.

'Jesus Christ, Tyler! Get out of there!' King shouted.

I clung to the ladder, panting hard, and threw up again. He reached down to help me up but I batted his hand away, sucking in long lungfuls of air.

'What the fuck are you doing?' he asked.

'Well I'm not here for the good of my health, am I?' I gripped the rungs harder to stop my hands shaking. That face, those arms, reaching for me... without my tablets, this was going to be a long journey.

'Katanga says the bilge pumps were taken offline.'

'By who?'

'They missed it when they were doing their sea checks, I dunno. Seb's tried switching off the ballast pumps to stop the water but he says the valve's stuck.'

'No wonder we're sinking.' I moved up a rung, resting my forehead against the cold metal.

The ladder trembled, I could hear King speaking to Katanga on the radio. I held on tighter and breathed deeply. I didn't need the drugs, I just needed to chill, I was letting things get to me again. Sleep, that's all I needed.

'The bilge pumps have just kicked in,' said King. 'He says even if the ballast valve's stuck open, the pumps should keep up.'

The walkie-talkie crackled again. 'I don't know what you have done,' said Katanga, 'but the gauge is showing aft peak tank is full all of a sudden.'

'Katanga says...'

'Yeah, I heard.' I looked down into the black water. 'And I owe you a new torch.'

'Oh man, really?' he stood above me, looking down. 'I've had that for years, not a scratch, and soon as I lend it you, boom, it's gone.'

'It's still down there if you wanna go get it.'

What I was more worried about was when I'd dropped the torch, I'd dropped the material that had jammed up the end of the tank's depth gauge.

I climbed up into the access space, King helped me shuffle across the floor then slammed the cover shut, kicking the lock across. Hopefully he'd locked my nightmares down there.

'Someone didn't want us to get far,' I said, shivering.

'You always were paranoid. Let's get the fuck out of here.'

'Give me a minute.'

I grabbed my jacket, pulled my knees in, and sat back against the hull, feeling the crashing waves through my spine. The auto bilge pumps being offline, the cover into the ballast tank being left open, the valve on the ballast inlet pipe sticking open. And someone jamming up the gauge that measured the depth of water in the tank, so that no one would notice any of those things until it was too late.

Whatever ghoul haunted these dimly lit passageways, it had an uncanny ability to interact with the physical world. If I didn't know better, I'd think it'd already taken a dislike to me.

Chapter Nine

Tiburon

King and I returned via the external stairs, opening the door at the same time as someone entered the bridge via the internal staircase. A short, rounded man with white hair escaping down onto his shoulders, leaving the top of his head empty to reflect the multi-coloured lights of the instrument panel. He closed the door behind him and turned, smiling.

The doctor was a welcome sight in more ways than one, another friendly face I'd known since I'd first used Miller's taxi service. I'd learned his real name once, but it was such a long time ago, and I'd been so drunk, that considering everyone else called him 'Doc' I didn't see any need to worry myself about it.

'My boy, my boy, come here.' He put a bag and a glass down on the desk then clasped my cheeks. He looked into my eyes for a few moments then pulled away, looked me up and down, and frowned. 'Soaking wet... You'll be dead of hypothermia before we reach England.'

I pushed my hair up from my face, threw my dripping jacket on the table, and reached for Miller's rum. 'All good, Katanga?' I asked.

He gave a thumbs up without turning. What I'd just done was apparently an everyday occurrence to these bandits. 'She's coming up again at the stern.'

It certainly wasn't an everyday occurrence to me. I unscrewed the bottle and took a gulp for my nerves, then a second to replace the rum I'd thrown up in the tank.

'Come here, come here,' Doc said, snatching the bottle from me and leading me to the chair.

'I think he's in worse shape.' I pointed to King.

Doc looked at King, at his hands on his head. 'Feeling a bit *Moby Dick*, are we? I have some seasickness tablets below.'

'I'm fine,' King said.

'Mr King, I'll remind you of the time you managed to contract malaria twenty-four hours after setting foot in Cambodia.' He looked over his glasses at the ex-para and cocked his head. 'Or your week of explosive evacuations in the Philippines. I'll fetch the tablets.'

King leapt up and ran for the door, a blast of sleety rain filled the bridge and then all I could see was a shadow leaning over the railings.

Katanga laughed and gave the horn a blast, Doc tutted.

King came back in, closing the door behind him but sticking close to it, back of his hand to his mouth.

'Now then,' said Doc, unfolding a pair of glasses, 'let's see why you require my services this time.'

I lifted my T-shirt to show him the wound. He took a cloth from his bag, and after rubbing at my ribs for a while, provoking more blood to spill out, he declared it a scratch.

'Really, you action men never learn. Two stitches, three at best.'

He should know, he'd originally stitched me up on a rolling ship in the eastern Med after a jolly fifteen years ago in Lebanon, and he'd had plenty more to do on me after that over the years. I looked past him at his glass sliding across the desk, almost empty but the brown ring halfway up told me why Miller had had difficulty rousing him. It wouldn't have been Doc's first glass, either. Fortunately his skills never seemed to be affected, he'd always done a decent job – though now I was getting on a bit I imagined I could feel his old stitches ripping across my kidney whenever I stretched.

'The Tylers were always injury magnets,' said King, still facing the ceiling with his eyes closed.

Doc reached for the rum bottle hanging under the chart table and poured an inch into the glass. He looked up at me, made a cheers motion and downed it.

'That's nasty,' said Katanga, I turned to see him looking at my side. He held something out in his hand. 'For the pain,' he waggled it.

King opened an eye, intercepting the joint Katanga was offering and pointing the twisted end at me. 'Didn't Tyler tell you? He's invincible.' He took a lighter from Katanga and sparked it up, blowing smoke upwards, it rolled around the ceiling. 'Made a deal with the Devil deep in the jungles of Colombia.' He smiled at Katanga, passing the joint to me.

Doc put the glass down, rummaging in his bag. 'And came out doing the Devil's work.'

I took a blast of the joint, Doc frowned, leaning in close to the wound, motioning for me to hold up my T-shirt.

Pain lit up behind my eyes, I shouted and pulled back, dropping the joint, fresh blood spilled across my jeans.

'Christ, Doc, what the hell?!'

King disappeared out the door onto the bridge wing again.

Doc held up a long steel spatula and a pair of tweezers. 'If I'd told you I needed to do that, you would have flinched.'

'A little warning would have been polite.' I picked up the joint, took another hit, closing my eyes. The pain died back. I took another long drag, holding the smoke down for a few seconds, then blew out and opened my eyes.

Doc wiped a tiny, congealed blob on the cloth and cleaned the end of the tweezers. He reached out and grabbed my T-shirt, jabbing his finger through the hole. 'Material had been pushed into the wound. It has to come out before I can sew it.'

'You got any morphine in that bag?'

'Mr Tyler, if I had morphine, I would not have had to take you by surprise.' He leaned round me and looked at Katanga. 'I wonder if he whinges this much under enemy fire?'

I passed the joint to Katanga before he could reply. 'Just gimme a minute, okay?'

No lights from other ships were visible in the darkness outside now, and the clearview windows were spinning overtime to battle the sleet coming in horizontally. King came back into the wheelhouse, dripping with sleet and sea spray.

Katanga swung his legs off the console. 'Turnin' now, friends.'

I looked outside, the sky in front was now lit in front with jagged fingers of lightning. After a couple of seconds I felt the difference too, a shift in the movement of the ship, rolling port to starboard more, pitching fore and aft less.

'Due west?' asked King.

'*Oui*, nothing in front of us now until North America.' He grabbed the radio handset. 'Sébastien, how's those engines looking?'

There was a pause and then, 'Port side still good,' the radio crackled back. 'Starboard engine's still running cool.'

'And how's that ballast?'

'We're half on three and four, aft peak full. We'll take a look at that valve when the bilges have emptied.'

'Lemme know about that starboard engine.' He hung the handset back.

I looked at the nav unit next to the table, the longitude and latitude, and then down at the chart. It showed us to be about five miles north of the Île de Ré's western tip, still seemingly sheltered by the great overhang of Brittany, but heading straight out into the Atlantic, into the deep water of the Bay of Biscay.

'Say that steering wheel got stuck; how far 'til we hit land?' King asked.

Katanga grinned. 'Two and a half thousand miles, give or take. Five days' sailing, but don't worry, we only have fuel for two.'

'Well, let's hope you don't forget to turn north,' said King. 'I don't want to be floating around the Atlantic for a week.'

'I don't have enough seasickness tablets, for a start,' said Doc.

'Oh no, you wouldn't be floating around that long,' said Katanga.

'How so?' I asked, taking another drag on the joint.

He laughed and went back to Mario. 'We'd be eating you and your friends long before then.'

Doc was looking at me impatiently. I didn't blame him – he was trying to help me, after all.

'Fine,' I said. 'Do your worst.'

'Not here, we need to clean and dress this wound properly, my boy. Come downstairs.'

I looked out of the streaked windows at the blackness writhing off into the distance, the flashes of lightning getting closer, then nodded at King. 'Stay here, keep an eye on my car.'

'Your *car*?' he crossed to the window, cupping his hands against the glass, looking from it to me and back again. 'What the heck?'

Chapter Ten

Château des Aigles
Twelve days previously

The German woman dropped a map on the coffee table and sat next to me on the sofa, pulling her long blonde hair up into a ponytail. She usually wore her hair down, when she tied it up it revealed a long scar. Glowing in the firelight, it ran all the way from her hair to her glass eye, then down her cheek to disappear under her T-shirt. She gave me a brief smile and picked up a steaming mug. She was comfortable here, in more ways than one.

The chalet I'd commandeered was a couple of miles further up the mountain from the target, an open-plan place, all golden wood and rough stone fireplaces with itchy blankets scattered over every chair. Huge windows looked down the valley to the village below with its multi-coloured lights twinkling against the snow, dark peaks rising all around us.

I spread the map out on the table, taking a swig of beer and putting the bottle on the corner to hold it open.

The woman put her mug on the floor and sat back. 'It cannot be done,' she said matter-of-factly. 'Not like this.'

The Scottish man leaned against the fireplace. 'That's the problem with Germans, no imagination.' He flicked a lighter and sucked through a joint.

She scowled. 'If I say it cannot be done, it cannot be done.'

The tip of the joint burned brightly, he pocketed the lighter and blew smoke up into the thick wooden beams. 'There's always a way.'

'The problem is here.' She leaned forward, wafted the smoke away from her, and ran a finger over the map. 'The access road for the electricity substation runs close enough to the target, but on this ridge we're exposed. They'll see us coming easily.'

'So we drive without headlights,' I said.

'I learned to drive in the Allgäu mountains, trust me: this is not a road to drive blind.'

'Is it a depth perception issue or are you just scared?' the Scot said with a wink. He passed the joint to me. 'I don't mind driving if…'

She shook her head, pulling out the hair tie and brushing it back down over one side of her face. 'Do you think it's clever to smoke that shit, am I the only professional here?'

'We could pull this job asleep,' I said. 'Enjoy the downtime before things get serious.'

'I do not want downtime, I want to be prepared. We cannot approach by this road, we are backlit here and here,' she pointed at the map, 'by the lights from the village.'

I smiled, blew smoke at the windows, passed the joint back to the man. 'We're convinced, okay?'

She was the best driver I knew, and had taught me plenty. The woman who'd recently outpaced me on the Nordschleife, me in my Audi and her in a diesel Golf. I stood and stretched, picking up my beer and walking to the glass wall looking down the valley. Lights twinkled far below, we could be in an airliner above a city at night. The chalet stood alone at the dead end of a winding Alpine road, secluded, no one else around but for an identical rental chalet a short distance further down, which was currently empty. We had the mountain to ourselves.

I took a sip of beer, leaning my forehead against the glass. One of the lights down there represented the house, the *mark*, the *target*.

'We'll drop in from above,' I said.

'Fuck yes,' said the Scot.

In the reflection of the glass he nodded and grinned behind me, pressing play on the stereo. The Beatles came on. 'A Day in the Life'. Christ, what I wouldn't give to sit and read a newspaper over breakfast, no *marks*, no *targets*, my only worry getting out of bed late and catching a bus to work.

The door opened with a whirl of snow, a swaddled figure entered and put down a bag. He slammed the door behind him, stamping his feet.

'Sorted?' I asked, turning to lean against the glass.

'No problem.' The newcomer pulled down his hood and started biting a glove off.

The woman said something rapidly in German, I caught the word *saukalt* – pig-cold – and something about saving a cow from the ice.

She smiled at my puzzled face. 'It is a saying, like what you think. It means, like, to pull something from disaster.'

'I wouldn't go that far,' I said with a smile, turning to the newcomer. 'That's why I hired him.'

The man was nodding as he took off his coat, still stamping snow off his boots and clapping his hands together. He'd lived in Sweden nearly two decades, since the day after he'd deserted Saddam's Republican Guard

– and been snowboarding almost as long – but he'd never really acclimatised.

'It may be why you hired me,' he said. 'But these radios are beautiful.' He blew on his hands.

'They better have been worth it, we already have decent comms.'

He opened the bag and took out a tiny earpiece. 'Russian undercover forces.'

The Scot put his joint in the corner of his mouth and took one from him. 'We need to talk about callsigns for the comms. I'm claiming *Wolf.*'

John Lennon had just started singing about Blackburn's many holes. I grinned, pointing my bottle of beer at each of the team in turn, the German woman, the Iraqi guy, the Scottish guy. 'Lennon, McCartney, Ringo.' I pointed at myself. 'Harrison.'

'You're the boss,' said McCartney, the Iraqi. 'Shouldn't you be Lennon?'

'George Harrison's the nicest one.' I winked.

'I like it,' said Ringo, the Scot.

'So I'm Lennon?' The German woman tutted, shaking her head. 'Let's hope I don't end up the same.'

McCartney smiled. 'Let's hope I live long enough to get knighted by your queen.'

'Peace and love,' said Ringo. 'Peace and love.'

Chapter Eleven

Tiburon

The ship was pitching and rolling more noticeably, a nausea-inducing motion that started on the port bow, slowly lifting the ship all the way to starboard side at the stern, then dropping it down and rolling it back. I've never suffered from seasickness but the thought of it worried me, a psychosomatic vicious circle that ended up making me feel wretched anyway. It also worried me because I had King and the others in mind – I needed them on their feet and not ill, at the mercy of this crew of pirates.

Doc had done a sterling job under the constantly shifting circumstances, taking me to his cabin to sterilise and dress the wound properly. Some of the best stitches I've had, not surprising when you consider he's an ex-Royal Navy medic who'd joined up way back around the time the *Tiburon* was laid down. That he'd been dishonourably discharged before I'd left school was inconsequent, since it hadn't been for his stitching ability. He was quick and thorough, but I was still thankful for the joint that Katanga had insisted I take with me.

He'd rechecked other wounds, too, a recent scar down my ribs that was healing pretty well considering I'd been snowboarding with it for the last couple of weeks, and a broken finger that was destined to be crooked for the rest of my life – however long that might be. Finally, with several tuts and a shake of his head, he'd discharged me from his care.

The passageways were damp, dimly lit tunnels of pipes and metal, which tallied with everything else I'd seen so far, but it was trippier down here; strange graffiti on the walls looked otherworldly in the flickering light and red emergency lighting. Faded Nineties neon paint ran down the walls, a ghost train of badly painted Simpsons characters and Sharpied quotes in German, lots about Dieter and Franke and other random Germans, their feelings on ex-Chancellor Helmut Kohl, long-gone band names, all from when the boat had been laid up at the end of the Cold War. *Drop acid not bombs* one piece said, I stumbled onward through a twisting crack den retro Laser Quest, both propelled and hampered by Marseille's finest Moroccan resin, swaying along the central passageway running fore and aft at the deck level of the superstructure. Doc had told me our rooms were belowdecks, in the dark belly of the ship, with engineering, workshop, and of course the engines.

A radio was playing somewhere, tinny noises rolling and bouncing around the steel corridors rendering the song unintelligible. It was coming from an open doorway ahead painted up as a huge mouth. Beyond it the passage continued to a crossroads. The lights flickered again and went out.

I pressed my arms out either side and braced against the clammy walls. Dim red emergency lighting ahead illuminated the floor and the bulkhead. I shuffled along the rubbery non-slip flooring, glancing into the mouth-doorway – a comms room, the radio tuned to some obscure station, a crackling and indistinct German voice, all staccato commands. A burst of static, a song cut in, '99 Red Balloons'. The radio crackled again and cut out completely, quiet but for the ever-present crash of waves reverberating round the hull. In the pauses between them I became aware of voices seeping out of the spaces between the rivets, as if the ship itself were whispering.

Ahead of me in the passageway something caught my eye. I stopped, eyes straining into the darkness.

'Hey, any chance you know where the stairs are?'

Something flitted across the passageway ahead. I rushed forward, grabbing the bulkhead and swinging through into the cross-passage running the width of the super-structure. I squinted into the darkness. Empty, a single door at the end leading back outside. I walked over to it, tried the handle. Locked. I was about to turn and check when the emergency lighting cut out completely, the passageway went black. I tried to follow the wall back but slipped and fell as the deck tilted.

'Tyler?'

The emergency lights kicked back in. Poubelle was standing in the middle of the crossroads back along the passage.

I rolled over and used the wall to climb to my feet. 'Health and safety nightmare.'

The lights cut out again for a couple of seconds, when they came back on Poubelle was swaying next to me. He pointed up at a bulb encased in a metal cage on the ceiling. 'We have shorts everywhere, she doesn't like rough weather.' He put a hand out to steady me. 'Or passengers.'

'She?'

'Has no one told you? You shouldn't be wandering around alone down here in the dark.' He mock-shivered and laughed, but the humour didn't quite make it to his eyes.

'Tell me about it, my lawyers will be in touch.'

He smiled, the lights flickered again, the smile dropped. 'This is a ghost ship.'

I frowned. 'Leave it out.'

'It's true.' He beckoned for me to follow him. 'Found adrift off Kolobrzeg in '83, no trace of the crew.' We walked back round the corner, he knocked on the open door to the radio room. 'Hey Nic!' he shouted.

I stumbled after him into the light spilling from a doorway, saw a young guy I swear hadn't been there a minute before. He took off a pair of earphones and turned from the ship's radio.

'Captain says to holler the instant you hear anything, got it?' said Poubelle, jerking a thumb over his shoulder at me. 'He says be on the lookout, no telling what this asshole's got us into.'

'Expecting trouble already?' I asked.

'His words, not mine.' He closed the radio room door, painted with fangs that completed the mouth, and turned the other way. 'Yeah, they think the crew abandoned ship when she lost power in rough weather, but who knows. They were never found.' He waited for me at the top of a narrow stairway.

'Bollocks.'

'Google that shit. Then there's the first mate who went mad in '87, stabbed four crew members to death before they locked him in the hold. Found him hanging in there when they arrived in port.' He smiled. 'No one knows why.'

'Poubelle!'

71

I turned to see Miller striding along the passageway. 'Get below and help Seb with that ballast valve,' he shouted. Poubelle nodded, I watched him descend into the flickering belly of the ship. 'Superstitions, give me strength.'

'I knew I should have taken the Chunnel,' I said.

'I'd rather you had.'

'Little bit of gratitude wouldn't go amiss, you know. I did just stop us sinking.'

'Don't over-egg it, you checked the ballast tank for water is all.'

He started to walk down the stairs, I grabbed his shoulder and turned him back. 'It was sabotaged.'

'Bullshit, these things happen…'

'I went in that ballast tank, Miller. I—'

'Jesus H. Christ, man, God knows the shit living in there. And at sea? What the hell were you thinking?'

'I found chuddy, Miller. Stuck over the gauge.'

'Chuddy?'

'Chewing gum. Someone had stuck it over the end of the pressure gauge pipe so it registered empty.'

He shrugged off my hand. 'I suppose you can prove that?'

'I dropped it in the tank.'

He nodded exaggeratedly and rolled his eyes. 'You expect me to believe someone on board wants to send us to the bottom?'

'We're not far from land, worth it if there's a big enough incentive. The cover was left open to flood the decks, and the bilge pumps were disabled. What are the chances?'

He narrowed his eyes. 'But like you said, no proof.'

'Of course not.'

'Then leave the ship to me.' He walked down the stairs, spun and pointed up at me. 'You just worry about these friends of yours.'

I followed him down, gripping the rail closely to avoid being pitched over the top of him. We turned at the bottom, past a huge bulkhead and watertight door that looked like it would lead forward towards the cargo hold and bow, but Miller led me back along another passageway aft. We stopped at the far end, cabin doors either side of us and between them, a heavy watertight door – the internal access into what I guessed was the area King and I had explored not long before.

'Why is this one welded up?' I asked, knocking on the door.

Miller grinned. 'Customs hate it, they spend ages trying to open it, I tell them it's always been like that, they decide it's suspicious. By the time they've got in through the outer hatch and found nothing they usually can't be bothered to search much more.' He placed his hand on the door handle to the right. 'You VIPs have got the master stateroom, you'll love it.' He opened the door, a woman inside turned, I looked past her at a man getting up off a bed, they both eyed me warily.

'I'm Tyler.' I shook the woman's hand.

'Martinez,' she replied. Despite being slightly shorter than me she was built like an MMA fighter. She'd opted for tactical gear from her native States – which was overkill – and, just like King, finished it off with an ugly-looking knife strapped to one thigh and a holster on the other – which probably wasn't overkill. The Walther that I guessed usually resided in it sat partially stripped on the bed behind her.

'Fields,' said the big guy ambling forward, seemingly the only person that had got the memo on dressing down, though he'd always struggle to travel incognito. Like me, he'd gone with jeans and a T-shirt, but unlike me he'd chosen both a couple of sizes too small to accentuate his physique. 'What the hell happened to you?' he asked, Glaswegian accent thick and strong. 'Simple transport job my arse.'

'Nothing for a big fella like you to worry about.'

'Aye, right.' He stuck out his hand suspiciously, I shook it much quicker than Martinez's as he tried the old alpha crush shit, but I'd already pulled away.

I stepped into the room. A symphony of grey steel and chipped plywood, decorated only with a few grubby pages from porn mags and a Wonder Woman poster, everything draped in a layer of dust. I noticed the beds had sick buckets next to them, though both were empty for now.

'Master stateroom,' I muttered, looking at the bent metal bedframes on each side, a wardrobe bolted to the wall, a tired old desk under the greasy porthole. An ensuite peeped through a creaking door, the grimy shower beckoned. 'This might be worse than the last place I stayed.'

Miller closed the door behind him, leaning back against it. 'I can see how it mightn't be as plush as a chalet, but what did you expect?'

I narrowed my eyes. I hadn't told Miller – or the others – that I'd spent the last couple of weeks in the Alps. What else did he know?

He smiled. 'It's my business to find out what I can about my passengers.' I opened my mouth to speak but he waved a hairy paw, pushing off the door and swaying across the room. 'Especially when it's you.'

'If it helps, our room's not much better,' Martinez said, still clinging to the bedframe.

'And where's that?'

Miller spoke for her. 'Just like you asked, right across the way.' He opened a cupboard above her head and threw a small box at me, I caught it with painful effort and looked at the label: codeine. I nodded my thanks, popped a couple of pills out of the packet.

Fields looked at my torn, bloodstained T-shirt and grunted. 'You planning on telling us what we're doing? We've been waiting ages in this coffin.'

I dry-swallowed the tablets. 'That's what you're being paid to do.'

'Well, we've been under way for a while now, I think we can ease up on the secrecy.'

I looked at my watch and nodded. 'It's time to bring in the cargo.' I looked at Miller. 'Show me the hold.'

'I can,' said Miller, 'but there's a reason I put you in here.' He waved for Fields to move out of the way, knelt on the floor and reached under the bed. 'Fuel tanks are below us, three of 'em. It's overkill for our purposes, this old thing could get halfway round the world back in the day.' He lifted a flap of grimy carpet to reveal a wooden panel set into the steel deck. 'Below us is the old centre tank.' He slid a bolt, lifted the hatch, and shuffled aside.

I knelt and looked down a ladder into the dim room below. Miller reached inside, flicked a huge spider onto the floor, and pressed a switch. I leaned down and put my head inside, brushing away cobwebs. The smuggling hatch was the size of a decent en-suite, illuminated by a couple of caged bulbs on the walls, which were rounded and unbroken but for a filler inlet and vent at the top and drain point in the middle of the floor. The spider scuttled towards the drain, disappearing between the bars of the grille welded across it.

Rum and stale smokes filled my nostrils as Miller's head leaned in next to me. 'For extra-special transport.'

I'd planned on using the hold, but this was too good to pass up. Only a few metres square but the bare walls and single entry point – from beneath my bed, no less – was perfect. I pulled my head out, smiled, and clapped Miller on the back. 'I don't care what they say, Miller, you're okay sometimes. Come on, you can give me a hand. Fields, come with me. Martinez, wait here. Be ready.'

'Ready for what?' She stood, sliding the magazine into her pistol and cocking it.

I shrugged. 'Trouble.'

Chapter Twelve

Château des Aigles
Eleven days previously

I stepped out of the shop into the cold evening. The snow had continued all day, the village was getting busier as we approached the holidays. I pulled my hat down low and walked down the steps to the German's disapproving look.

'What's up, Lennon?'

She wasn't taken with her callsign but they'd stuck, so not much she could do.

'Was that necessary?' she asked. 'I thought you wanted to tail them, not go shopping.'

I pointed at the orange jackets bobbing around further down the street. 'We could go to the pub for an hour and we'd still find 'em within a couple of minutes. These guys think they're untouchable.'

'What did you buy?'

I took the box out of the bag, a fancy new smartwatch with integrated standalone GPS and a host of fitness features.

'You need to take up jogging, you're getting old and soft.'

'Ouch.'

She meant it, too. I dropped it into my rucksack, throwing it on my back. 'Come on then, let's see where they're going.'

The target was easily visible in the glow from the shop windows; Bob had finished his evening ski but unusually he'd headed straight into town after. We'd christened him Bob while poring over the files and McCartney's surveillance photos. Band Aid had come on the radio and Ringo, the Scot, had cracked a joke that the target was the spit of Bob Geldof. Of course it'd stuck – and prompted a whole host of ridiculous codenames for the other bodyguards.

Sting and Midge Ure stalked on either side of Bob as ever, carrying the gear, with the big bastard Branko – or Bono, as he was now known – bringing up the rear as always, eyes alert for trouble. No prizes for guessing why he was head of their 'security', he was the best of the bunch – if by best, you meant the one most likely to give us trouble.

I walked along the top side of the square with Lennon. Past its enormous twinkling tree, lights reflecting off compacted ice in the gutters, past the children shouting and squealing on the small ice rink, through clouds of *vin chaud* steam, caramelised nuts, stalls selling biscuits and Nutella crêpes.

Lennon squeezed my hand, I saw the Rolls Royce SUV pull up in the corner of my eye, taking up two disabled bays outside a chemist. Sting and Midge loaded the ski gear then climbed inside with Bob. We watched for a couple of minutes as Bono scanned the cars on the road, one hand never straying far from that Desert Eagle nestled under his enormous sweaty pit.

Lennon turned away, starting to walk back to where we'd parked our car, but I grabbed her hand, pulling her back. Bob had ditched the skiwear and emerged in jeans and a shirt. He shrugged on a woollen overcoat and nodded to his two bandmates, now similarly attired. The three of them walked in the opposite direction as the Rolls pulled away. Bono hovered for a few seconds more then followed several paces behind.

'Call Ringo, tell him we're off out for tea,' I said.

She raised a scarred eyebrow, looking herself up and down.

I pointed at the Rolls at the end of the road. 'They can't be going anywhere too fancy if they're walking.'

We followed at a distance, Lennon on the phone to McCartney and Ringo getting out of the bubble lift. Bob looked smaller in his civvies, squeezed in between the two bodyguards.

McCartney had fished out more intel on the core security team. Sting was a Brit ex-para like my brother, with a matching dishonourable discharge, but unlike my brother the reasons were numerous and varied. Midge was ex-Spetsnaz, Russian special forces. Bono, their Serbian head of security, was a wanker with a blurry history of war crimes going back nearly thirty years. The random goons back at the house were mostly deluded thugs, with a few ex-military dregs thrown in. More DDs for those guys, they weren't exactly a shining endorsement of their respective countries' armed forces. Dutch, Belgian, Brits, and – like Bob – Aussies. A real mixed bag but they all had something in common; they were all weapons-grade arseholes.

I patted Lennon's arm, she hung up the phone and accelerated ahead, heading for the restaurant Bono had just disappeared into. *Le Cerf Sauvage*, a heraldic-looking stag carved above the door scowled down at us.

I left, doubled back down an alley, came round, waited for a couple of minutes by a jewellery shop window to make sure no one else was following. When I was satisfied

I mounted the steps, ignoring the disapproving look from the stag, and pushed through the door.

The warmth hit like a wall, like leaving England in February and stepping off the plane onto a runway in Cuba. A rustic alpine restaurant with a bar at the back, three-quarters full with the type of people who use 'winter' as a verb. I took off my jacket and scanned the tables, Bob & Co. had taken over a large booth over by a side window. He was leaning back in his chair, shirt buttons straining, talking loudly to the thugs either side. Lennon was seated four tables away, pretending to look at a menu but I knew she was watching the door in the mirror behind the bar. A waiter smiled and started towards me but I waved at Lennon and swooped over to her.

I put my hand on her back and leaned close to her cheek.

'Bono is in the toilet,' she whispered. 'He kept his coat on.'

I sat on the bench so I could see both the door and Bob's table. 'Ten quid says he waits in the car again.'

She nodded in agreement. Bono appeared at the far end of the room, shoulder barging a teenage girl waiting for the toilet. I picked up a menu, occupying my hands to stop myself jumping up and putting a fist through Bono's face as he strode past us and out the door. Headlights flashed outside the window, he crossed the road and climbed into the Roller that'd just pulled in.

Lennon shrugged out of her Bogner jacket and removed the fleece underneath, quickly smoothing her hair down to cover one side of her face. Contrasting with the expensive jacket, she was wearing one of her various faded racing-brand T-shirts, always long-sleeved to cover the scars. I pulled off my beanie, ruffled my hair, and turned slightly to eye up the Roller. It pulled away from the slushy kerb and reversed into a side street to watch the restaurant. Lennon nudged me.

The waitress had arrived at Bob's table, his hand hovered behind her skirt. As she bent to take Sting's order Bob's hand shot up, she stood bolt upright. He gave her a leer and turned back to the menu.

'I can't stand looking at him,' Lennon said, mouth turning up into a snarl of pure disgust.

A man on the table over from them grunted his disapproval. Sting turned and stared at him. The man's young son looked between the thug and his dad, Sting's lip curled, the man looked down into his menu, holding it up in front of his son.

'I'll drive to Spain tomorrow to finalise the transport,' I said. 'You hold the fort here.'

'Don't be too long,' she said, eyes still boring into Bob's back. 'I might kill this bastard before you return.'

Chapter Thirteen

Tiburon

The ship corkscrewed through the black, rain coming at us from all angles. As we climbed up to deck level and navigated the passageways to the port-side door I pulled on my soggy jacket, transferred my pistol to the pocket, and zipped it all the way up. The air was freezing but fresh, welcome again after just a short period in the stale air of the old ship. In the dim spotlamps, Miller was already striding through the rain pounding the deck, I left the safety of the doorway to follow him. Waves boomed against the hull, launching up over the prow and dropping an extra deluge on us.

I paused to shelter by the rearward deck crane as the water washed about my ankles, Miller continued to saunter along as if we were on a summer cruise. My car was lashed down to the huge forward cargo bay doors, half the length of the ship away. In front of it the prow crane strained against its ties with every twist of the deck, threatening to collapse onto my pride and joy.

I clung to the railings and looked up at the glowing wheelhouse, Katanga peering through the streaked windows. I turned to see Fields still huddled in the doorway, he nodded, stepping out onto the deck, pistol up. He soon gave that up as he slid sideways. I let go of the railings and ran back towards him as a wave broke over the side, he flailed as he was lifted clean over the railings by the motion of the ship. I grabbed his arm before he was pitched overboard, pulling as he flailed in the spray, dragging him back onto the deck.

The ship heaved the other way, we slid across the deck and slammed into the superstructure. I was wearing Converse, great for driving but not renowned for grip on a wet deck. Still, they were a damn sight better than Fields' heavy boots, I kept hold of him as we rose on another wave, scuttering and sliding like Bambi on ice.

He gripped the external staircase and pulled himself to his feet, looking out over the churning sea. 'I dropped my weapon!'

'You absolute dickhead,' I shouted above the waves. 'What did you think you were gonna shoot out here?'

I pulled his arm, sticking close to the superstructure and holding on to the lifelines and grab handles as we shuffled forward. Up ahead, Miller was already standing at the boot of my car, hands behind his back, experienced sea legs flexing as he rocked with the motion of the deck.

'You fellas nearly went for a swim there,' he shouted as we approached, grinning through his drenched beard. 'Remember, there's no turning round if you take a drink.'

'Fuck off, Pugwash,' Fields said, but the edge was taken off by his inability to move without squatting and spreading his arms out, ready to grab the nearest thing, which at the moment was me.

I blipped the car, the indicators lit up the seawater washing around our feet. Miller waited for a wave to crash over the bow and the ship to begin the next climb, then made to open the boot.

'Hang on,' I shouted, handing Fields off to Miller and grabbing the boot lid myself. With a glance back at Katanga and King watching us from the bridge, I swung it up.

A pile of clothes was pushed up against the back of the seats, bulky skiwear and a bright orange jacket, huddled like a scrunched up sleeping bag. It shook when I climbed into the boot, whimpering, pressing further away.

'Shite,' said Fields. 'You didn't tell us the cargo was alive.'

'Listen to me,' I shouted to the shape in the boot. 'We're on a ship in the middle of the ocean, there's nowhere to go. You make any moves, you'll go straight over the side, you got me?'

A slight shudder of the canvas shopping bag on his head, another whimper said he got me. He was in no mood to argue, and couldn't anyway, given he'd a big strip of duct tape over his mouth. I slid a penknife out of my pocket, flicked it open, cut the cable ties binding his hand-cuffs to the load anchor points, dragging him across the boot. I noticed a dark patch on his trousers even though we'd made a toilet stop an hour and a half before meeting the ship. Maybe the stress was having a detrimental impact on his body. That or the ket and thiopental cocktail I'd been using to keep him sedated.

'For fuck's sake, I've had this valeted not long since.' Still, the bullet holes and BMW-coloured scrapes down one side had already ruined that.

I stepped down to the deck, steadying myself on the car, and shouted at Fields, still hunched over and clinging to Miller. 'Give me a bloody hand then.'

Fields leaned into the car and helped me lift my captive out of the boot, the three of us sliding as a wave tossed us sideways. Miller leaned in to steady us, I reached back in, grabbed a rucksack, and slammed the boot. We waited to complete another circuit of the corkscrew motion then shuffled as one across the deck, back to the superstructure, a journey made more difficult by the worn tread plates and relentless, driving, freezing water.

The man's boots clattered and slid on the deck, ski boots not being suited to graceful movement at the best of times, least of all on a ship at sea. Finally, Miller opened the door and half-fell inside, dragging us with him. Fields rested back against the wall, panting.

The man stood shivering and shaking in handcuffs. Miller looked him up and down, ending at the bag tied around his head, and scowled. 'I've told you how I feel.'

'Don't grow a conscience now,' I said. 'Come on, Fields.'

The man screamed and shouted into the duct tape, making a half-hearted attempt to ward us off, but with a bag cable-tied around his neck and looking like a deflated orange that'd been through a washing machine with no spin cycle, he was in no position to argue. We took an arm each, the captive sounded like he was imploring, fingers digging into our wrists as we dragged him between us like drunk mates on a pub crawl. King met us at the foot of the bridge staircase.

'Christ man, *item of value*, you said. I was surprised at your car but I'll be honest, you've gone one better.'

'Shut up and get him below,' I growled.

King knew better than to argue, or ask questions – for now anyway – and took over from Fields, who'd turned a shade of green and followed us by sliding sideways along the wall.

Miller paused by the steps up to the bridge, frowning. 'Doc will bring some breakfast down.'

Fields retched and threw up across the wall. King shuddered next me, he'd be next if we didn't get a wriggle on.

Miller shook his head. 'Keep to your cabins, and try not to wave any guns at my crew – some of them get kinda touchy about it.'

I gave him a nod, he stamped up the stairs.

A woman screamed behind a swinging doorway, I glanced in, saw people running around on a TV fastened to the wall. A man was watching, he turned to see what was happening, saw us and got up.

I slammed the door shut and continued aft, Cons squelching and slipping across the little round supposedly non-slip circles on the floor, dragging the man down the flickering passageway with Fields lurching behind us.

A head poked out of the mouthy doorway up ahead, the young guy in the radio room.

'Inside,' I barked, he dodged back. As we passed, he was half-hidden round the door. I glared, he turned and pretended to go back to monitoring the radio, briefly looking up as he put his headphones back on.

The lights buzzed and went out, we struggled on in the dim red emergency lighting. I stopped at the crossroads, looking back towards the radio room, trying to gauge my location. The German and Russian signs on the wall were no help, it all looked the same – that's to say, it all looked like a dystopian sci-fi nightmare in steel, pipes and riveted seams, flickering light interspersed with gloomy red. Graffiti scrawled in various languages mingled with badly drawn cartoon characters, it was all a bit *Das Boot* on too much acid.

'Here,' King said, taking the lead down the stairs. Behind us, Fields fought to remain vertical as he bounced from wall to wall, staying upright made more difficult with one hand over his mouth.

'Down,' I prodded the hooded man in the back, 'and hold on tight.'

I forced him on, slow going as he crab-walked sideways down the open stairway. My foot slipped out from under me, I gripped even tighter. He was fortunate to be wearing the bag on his head. He couldn't see the tight, steep metal steps, the rolling motion threatening to pitch us over the handrail onto the crates below. Above us a door opened, raised voices filled the corridors.

Martinez was waiting at the bottom, fingers twitching next to her thigh holster. She stepped out of the way, glaring behind us at the noisy crew members congregating at the top of the stairs.

We shuffled along the passage and threw the Michelin man into my room, Martinez closed the door behind us. Fields collapsed onto the nearest bed, grabbing a bucket, King shoved the prisoner out of the way and sat down.

'What the hell is this?' asked Martinez.

'Too late to ask questions now,' said King. 'If you had any qualms about the job, you should have specified them before taking the money.'

I gave him a nod of thanks, dropped my rucksack on the floor, and dragged the man to the hatch.

'Sit down.' As he did I knelt to open the wooden panel. 'You're going down a ladder. Don't slip or you'll break your leg.'

He mumbled something as I helped his boot onto the top rung then forced him down. As he descended I swung my legs into the hatch.

'Hand me that chair,' I said to King as I started to climb down.

King passed it to me, I reached the bottom and stood it behind the man, leaning in close.

'Co-operate and you might still survive. Sit.'

He sat on the chair.

'I'm going to take off your boots. Your gear can stay on, it's bloody cold in here. Nod.'

I knelt and loosened the ratchet. As I unhooked one of the catches he kicked out, just missing my nose and catching me painfully on the shoulder. I fell back, he made to stand, but I was quicker to my feet.

I shouldn't have hit him quite so hard, but you'll have to trust me: the guy deserved worse. The chair rocked, I caught it and straightened him up, pulling several thick cable ties from my jacket. He attempted a half-hearted struggle but the fight had been knocked out of him hours ago back in the mountains; within seconds he was bound to the chair. Leaving his uncomfortable boots on, I stepped back, watching his head jerk side to side, the chair sliding on the floor. I climbed up the ladder, when my head reached the top all three of them were staring at me.

'Don't feel sorry for him,' I said, closing the hatch and kicking the carpet back.

'We're professionals,' said Fields.

Martinez shook her head. 'This is looking more and more like some gangland shit. Kidnapping ain't my thing.'

'The guy's a wanted man.' I swung my bed down and sat on it to untie my laces.

Martinez was still shaking her head. 'That's what police are for. Abduction and extraction from European countries ain't—'

'Isn't *what*? Why's it okay when it's some Al Qaeda leader in the Middle East, but not here? He's a traitorous, murdering scumbag, and he's going to face justice.'

'So bad we're ferrying him to England?' said Fields.

'And being paid very well to do so.' I kicked my trainers under the bed then stood to peel off my sodden jacket.

'The money might not be worth it if you've made us important enemies,' Fields muttered.

'You think he'd do that, with his penchant for self-preservation?' said King. I appreciated the backup, and he'd tried to inject levity into it, but I could see he was thinking along the same lines as the others.

I hung the dripping jacket over the en-suite door then peeled off my socks, launching them into the sink. 'Look, we're covered. This time tomorrow we'll all be back home and considerably better off.'

King and Fields continued to argue it out. I grabbed my rucksack and rummaged through the clothes. Martinez sat silently watching me as I pulled out a rugged, waterproof satphone.

'Hold the fort, I'm making a call.'

She nodded and closed the door behind me as I stepped into the corridor. No faces upstairs now, no shouts, just the waves booming against the sides and the constant thrum of the diesels. I walked to the end of the corridor and turned by the engine room, passing the stairs and heading to a black porthole set into the wall, rhythmically dipping under the water. I pulled the antenna up and held it near the porthole, the display showed what I hoped was just enough signal.

The call was answered immediately.

'What time do you call this? Update.'

I'd often criticised Colonel Holderness' management style, brusque at the very best of times and downright shitty at all others, but the relationship had soured recently.

'I was instructed not to call until the parcel was in the post.'

'Any problems?'

'A little traffic. Still managed to catch the post office before it closed.'

'Trip going well?'

'Everyone's enjoying it so far.'

'Take care. We know children can act up on long journeys. Update me again at a more suitable hour.'

The phone went dead.

Chapter Fourteen

Tiburon

I pushed the satphone into my pocket, was about to go back in my room when I heard footsteps on the stairs. Doc, carrying a tray, like a mountain goat somehow managing to make it down in perfect co-ordination with the rolling of the boat.

'A spot of breakfast before you turn in,' he raised the tray. I followed him back to the cabin.

At the opening door, three pistols clinked in unison as the mercenaries inside cocked and readied, then relaxed. I stood to one side and ushered Doc in.

He looked at King's green face and smiled, placing the tray on the desk: croissants and mugs of coffee. Martinez picked up a mug.

'I don't wanna sound rude,' I said, picking up a mug and turning up my nose, 'but you got any tea?'

'Miller doesn't trust anyone who doesn't drink coffee.'

I put the mug down in disgust. 'Nor should he, but the question stands.'

'I'll have a forage, my boy. But first...' He pulled out a bottle of capsules and tipped one out, handing it to King. 'For the *mal de mer.*' He tipped out more pills for Martinez, Fields, and me.

'I don't get seasick,' said Martinez.

'Everyone takes the tablets,' I said.

'My dear Ms Martinez,' said Doc, handing her a pill. 'We are heading into the Bay of Biscay in December. You may have observed the current motion of the boat…'

King put a hand to his mouth.

'…but trust me, this is but a millpond compared to what we'll be facing in a few hours. Do not let that tablet resurface, Mr King.'

I took the pill and swallowed it. 'I need you all in good shape. There's no sick pay.'

Martinez pulled apart a croissant and nodded at the floor. 'You need to feed your friend down there.'

Doc nodded. 'I don't know who it is you've brought on board, but as a doctor I must agree with your colleague.'

'He'll be fed in England.'

Doc shook his head. 'When was the last time he ate?'

I thought about it. 'Maybe thirty hours or so.'

'Out of the way, out of the way,' Doc bustled Fields across the room and bent over the breakfast tray. 'Stress is a terrible thing. It's almost twenty hours to Poole, that's two days with no food or drink, captive in the boot of a car and then the stinking hull of a pogoing boat in a storm. I suspect your employers will be very much aggrieved if you deliver a corpse.'

He was only half right. I stood and lifted the bed.

He put a seasickness pill and bottle of water next to a croissant on the tray and passed it to me. 'Doctor's orders.'

'Clear off.'

He closed the door behind him. Martinez was already halfway through a croissant, inhaling the mug of coffee.

'You two,' I waved my finger between Fields and King, 'make sure you eat. I wasn't kidding: you're not being paid if you're too sick to aim a weapon.'

I opened the hatch once again and climbed down into the hidden room, placing the tray next to the chair. I pulled the bag off his head, dropped it on the floor. The man blinked in the lights, made more difficult and more painful by the broken nose and two black eyes I'd given him a few hours ago. I peeled the tape off his mouth.

'Don't say a word. I'm gonna cut one arm loose so you can eat something.' I nodded at the tray and flicked open my knife.

'Please, I didn't mean—'

I clenched a fist, glanced up at the hatch in the ceiling then fixed him with a hard stare, he closed his mouth. Everything about him repulsed me, I was itching to beat the shit out of him and wondered, not for the first time, how cops managed it. Fortunately, I didn't have to; I'm not one of the good guys.

I sliced the cable tie on his right hand and stood back. Bound to the chair he was unlikely to attempt anything, and the guy was a cowardly rat anyway. But cornered rats can be unpredictable. He picked up the mug and drained half in one go.

'If you so much as make a sound...' I let him decide what I'd do, left him to it and climbed up.

King was busy showing off his fancy new Glock again.

'Nice,' said Fields, dropping the mag and sliding it back in.

'You'd best get that back off him,' I said to King. 'He's already lost his over the side.'

'Got another in my cabin,' Fields said. He squinted along the pistol at the door. 'What do you think, Tyler?'

I shrugged. 'I always thought the person holding it was the important bit.' I kicked the hatch cover closed. 'Suppose he needs all the help he can get.'

'Seems you're the one needs all the help,' said King, pointing at the bloody tear in my T-shirt, 'since you've got us along to babysit you.'

'You guys go way back?' Martinez asked.

'Too far,' I said.

Fields finally put the gun down and started picking at a croissant. 'You served together?'

I shook my head and leaned against the wall to brace against the rocking motion. 'I'm not military.'

She looked puzzled. 'Weird career choice, then. How'd you get into it?'

'I knew someone who knew someone.' I looked at King.

He coughed and picked up his coffee. 'Ranger, aren't you?' he asked her.

She nodded. 'Past tense. You?'

'Paras. Long time ago, now.'

'Royal Marines,' said Fields. 'Probably even longer ago.'

'You guys all been private a while?' she asked. I knew she'd not been freelancing as long, similar age to me but a career soldier.

King nodded and held his hand up. 'G4S, Aegis, Bidvest. Over fifteen years.'

'Same,' said Fields. 'Started with Cresswell in '08.'

'Where have you worked?' Martinez was looking at me but, since I didn't answer straight away, Fields jumped in.

'Mostly Afghanistan. Iraq late-on, Syria, some protection in South America.'

'So you're the odd one out?' Martinez persisted in aiming questions in my direction.

'Don't let that fool you,' said King. 'He's been in more shit than all of us. His brother was...'

'My brother was an idiot.' I gave King a cold look.

The speaker outside the door burst into life with a crackle and a hiss.

'What was that?' Martinez stood, opening the door.

'Tyler to the saloon,' the speaker repeated.

I sighed, chances of getting any rest were diminishing. I looked at my watch, quarter to four. Grabbing a roll of duct tape and a rope from my rucksack I stretched, opened the smuggling hatch, climbing down and pulling it shut again above me.

The tray was empty, he'd wolfed everything. I tore a strip of tape off, he started shaking.

'No, not that...' He shut up when he saw my balled fist.

I stuck his mouth shut, placed the bag back on his head, and pulled a new cable tie out of my pocket, securing his hand to the chair. I looped the rope around the chair and through the bars of the grill in the floor to prevent him sliding around too much. After checking everything to make sure he wasn't going anywhere I scooped the tray and climbed back up, flicking off the lights and securing the hatch.

The speaker out in the corridor crackled again. 'Tyler to the saloon, *now*.'

The others were on their feet. I ushered them into the corridor and locked my door, pocketing the key. I looked to King and Fields, still cradling their coffees. 'Stay here. No one enters this room, *no one*. Martinez, with me.'

She gave me a nod, happy to be finally doing something.

My bare feet slapped the rubber flooring, a lot easier than wet trainers but the flickering lights and flaking rust made me question the wisdom of it.

'You can call me Anna, you know.' She swayed in time with the walls better than I was managing to as we walked to the stairs.

'Don't use full names around the crew, they're not that friendly. Martinez will do.'

'Make it Marty then. Look, I didn't wanna argue in front of the others, but this op is bullshit.'

'King said you weren't much of a talker.' I gave her a look. 'Probably for the best.'

'I get the secrecy,' she persisted. 'But you said this was all about gathering intel, not people. And why me? You and King go way back, Fields is a Brit too...'

'Don't let him hear you say that.'

'...but we've never worked together.'

'That's exactly why you're here.'

She bounded up the stairs two at a time. 'Are you gonna be cryptic all the way? Cos if you are, the price just went up. I need to know what I'm into.'

The speaker at the top of the stairs crackled. 'Tyler! Saloon!'

I followed her up the stairs more cautiously, wincing on the ribbed metal treads. 'You're new to this, so I'll cut you some slack. The price is good and you should have specified if you were squeamish.'

She stopped and raised her eyebrows at me.

'How good's your French?' I asked.

'Non-existent.'

'Peachy.'

We carried on, at the top the lights flickered and went out. There was a commotion up ahead, a door swinging and banging with the motion of the sea, the room beyond was still lit with the multi-coloured glow of the TV. Marty stood to one side, I overtook her and pushed the door open.

Saloon was right, it was like stepping into the Wild West, the commotion stopped instantly. Marty closed the door behind us as I looked round the room, taking in the new faces. Miller had shed his outdoor gear and squeezed into a grubby Led Zep shirt. He was leaning on a counter that ran the length of the room, pouring himself a drink and managing to get every drop in the glass as the stream swayed in time with the motion of the ship. Next to him sat Doc, deep in thought, whether about our situation or simply whether to go with rum or gin next, I wasn't sure. The young guy from the radio room – had Poubelle called him Nic? – was stood in the corner, eying me intently. There were two other men, the big bald dude I'd seen watching TV earlier and a smaller ferrety guy, both dressed in grimy overalls, oil smeared on their faces, these must be the two new engineers, Sébastien and Vincent. They reminded me of that childhood rhyme:

Fatty and Skinny went to war
Fatty got shot by an apple core.

'Something funny?' asked Fatty in singsong rural French, rolling the vowels round slowly. I stared blankly, pretending not to have understood, he looked at my sodden jeans and bare feet, smirking. I glanced at the muted TV over his shoulder, *Jaws* with French subtitles.

Miller spoke first, in English for our benefit. 'Tyler, the crew is… unhappy.'

Fatty took over, switching into perfect English himself. 'You brought somebody on board.'

'I've hired this tub, my cargo is none of your business.'

'It is definitely our business,' Fatty said.

'Seb's right, it's our business if it gets us killed,' Miller said.

So Fatty was Seb.

'We were told four passengers,' said Nic, the radio guy, in French. I understood perfectly fine, but stared at him while waiting for Miller to translate.

When he'd finished I laughed. 'Health and safety concerns?' I shook my head. 'Stick to drug-running, is that it? Arms? Gimme a break.'

'We shouldn't be takin' no passengers, you know that,' said Skinny. 'She doesn't like it, not at all.'

'Shut up, Vincent,' said Miller.

So I was right, Skinny was the second new engineer, Vincent.

'It's true, Captain,' said Vincent. 'These passengers will bring the curse down on...'

'Shut *up*.' Miller looked at me. 'Things have changed,' he jerked a thumb at the young radio operator. 'Nic here's been listening. There's a bounty out, on you and your "cargo".'

Everyone looked at Radio Nic. He leaned forward, a serious expression on his face, switching into broken English.

'There was interference, it was difficult... but someone was out there. Dead or alive, they will pay for the return of their friend. One million euro.'

Marty was holding her breath. Behind Nic, Robert Shaw began a subtitled monologue about never putting on a life jacket.

I looked at Miller. 'I hope for your sake the call went unanswered.'

He spread his arms out and gave me a lopsided smile. 'It's more than you're paying.'

The temperature in the room seemed to drop by several degrees, everyone was silent, the room creaked with the crashing waves. Skinny flexed his knuckles and slowly reached into his pocket. Seb patted the wrench into his free hand. Sod's law had already told me this wouldn't be plain sailing, but things had taken a turn much quicker than I'd expected. Lightning flashing through the windows, glinting off tensed jaws sheened with oil and sweat, narrowed eyes. Nic slid away from the wall, reaching behind him. His hand came out with a large knife, one of those evil black tanto types the Bundeswehr use. The fact he was wasting time posturing with it meant he was young *and* stupid. I always think the first time anyone should know you're carrying a blade is when they're wondering why they're bleeding out.

Marty took a step forward, shoulder to shoulder with me, flicking the cover off her holster. Intakes of breath as she slid the Walther up just an inch.

Miller's eyes darted between her, his nervous crew and me, still no one breathed. Vincent continued to fidget with his pocket, which I noted was distinctly revolver-shaped. Marty's fingers twitched at her side as we leaned one way then the other with the ship, swaying in unison like a poor man's Michael Jackson video.

I put my arm out, across Marty, waving her hand down, and looked at Miller. 'You know who I'm working for. You'll make some powerful enemies if you double cross me.'

'We are not kidnappers,' Vincent said, turning the revolver, still in his pocket, to point towards me.

'Easy, Vincent,' said Miller, waving his hand back at him and his revolver-shaped pocket.

Doc finally made his decision, pouring a glass of rum. 'Gentlemen, this is all very confrontational. You know I abhor violence.'

'Says the man discharged for affray in a South African bar,' I said with a wry smile.

'The fire of youth, Mr Tyler.' He looked round his shipmates. 'We may not agree with Mr Tyler's ethics, but neither do we make deals with despicable racists and bigots.' I raised an eyebrow, he smiled. 'It is not difficult to put two and two together and know who you have brought aboard, Mr Tyler.' He looked at Miller. 'I think the quicker we get to England and help Mr Tyler on his way, the better for everyone, hmm?'

Miller looked round the crew then stared at me, taking a drink. He gulped it down and slammed the glass on the countertop. 'From now on, no one uses the radio. Let's get these bastards off our boat as quickly as possible.'

He wiped his beard with the back of his hand and strode across the room, Marty's hand flexed on her gun, the others leaned forward. I stood aside and let him push past, the cue for everyone to stand down. I followed, backing out of the room, Marty did the same, never taking her eyes off them. The way she moved, the way she held her nerve, fingers hovering close to that pistol; she hadn't been cheap, but like a bottle of L'Oréal she was clearly worth it. I'm pretty sure she could have put bullets through the eyes of every man in that room before they knew what'd happened. I shuddered as I pictured the last time I'd seen someone point-blank put a bullet through someone's eye.

Marty closed the door behind her, gave us both a black look.

I grabbed Miller by the lapels of his shirt, slammed him against the dirty wall. 'What the hell was that?' He pushed against me but I slammed him again, his eyes went wide. 'Thanks for the backup,' I said close to his face.

'How long have we known each other, Tyler?'

'Since Sierra Leone.'

'Fifteen years, give or take, so I'm gonna be frank. I don't like it.' He nodded at Marty, still scowling at us by the door. 'And it looks like your own team feel the same.'

The saloon door opened, I couldn't see who it was because they didn't make it to the threshold before Marty had her pistol drawn. Several shouts sprang up inside the room, Miller leaned round me and waved his hand.

'Shut the goddamn door,' he shouted. It slammed. 'I don't like it, Tyler, and neither do my crew.'

Marty watched us carefully, one hand on the door handle, the other still gripping her pistol down low. Her eyes flicked as she assessed which was the biggest threat – the crew, Miller, or possibly me. I let go of Miller's shirt.

'Didn't tell us what you were transporting, did ya?' he continued. 'We smuggle drugs, Tyler.' He waved for us to follow him, striding along the tilting corridor, swaying in time with the floor while I staggered and bounced in his wake. 'We smuggle drugs and bullion and guns and pretty much anything else UPS won't carry.' He stopped at the top of the stairs. 'We don't smuggle people.'

I paused, gesturing for Marty to go below. 'Fifteen years... Bit late to grow morals.'

He looked like he wanted to say something else but saw the anger in my eyes and stopped himself. I left him, following Marty down the stairs into the cold bowels of the ship.

He found his voice when I was out of arm's reach. 'Fuck you, Tyler,' he shouted after me. 'You know which ships carry people? Slavers.'

Marty was hanging on to the railings at the foot of the stairs, face flushed, eyes burning. 'He's right,' she hissed quietly, finger in my face. 'And I gotta be honest, right now I'm siding with those guys.' She marched along the corridor away from me, I jogged to catch up.

'Transporting people, transporting intel, same thing,' I said. 'Don't go all saintly.'

'I'll back you up in front of the crew, but I swear to God...' She stopped, bracing against the wall as the boat heaved and dropped.

I pushed past her and rounded the corner. King and Fields were still waiting outside the room, neither looking overly anxious, though a full holster and fifty years' combined combat experience can do that. Their complacency worried me, though it was somewhat offset by the fact they were both looking a little pinker; the seasickness pills were taking effect.

I unlocked the cabin door and walked in, throwing my pistol on my bed.

'Bad news?' asked King.

'Mutiny isn't out of the question,' I replied.

King gave Marty a wink. 'Welcome to Tyler's world.'

'Does he always have to rely on retirees to save him?' she said. 'If that doctor hadn't talked them down...'

King laughed. 'Doc's a tougher old devil than any of us.'

I shrugged. 'There isn't a person on this boat who isn't going straight to hell.'

'And you at the top,' said Marty. 'Extraordinary rendition. There are laws, you know.'

'There are laws against a lot of things we do, it's never stopped any of us before.'

'I'm serious, it's not what I do.'

Fields leaned on the desk, shaking his head. 'Look, I don't really care about the niceties, all that matters is who's paying and how much.'

'See, there's a man with the right attitude,' I said.

Marty could see she'd lost the argument, the others were staring at her like morals were a bad thing. After another few moments she sat on the bed, sighing.

'Well I'm gonna lose ma nut down here,' said Fields. 'Like a fucking iron tomb.'

King nodded. 'Can we at least get one of the topside cabins?'

I stepped into the en-suite and peeled off my wet T-shirt. 'This is the most secure part of the ship, only one way in and out.'

'Aye, that's what bothers me,' said Fields.

'And you a Sea hat as well?' King smirked.

'A what?' Marty asked.

'Paras think they're hilarious,' Fields said. 'Anyone who doesn't have wings is a hat. I'm a Marine, so...'

'Yeah yeah, I get it. Airborne have the same sense of humour, they call us legs.'

I dropped my soaked T-shirt in the sink with the socks, stretching, feeling every muscle tighten, wincing every time something clicked out of place. When I returned to the room the others stared at me.

King pointed at my arm, at the black outlines wrapping round it. 'Collects tattoos from everywhere he's done jobs. I don't know why, when he picks up so many scars from them for free.'

'That's recent,' Marty said, pointing at the line running down my ribs, the fresh red puckered skin where the staples had been removed.

'Got it in Scotland, would you believe?'

Fields laughed. 'I've known English folks to drink in the wrong pub, but that's ridiculous.'

'Thought you'd been sunning it up on an island?' asked King.

I smiled, looked at my watch, just gone four in the morning. 'Fields, Marty, you guys turn in, get some rest. We'll regroup at 0900.' No arguments from either of them. 'And be ready.'

Marty narrowed her eyes. 'For trouble?' she asked sarcastically, arching an eyebrow.

Chapter Fifteen

Château des Aigles
One week previously

I turned off the ignition, the Audi shuddered and went quiet.

'On yesterday's run I took it further up the road,' said Lennon from the passenger seat. 'There's a cabin below the drive where Bananarama live. Nice early warning system.' She reached up and flicked the interior lights off. 'That Beemer of theirs followed me back as far as the village.'

'I told you to be careful.'

She scowled. 'Maybe you should have been here instead of pissing about in Santander whorehouses?'

I gave her a matching stare. 'Well I'm back, so we'll use the Audi from now on. We need the Porsche to stay clean.' I wound down my window and reached over to the glovebox. The target's house was over a mile away across open white fields, lit up brightly, all glass and steel making the night recces easier. I pulled out a pair of binoculars and put them to my eyes. 'Looks like Bono's already having his fag on the deck.'

'He is early tonight.'

'I still think that snowdrift might cause access issues. Hang on. Yep, he just walked round it and the security light came on.'

I glanced at Lennon, she opened a pad and started scribbling notes, then held a rifle scope to her good eye.

'Bob's having fun at least,' she said.

I adjusted the focus as I panned upstairs, a naked woman was bouncing on the bed, Bob's lank hair flailing, balding head flashing in the dim bedside lamp. I took the binoculars away and looked at Lennon. She was leaning on the doorframe looking through the scope, adjusting the magnification with minute clicks. Her hair glowed in the faint light off the snow-covered meadow.

'It's the girl from the bar again,' said Lennon. 'What are these actually for?'

I looked down, she was holding a bulging prescription box in her hand. I snatched it, threw it back in the glovebox, then put the binoculars back to my eyes.

I panned across the wide picture windows of the open-plan living area to where several other Band Aid members were visible. 'Another one just entered the kitchen. And Boy George… yep, he's in his favourite chair. He's gonna have to get up again soon, the fire needs another log.'

'Sting is on the prowl upstairs,' said Lennon. 'You know the pills are just a crutch.'

'What did I tell you, Boy George is off to get more logs.'

'They only work if you get help, real help – I mean from a professional. They're not a substitute for dealing with your problems. Do you remember Martijn?'

'The Dutch butcher? He died a while ago.'

'He wouldn't get help, just kept taking more and more pills.'

I lowered the binoculars, gave her a grin. 'As I recall it was a bullet that disagreed with him, not a pill.' I focused on the upstairs windows again.

'They took off so much of his edge he was rounded. How long before you're too dosed up to dodge the bullets?'

'Can we keep on the job? No sign of Simon yet,' I said. 'Two more goons on the landing.'

'Take some responsibility.' Lennon sighed, putting her hand on my knee but taking it away after a few moments when she could see the topic was closed. 'Anyway, I have told you, Simon Le Bon was not in Band Aid.'

I put the binoculars down. 'Look, I don't know how it went down in Germany but in my neck of the woods Band Aid's a national institution.' I lifted the binoculars again.

'You are thinking of Paul Young.'

'It's our karaoke song all year round, why would I get Paul Young mixed up with Duran fucking Duran?' I panned across the house, Bono puffed smoke up into the freezing night air.

'Simon was not in Band Aid,' she muttered again, scope pressed into her eye. 'We should redesignate him George Michael.'

'I'm telling you, Simon Le Bon sings the verse *after* George Michael.'

'There are more guards tonight.'

'You sure? Maybe we missed some before.'

'There were more in town with him too.' She took the scope from her eye. 'I wasn't sure at first, but they've upped their security.'

In my binoculars Bono flicked his cig off the decking and clapped his enormous hands together. 'And?'

'This is getting too much. We need a bigger team.'

I put the binoculars down and gave her a look. 'These guys are hooligans, we can do this job in our sleep.'

'Not if they know we're coming,' she muttered.

'What's that supposed to mean?'

It was her turn to give me daggers. 'You know exactly what it means. We have a rat.'

I chuckled and put the binoculars back to my face. 'You're getting paranoid in your old age. We'll do one more recce tomorrow night. All being well, we go the night after.'

I wasn't looking at the cabin any more, truth was I'd put the binoculars up to hide my face. Because she'd just said aloud what I already knew.

Chapter Sixteen

Tiburon

Like the distant explosions of a war zone at night, crashes echoed through the empty cargo hold every time we slammed through a wave to begin our descent into a trough. A boom as we hit the bottom, tilting, the ship straining and creaking and holding its breath to see if it would rise up again or remain submerged, before climbing up the rollercoaster ride to do it all again.

In the lull between waves, I could hear King shuffling in the bed on the other side of the room, tossing and turning more than the ship. I looked over at him, could just make out his bulk on the bed in the dim lava glow of the emergency lights creeping under the door. I looked at the luminous hands of my watch. Six a.m.

'How the hell do the crew sleep?' mumbled King.

'Remember Spitsbergen?' I said.

King chuckled. 'I don't think that was as bad, was it?'

'Take off the rosy glasses, it was much worse.'

'Why put up with it, what happened to getting out? Last time we spoke you had a plan.'

'I've got a debt to work off first.'

'All these lucrative contracts you pull, how the hell did you end up in debt?'

'A debt isn't always money. Don't ask.'

'Not sure I want to be working for these employers. Is it really the government?'

'Don't ask.'

'It's bad juju, man.'

'You always think that.'

'I had bad vibes in Zurmat, remember?'

Of course I remembered Afghanistan, only too well. Supposedly an easy job but King had refused to travel with my brother and me that day, and only I'd returned.

King turned over again. 'You've changed, and not for the better. I'm talking to the outer shell. Where's the man?'

'You do this for long enough, you harden. You know that.'

'The harder something is, the easier it cracks.'

'What fortune cookie did you pull that shit from?'

He sighed. 'Why now, John? Why me, after everything?'

'I told you, I need someone I can trust.'

'And you knew I wouldn't refuse. You're a dick, you know that?'

'It's complicated.'

He breathed deeply. 'You know how hard it is for me. I see you, I see him.'

'That's why it had to be you.'

'If this is about your stupid crusade for justice…'

'Easy for you to let it go,' I snapped. I'd put a little too much into it, I knew it was far from easy for him.

'Don't you dare, we both loved him.' He sat up in bed, shaking his head. 'Jesus, man, your brother died in a war, I'm sorry for it, Christ you know I am, but that's the job.'

'He didn't *die*, there was nothing passive about it, he was fucking murdered.'

'And lugging a suitcase of survivor guilt around with you does fuck-all. Why do it to yourself? And why drag me into it?'

I took a deep breath. Time to fill him in. 'They're here, okay? The person responsible for the bomb.'

It took him a long minute to answer, when he did his voice had dropped to a whisper. 'You tracked them down? After all this time?'

'I got a break last month.'

'That's who you've kidnapped?' He swung his legs off the bed and pointed at the floor, voice rising again. 'That guy...'

'There's more to this. I need you to be cool, I've got a plan.'

Movement skittered in my peripheral vision, the dim light in the room flickered. I held my breath. It was still pitch black and raging a storm outside, spray crashed against the porthole. A shadow moved in the red glow, shoes outside the door.

I slid out of bed silently and crouched, retrieving my pistol from under my pillow.

'What is it?' asked King.

I held a finger to my lips and motioned with the gun towards the door.

In a second King was out of bed and alongside me, Glock in hand. I held my own pistol down low, reached a shaking hand to the handle, and threw open the door.

The passageway was empty.

I looked down the length of it but no sign of anyone. King joined me in the doorway.

'What was it?' he whispered.

'You didn't see it? Someone was outside the door.'

He took off down the passageway in his bare feet. I watched him disappear round the corner at the end. A few seconds later he came padding back, Glock held low by his side.

He shook his head. 'No one there.'

I switched the lights on, rubbed a hand across my face. 'I swear, there was someone there.' I saw the way King was looking at me and wondered if I'd imagined it. 'I need a brew.'

King slid out his trainers from under the bed, pulled on his jeans. 'I need a coffee, shall we shake something up?'

'I need to stay here to watch him,' I pointed down at the smuggler's hatch, unlocking my phone and automatically swiping onto the fitness tracker.

I froze, staring at the screen. 'Get Doc, now.'

The heartbeat monitor synced to the smartwatch on our passenger's wrist had flatlined. I clicked to refresh the data, the Bluetooth signal was weak but after the icon on screen had spun a few times it re-synced. The line was still flat.

I looked up to see King staring at me intently. 'What's happened?'

'Just get him, now! Miller, too.'

He nodded, running from the room.

'King,' I hissed after him, he skidded and looked back in. 'Don't tell them anything. And tell no one else.'

He nodded again and left.

I closed the door, flipped up the bed, and rolled back the carpet. The hatch was still securely bolted shut. I slid it back, lifting it, looking down into the dingy space. The bulky orange ski jacket was just visible, huddled in the dim light falling through the opening. I reached in, flicked the lights on and realised at some point during the night our companion had fallen over. The chair was on its back with him still cable-tied to it, sliding around with each wave. I breathed – the watch had malfunctioned, that's all, maybe he'd fallen on his wrist and broken it. He hadn't *actually* flatlined. I climbed down the ladder, hoping that was it.

I crouched, pushed my fingers up under the bag and worked them into the bulky collar, feeling for a pulse. Nothing. I tugged at the bag but the string had caught on his jacket, I hooked my fingers under and pulled, tearing the material from his head. My stomach dropped.

The man's face was contorted in a snarl of pain or fury, maybe both. It wouldn't change now, as he was certainly dead.

Nausea crawled up my throat despite the seasickness tablet, I stood and grabbed the ladder to steady myself. Unexpectedly coming face to face with a corpse is never fun, but rolling around in a storm in the stinking hold of a decaying ghost ship the effect was magnified. Waves echoed through the hull, I took a few moments to breathe deeply while the chair scraped around on the metal floor behind me.

I turned and looked again at the body. Looked like he'd been dead a while, the bruises on his cheeks that would never fully form looked angrier against his clammy white skin. No obvious cause of death but it hadn't been pleasant. His hands were puffy and bloodied where the cable ties had cut into his wrists as he'd strained. Heart attack, most likely, but I decided to hold off guessing until Doc arrived. He'd been right, of course – tying someone up in ski gear for hours in a car boot and then a heaving ship's hold must have been too much for him. That plus the cocktail of drugs swilling round his system. Obviously

I'd expected an attempt on his life, hence the security and secrecy, but I hadn't considered it'd be me that'd kill him.

I climbed back up into the cabin, kicked the en-suite door open, and ran the tap to get it good and cold. The water sloshed side to side in the grubby sink, I splashed a few handfuls across my face and stared into the mirror. More wrinkles, more scars, more greys, stress was an understatement. *Well if things go to plan this'll be the last job I pull for Holderness and his cloak and bloody dagger department.*

I went back into the cabin, opened my rucksack, took out fresh jeans and a T-shirt, rooting around in the bottom for a pair of dry Adidas.

Footsteps sounded in the corridor, I threw the clothes on, slipping my feet into the trainers as someone hammered on the door. I opened it to find Doc in his dressing gown carrying his bag, followed by Miller in his usual attire carrying a mug of what looked like coffee but left the aroma of rum in its wake.

'I wish to God I didn't need the money, Blofeld,' he said, taking a gulp. 'Because I'm *this* close to pitching you and your buddies over the side.'

'Wait there. Doc, come with me.'

'I swear, Tyler...' growled Miller, cradling his mug and leaning on the doorframe.

'Get out of the way,' said Doc, pushing me aside and climbing down into the hatch. He reached back up for his bag.

'You won't need that,' I said.

He tutted and gave me a raised eyebrow. 'Did I not impress upon you that the current conditions were not conducive to keeping a man tied to a chair with a bag upon his head, not least without sustenance?' He grabbed the bag anyway and climbed down.

'I know you're not a pathologist,' I said, looking at the top of his head shining in the lights, 'but I want a best guess at how he died.'

Doc placed the bag on the deck, stared at the body, then looked up at me. 'Have you moved him?'

I shook my head.

'Checked him over in any way? This is how you found him?'

'All I did was check for a pulse.'

'What the hell's going on?' Tired of waiting, Miller had stepped into the cabin.

'Keep him out of here, please, Mr Tyler,' said Doc, waving his hand.

I stood to intercept Miller as he tried to get to the hatch. He growled, shrinking back to stop his Barbadian coffee from spilling across the wall.

I pushed him back out of the room and held an arm across the doorway. 'My charter, my cabin, for the time being anyway.'

'So why did you want me here?'

'You need to know.'

'Know what?'

'Murder,' Doc's voice drifted up from below.

I turned back to the room, dropping my arm to let Miller pass. He knelt by the hatch and put his mug on the floor, I joined him and crouched to watch Doc pointing excitedly at the body.

'As you say Mr Tyler, I am no pathologist,' he continued, eyes shining, 'but I can tell you that a blade through the heart in such a manner as this is very likely to cause immediate cessation of life, and is seldom self-inflicted.' He hitched his dressing gown and moved out of the way so we could see. 'Particularly when the deceased is tightly bound to a chair.'

Doc had rolled him over and unzipped the bulky ski jacket so I could see the T-shirt underneath, stained red around the handle of a knife protruding at an angle from his chest.

'Again, I would like to stress my lack of qualifications in this area, but if I may posit a theory, I would suggest at some point in the last couple of hours your companion was attacked thus.' Doc stood and brought his arm up in an arc. 'The blade has penetrated between the sixth and seventh ribs in an upward motion which is consistent with being seated in front of his attacker.'

He carried on this extremely good impersonation of a Home Office pathologist, but there were three questions occupying my mind as I sat back against the wall. The first was fairly mundane, and the same question Miller and Doc would presumably also be asking themselves, which related to the identity of the murderer among us – unless they really did believe the ghost ship nonsense. The second was whether they realised the matt black steel handle of the knife sticking out of his chest belonged to Nic, that young radio operator, and if they did, whether they'd mention it. But the third question was something probably only I was thinking about for now, so I decided that was the most important question. That of how, on board a corkscrewing boat in the middle of the sea, someone had got past me, into a sealed room, to kill my prize.

Chapter Seventeen

Château des Aigles
Six days previously

The last rays of late-afternoon sun and the frenetic opening chords of the Beatles' 'Helter Skelter' cut through a haze of weed smoke. Photos were spread across the polished oak floorboards, Sharpie circles drawn around the bodyguards on some of them, notations and statistics scrawled under ugly, purposeful faces. Other photos showed the target chalet, annotated with distances, angles, windows and blind spots. A printout of the site from Google Earth was scribbled on with more notes, a map spread next to it was marked with different-coloured arrows. In the middle of the floor Lennon had laid out a large-scale drawing of the chalet, noting every window, every door, interior rooms and dimensions, furniture, even the Christmas tree at the end of the lounge.

I put my mug of tea down, plucked the joint from Ringo's mouth, and stubbed it out in an ashtray.

He scowled. 'We can still walk this job with both eyes shut.' He looked at Lennon. 'Or at least one eye shut.'

She gave Ringo a tight-lipped smile over her mug.

'Don't get complacent,' I said. We'd discussed the implications of the increased security, but the other two hadn't yet brought up the elephant in the chalet; the fact that more protection suggested the mark knew we were coming. 'Let's go over it again.'

Ringo rolled his eyes. 'Some easy off-piste, I take the shallow route from the north-west and hold at the corner here.' He pointed at the chalet photos and looked at McCartney.

'I drop in from the ravine further east,' McCartney said, running a finger across the map, 'and come in on the blind spot by the garage.'

I looked at him. 'You're sure on the jump?'

He nodded. 'No problem.'

'You don't look sure,' said Ringo.

'He's the best snowboarder I know,' I said.

'That's not saying a lot if most of your friends are Iraqis.'

'What's that supposed to mean?' McCartney asked.

'I mean, Iraq's hardly famed for its winter Olympics team.'

'Concentrate on your own task,' Lennon spat. She gave him a hard stare until he looked away, then jabbed a finger at the map. 'I bring the Porsche halfway up the road to this layby and await the signal.'

I moved her hand and tapped on a tree symbol. 'I swing round west and come in through the woods, ending up at this point below the front of the house.'

Ringo leaned over the map. 'Maybe I should play sniper.'

I shook my head. 'You might be a better skier than me, but you're a shit shot.'

'If you smash into a tree it won't matter how good your eye is,' he smirked at Lennon, 'no offence.' He looked back at me. 'I think you're scared of getting your hands dirty.'

Lennon looked livid. 'He may be a lot of things, but scared is not one of them.'

I gave her a little nod of thanks, sat back, picked up my cup of tea. 'Besides, if I do hit a tree you can all walk away.'

'And miss out on the rest of the money?' McCartney sparked up a cigarette and looked at the others. 'It's Tyler's show, let him try it.'

Ringo shook his head. 'They're risks we don't need to take, man.'

'Like he said, it's my show.' I picked up a Sharpie and drew a cross through a photograph of their head of security smoking on the decking outside the chalet. 'Once Bono is down you move in.'

'Via the front door,' Ringo said, 'where the real action is.'

McCartney blew smoke up into the beams. 'Then I'm through the roof window, incapacitate the target, hold the bedroom until the cavalry arrives.'

'This is the point the shit hits the fan,' said Ringo, looking at me. 'So you better be damn quick on the trigger.'

'You just worry about the entry, let me take care of the rest.'

Lennon cleared her throat. 'At the signal I drive from the layby here,' she said, tracing a finger along the road, 'up to the house, waiting on the driveway on the east side.'

I nodded. 'McCartney and Ringo get the target in the boot, you guys drive down and meet me outside the village. Then it's west in the Porsche, La Rochelle or bust.'

'Shame we can't head to my place near Geneva,' Ringo said.

He hadn't shut up bragging about his house on the bloody lake. 'We can't afford to stop moving,' I said. 'We run straight for the coast.'

Lennon smiled. 'Tomorrow night, then.'

I stood and walked to the window, looking down towards the target chalet. 'Easy money.'

Chapter Eighteen

Tiburon

Miller was unhappy, ranting that I'd brought a murderer on board. Never mind that his crew were the flotsam found drifting in French ports, and that the murderer was more likely to be one of them – especially with a million euros on the table. He did have a point, the three I'd brought along were killers for hire – but they'd be shooting themselves in the foot pulling this.

'Who has a key to this cabin?' I asked, stopping his rant mid-flow.

He didn't even need to think about it, eyes flicking to the shelf by the door. 'There's only one key.'

I'd locked the door and taken the key with me when I'd been called to the saloon. Fields and King had been on guard outside until I'd returned.

'It's your fella,' said Miller, his train of thought mirroring mine. 'The big guy.'

'Fields?'

'Him or King.' He saw my expression and added, 'A million euros, man. Wicked tempting. When did you leave the room?'

'Only when you called me to the saloon. Been in here the rest of the time.'

'There you go, then. Doc, go fetch Sébastien and Vincent, make sure they're tooled up.' He looked at me. 'We need to detain your people. All three of them.'

'Wait, Doc,' I grabbed his arm. 'I'm sure King's not involved, he must have left Fields alone. Let's ask him when he gets back, before stirring any hornets' nests.'

'When he gets back?' Miller looked puzzled, looking round as if noticing for the first time there were only three of us in the room. Alive, anyway. 'Where is he?'

'He went to fetch you after rousing me,' said Doc, looking at Miller.

'Yeah, he came up to bridge to get me. Said he was making his way back to his room while I waited for Katanga to relieve me.'

'Shit,' I said simply. The implication was not good; despite not wanting to believe he was to blame, King was on the shortlist of suspects – and now he'd taken the opportunity to disappear.

Miller's thinking was along the same lines. 'There's a killer loose on my boat,' he said. 'I need to warn my crew, tell them what's happened.'

'No, keep it between us.'

'Why would I do that? The man's dangerous.'

'Firstly, we don't want panic. Could make relations between the crew and my team even frostier.'

'I rather suspect they couldn't be much frostier, but I agree with your general point,' said Doc.

'I gotta warn them, Blofeld.'

'Secondly, you tell your crew, they'll get jumpy and put a bullet in his head before we can talk to him. Or more likely they'll end up on the receiving end, either way it's not good. Give me a chance to find him first.'

'I'm warning you…' Miller inhaled slowly, giving me that same look I always ended up getting from him. 'You've got fifteen minutes before we lock down this ship.'

Chapter Nineteen

Tiburon

I checked my HK again, sliding out the magazine, checking the brass, sliding it home. Like checking your passport in your pocket every five minutes as you walk through the airport, except here if that magazine wasn't loaded it could mean a very different trip, one way. I laid it on the bed, picked up King's paperback and grabbed a pen off the shelf, turning to the blank title page to scribble a timeline while it was fresh in my mind.

03:45 – called to the saloon, the last time I'd seen my prisoner alive. I knew the time as I'd checked my watch, knew he'd been alive and well as I'd secured the bag on his head and locked him in.

03:55 – I'd returned to the room. Again, I'd checked my watch to see how long until we regrouped – five hours' rest, I'd given them, until 9 a.m.

Since then I'd been lying in bed right on top of the hatch.

06:00 – I'd got out of bed and found him dead.

I drew a big circle around the ten-minute window, 03:45 to 03:55, the only time I'd been away from the room.

Locks are easy to pick, and on a boat carrying only mercenaries and drug smugglers a locked door meant nothing. I just couldn't see King doing it, so I scribbled a list of everyone's locations.

Me and Marty, Captain Miller, Doc, Seb, Vincent, Nic.

We'd all been together in the saloon during that time. So who did that leave?

I came straight back round to Fields and King, wrote their names first, followed by Katanga, who'd apparently been at the helm but since that hadn't been in my eyeline, in my book it made him a potential suspect. That left one crew member unaccounted for; Poubelle.

Four suspects, but realistically it had to be Fields or King, or both of them, unless maybe Poubelle had lured them away from the room long enough to get inside and stab my captive.

And where the hell is King?

Time to find out.

I pushed my pistol into the holster, locking the door behind me. The corridor was almost pitch black, not only were the lights off but the red emergency lighting had knocked off, too.

Fields and Marty were directly opposite, I looked forward along the passageway that led down the centre of the ship, towards the dim shaft of light falling down the stairwell, illuminating the huge waterproof access door to the engine room. Nothing moving there. I held an arm against the opposite side of the corridor and tried the handle, it was locked but something moved inside.

I knocked. 'It's Tyler.'

After a few seconds' shuffling inside, Fields opened the door, rubbing sleep from his eyes.

'What's up?' he asked.

I looked around again, the corridor was empty. 'Where's King?' I watched Fields carefully but he didn't react.

'It's not even dawn, isn't he with you?' he said.

I gestured for him to open the door, stepped inside and closed it behind me.

Fields yawned and sat back down on his bed. 'Nine, you said.'

In the bed on the other side of the room Marty was watching me, I could see her pistol peeking out of the covers.

I leaned against the door and looked back at Fields. 'Earlier, when we went to the saloon, you and King were on guard outside my cabin.'

He looked at me blankly like he was waiting for me to carry on, after a moment he nodded. 'So?'

'What happened?'

His face didn't suggest anything amiss, it was set at the right level of puzzled without looking like he was trying to look puzzled.

I pressed him. 'Did you guys leave the room?'

He shook his head. 'We were outside the door the whole time. Well, I went for a quick piss, but King was there the whole time.'

I didn't like it, but there was my answer. He must have known he'd be found out, so where had he gone? Where do you hide on a boat no bigger than a few buses?

'Tell me if you see King. And lock your door.'

'Slim chance of seeing him then.'

I left them wondering, jogging forward to the stairs.

I'd known King for twenty years, been with him through all kinds of shit. This job was nothing, not even a walk in the park. To him, this was sitting on the settee *thinking* about walking in the park. I refused to believe he'd fuck me over, but what other answer could there be? Why would he kill someone he didn't know? Just money? More importantly, where the hell was he now?

I looked up the stairwell. Low voices tumbled down, impossible to tell whose or even what language, competing as they were against the booming waves. I climbed up, the deck swayed more with every step until I reached the top, pitch black save for a dim glow spilling from the crack in a door, the radio room. I paused outside, peering in at Nic seated at a desk with his back to me, headphones on. The wire snaked across to the huge set built into the wall; he reached up and adjusted a dial.

I crept onward, past closed doors, following the voices up the stairs to the bridge. Miller and Katanga were arguing. I gripped the handrail, pausing at the top to look out of the window over the stern, watching the flag flapping wildly in the gale.

Through the window set into the bridge door I watched Miller and Katanga staring intently at the console.

'Again?' asked Katanga on the other side of the door.

'Pays to be sure. Make another turn, ten degrees to port,' said Miller.

They were changing direction.

I opened the door, Katanga and Miller looked round.

'What are you doing up here?' Miller asked. 'I told you to stay below.'

Katanga shifted on the seat and looked back out of the window, holding the wheel.

'Don't you dare take us off course, Katanga,' I said.

'Tyler, get below. This is my ship.'

'I'm paying to get to England in one piece, Miller.'

Katanga steered, a moment later I could feel the rhythm change under my feet as the waves assaulted us from a few degrees further round. I pulled my pistol out of my waistband and held it down low. 'Keep this ship on course or I'll steer the bloody thing myself.' I glanced at the instruments, looking for a compass or nav unit.

Miller shook his head. 'A hard man you may be, Tyler, but a sailor you are not.' He pointed through the windows. 'How far do you think we'll get if we start taking those waves on the beam?'

I crossed to the windows and looked out, up ahead the boot lid of my car was just about visible but beyond it the bow was in darkness, only the white crests of the waves blowing across the ship were visible.

'The storm hasn't changed direction,' I said, backing away and sitting on the desk against the wall. 'Why have we?'

Katanga turned. Miller nodded at him.

Katanga pointed at a control unit on the left, a screen and buttons. All I could see was a green glow. I walked over to look, Miller leaned in, I gave him evils, he backed away with a sigh, folding his arms. It was the radar, though it didn't look anywhere near as old as anything else on the ship. Made sense, given her occupation.

'All right, other than what looks like my old Speccy 48k, what am I looking at?'

The screen was awash with fuzzy snow, the effects of the storm, I presumed.

'Spotted him a couple of hours ago, about sixty kilometres out,' said Katanga.

Miller jabbed a chewed nail at the screen, at a small green blob at the bottom right. 'We turned north, he turned north. We turned west, he turned west.'

'You think we're being followed?'

'More like hunted down. They've made up five kilometres in the last two hours.'

'Coincidence?' I asked, knowing that was optimistic.

'Always a possibility,' said Miller. 'But a remote one. You see any other ships out there?'

There were a couple, but the trails showed they were headed either away across the Atlantic, or south towards Spain. We watched the screen intently, after a minute or so the green dot at the bottom right flickered and showed a course change, now heading north.

'West again, Kat,' said Miller. He slapped a pad of paper on the dash, full of scrawled data and calculations. 'It's not exact, with the storm, heading, speed, but…'

I ran a finger down the pad, he'd circled seven p.m.

'What happens then?'

He arched his eyebrows. 'One of two things. Either we hit the Cornish coast, or…' He shrugged.

'Or maybe they hit us,' Katanga finished, spinning the wheel.

Chapter Twenty

Château des Aigles
Five days previously

The wind's attitude had taken a turn for the worse, whipping the day's snow off the fields and hurling it at us angrily as we stood in a line outside the chalet. Below us, the village twinkled cheerily between sheets of white, oblivious to the three armed, camouflaged figures looking down on it.

McCartney stood on my right in his Russian gear, baggy white smock and overtrousers covered in dirty-looking splodges. Ringo stuck to US stuff for some reason, he was on my left dressed all in white with patches of blue-grey digi camo. I get my gear from everywhere, tonight crisp white Royal Marine Arctic overclothes covered my civvy snowboarding gear. The scientific process by which different countries come up with entirely different concepts for what constitutes the best in camouflage never fails to astound me.

The three of us were wearing military webbing and straps securing weapons, gear, and ammo pouches to our bodies, ready for the ride down the mountain. I looked between McCartney and Ringo, faces set into the blizzard, no jokes, no beer, no weed, all professional now that the job was on. My hands shook, I felt my own surge of adrenaline as I looked down the couple of miles of rock-strewn pasture. The unmarked, unlit, ungraded off-piste mountainside had been impossible to chart, too close to the target chalet to recce or practice. Google Earth had shown us a summer view, which right now didn't mean shit. On this cloudy night, we were truly alone.

The red lights of Lennon's Porsche SUV glowed away as she drove to the staging point on the road below to wait for the signal. The target chalet's windows gave uninterrupted views over the roads and all routes in from the front. We'd stick to the mountain's shadows and close in from the blind spots before they knew we were there.

McCartney reached round to his back and ripped off the Velcro strap securing his PP-19 Vityaz submachine gun to his webbing, holding it out to me. I took the strap and pulled it tighter, patting it down on his back. Ringo adjusted his leg holster then, for the tenth time, checked the suppressor on the Heckler & Koch MP5 strapped across his chest.

I pulled my glove back and looked at my scratched Bremont. The illuminated hands ticked round to eleven p.m. I reached out and patted McCartney on the back. 'Go.'

He jumped up, spinning round to point his board down the hill, hissing away across the ice-crested powder.

Ringo turned to me. 'Good luck.'

I nodded, he dug his poles in and shot forward, his skis slashing away at an angle. Within moments they were both lost to the darkness.

I tightened the straps on the G28 Marksman rifle slung across my back, tapped the leg holster holding my trusty VP70 pistol, pulled up my fleece snood. I rocked down, clicking into the bindings on my snowboard, shuffling forward to the edge, turning side-on to the steep slope. I'd moved the bindings on my freeride board back and adjusted the angle into a slightly forward-facing stance, ready for the deep powder.

I pulled my mask down and jumped forward, following into the same darkness.

Chapter Twenty-one

Tiburon

I looked at the ominous pulsing dot on the radar screen, thought about that Beemer in La Rochelle that'd tailed me from the Alps. 'Can we pour on more speed?'

'No suh, not in this!' said Miller. 'We're pushing as it is, and only making fourteen knots now. I'd say they're making closer to seventeen, eighteen.'

'You said our top speed's thirty, why have we slowed?'

'Look, we'll be turnin' north soon, runnin' with the sea. We'll increase speed then.'

'Problem is, so can they.'

'Kat, get Blofeld a drink, he's finally catching on.'

A flash of lightning briefly lit up the churning evil. The lights and gauges flickered, Miller thumped the console to coax them back into health.

'Looks to me they've charted an intercept,' said Kat, turning from the wheel.

'Faster than us, wonder what it is?' I said. 'Law enforcement? Military?'

'Not out here, not in a storm like this. Only things out now are the hardcore trawlers and the big freighters. They can't stop for storms, they lose money. The law – not so much, they don't get paid to go out in this. Besides, we know what she is.' Miller tapped a screen next to the radar set. 'She's a hundred-thirty-foot superyacht outta La Rochelle, which means they're not too smart.'

'How so?'

He tapped the screen again. 'They left their AIS active.' My face must have been blank as he continued for my benefit. 'Auto ID system. Transponder. Boat information.'

Katanga turned again. 'They're not that stupid. They're catching up, but not pushing too hard, not too risky.'

'Who's on board?' I said, to myself and mostly rhetorical.

'We were kinda hoping you could help us with that.'

I gave him another blank look.

'Fuck, Tyler. You treat this like it's a game.'

'Because it is. Because if it's more than that, then...' I shrugged.

'You've kidnapped their guy, using my boat for some kind of extrajudicial rendition shit, they've been on the radio. You're gonna have to start sharing some information real soon or we're all gonna be in the shit.'

'I chartered your boat "no questions asked", do I need to get the crayons out to explain what that means?'

'It's not a game, Tyler, not to us!' He slammed a hand on the dash. 'Not to my crew!' He dismissed me with a wave but I didn't move. 'Kat, bang a U-ey,' he said, snatching his pad of paper with his calculations back. 'We can put into Brest before they catch us, dump these motherfuckers, and get back to the Med where we belong.'

'Brest?'

'Should reach it by lunchtime if we pull out the stops.'

'Brest, the home of the French Navy? That Brest?'

'They won't look twice at us.'

'They will if I put a call in.'

Katanga looked at Miller, hand still hovering on the wheel as he decided whether to listen to his captain or the man who was paying him.

'Put it this way,' I continued. 'I'm paying you to take us to England. No England, no pay.'

In the corner of my eye Katanga made up his mind on which way it'd go, settling back into the chair.

'Goddammit, give me *something*, Tyler. I need to know what's gonna happen when they come over that horizon.'

'Bad things.'

His stare dialled down several degrees.

'Just hold your course,' I said, jabbing a finger at his chest.

I left the bridge, swaying down the stairs. Like Miller said, it'd be fairly easy to know if the ship drastically changed direction, simply by taking note of which wall I fell into.

The lights winked out. Eerie music drifted out of the radio room, I spun as someone whispered close by but there was no one there. The red emergency lights kicked in, the music faded away, I slid along one wall until I reached the glowing fangs of the radio room doorway. Nic was still sat in silence with his back to me.

Filing cabinets and charts covered one wall. Impressive and expensive-looking but largely obsolete radio equipment filled another. All overkill for a light freighter, but obviously a relic of the vessel's previous occupation. I remembered the last time I was in a cramped radio room. Despite the previous circumstances, this one was in a far worse condition. I noticed some of the radio equipment was missing the knobs from the dials, cracked glass, frayed wiring.

The lights buzzed and flickered again. Nic closed a laptop and pulled out a cigarette from a pack on the desk, made a meal out of lighting it, turning to the radio, blowing smoke. A bobble-head Father Christmas nodded at me from the windowsill, going crazy every time a wave pummelled the ship.

'Hey,' I knocked on the door, 'seen my friend?'

Nic jumped a mile, banging his legs on the desk, the headphones clattered to the floor, pulling the wire from the socket. Static and faint voices burst into the room. He scrabbled to plug it back in, dropping his cig in the process. I scooped it up and held it out for him.

He put the headphones on the desk, cleared his throat and spoke, with a melodic Marseillais accent that I had to concentrate on to catch fully. He was moaning about me being in there.

I shrugged and spoke English again, slower this time. 'My friend. King. He been in here?'

'I have not seen him.'

'Convenient,' I said as he slipped the headphones back on.

'Tyler!' Miller barked, I turned to see him standing in the doorway, face the colour of bacon left in the fridge too long. 'I thought I told you to get below, you've got no business in here.' He slammed a palm against the bulkhead, the lights buzzed back on.

I nodded, stepped towards the doorway, holding the frame as we rocked.

'Nic, isn't it?'

He turned in his chair, holding his earphones off his head.

'That's a nice knife you've got.'

He frowned.

'The one you had earlier. What is it?'

He smiled. 'It's a Bundeswehr knife, why?'

'I thought so. Can I see it?'

Miller grabbed my arm, with the help of the rolling ship he pulled me from the room. I stumbled against the far wall, grabbing the hot pipes to keep upright.

Miller was leaning across, waving his hand in my face. 'You might be paying but this is my ship, Tyler, my crew. You don't go throwing your weight around.'

'Like I said, I'm paying for safe delivery of my cargo to England.' I recovered my balance and slammed him against the wall, he pushed back but I gripped his shirt and slammed him again. '*Safe* delivery!'

His eyes were wide, he pulled his hands up to his face, thinking I was about to stick the nut on him. 'You never told me the cargo was alive, and we'd be chased all the way!'

'It doesn't change a thing. I'm half minded to get a refund.'

'A refund when your own man killed him?' Miller shoved again, almost trying for a punch but thinking better of it, he knew he'd still come off worse even if I had my hands tied. I let him go and moved back against the opposite wall, staring into his eyes. They were black, chest rising and falling, a man on the edge, though on a totally different one to me. The lights buzzed and flicked out again, we continued to stare at each other in the red glow.

'My cargo is lying in a room you told me was secure, with a knife sticking out of his chest that belongs to one of your crew.'

'Find King, get to your cabin.'

'Confined to quarters now, is that it?'

'Since you came on board my boat you've been waltzing round like you own it. You think you're tough, but my crew aren't choirboys and you're outnumbered two to one.' He gestured around the passageway. 'We see *any* of you out of your cabins before we hit the Channel tonight, I won't be responsible for my crew's actions.'

He retreated back up the stairs to the bridge, I let him, he was in no mood to help me. I wasn't worried about him – what worried me were the odds, which he was right about, and I'd seen they had the hardware to back it up. The closer that pursuing boat got, the longer King stayed hidden somewhere, the more precarious our situation would become.

And worse still, someone had killed my captive. Someone had plans of collecting that bounty. And not King, I was sure of that. Someone on Miller's crew.

I'd been in far worse situations, had faith in Fields and Marty, but still, things had the potential to get very ugly, very quickly.

I looked back at the radio room door, then around the others leading off into what I presumed were the crews' quarters. I waited until I heard the bridge door slam above and then hit the room opposite, closing the door behind me and flicking the light on, past giving a shit if it was occupied.

It wasn't. The cabin was furnished in a similar way to mine, fehgrau steel softened with splintered Seventies wood veneer cladding two walls, chipped plywood cupboards, and a desk with every surface and corner so obliterated I presumed at one stage it hadn't been bolted to the deck as securely as it now was. There the comparison to my cabin ended, as this room was single-occupancy, and clearly for the long-term.

A flat-screen TV was screwed into the desk with a PlayStation 3 bungeed to the drawers below. Above the desk the dark sea rolled behind a deep window ledge, spray flecking the glass.

A high-sided bed was also bolted to the floor, above it a lipped shelf ran the length of the wall. An elastic bungee ran across to hold books on during a storm but at the moment it was being stretched to breaking point round a stack of PS3 games leaning precariously out over the bed.

I bet myself it was Katanga's cabin.

I rummaged through the drawers and confirmed it when I found his passport, or more correctly, several of them, in differing nationalities – some better forgeries than others. A stack of cash suggested he trusted the rest of the crew, the ammunition rolling around in the bottom said he wasn't entirely trusting by nature. The door opposite the bed covered a wardrobe, which smelled strongly of weed. There was nothing to be gained by hanging around: it was Nic's room I was interested in.

I opened the door slowly, checked the coast was clear, and closed the door softly behind me. I listened again, satisfied no one was coming, opened the next door and slipped inside.

The room was the same size but double-occupancy, we were obviously further down the hierarchy here. The beds either side were unmade, sheets hanging on the dirty floor, clothes kicking around. Dirty jeans, odd socks, a pair of oily overalls hung on the door behind me. I swept a hand along the shelf above the bed next to me, knocking off a clock, a gun magazine, a phone charger, some dust. The shelf above the other bed held even less, but did have a rogue spanner. That was interesting; it was clearly the room Seb and Vincent shared, but I don't know many decent engineers who didn't take pride in their tools, and who wouldn't have put that straight back in its rightful place.

Lockers held more clothes, empty cig packets, broken lighters. Nothing to go on, nothing at all that told me anything interesting about the occupants of the room.

Every other time I'd used Miller's transportation services his chief had been Étienne, a Basque ex-Marine Nationale engineer, and a damn good one. I'd spent hours down in engine rooms with him. All irrelevant now, but what was extremely relevant was that he'd been murdered not long before I'd stepped on board, his place taken by a couple of new guys who I knew nothing about – and, by the state of their room, it would remain that way.

I crouched, looking under the bed. A distinctly Mediterranean-looking spider reared up then scuttled away. It'd been guarding nothing more than empty food wrappers and underwear. Under the other bed was a greasy streak along the back wall and rat droppings next to a vent cover, I could hear banging echoing up from the engine room below.

My knees groaned, I shifted and put a hand out to steady myself and that's when I saw it. Scratched into the grey painted steel of the bedframe, a tiny symbol. Like a cart wheel with broken spokes, it was a Sonnenrad, or Black Sun. A symbol commonly used by far-right and neo-Nazi organisations. I traced my thumb across the scratches, smearing grease across it. It was fairly new, likely carved by one of the room's occupants.

So we had the regular engineer of years, murdered in an unrelated scuffle days before we sailed, replaced by two new guys who didn't bring any personal effects with them but did carve white supremacist symbols into the furniture. Cool, cool.

I opened the door again to footsteps approaching down the bridge stairs. Split-second decision: back in the room or out into the passageway. I went for the passageway in case it was Seb or Vincent, not wanting to explain why I was snooping round their room.

It was Katanga, frowning. 'Still holding course, Mr Tyler. For now.'

'For now?'

'For now. You were looking for Mr King?'

'Yeah, seen him?'

He nodded. 'I just told the captain. He'll get himself killed before we get to England… if he isn't dead already.'

The way he chuckled didn't sound threatening, which is always good. 'Why do you say that?'

He pointed to the door at the end of the passage.

'He went outside? Why?'

He shrugged. 'I assume for the same reason he's been going outside every five minutes since we left La Rochelle.' He comically mimed throwing up.

I walked to the door and grabbed the handle, Katanga's face dropped. 'What are you doing?'

Water lashed the porthole as the boat lurched and twisted, I looked back at Katanga. 'Scared of a bit of rain?'

He walked to me, leaning on the doorframe. 'Going outside in this storm is not wise.' He looked out of the porthole and crossed his arms.

'So what you waiting here for? Can't turn the ship around if I get washed overboard.'

'I'm watching so that if I see you get washed overboard I can tell Captain Miller we can all go home.'

I opened the door, rain and spray blew in, soaking me immediately. Beyond the spray there was nothing. We were heading away from the sunrise, whenever it finally came, still forging into darkness, into the unknown.

Chapter Twenty-two

Château des Aigles
Five days previously

Somewhere in the distance an animal screeched, cut short by a gust shrieking between the pines. I lay on my back in the snow, motionless, waiting, listening. Nothing, no shouts, no engines, no lights flared in the whirling snow above me.

I'd glided across fresh powder towards the copse, entering at high speed before slowing in the cover of the trees, weaving between narrow trunks and piles of fallen snow, sheltered beneath bowing branches. Leaving the treeline, I'd hit the deep snow on the fields and cut sideways, dropping backwards, falling into the snow. I'd been lying on my back, watching the thick clouds dropping more snow on me, only too aware that if any of the inhabitants in the house chose to shine a powerful torch across the mountainside, they'd see three different sets of tracks cutting a path straight to each of us.

At this hour, torch beams were doubtful. We'd planned carefully, knew their routine, worked out the blind spots, where McCartney and Ringo could approach the house unseen. The biggest risk to the job was me, leaving the safety of the pines to cross in front of the house and its sweeping fields, Lenor-fresh blankets of unbroken white.

I rolled over, sinking further, staying low as I unclipped my boots from the bindings. I unravelled a strap attached to the webbing over my shoulders, snapped a carabiner onto the board then crept forward, hunched over. The snow was thigh-deep out of the cover of the trees and the going was slow, towing my board behind me. To my left, about 400 metres up the slope if I'd got my approach angle right, the lights of the house blazed a wide swathe, highlighting the swirling snow.

The unending white was utterly featureless, no undulations, an entirely flat carpet, dropping steeply away to the lights of the village below. A perfect killing zone, if one needed it, akin to the stretches of woodland razed around a castle to give defenders a good view of attackers. An unbroken field of fire, me right in the middle.

But 400 metres from the house put me deep in shadow. Someone at the windows staring straight down would struggle to pick me out in daylight, let alone at night in a blizzard.

I stepped forward again, deep snow creaking and squeaking beneath my boots. The heavy snow of the last twenty-four hours had settled on top of the layer of the last few weeks and hadn't had time to bond. I reckoned on the slope being a little over thirty degrees, not good conditions. I was acutely aware I was cutting a potential break line across the meadow, risking fracturing the slab and sending the lot down. This wasn't a particularly dangerous avalanche zone, but even the slightest slip could take me with it, onto the rocks below. It'd also bring everyone in the house out, not that I'd care if I was folded around a pine tree a couple of hundred metres down the hillside.

I dropped, suddenly and without warning, down until the snow reached up to my chest. I held my breath, the ground felt solid beneath me. I crawled forward, pulling myself out and lying face down. The snow creaked. I'd dropped through a weak spot in the layer, a sure sign the slab was unstable. I crawled forward on my belly, still towing my board behind. A *whumpf* sound came from below me, a crack raced along the slope. I paused.

'In position,' said McCartney in my ear.

There was a crackle and then Ringo said, 'Been in position for five minutes. Where the hell are you, Harrison?'

'Almost in position,' I whispered.

'Confirmation target is in the house,' said McCartney. 'Bob is heading upstairs.'

'Roger that,' I said.

'Roger who?' asked McCartney.

'Roger Taylor,' said Ringo with a chuckle.

Another *whumpf* sound, the fissure widened.

'Cut the shit,' I said. 'Two minutes.' I checked my watch, I was on track. 'Anyway it's Phil Collins, not Roger Taylor. Queen did Live Aid, not Band Aid.'

I dragged myself across the creaking snow, after another minute's struggle I had a good angle on the house. I pulled the snowboard in front of me, turned it on its edge and pushed it down into the snow, creating a small wall and, more importantly, a stable firing platform. I reached over the front to scoop snow against the board's dark underside to provide additional camouflage.

The lights from the house lit up a decked area and garden but failed to penetrate beyond. I knew from our recces that in the shadows beneath the overhanging roofs, snow had been swept into piles to create a walkway for the guards to pace circuits without changing into boots. We'd watched the one we'd dubbed Bono wearing a path around the house around eleven p.m. every night that we'd observed them.

We could have waited until four a.m. for our assault, when everyone was likely to be in their beds and experience told us there'd be only one bodyguard on the prowl in the house. Problem with that was we didn't know exactly where all those other bodyguards would be, or how close they'd be to a phone. Eleven; late enough for them to be relaxed and well oiled. Those that could drink would have been doing so for a while. They felt safe in their eagle's nest, especially now with the beefed-up security. Heavily armed, nothing but an expanse of white around them, more guards posted in a cabin near the bottom of the road to warn them if anyone came up. And who would try anything here, in Western Europe? What did they have to fear? Especially now, with mainstream discourse veering further to the right thanks to the media they financed fuelling hate from Budapest to Liverpool.

Their complacency was underlined by the lights blazing from every room in the open-plan retreat, no curtains or blinds to obscure their view of the village and mountains across the valley, but importantly nothing to obscure our view of them behind all that glass. Their attitude was marked in the way they went about their routines without variation and without care for who was watching. Sure, we'd seen how efficient they could be – when a crowd closed up in the village, or a passing car slowed, or someone got too close on the slopes; they were professional in an instant, a moving cordon, warding people away, assessing threats with hawk eyes and ready to pull various armaments from under their clothes. But up here they acted like a bunch of middle-aged businessmen on a jolly away from their families.

'Bedroom light is out,' said McCartney.

'That's Bob in bed,' said Lennon.

I scooped snow underneath me and sat down, the barest sliver of my hood protruding. I loosened the straps holding the rifle securely to my back, lifting it over my head and laying it on the edge of the upturned snowboard. A perfect match for the surroundings, it was Plasti-Dipped white and grey over its normal dusty sand colour and, like my suit, hung with torn strips of white fabric, collecting snow.

I shuffled in, getting comfortable, pulling my goggles off, looping them into one of the straps on my chest. I switched on the big Schmidt & Bender scope and flicked up the lens protectors.

'In position,' I said quietly.

'Check,' came three hushed replies.

I put my cheek against the freezing stock, blinked a couple of times and watched the scope's illuminated reticle dance over low eaves piled with snow, so close I felt I could touch it, deep shadows beneath. I swept across until I found the front door, placing the red dot on the handle.

I'd sighted the rifle in for 400 metres. I moved my eye up to the thermal imager on top with its laser rangefinder and got a reading: 427 metres from the scope to the front door, not bad going at all. I took a reading on the gusts blowing down the valley. Even with the suppressor the shot would be loud, but at this distance and with the wind blowing towards me, it wouldn't be heard inside the house. I adjusted the scope for the added distance and wind, tiny soft clicks, then locked it back in, I'd been using the rifle long enough to know it instinctively.

I put my eye back to the scope and panned across from the door, checking the outside first. Beyond the porch and covered deck, the obscene Rolls Royce Cullinan sat side-on. I traced over the empty ski rack on the roof, down over its ridiculous wheels, and over to a Range Rover that I hadn't seen them use yet, just peeping out from a timber garage. I worked my way around it and saw a small mound of snow piled against a log store. I zoomed in on the scope.

'McCartney, I can see your boot,' I whispered.

A slight twitch of the snow and it was gone. I moved the red dot up the long low roof, deep with white, overhanging huge windows. The top floor was black, I squinted down the scope at the dark room but couldn't make anything out, no show tonight folks. I raised my head, flicked on the FLIR night-vision scope and zoomed in. The snow disappeared, everything morphed into shades of grey, a shadow of a bed, a slight shade variation on top of it.

'Looks like Bob's in bed.'

'Sting's in the kitchen,' whispered McCartney.

'Copy,' said Ringo. 'Had eyes on Bono but I think he's gone back in the lounge.'

I continued to check the upper floors, then dropped back to the better scope to cover the ground floor, sweeping across the lit windows.

'Yep, he's filled his glass,' I said. 'Watching TV with Tony Hadley.'

In my circle of vision, a bodyguard threw a log on the fire then slumped in a chair over on the far side of the room. Boy George, who our intel had told us was a roid-rage English thug with a string of hate crimes behind him. He took a gulp from a bottle as I panned across an enormous, garishly decorated tree. Another two bodyguards sat on a low-backed retro sofa that probably cost more than my car, hunched forward over a coffee table, cards in hands. Behind the sofa, another guy was pouring a drink from a bar against the wall.

'Car just passed me,' said Lennon.

'Coming up?' I asked.

'The BMW, heading into town,' she said.

'Didn't come from the house,' said McCartney.

'Must be from the cabin below,' said Ringo. 'That's good, means they've got less backup nearby.'

I inhaled, blinked a few times, put my eye back to the scope. 'Perfect timing. Just waiting for Bono to fancy a smoke.'

I stared at the house for another fifteen minutes, cold burning my cheeks and eating up into my legs, flexing my fingers in the thin gloves, grateful most of the biting wind was being diverted above my head by the little wall I'd created. Fresh snow had drifted against the board in front of me, better camouflaging where I'd scooped out the snow. I looked to my left, it'd almost filled my tracks, reducing them to a slight depression running back to the treeline, and even that would be gone soon. We were fairly safe from watching eyes now, me in my hide and the other two huddling down, awaiting my signal.

A light came on at the house, I put my eye to the scope and watched the front door.

'Showtime,' I whispered.

Ringo hummed the Pearl & Dean tune in my ear.

'Okay McCartney, you're up.'

'Moving in.'

I continued to monitor the lounge, no changes there. I panned back towards the garage where McCartney had emerged from one corner, submachine gun at his shoulder. He approached the house side-on, using the brickwork of the chimney to mask his approach, a blind spot out of view of the chalet's expanses of glass that offered an easy route to the overhanging eaves. He pressed his back against the chimney and looked straight at me, even though I knew he couldn't see me.

'You're looking good,' I whispered.

He gave a slight nod. The door opened, a huge man shuffled out, shrugging on a thick bright orange ski jacket, the familiar granite shaved head scowling into the freezing air.

'Bingo, Bono's fag break. Everyone check in.'

'Ringo, go.'

'McCartney, go.'

A slight pause and then 'Lennon, go.'

'Okay, he's lighting up,' I said. 'On my mark.' My thumb flicked the lever to safe, I pulled on the charging handle and settled in.

The reticle wavered over his face as he sucked on his cigarette. The wind kept blowing the lighter out, he cupped his hands round it, trying a couple more times before finally succeeding. He blew the smoke up into the cold wind then pulled up his hood.

'Go, McCartney.'

I watched Bono take another drag than panned across to the other side of the house in time to see McCartney's boots disappear behind the chimney on the low roof. From there it was a short walk up the incline to the skylight over the master bedroom. Back to the door, Bono was picking baccy out of his mouth with his bratwurst fingers and spitting on the ground.

'Nice work, McCartney. You're still clear.'

'Copy,' he said. 'Standing by.'

'Ringo?'

'Check,' said Ringo. 'I have four tangos in the lounge. No movement upstairs.'

'Lennon?'

'I'm still go,' she said.

'On my signal,' I said.

I moved the reticle down onto Bono, a straight-on shot as he stared out at the dark. I pictured the shot from the other side, the white fields stretching below him, me right in the middle, the small black opening at the end of the white-painted suppressor.

My finger twitched, I flicked the safety down and hummed the Band Aid song. I got as far as the chimes clanging Bono's doom, then exhaled and settled in. The red dot wavered over his chest, at this distance the high-velocity bullet would pretty much remove his heart or a lung. A smile twitched at the corner of my mouth. Well tonight thank God it was him, instead of me.

My heart stopped, time stopped. His hood lit up as another light came on in the house, somewhere above. I eased off the trigger, sweeping up to the master bedroom. The light was on, Bob was out of bed.

'Wait,' I said.

Bono was stamping his feet.

'What's the holdup?' Ringo hissed.

Back to the bedroom, the target was talking to an unseen person in the doorway.

'There's someone else in the bedroom.'

'His cigarette is not going to last much longer,' said McCartney.

Bono started walking across the front of the house. I had to take the shot before he got to the big windows in front of the lounge if I was to give Ringo a surprise entry.

It'd be unfortunate if every bodyguard in the house saw their head of security being spread across the glass.

'Take the fucking shot,' whispered Ringo.

I panned up to the bedroom. A boy, maybe four or five, walked into the room rubbing his eyes. Bob ruffled his hair, a woman sat up in bed.

'Shit. Abort.' I flicked the safety back on. 'Abort.'

'What do you mean, abort?' said Ringo.

'I mean fucking abort.' I followed Bono's progress, he'd stopped at the edge of the porch. Upstairs, the kid climbed in bed with his parents.

'We can't abort,' said McCartney. 'Any second now Bono will walk round here and I'm perched on the roof like a bloody robin.'

'We go, now,' said Ringo. 'Take the shot.'

'There's a kid in there.'

Silence over the radios for a moment.

Finally Ringo spoke again. 'We're going in.'

'I said there's a fucking kid in there, his family have turned up for Christmas. Must have arrived while we were gearing up. This is done, we're out.'

'I'm not saying goodbye to my fee because someone got squeamish,' said McCartney.

'Harrison, think about this,' said Lennon.

'There's no more time,' said Ringo. 'Fuck this, we're going in right now.'

Movement flashed by the doorway, Ringo was at the corner, about to make his entry. Bono was still over the other side of the decking. I panned back to the far corner of the house, could see Ringo, submachine gun up, ready to pop round the corner guns blazing.

'Ringo, you take one more step I'll drop you.'

His head spun, I could see him squinting into the darkness.

Bono finished his cig and fired it off the deck into the snow, walking back to the front door. Metres from him, Ringo wasn't moving. I flicked the safety off, centred the cross hairs right on Ringo's chest, squeezing ever so slightly. 'If you move a centimetre I'll shoot you now.'

'Did you care this much about the children on the streets of Iraq?' asked McCartney. 'Or is it just the white children?'

'A kid's a kid,' I hissed.

Bono paused outside the door, took one last look around, and disappeared inside. The door slammed behind him. Round the corner, Ringo dropped his submachine gun, letting it dangle by the straps, holding his hands up to his head.

'There'll be another opportunity,' I said.

'When?' asked Lennon. 'We've been planning this for over a week. Intel says he's leaving for Switzerland in a couple of days.'

I stood, flicked the lens protectors down on the scope, slung the rifle onto my back. 'Rendezvous at the car as planned. Out.'

Chapter Twenty-three

Tiburon

The waves crashed, I pressed my back against the wall and shuffled sideways along the slippery deck, out of the worst of the ceaseless walls of water washing over the railing and assaulting the superstructure. I shivered in my T-shirt, no time to get my jacket, no point now, I was soaked to my bones. I wasn't overly bothered by it, but it was another good pair of trainers ruined.

Katanga waved at me from the doorway then slammed the door shut, peering out from the porthole.

The horizontal rain highlighted the soft glow from the windows above. Somewhere up there, Miller was at the wheel, rum in hand, squinting into the darkness. I looked forward at the white water over the bow, swamping the forward deck crane and washing around the raised cargo hatches, spraying across the front of my car.

I clung to the railings as I edged around the number two deck crane, watching the furious sea nervously. The boat surged down the slope of a wave, hit the bottom, climbed the next, every crash of water threatening to dislodge me and send me sliding over the edge.

Why the hell would King have come out here, on deck, in the middle of the night in a storm? I looked back at the door. Had Katanga tricked me into going out here, where

I'd be washed overboard, or even shot and thrown over, without anyone noticing?

Then I saw it. Difficult in the rolling seas, obscured by the rain and waves and due to me concentrating on not going over the side, but in the darkness at the bottom of the trough it was just visible. A tiny, dim light in the darkness.

My car's interior light.

Someone had been in my car while it had been on deck, sometime since I'd locked it. King? Or like me, moth-like, had he been drawn to the light, too?

I edged further out and looked up. Miller's head was just visible through the spinning clearview windows. Into the next trough, his eyes would be up, scanning the horizon way above me as we angled down, deeper into the sea. I went for it.

A short distance, I sprinted across the deck, trainers skidding on the metal plates. As I approached, I saw the passenger window had been smashed. I slid behind my car, dropping to my knees, grabbing the rear wheel and clinging on. We hit the bottom of the trough, the *Tiburon* groaned in pain beneath me. The keel shuddered, every rivet and weld working overtime. Water crashed, we rose again. Seawater cascaded under my car, I held on and poked my head up.

Miller was fuzzy through the windows but hadn't moved, hadn't changed position, didn't seem to have noticed me. Now I was out of reach of those dim spot-lamps bolted to the superstructure, there was no one to see me if I did go over the side, certainly no one would care. I crept backwards, one hand on my car's door handle, the other pulling out my gun. I brought it up and looked in through the broken window in one movement.

The interior light had been switched on manually, I was dismayed but not surprised to see my favourite car full of seawater. I don't know if I was more upset about that or the tiny cubes of glass washing around the passenger seat and still dropping from the doorframe with every movement of the ship. The former meant stripping my car, the latter was easier to fix but the implication was far worse – someone had done it to get inside. For what, I didn't know – I'd removed the valuable cargo hours ago, everyone knew that.

The glovebox was open, its contents washing around in the footwell, several soggy OS maps which I'd used to plot the route from the Alps to La Rochelle. Another of Dorset, which I'd used to check over the roads in and around Poole and up to the Army base. The centre console box was open too, its contents on the driver's seat, sweet wrappers, vintage Ray Ban Aviators, and some Nurofen: hardly interesting.

Someone had smashed my window to turn over the inside, looking for something. Surely not King, why would he do that? He'd been in my car enough times, we'd lived together for a while for God's sake, he'd have no reason to go rooting around in my car.

Various cargo straps lashing my car to the deck prevented me from opening the doors, so with another look up at the wheelhouse, I pushed through the window. I dragged myself through the falling cubes of glass and lay across the front seats to get my breath back as waves broke over the bow and spray slammed the windscreen.

I angled myself round, turning to look in the back seat. Nothing to see there: my G28 rifle, out of bullets, my bloodied snowboarding jacket, mostly avoiding the worst of the seawater blowing in the window.

Something moved in the boot – the boot which should have been empty. It poked up above the headrest and then bobbed down again.

I held my pistol close, hugging the driver's seat, looking through the gap in the headrest. I reached down, pulled the lever to slide the seat back, then stretched out my left arm, reaching the lever to flip the back seats down.

I pulled, the waves crashed, we tilted, the rear seatback folded down. My finger was ready on the trigger but straight away I could see I didn't need it.

King was dead.

Chapter Twenty-four

Tiburon

I gave King a once-over in the dim light of my phone torch. The wet, matted hair, the lack of other wounds suggested he'd been knocked on the back of the head. I put my fingers to the torch to have a look at the cause of the wetness, then brought the light close to his head for a better look. He'd been knocked on the head damn hard. Obviously King hadn't smashed my car, he hadn't ransacked it. He'd seen something, or someone, and, cat-like, his curiosity hadn't done him any favours.

I switched off the torch, throwing the phone onto the driver's seat, lying there in the dark, legs still in the front of the car, head in the boot with King, staring at nothing. I don't know how long for, time was immeasurable, just the rolling sea and the constant crash of waves.

Ever since Justin had died, I'd still considered King my brother. An estranged brother maybe, since he hadn't wanted to work with me, even see me, for a long time. Always said seeing me made him remember. He was right – I'd begged and bribed, knew he wouldn't turn me down. He'd given in, and this is where it'd led him. If I'd told him the real reason I wanted him here he'd never have agreed. Yet another person I loved now dead, another victim of my hubris, my arrogance, my overwhelming desire for revenge above all else.

I breathed out. Hiding in the boot of my car in the middle of the ocean wasn't going to help anyone, so I did what I always do – pushed everything down as far as it'd go, down to the place from where it only crawls out at night. *Ignore it, get up, go on the offensive.*

My main problem wasn't the question of who'd killed my captive – and therefore also King. The big problem was *how* they'd done it. How mattered more because it would tell me whether anyone else was involved, and how worried I should be.

The other question was how I'd kill them – because I surely would – without being discovered and thrown overboard by the rest of the bloodthirsty crew.

I climbed back out the window and, after another glance up at Miller on the bridge, slowly edged my way back aft along the railings, across the rocking deck to the superstructure.

I slammed open the door and pushed Katanga out of the way, lurching off down the corridor.

'What happened?' he shouted after me. 'Did you find Mr King?'

The door to the radio room was shut, I opened it and looked inside. He was still in there, Nic, his back to the door, headphones on, tapping a pen against the desk to a beat I couldn't hear. Katanga was coming up behind me, I closed the door on him and stepped silently behind Nic. The Father Christmas bobble-head moshed in time with the waves.

Nic's knife was buried deep in my prisoner. I'd been content to take my time, question him later, more discreetly, but that was before I'd found King.

I grabbed a fistful of hair, bouncing Nic's head off the desk with just enough force to get his attention. Wobbling Father Christmas fell to the floor, his head rolled under the desk. Nic screamed, reaching up behind his head and getting tangled in his earphones. I swatted his arms away, dragging him backwards out of his chair and slamming him to the floor, kicking his belly. The scream cut off instantly, he writhed, mouth flapping like a fish.

The door opened, Katanga looked in then put his hands up and backed away. 'Woah friend, what the hell are you…?'

I kicked the door shut, crouched, patted Nic down but couldn't find any weapons. Leaning in close, I grabbed his hair again, lifting his head.

'Talk.'

He finally managed to suck in a breath, tears welling in his eyes.

'Tell me everything,' I hissed into his ear. 'Give me a reason not to drag you out that door and drop you over the railings.'

'I…' he struggled for air, voice cracking. 'I told you. The radio.'

'I'm not talking about the radio, I'm talking about your bloody knife.'

'My knife?'

'Big black German thing. Where is it?'

Outside the fire alarm started blaring.

'It's in my room.'

I bunched up his collar in one hand, picked him up, flung open the door. The passageway was empty, pulsing red in time with the wailing alarm.

'Which is your room?'

He pointed to a door at the end, past the stairs. I dragged him, spinning him round and pushing him forward, slamming him against the door. He screamed out in pain, I turned the handle, bundling him inside.

'Where's the knife?' I said, still holding him by the collar.

He pointed at a shelf above his bunk.

I pushed him roughly against the far wall, backed up, not taking my eyes off him, and reached up behind me. My hand brushed along the deep-lipped shelf, knocking everything onto the bed. A couple of grubbily thumbed porn mags, an even grubbier paperback, a chipped mug full of brown stains. No knife.

'Where?'

'It's there.'

I lunged, he flinched away but I grabbed a handful of T-shirt and whirled him round, throwing him on the bed. 'Find it, now.'

He knelt on the bed, eyes wide when he saw the shelf was bare.

'It was here… Someone must have taken it…'

The door flew open. I grabbed Nic, pulling him in front of me. Katanga brought up the AK-47 as I reached into my pocket and brought out my pistol.

'Let him go,' growled Katanga, rifle dead steady.

I held my own pistol on him just as steadily. 'Put it down.'

Feet pounded outside, another gun barrel appeared in the doorway, this one belonging to an ugly revolver held by Miller, who squeezed beside Katanga.

'I told you, Tyler,' he snarled. 'My boat, my crew.'

I looked at them in the doorway, reckoned I could get a shot off at both of them before they squeezed their triggers but I'd rather not if I could help it.

'It was his knife, Miller,' I said.

'You don't know that.'

He fired off a barrage of French at Nic. A heated discussion ensued which concluded with the radio operator having no idea where his knife was or who could have taken it. Katanga joined in with some choice words, there was clearly no love lost between the two shipmates. I glared throughout, still holding my pistol on the pair in the doorway.

'He says he doesn't know where it is,' said Miller.

'Convenient,' I said, but two things struck me. Neither Miller nor Nic knew I spoke French, so their conversation was likely genuine. That meant Nic was either telling the truth, or he was lying to Miller. Either way, it suggested Miller wasn't involved.

'You can't go around accusing people, Tyler,' Miller said. 'Not on my boat.'

'Someone on your boat's a murderer,' I said. 'And you don't seem to be doing much about it.'

'You brought the hired killers on board. And you're outnumbered.' He waved the revolver, gesturing for me to leave the room.

'Outnumbered, but not outgunned,' said Marty from outside in the passageway.

Miller looked over his shoulder, held his revolver up and backed away. Katanga did the same, reluctantly lowering his rifle.

I advanced through the doorway, keeping my pistol on Miller. 'Check, I think.'

Marty was standing to one side of the corridor, gun on Katanga. She was dripping wet, I figured she must have braved the storm to slip out one of the aft doorways and back in at the front, below the bridge stairs. Out of the corner of my eye I could see Fields half-hidden round the corner at the other end of the corridor, a submachine gun pressed into his shoulder. They were positioned to create a killing zone right in the middle without hitting each other, the 180-degree spread made it impossible for Katanga and Miller to respond.

Katanga's fingers twitched on the assault rifle but his expression looked vaguely amused, unlike Miller chewing glass next to him. I kept my gun on Miller.

'King's dead.' I kept emotion out of my voice. Fields shuffled, Marty gave nothing away.

'What?' Miller's expression softened, this was clearly news to him. 'I'm sorry, Tyler, I am. I know what he meant…'

'He was my fucking brother, Miller,' the gun shook in my fist, 'and one of your pirates killed him.'

'Who was it, Tyler?' Fields growled behind me. I appreciated the backup but could do without him losing his shit.

Miller pushed the revolver into the waistband of his oily jeans and spread his arms wide. 'Let's all calm down, eh?'

There was a scuffle in the corridor behind me somewhere, I heard Fields mutter under his breath. Miller grinned.

I chanced a glance over to see Fields, gun now lowered, with the barrel of a revolver held to his head by Poubelle.

'And that's checkmate, Tyler,' said Miller.

'Jesus Christ, Fields, you've just been outflanked by a fisherman.'

Katanga had his AK back up again, this was taking us nowhere good. Miller must have been thinking the same, as he broke the stalemate first.

'This is my boat. I'm sorry about King, you know I am, but it's got nothing to do with my crew. You've hired us to do a job, all right, we'll deliver, but I can't let you go round attacking people.'

I didn't waver. 'It's going to be a long journey if we do it all like this.'

'Won't last too much longer, not without anyone at the helm.'

'So what do we do?'

'Get below. Any of you step a foot outside your cabin before we reach Poole, you go over the side, you hear me?'

'Yo ho ho,' Fields muttered, smirking and looking at me.

I wasn't laughing, I'd seen him do it. 'Loud and clear,' I said.

Marty held her gun up and walked slowly to me, the three of us backed away, passing Poubelle as he came the other way. They waited in the middle of the passageway, completely at home swaying with the motion of the boat as we stumbled backwards, round the corner and down the stairs.

Chapter Twenty-five

Château des Aigles
Four days previously

McCartney placed a tray down on the floor, hot croissants, three cups of coffee. As usual I was left to make my own tea. I watched the three of them poring over the familiar map, the pictures of the target, his chalet, the bodyguards. Each of them had woken up with a new plan, and each was as shit as the next.

Last night it'd taken a while for them to speak at a normal volume in the car on the way back, despite me reminding them who was paying their wages. Ringo had been last to calm down, and when we got back to the chalet he'd spent a while pacing furiously in front of the big windows, looking down on the oblivious target who'd so narrowly evaded us through sheer luck.

The target could be the worst person on Earth (he was definitely in the running), but his kid was innocent. Doubtless he was bringing the kid up in the same mould, teaching him hate and prejudice directly and subconsciously, but until that kid was old enough to know better, I refused to let him be collateral damage. We could have been careful but three armed men breaking in and killing all the bodyguards before abducting your dad, subjecting him to that, making him, in the best-case scenario, a witness – that's not really something I go for.

Our planning of the last week or so was down the drain, we had twenty-four hours to come up with something new, maybe another twenty-four hours to carry it out.

Ringo's plan had been shot down immediately – a dawn raid on the chalet with one of us tasked to secure and protect the kid, thinking that'd get me on side. Non-starter. Then McCartney had suggested a post-breakfast hit as they got in their car, knowing the wife and kid would be safe inside. Mildly better, but out in the open against the whole team, with the second team at the foot of the hill behind us and the wife safely next to a phone? Too many variables, too many risk factors.

Lennon's had been the most sensible. She'd suggested a hit on their car in-transit.

I stirred my tea, watching the brown swirling, shuddering at a memory, the imaginary scent of gas crept up my nostrils. 'I don't like it,' I said.

She put her cup down hard on the wooden floor, coffee spilled onto the map. 'Don't like it because it won't work, or because you didn't come up with it?'

I squeezed the teabag against my mug and fired it off the spoon into the bin. 'Too many unknowns.'

'You've done a lot of criticising,' said Ringo. 'You know what I think?'

'You're gonna tell me anyway.'

'Nothing will satisfy you. You're looking for reasons to pull the plug.'

'You don't think I wanna get paid?'

'You're too old. You've lost it.'

'If by lost it you mean don't wanna die…' I rubbed my eyes and sighed. 'Here's the thing. First, we find a stretch of road we can guarantee they'll be on at a given time. Then we need to separate the cars – we're only interested in the Rolls, so the backup needs to be split from them. Gotta do it in a non-violent way so they're off guard. So we split them up with traffic. That takes at least one of us to handle. Once the Rolls enters the kill zone we gotta block the road off – in both directions. That's at least another of us, probably two.

'That leaves one of us to deal with a moving vehicle and three armed guards – who we can't shoot at because they're too close to the target. Please, tell me how you plan on doing that?'

Lennon scowled. 'It's the best we've got. I haven't heard anything from you.'

'We need to isolate him from the bodyguards as quickly as possible. There's only one place we can do that.'

I pointed out the window, across the valley, beyond the village, at the tiny string of gondolas climbing the mountain. They looked, shaking their heads.

'I've been thinking,' I continued. 'Three bodyguards plus the target go up the mountain. Midge sits in the restaurant, only two bodyguards ski with him, so straight away we've bettered the odds.'

'Yeah but one of 'em's that big bastard,' said Ringo.

Paul nodded. 'Bono counts for three men.'

I shook my head. 'Won't matter how big he is if that Ruger ammo is as good as you say. Look, they always ski in formation, right? We've watched them. Always Bono first, Bob in the middle, Sting bringing up the rear.'

'We talked about this,' said McCartney. 'We'll have to kill the bodyguards, because otherwise how will we get

Bob away? How do we kill two bodyguards on a ski slope in front of hundreds of tourists without having the cops on us before we get down?'

'And *how* do we get down?' said Ringo. 'Dragging the target between us who, let's face it, is hardly going to come quietly.'

'As per the original plan, we'll drug him.'

'Fine. So we kill the two bodyguards in front of all those holidaymakers, then we carry a drugged and incapacitated man onto a cable car?' asked McCartney. 'And we just what, sit down next to a family and make small talk?'

'Can you imagine us standing in the queue with him?' said Ringo. 'Fucking *Weekend at Bernie's.*'

I took a gulp of tea, put the mug on the sideboard, and knelt on the floor, spinning the map around.

'We know their routine, they don't take the cable car down.' I pointed at the map then traced a path. 'Each day they do this black run, then go off-piste for a kilometre, and join up with this blue run. Between these two points they have the mountainside to themselves.'

They looked at the map, comparing it to a cartoonish resort piste map. McCartney leaned in close.

'Okay, so we could in theory hit them there – if we could deal with the bodyguards.'

'Only two bodyguards,' I reminded them.

'Armed bodyguards, nonetheless,' said Ringo. 'But let's say we could do it, and drug him. We've still got to get him off the mountain. The only way down from there is the blue run below, in full view of the restaurants and the cable car running overhead.'

I shook my head. 'It's like Piccadilly Circus down there, only with more lights.'

'Exactly, so the only way is to carry him back to the cable car with all those witnesses,' said McCartney.

'Stretcher?' said Lennon, thinking outside the box for the first time. 'Use a Skidoo, make out it's a medical emergency?'

'Too noisy, too obvious, too memorable. There's a much easier way.' I jabbed my finger at a narrow stretch annotated with warning signs. 'Here. This pass is the exact spot we hit them. Out of sight of the resort, away from the cable car, the piste, away from everyone.'

'You're missing the point,' said Ringo. 'It's a long way to get down off the mountain from there, and there are a hell of a lot of witnesses in between. Skidoo idea is good, but then there's the rest of his bodyguards waiting for us at the bottom.'

'Look again.' I tapped the point on the map. 'This the shortest route off the mountain.' I took a Sharpie and drew a circle around the section of mountainside, a centimetre of closely packed contour lines. 'At this point here it's only one hundred and twenty metres to the road.'

McCartney squinted at the map then looked at me, face screwed up. 'One hundred and twenty metres... straight down.'

Chapter Twenty-six

Tiburon

I'd brought Marty and Fields up to speed, which hadn't taken long. Showed them the body still rolling around the hatch beneath my cabin, then sat on King's bed and told them how I'd found *his* body up on the deck in the boot of my car. All the while, Fields was pulling out and pushing in the magazine in his Glock, leg bouncing up and down, looking at me nervously.

We were well and truly in the shit, no doubt. Stuck on a boat, tossed around by a storm in the Atlantic, miles from anywhere. A killer on board with us, the crew set against us, our transport job dead with a knife sticking out of his chest. I pictured his face forever set in a grimace of pain, the traces of red staining the T-shirt where it'd escaped around the blade still wedged between his ribs.

'We should strike now,' said Fields.

I looked up at him, sat on the desk, eying the door nervously. 'Strike at who?'

'Them. The crew. Threatening us like that.'

He looked strung out, maybe Miller was right. After all, he and King were the only two people on guard while Marty and I had been upstairs in the saloon.

Marty's voice came up from the hatch. 'Someone wise once told me to the route to victory doesn't lie in knowing when to attack, but knowing when *not* to.'

'You get that from a cracker?' I asked. 'That's some bullshit that sounds wise but when you think about it, it's exactly the same thing.'

'No it's not.'

I stretched, then crouched and looked down into the hatch. 'I mean it is, but sure, go off.'

'Hmm.' Marty didn't sound convinced. She crouched by the body, looking at the grate in the floor, then up at the ceiling. 'There must be another way in.'

'It's welded shut.' I followed her eyeline to the grate at the top marking the fuel inlet and ventilation valves.

'Where does that come out?' she asked.

I climbed down the ladder to join her. 'Somewhere under the passageway outside the rooms I guess, but there's not enough of a gap between the decks for a person to crawl through.'

'You sure? Maybe someone dropped down, killed him, welded it shut after?'

'Not done much welding, have you?' shouted Fields from above. 'It'd stink for a start. Plus, you'd have to be tiny to fit through there.'

She stood on her tiptoes, tracing the outline of the opening. 'I think I could fit.'

'Not welding it up again after,' I said. 'No way.'

I placed the chair upright, with his body still bound to it, then stood in front of it, mimicking the actions needed to stab him.

'The killer unzipped the jacket first,' I muttered.

'Get a clean thrust at the heart?' offered Marty.

I nodded. 'Yeah, I guess. Why zip it up again after?'

'To hide the knife? Although you found it anyway, so...'

'Jeez, I guess this is why they have detectives, eh? I'll never mock them again.'

'Blood spray?' asked Marty.

'You could be onto something. Maybe removing the knife had been a risk, the killer didn't want a mess everywhere? Didn't wanna get sprayed with blood themselves I guess.'

'Exactly. Leave the knife in, zip the bulky jacket up over the handle to hide it from a casual glance, no blood no mess.' Marty stood and put her hands in her pockets. 'Most importantly, no mess on the killer.'

'I think you're probably right. This detective shit isn't that hard after all, is it?'

She smiled. 'Nice to know there's a career waiting for me when I want to settle down.'

'Problem we've got out here is we don't have any forensics. I bet there's DNA all over the body, fingerprints too. I've got a cousin in Sheffield who's a copper, this is his realm, but out here the killer knows there's fuck-all we can do about it.'

'There'll be no autopsy either, I'm guessing?' Marty said. 'No time of death, no other clues they throw in on *CSI*.'

'Wait, time of death?'

'I just meant like they do on TV. We already know the time of death, right?'

'We do,' I said, patting my wet jeans.

My pockets were empty. I climbed back up into the cabin, waving Fields out of the way to check the desk, nothing there. He watched as I pulled down my bed and shook out the blankets, threw the pillows on the floor, checked the shelves above.

'What is it?' Marty shouted.

'Something that tells us how he was killed?' asked Fields.

I grabbed the paperback off King's bed and flipped it open to the first page, my timeline. 03:45, he was locked in, alive. 03:45 to 03:55 – Marty and I were in the saloon. From then on King and I were getting some uncomfortable broken sleep, until I found the body at 6 a.m.

I tore the page from the book and stuffed it into my back pocket. 'Anyone seen my phone?'

Fields reached up to the shelf above my bed, holding up my satphone.

'No, no, my iPhone.' I patted my jeans again.

'Won't work out here,' he said.

I gave him a look, then flipped my bed back up and started to climb back down into the hold. 'Phones do more than make calls these days.'

I reached the bottom, turning to Marty. She looked sceptical, I held up the dead man's arm. 'Poor man's tracker.'

I pulled up his sleeve to reveal the smartwatch I'd fastened round his wrist, hastily bought from a French electronics shop. No phone signal out here to track it over distance, but it'd still been downloading me his vitals via Bluetooth whenever I was close enough to pick up a connection.

'I need my phone to access the history. I had it earlier…' I trailed off as I pictured King's bloodied hair in the dim light from the tiny LED phone torch. What had I done with it? Everything from that point was a blur, the mist had descended right up until Katanga and Miller had stopped me in Nic's cabin.

Which is probably why I'd left it there, on the driver's seat of my car, now inaccessible to me, outside on deck, behind a wall of angry smugglers with AK-47s.

Chapter Twenty-seven

Tiburon

The lights went out, I crept forward to the end of the passageway by the red emergency lighting, pausing outside the huge engine room door, listening to the regular train-like throb through the bulkhead. Voices tumbled down from the superstructure directly above. A single grimy bulb buzzed in the stairwell above, casting a sickly amber puddle across the wall. The voices upstairs were close. I took out my pistol, screwing the suppressor onto the modified barrel. I didn't want to shoot these people, but many are the passengers who never made it to port on Miller's ships; his threats were never idle.

I held the pistol down low as I stepped up, craning to see the deck above. The voices rose in volume, coming closer.

I dropped back down, looking round. No external doors here deep in *Tiburon*'s belly, no route to my car but through those armed crew members. I held my pistol up, looked back along the corridor towards the stern. Fields was kneeling at the far end. He nodded me on and disappeared back round the corner as the voices upstairs closed in.

Despite being outnumbered I'm fairly sure we could have taken the ship, but aside from not wanting to risk everyone's lives, Nic's insistence kept coming back to me. He'd seemed genuine. Miller wasn't the enemy here, someone else was. I just had to find a way to prove it to him.

The engine room was forward of the accommodation, better to keep moving in the direction of my car than retreat. I turned the heavy handle in the centre of the engine room door, unlocking the dog latches around the watertight frame. Light spilled out, the noise increased several-fold as I quickly stepped over the thick metal threshold and pulled it shut behind me. I looked down on the mechanical guts of the *Tiburon*.

Half a level below me the engines occupied most of the open space, great wedges of cast iron and pipes and gauges. Pistol ready, I jumped down the steps from the platform onto the walkway running between them, steadying myself on the hot coolant pipes, looking down into dirty water slopping around beneath the criss-cross tread plates. The noise was overwhelming in stereo, hot and damp. The smell of oil, diesel fuel, and various other chemicals swished back and forth through the air in time with the murk beneath my trainers.

In contrast to the rest of the boat – and indeed to most others I've been on, including Miller's previous tubs – the engine room was comparatively clean, the diesels obviously far newer than the rest of her and no expense spared in their maintenance. Clearly this was where a large percentage of Miller's considerable profits was reinvested, along with the generous pay for the crew – both necessities for a rapid and efficient smuggling operation. I hoped his new engineers, Seb and Vincent, were up to the vacancy left by poor Étienne's departure.

My hunch looked to have paid off, at the far end of the walkway was a short ladder up to a matching platform and door leading forward. I climbed up, it was another watertight bulkhead door, this one stiffer as I unlocked it and swung it open, heading in gun first.

No lights in here, I swung the door shut behind me, felt around and found a switch. Again the smell of oil and machinery, but this time mixed with acrid burning. The workshop, grubbier than the engine room, rows of cabinets and workbenches along one wall, huge grimy floor-standing power tools along another – a press, a pillar drill, a huge circular saw, a grinder, everything covered in used oil and a million dirty fingerprints. The strip lights were barely adequate, flickering and emitting a constant buzz like they were about to give up any second. I walked straight through to a door at the opposite end, it opened with a creak into a short, red-lit corridor, and slammed behind me with the help of a wave. Welded to the wall was a ladder up to a hatch. I worked out the distances in my head and decided it must come up on deck just forward of the superstructure. I was aft of the cargo holds so I'd certainly be able to get to my car, but I'd probably come up in full view of the bridge windows and those spotlamps right under Miller's nose.

I tried the only other way, a short passage to my right which ended with yet another enormous watertight bulkhead door. This one was stiffer, the wheel in the centre was tight and tinged with rust rather than the well-greased levers on the other doors. Eventually the dogs round the edges groaned off their stops and creaked open.

A symphony of percussion hit immediately, the echo of waves against steel plates. A cavern yawned away into darkness in front, above, below, the greasy bulbs around the walls were set too far apart to accurately gauge the size. No bulkheads separating the holds, just one open space. I thought back to all the kids' books that measured everything in double-decker buses, this looked like it could comfortably swallow a few lengthways. This was the area that, back in the good old days of Brezhnev, would have been taken up by enormous fuel tanks and spare parts, refuelling and servicing the Baltic fleet, perhaps out into the North Atlantic for weeks on end to rendezvous with the huge Typhoon-class subs.

The stubby walkway overlooking the hold ended at a ladder down. I crouched, pointing my pistol through the railings, at the steel ribs along the wall on either side, the innards of a gigantic whale. With each wave water cascaded from above, between the slim gaps in the cargo hatch doors, I hoped the hum of the bilge pumps somewhere below was enough to keep up. My car was lashed down to the front cargo doors, towards the bow.

Waves boomed, echoing around the empty space, no chance even to die away before the next hit. With every crash the dim lamps flickered, casting eerie shadows across the neon graffiti daubed on the walls, German phrases, anti-establishment slogans, acid-house smiley faces, Nineties satire. On one wall an enormous pear representing Helmut Kohl was flaking in brown stains running down the steel plates, I remembered when my brother was stationed in West Germany at the time that this was how Nineties magazines often depicted the ex-Chancellor.

I stood and leaned over the railings to look down at a network of steel girders and mesh-like tread plates with a few empty cardboard boxes slowly rotting on them. Below that, the huge ballast tanks made up the space down to the keel. I was in the naked unadorned belly of the beast. I pushed my pistol into the holster, and climbed down the ladder.

A whisper came from down below, on my right. I paused on the ladder, withdrawing my gun again. The lights flickered and blinked out.

No emergency lighting in here, I gripped the ladder, pointing my pistol down. Something scratched at the tread plates, using the cover of darkness to move towards me. The faint sound of nails on rusty steel. I wrapped my left arm through the ladder, pulled my legs up a rung, swung the pistol down, tracking the sound. My finger twitched on the trigger.

Another whisper came from the other side, answering the first, I looked round, eyes straining into the black. Patches of glow-in-the-dark paint, bright words and drooping faces lent a soft glow to the walls but weren't enough to touch the shadows. The same scratching came from the tread plates below as it approached.

I swung my arm side to side as the sounds closed in, pointing the pistol straight down as they converged at the foot of the ladder. The hold was in darkness, water poured from the bay doors above, making it impossible to understand what the voices were saying.

The ladder trembled slightly, the lightest vibration, another scratch. They were climbing. I reasoned whoever they were, they weren't friendly.

The gunshot lit the ladder, a shadow scuttled away. I fired again, it retreated, three times I fired, the flash briefly lighting up another shadow round the back of the ladder.

The lights buzzed, fizzed, pinged back on. A pile of cardboard washed around in the dirty seawater at the foot of the ladder. I dropped, hitting the floor and rolling backwards, swinging the pistol up. Nothing, I came up onto my knees, aiming into the corners of the room. The hold was empty.

I massaged my eyes, yearning for sleep.

Chapter Twenty-eight

Château des Aigles
Three days previously

The sun had already dipped behind the peaks, the sky was darkening as the cable car creaked up the mountain. My gondola was empty; no one else was braving these temperatures, most were heading down the mountain to get changed for tea.

The wind had picked up. I gripped the seat and closed my eyes as I swung upwards, trying not to think of the long drop to the trees below, the soft white duvet concealing hard, sharp rocks.

'They're getting off,' said McCartney's voice over the comms, waiting for me at the top. I forced my eyes open and looked up, two cars in front, where a gondola was entering the station.

'Don't get lazy,' I said. 'These guys are dangerous.'

'We can't lose them,' said McCartney. 'We need to make sure they're still sticking to the route.'

'Just don't get too close.'

'Okay, they're heading further up. Bob, Sting, and Bono.'

'Where's Midge?' asked Ringo from the gondola in front of mine.

'Still in the bar,' McCartney said. 'Looks like he's finishing up now.'

Through the radio came the sound of crunching snow, I could picture McCartney making his way up the slope from the bubble lift station to the plateau, where the chairlifts would take us up to the start of the runs – and the black run through the tight valley to the start of their favoured off-piste.

'Hold there,' I said.

'I'm waiting at the top,' said Ringo. I opened my eyes, above me his gondola had reached the station.

'Nearly at the chairlift,' said McCartney.

'Hold and wait for us,' I repeated.

'I'll get on behind them.'

'Hold and wait, for fuck's sake!'

I stood, holding the guardrail, and made the mistake of looking down at my boots. Far below, black rocks stuck out like islands in the snow. Lego-sized pines bent and swayed with the gusts whipping through the valley. My heart pounded, I screwed my eyes shut.

The gondola swung and slowed, the doors slid open. I stepped onto the metal ribbed walkway and propped my board against the railings to pull up my scarf over my nose. Ringo was leaning on the wooden railings of the outdoor restaurant area, next to a crowd preparing to travel back down. I grabbed my board and walked over the hard-packed snow as the group trudged past me.

He nodded and picked up his skis as I approached. I glanced sideways to see the third bodyguard pushing outside through the restaurant doors.

'Midge is on his way down to you,' I said.

'Copy,' said Lennon from where I'd left her in the cafe at the bottom.

I patted Ringo on the shoulder and headed for the chairlift.

'Two minutes, McCartney,' said Ringo beside me.

'They're two seats in front of me,' said McCartney. 'They've just got off.'

'Jesus Christ, McCartney, what don't you understand. Wait at the top of the chairlift, we're coming up.'

'We can't lose them,' said McCartney.

'Don't worry, we know where they're headed,' said Ringo.

I put my board down and clicked in, skimming down the short incline to the chairlift with Ringo alongside. The seats came round and plucked us into the air, I pulled the bar down quickly and held it tight.

'Christ, I thought you were supposed to be a hard man,' Ringo said. 'Show a little backbone, will ya?' He pulled on the bar, swinging the chair side to side.

I gripped tighter. 'Cut that shit out. Where are they now?'

The chair swung again as Ringo leaned out to see past the cable support tower. 'McCartney's getting off.'

A minute later it was our turn. Ringo tapped me and pulled up the bar, I opened my eyes and braced, jumped up, riding the short slope off the chairlift. No sign of McCartney. Ringo overtook me on his skis, hooked a tight turn, headed straight over the berm to the right and dropped over the edge. I leaned and cut across, following in his wake.

'McCartney's gone ahead,' shouted Ringo, pointing at the four sets of tracks.

The bashed snow of the run changed as we cut over the drifts and off the piste, dropping steeply on the far side. Ahead of me Ringo was already slowing, ready for the thick pines. No one else was around, the temperature was plummeting quickly, the snow had already obliterated anyone else's tracks that might have been through here. Everyone except the three targets, and their three hunters.

Snow hissed under my board as I weaved across the steep slope. Ringo had disappeared into the trees but I could hear his skis slicing the deep snow in my radio earpiece. There was a sharp crack, a muffled banging sound like a mic in a tumble dryer.

'McCartney, check in,' came Ringo's voice.

I could see Ringo now, he'd waited for me, crouching just inside the treeline.

More banging on the radio, McCartney mumbled something then a grunt, more rustling.

This side of the mountain was almost dark, the lights of the cars below twinkled between gusts as flakes were whipped down from the sky and up from the ground like mini tornados sweeping the mountainside.

I leaned sharply, sliding to a stop next to Ringo, lifting up my goggles and squinting into the trees.

'...Don't ski...' came a voice. Bono, the big Serbian, over McCartney's radio.

'Any sign of them?' I asked.

Ringo held a finger to his lips and tapped his ear.

Faint laughter, muffled, as if McCartney's radio earpiece had been wrapped in cotton wool. Or fallen into the snow.

I nodded, reached down and unclipped my board, stepping off into the deep snow. The laughter continued, a few choice insults about McCartney's ethnicity half-caught between snatched breaths. I unzipped my jacket and pulled out my pistol, set off jogging through the trees with Ringo right behind me.

'…skiing is for whites…'

The pit of my stomach dropped, I picked up the pace, deeper into the trees. More muffled words came through my earpiece, shouts that I could only hear over the radio but not above the wind, they couldn't be close. I pushed harder.

'…can't ski, maybe you can fly…'

'Guys, what's happening up there?' asked Lennon, panic creeping into her voice.

'Keep it clear, no chatter,' I said, one eye on the shadows between the pines, the other on the tracks slicing deep through the powder.

A crackle of static burst in my earpiece, the radio cut out. I slid to a stop, holding up my hand for Ringo to halt. Nothing to hear other than the wind skimming the swaying treetops above.

We set off again, whipping through snow-laden branches, still following the tracks. A piled of disturbed snow, a bunch of prints cut sharply to the left, a huge impression in the snow, as if something had been dragged.

I dropped to my knees, panic starting to creep up my spine. When I turned, Ringo had his Glock up and ready.

I pointed to the tracks. 'They're on foot.'

He made to run.

'Wait,' I hissed.

He looked back, saw my face. I held up my fingers. Blood. Spots were spattered across the fresh white, a small puddle a little further away melting a valley into the fresh snow.

He nodded, we sprinted through the trees until the snow grew brighter, the edge of the treeline. The tracks continued, I made to follow but Ringo tapped my shoulder and pointed to the right. I followed his gloves and saw it, on the edge of the hill a faint line of ski tracks slicing back across to the piste, disappearing over the edge of the plateau.

We ran, continuing to follow the boot prints. It didn't take long to find the end.

The snow was kicked up, spots of red still clearly visible even in the ever-darkening light. A depression and more blood marked where McCartney had been dropped on the ground after being dragged out of the trees.

We looked at the tracks where the three attackers had disappeared, long gone now, it would take us several long minutes just to get back to our skis. Six clear lines cutting deep through the fresh snow, three pairs of skis.

I pushed my pistol into my pocket and crept further forward, fear climbing higher up my spine the closer I got to the edge. The ground dropped away in front, black, a vertical rock face slashing through the mountain, the head of the valley that eventually widened to envelop the village. I lay down, pushing forward on my front, towards the precipice.

The sharp rocks dropped steeply into dark shadows. A beam of light shone down as Ringo clicked his torch on, peering over the edge next to me.

'Lennon, come in.'

'What's happening?' She sounded worried.

'McCartney's dead,' I whispered. 'I'm sorry.'

The drop looked lethal enough, a good twenty metres or so, but the direction of his limbs and the angle of his head meant it was a sure thing. Snow was already settling on him, melting where it hit the streaks of red.

There was a pause and then Lennon's voice again. 'Accident?'

'No.'

'We need to get down there,' said Ringo, looking around, panning the torch across the rocks, landing on McCartney's broken snowboard.

I shook my head and rolled onto my back, closing my eyes. 'Snow'll cover him soon. He won't be found until spring, and even then maybe not.'

Lennon was jabbering in my ear, I pulled out the earpiece and pushed it into my pocket, climbed to my feet, started walking back to the trees.

Ringo grabbed my arm, spinning me round. 'We don't leave anyone behind.'

I shrugged him off. 'We do if it's minus ten and dropping dark on a mountainside, without climbing gear.'

'You can't be serious?'

'If we pull him up, what then?' I shouted. 'Carry him off the mountain? In full view of everyone? The police, the questions, what then?'

'We can't leave him there.'

'We can't jeopardise the mission.'

'I'm talking about the fucking mission! What if they find his gun? His radio? What happens when they ID him?'

'Nothing ties him to us, he doesn't have anything on him. He didn't even know your real name, for Christ's sake.'

'Listen fella,' he jabbed a hand at my chest. 'I'm getting fucking paid!'

'You listen!' I brushed his arm away. 'I've known him near-on ten years, you think I like the idea of him buried on a French mountain? We carry him out, call in mountain rescue, we do anything at all and this whole gig is blown.' I waved a finger in his face. 'And that means *I* don't get paid.'

I turned back to the trees and stamped through the snow, trying to shut out the mental image of the body splayed out on the rocks. Another name for the list, another ghost to hound me.

Chapter Twenty-nine

Tiburon

I clung to the top of the deck ladder, with my head underneath the forward access cover, listening to the sea washing over the steel centimetres above. The ladder leaned back, threatening to tip me down into the hold, we were climbing again. I wrapped my legs round the rungs and grabbed the wheel on the underside of the hatch cover, straining to get it unlocked. It was heavy, I had to let go of the pitching ladder to push with both arms, then the salty air was pouring in, bringing freezing water with it. I pushed all the way, swinging it back against the deck with a thud, following up the final rungs out into the open.

I found myself looking straight out over the prow, the folded deck crane straining against its ties, bucking and banging with every movement of the ship. I'd come up on the darkness at the foredeck, right in front of my car's bumper. It hid me from view of anyone on the bridge, but even without the car they'd have a job on against the dark waves.

The deck pitched, I grabbed the spokes of the front wheels, kicking the hatch shut, bracing myself under the front of the car as the ship slipped off the crest of the wave and down towards the next crash.

When it came it took my breath away. Freezing water submerged me, I held my head up and turned to the side, pressed up under the front bumper in the wash of seawater. My fingers were numb but burning, gripping tightly to the filthy wheels as the wash tried to pull me across the deck and take me over the side, out to sea.

I let go of one wheel, let the water carry me round the front of the car, swinging round the passenger side. The deck levelled, I jumped into a crouch, one last look at the wheelhouse and the faces behind the dark windows, I dived through the smashed window of my car and onto the passenger seat.

I pulled in my legs and turned. Hunkered in the bucket seat it was more like a roller-coaster as we pitched and bucked in the night. I scrabbled on the driver's seat, no phone, I leaned over, feeling round the floor, and found it washing around by the pedals. I leaned off the seat, pushing it into my pocket as we hit again, water spraying in through the window.

I waited until the water on deck had receded then climbed out, crouching, holding the door handle. Still no movement or sign of alarm from the superstructure, only one way to keep it that way and make it back to my room. Back the way I came.

I crouched, sliding back round to the hatch and grabbing the big heavy handle. It wouldn't budge. I heaved again, one eye on the incoming wall of water as the ship lurched, I hadn't locked it down but it refused to move. The water loomed, I spun across the deck, my back to the incoming wave, bracing my trainers against my car wheels. The handle gave a millimetre, my fingers slipped on the freezing metal. One of the slower fingers of my left hand snagged, catching in the spokes of the little hatch wheel, bending it back. Nothing much but I'd broken it three weeks previously and the resulting agony cost me a couple more seconds.

I pulled out my pistol, jamming the long suppressor down into the spokes at an angle, yanking the wheel with the additional leverage. Millimetre by millimetre the wheel grated until finally it slipped free, I pulled it upward just as a crash of water hit the bow.

I dived through the hatch, propelled by a ton of water, one hand grabbing for the top rung of the ladder. I caught it, swinging through 180 degrees, bringing my feet up and snagging them on a rung. I hugged in close as water poured in, reaching up behind me to pull the hatch shut then dropping down the ladder to the rusting platform, slumping against the wall to catch my breath. Spray-painted across the wall next to me a washed-out and flaking cartoon DJ was spinning decks, clearly the cathedral-like hold had seen illegal raves in that no man's land when the Berlin Wall came down. Ironic that the same space now carried drugs into Europe.

I pulled out my phone, unlocked it, swiping to the fitness app. It showed an error message, the watch on the corpse's wrist in my cabin was too far away to pick up the Bluetooth signal – not to mention the layers of steel separating us – but that didn't matter. Last time I'd been in there it'd synced up and downloaded the history. Marty's words of inspiration flashed back through my mind. *Like* CSI, *no time of death…*

I scrolled left through the tracker, following the flat line back in time. 6 a.m., 5:50, 5:00, onwards, still a flat line. 4:45, 4:30, 4:00, the line jerked and started back up, my prisoner was alive. I scrolled forward slowly until I reached the interesting part, which happened at 04:12. The ECG line jumped, then started skipping erratically, presumably as his heart sucked in air and pumped blood into his chest cavity. Seconds later it flatlined.

I reached in my back pocket for the crumpled timeline I'd scrawled in King's paperback, smoothing the wet paper out on the metal tread plate. 3:45 a.m. – called to saloon. 3:55, returned to room. My prisoner had been alive at that time, he hadn't been knifed until nearly twenty minutes later. I thought about it, King and I had turned in almost immediately. The implication was just as alarming as it was confusing. He'd been stabbed through the heart as I'd been going to sleep right above him, on a bed which had to be moved to gain access down into his room. By the time we found him with the knife sticking from his chest he'd been dead nearly two hours.

The other implication was something I already knew, but it was satisfying to have it confirmed – King couldn't have murdered him. At that time, he'd been in my eyeline.

It wasn't suicide, because my captive had been tied to a chair. It wasn't some freak accident like falling on a knife in the rough weather, because it'd been pushed up right between his ribs, his jacket zipped up afterwards.

Crouched in the stinking hold of a ship in a storm, surrounded by angry smugglers and pursued by people who wanted me dead, I had enough problems. This information brought with it a whole bunch of new shit. I was holding in my hand proof that my prisoner had been stabbed by human hand while I was lying across the only entrance.

Chapter Thirty

Château des Aigles
Three days previously

I poured another generous slug of rum into the glass, topped it up some more for good measure, then drained half of it. Ringo had turned in a few minutes ago, still arguing with me even as he climbed the stairs. On the coffee table his half-smoked joint smouldered. I put it between my lips, sparked up the lighter, staring into the blazing fire. The broken body at the bottom of the ravine stared back.

'To live on in hearts is not to die,' I muttered, lying back on the sofa, staring over at the windows and colourful lights in the valley. 'Or in nightmares,' I added.

'You're drunk.'

I collapsed back, head upside down over the arm of the sofa, to watch Lennon walking down the stairs into the open-plan lounge.

'You need to keep a clear head,' she continued.

I didn't tell her that a clear head lets in other things. Instead I sucked on the flame and blew smoke up into the deer antlers above the fire.

'All he cares about is money.' Lennon walked around the back of the sofa. 'That's why he's angry.'

I tossed the lighter on the table. 'I'm gonna kill every single one of those motherfuckers.'

'No you're not.' She put her hand on my shoulder. 'You're going to do the job, because this is business.'

'They didn't know that though, did they?' I took another drag and flicked ash on the floor. 'They killed him for sport.'

'That's not your fault.'

'Letting him tail a group of white supremacists wasn't the best decision.'

'But it was *his* decision, he knew the risks.'

She didn't know the half of it. If she knew the real reason I'd got them here… 'I should have been on point.'

She shrugged. 'He was the better snowboarder. It made sense.'

I grunted and inhaled again, blowing smoke up. It spiralled around the antlers, up into the beams.

She plucked the joint from my mouth and threw it into the fire. 'We take the job, we accept the risks. If I die tomorrow don't cry for me.'

'No point living if you've nowt to die for.'

She smiled a sad smile, took my hand, pulled me up off the sofa. 'Come to bed.'

She led me upstairs to her room.

Chapter Thirty-one

Tiburon

I climbed the ladder up from the hold carefully, trainers slipping on the thin steel bars. When I reached the top I took a second to steady myself on the platform before reaching for the door.

It opened before I got to it, I barely managed to duck a wrench whistling through the air. I spun to my left, the wrench bounced off the railings with a reverberating clang lost in the crash of waves on the hull. I carried on sliding along the railings as the ship tipped, then grabbed on with one hand to steady myself.

Seb was already snarling towards me, having no trouble launching across the tilting walkway. I grabbed for my pistol but he swung the wrench again, I ducked, bouncing against the bulkhead and rolling away. The ship lurched the other way, I slid back towards him just as quickly. He swung again, I scrabbled and managed to bring up my pistol, the wrench connected with the barrel. The suppressed shot died away in the hull, the bullet went wide, ricocheting away, my pistol sailed after it into darkness.

Seb smiled, holding the wrench aloft. *The wrench that had stoved King's head in?*

The deck tilted again, I slid away with him looming after me. I scrambled to my feet, ducked a half-hearted swing, landing a fist into his gut. He didn't flinch, and Fatty had been a complete misnomer because it felt like I'd punched a wall. I dodged sideways, trying to get to the door, he threw the wrench. It struck me in the side just as I got through, I stumbled, hit the opposite wall hard, landing on my knees, winded. As the boat pitched again the door swung shut, I grabbed for the handle, spinning the dog latches closed just as I felt him pulling on the other side. The wheel turned through my hands, I grabbed the spokes, looking around for something to brace it but there was nothing, and he was far stronger.

I let go, ran back through the next door into the workshop, slamming it shut behind me. I heard the other door clang open, then he was turning the handle of this one. With one hand gripping the latch I reached for the tool rack on the wall, for something to give me some leverage, my fingers burned with effort, slipping on the metal, fingers twisting. I let go, colliding with the workbench, spinning me round as the boat pitched beneath me. I stood firm, raised my arms ready to fight, but amazingly the door stayed shut.

Contrary to what every hero on film believes, running is always a better option than fighting if it's available, so I staggered to the door at the other end of the workshop, glancing back over my shoulder, waiting for those latches to slam open. They didn't, and I'd made it.

I eased open the door into the engine room, stopping abruptly when I saw what awaited me. I closed the door quietly, slowly turning the handle and pulling it tight. On the other side of the door was another of the crew members, back to me, leaning on a railing sparking up a cigarette. Thankfully they hadn't heard the door over the hammering engines.

It wasn't necessarily the crew member's presence which worried me, but the AK-47 hanging from his shoulder, one hand on the grip, finger already curled around the trigger as he brought his lighter up in the other. And it wasn't even the AK-47 per se, but the knowledge that if that finger pulled the trigger, even if the bullets didn't make it into me, they'd summon everyone on the ship. A swift trip to hell, or more likely, a long one over the side of the ship.

I glanced back, Seb still hadn't arrived, and then I realised why: he'd gone down into the hold to get my gun.

I grabbed a crowbar from the rack, slipped it through the handle spokes of the door into the engine room, jamming it down against the bulkhead to prevent the crew member on the other side getting in. I had seconds to find a weapon. I looked round the workshop: there were a hundred improvised weapons hanging from the walls and in the drawers under the workbenches but unfortunately none which matched the effortless lethality of a Heckler & Koch VP70.

I went for a chisel and a screwdriver, holding them down low as I crossed back to the other door, just in time for the handle to turn. I threw myself against the wall, holding the workbench for balance against the constant motion of the room.

My gun crept into the room, long suppressor first, I seethed as I saw it clenched in that murderous fist. I whipped the chisel up, embedding it in the bulging tendons across the back of Seb's hand. He screamed, I dragged the chisel upwards, his hand sprang open in a shower of blood, the gun clattered across the greasy floor. I leaned my weight against the door, swinging it shut on his arm, bringing the screwdriver up, ready to drive it through his wrist.

Before I could he growled and shoved back, using his weight advantage and an inconveniently timed wave to throw me off balance, away from the door. I dropped the screwdriver, leapt for the gun, felt the world shift as something collided with my head, pushing me away from the gun, across the room. Everything spun more than the waves accounted for, I looked at him swimming in and out of focus, cradling his injured hand against his chest, gripping the huge wrench in the other. Pain erupted behind my eyes, I screwed them shut, put my hand to my head, it felt warm and wet.

I shook my head, opened my eyes. His whole body was rising and falling as he panted, short, angry breaths, eyes darting for the gun. The screwdriver rolled across the floor, I got my feet under me and grabbed it, ready for the attack. He was already halfway across the room, scooping up the pistol and aiming it at me while I was still trying to shake the fog from my head. What is it they said about bringing a knife to a gunfight? And all I had in my hand was a screwdriver.

He smiled. 'You took something from those mountains that doesn't belong to you.'

'Did you kill King?' I hissed through gritted teeth.

His savage grin was answer enough, he steadied his feet as the deck shifted, levelling the gun at me.

I stared into the suppressor barrel. 'You're fucking up in a big way pointing my own gun at me.'

'You messed with the wrong people.' He squeezed the trigger.

A very heavy, very crunchy, very unexpected 20lb trigger pull to someone unfamiliar with the pistol.

I kicked out with my left leg, slamming my shoe against a big green button on the workbench.

Startled by the sudden whirring noise right next to his head, he turned, still squeezing the trigger. His arm followed his eyes as he looked at the big circular saw, unable to stop the gun drifting with his head. The bullet buzzed past me, tearing up the rubberised flooring as I launched forward. He leaned back, putting distance between us, squeezing the trigger again, but I was too close now for him to turn the gun onto me, especially with the unwieldy suppressor attached.

I punched his arm as hard as I could, it turned, the gun coughed again three times in rapid succession, bullets spat at the wall this time. I pushed his arm, he carried on squeezing the trigger as his wrist hit the safety guard of the circular saw, I grabbed his right arm, forcing it down towards the spinning blade. Inch by inch, closer to the buzzing steel. I had the advantage, pushing down, even so it took all my strength. His wrist was a centimetre from the whirling teeth, I put all my weight behind it.

He reached behind him with his free left arm and pulled the plug from the wall, the noise stopped, the blade whined slowly to a halt. Seb smirked.

I brought my right arm round in an arc, burying the screwdriver to the handle in the side of his now unguarded neck, instantly severing his carotid artery. *Ambushed by a saw.* He spluttered, eyes wide, pulling the trigger over and over again even as he slumped backwards, bouncing off the workbench and rolling onto the floor. His mouth flapped, trying to take breaths to displace the blood filling his lungs. I prised my pistol from his fingers, slid out the magazine. Empty. I looked back at the door; the handle hadn't moved. His mate in the engine room hadn't heard the commotion, still stood in between those two thrumming engines.

I grabbed a roll of paper towel from the bench and mopped it through the blood pumping across the floor, thankfully with the screwdriver still embedded there was far less than there should have been, most of it was pumping out on the inside. One of his hands was on his neck, the other reaching for me weakly. His eyes were glassy, breathing shallow, I swatted his hand away from his neck and lifted his head to mop under it, then slid a plastic rubbish bag over his head to catch the rest, wrapping some duct tape around his neck to hold it on. I stood, hands on my knees, thinking of my next move as the plastic bag moved in and out with his gurgling breaths.

He'd followed me in here, attacked without asking questions, and the few words uttered suggested he was friendly towards my pursuers. Unfortunately, it'd been over before I could get more information, and he was beyond speech now. Had he killed King? Almost definitely. But had he somehow broken into my cabin to kill my captive?

The man out there in the engine room could probably tell me more, but I didn't fancy a one-sided conversation with that AK-47, not when a single shot could bring the whole ship running.

Then everyone would find me in here, standing over the dead body of one of their crew mates with his bloody head wrapped in a plastic bag. Not a good look if, as I did, you want to make it home to England.

Like I said, subterfuge is always preferable to conflict, running and hiding a better policy than standing and fighting. It's not cowardice, just facts bred of experience in war zones. If you have an out, that's better odds than facing down a gun. Take the odds.

I picked him up under his arms and dragged him backwards through the doors, into the cargo hold, leaving him on the platform while I ran back to check the workshop. The place was already filthy, a few wipes with paper towels and you'd never know anything had happened. I scuffed up a couple of new gashes in the rubber-coated floor, wiped an oily rag across a couple of dings on the wall made by ricocheting bullets, grabbed a few shell casings rolling round the floor and put them in my pocket. Couldn't find them all but amongst fifty years of detritus I wasn't too concerned. Good as new, or rather, as good and grubby as it had been.

I grabbed a rope looped from a hook on the wall and went back into the hold, closing the doors behind me. As I stepped over Seb I noticed the plastic bag on his head was barely moving now.

Chapter Thirty-two

Tiburon

I paused at the top of the ladder, tied the rope off on the top rung. Crashing surf swooshed above my head again, on the other side of thick steel plates. I held on tightly as the ship dived down another trench, waited until the waves had broken over the bow, then turned the handle and pushed the hatch open. I caught my breath as seawater poured through, freezing me to the bone. I pushed again, moved up a couple of rungs, heaving it all the way open, head and shoulders out onto the deck. The water cascaded away off the sides, I climbed up again as the boat climbed the next wall of water.

For the second time I hauled myself up and over the raised threshold of the hatch as we reached the top of the wave, the ship hanging in mid-air for a second before groaning and shuddering, pointing straight back down again. I used the momentum to roll up and onto the deck, swinging the hatch closed behind me and sliding underneath my car as we reached the bottom of the trough. Again, a wall of water descended on the deck of the boat, drowning everything. I braced myself against the wheels as the water raced away again, threatening to carry me over the side with it.

As soon as we were on the up I opened the hatch again, reaching in and grabbing the rope. I pulled the first few loops arm over arm, picking up slack until the line went taut. I spun round, sat on the edge with my feet braced against the other side of the hatch, the rope disappearing between my legs. I heaved, lifting the dead weight, trying to use the rolling of the boat to my advantage. Another wall of water loomed, this time I just closed my eyes and mouth, letting the deluge hit, wrapping the rope round my arms. Water poured down into the hold, dragging on the weight in my hands. I carried on hauling as we rose out the other side.

My arms burned as the rope pendulummed around the hold with the motion of the ship, harder at first as it swung in long, heavy arcs, but it got easier as the rope shortened and the arc shortened. Several waves later, Seb's head, still shrouded in the plastic bag, reached the top of the ladder.

I waited until we were crawling up another wave to haul Seb up onto the deck, untying the rope from the ladder and slamming the hatch closed.

Here we were in darkness – just the small navigation lamp at the prow beaming into the inky black – but I knew if anyone on the bridge saw anything they'd flick on the work lamps and I'd be frozen like a rabbit, standing over the dead body of their pal.

We started down into another black trough, I braced against the front of my car again and took some time to get my breath back. A jarring crump as we hit the wall of water, it curved over the bow and then everything was drowned. The freezing water poured away again as we rose, the rope slipping through my numb fingers, Seb's body was almost swept out past my car.

I looked up at the wheelhouse, could just about make out a figure through the blurry glass. No panic, no excitement, it looked like they were just staring ahead, trying to keep course. Above, the running lights on the mast winked in the driving rain. I noticed the sky behind was lighter now as the grey dawn approached the horizon in the east.

I dragged Seb back across the slick metal, slipped the loop of rope off his body, wrapping it over my shoulder. Now at the top of the wave, hanging in mid-air for a second before teetering and dropping back into the abyss, I crouched, dragging him by the arm towards the railings. The wall of water was approaching.

Barely visible was the low metal wall, punctuated with small holes to let water drain from the deck back into the sea, while also hopefully preventing an unwary crew member from being swept overboard. I grabbed it and dragged Seb closer, lifting his head, his shoulders onto it. An arm jerked out, gripping onto me, the blood-filled plastic bag turned, his other arm reached for me. I grabbed onto the railings as water crashed over the bow again, pulling me off the deck, he grabbed for my legs, fingers tearing at my jeans, briefly underwater. When I could take a breath I realised I was on the wrong side of the railings, being dragged off the ship, into the whirling Atlantic.

I looked down at my leg, Seb was clamped to it. I uncurled my other leg from the railings, let myself hang over the side of the ship, swinging round, and aimed a kick into the plastic bag. I felt the tug on my leg as my foot connected, the brief squash of flesh against my heel, and then he was gone, dropping into the black.

I used the motion of the ship to swing my legs back up, managing to hook them around the railings as we reached the zenith of yet another crest. Still the face in the window stared past me, fixed on some point on the rolling horizon. I jumped to my feet and launched across the deck, gripping my car as the ship tilted up, trainers sliding on the deck plates. I crouched for a moment as the ship stabilised, I didn't have to look behind me to know we were on the crest, I took advantage of it and ran aft towards the superstructure.

I didn't get far before the deck tilted the other way, bow angling down steeply, a big one, I ran harder. The deck pitched forward ever steeper, I leaned into it, running uphill on wet steel in trainers without decent grips, trying to make it to the superstructure and back inside, but it was no good. The impact at the bottom of the wave knocked me off my feet, sent me stumbling backward, I spread my arms and reached out, managing to grab a cargo strap before I was pitched into the beam of the deck lamps. Seawater enveloped the bow, most of my car, sweeping back across the deck, wrapping itself around me as the ship tilted the other way. We climbed again, the strap slipped between my fingers, I was tossed across the deck like a takeaway cup going over a waterfall. I threw my arms out again, ready to grab the railing, but didn't make it that far as I slammed against the superstructure, spinning round, fingers finding the doorframe.

The water washed away. I grabbed the door handle, pulled myself up then ducked back down quickly, reversing away from the door. A figure had been stood just inside, back to me, rifle in his arms. I wrapped a hand round the skeletal external staircase up to the bridge wing, pulled out my pistol. It was empty but anyone confronting me wouldn't know that, it could still be useful.

Fortunately, no one opened the door, I hadn't been spotted. I waited another minute, spent another couple of cycles of waves clinging to the stairway, then rose again to peer inside. The figure hadn't moved, back still to the door, rifle ready as if expecting trouble. Miller must have posted them around the ship, had them all wound so tight they'd shoot if a fly buzzed past. I needed to get back to my cabin without being seen. Seen meant implicated, especially when Seb's disappearance was noticed, and out here, with this lot, that would mean death, unpreventable with my ammo back in my cabin.

A number of hatches peppered the deck, including the one I'd come out of, but they all led to the hold or access spaces, all of which funnelled me into that same corridor outside the engine room and didn't solve the question of how to get to my cabin. There was no telling how the crew was dispersed, who was roaming the passageways.

I leaned over the railings, looking down into the sea. The lights from my cabin glowed out across the dark water below. I ran back to the superstructure and stuck to it as I made my way aft, careful to duck under the windows at deck level. The crashing water didn't make it back this far – easier to walk gripping the various grab-handles and window frames. I stopped as the deck rounded towards the stern, ducking under the lifeboats hanging from the davits and pausing by the tattered flag flapping in the gale. Dawn was definitely on the march, it'd be light soon. The brighter sky was further round to starboard, we must have turned north earlier than Katanga's plan.

I briefly considered taking refuge in the bilge access King and I had used earlier, but that was a pointless dead end. I ducked back under the lifeboats and ran to the starboard side, leaning over the railings there. A light in

Fields' cabin glowed weakly, just a couple of metres below my feet. I uncoiled the rope from my shoulders, slipped my arms through the loop I'd used to hoist Seb's body up the ladder, and with one last look out over the writhing black, I slipped the rope around the railings and jumped overboard.

Chapter Thirty-three

Château des Aigles
Two days ago

The red dot shone bright against the white canvas as I swept the cross hairs over the mountain. I took my eye away from the Ruger rifle's Viper scope, blinked a couple of times, looked out across the distant peaks, towards Mont Blanc. The last few minutes of afternoon sun seemed to set fire to the peaks, sparkling copper off the compacted snow of the piste further up to my right. The wind was picking up again, beyond the piste a line of pines shivered, dropping the last hour's-worth of snow and springing back, ready for more.

I bit off a chunk of Toblerone and squinted at the pass a few metres beneath my snow bank. Here the snow was still deep: skiers stayed away from this section of the mountain, with its rocks and inclines leading only to the thick trees and the village a kilometre below. Today no one had been through. I knew, I'd been watching through a slot the size of a paperback since I'd dug in hours ago.

Gore-Tex gear and the mat spread under me had prevented the damp from seeping up, but not the cold. Nor had the Belleville boots prevented my toes going numb. I'd got used to it around midday. Used to it, but not immune. I wiggled my feet again and shivered, an involuntary spasm shaking my arm. I swore under my breath and flexed my fingers, took a slow breath, rested my cheek against the stock of the rifle and put my eye back to the scope. I angled up, looking towards the tree that marked the turn onto this section. Out of focus white blobs drifted lazily in the magnified image as the snow started up again.

Ringo buzzed in my ear. 'Two minutes to the turn.'

'Two minutes, aye,' I replied, bringing the rifle down slowly, looking for the stick I'd stuck in the ground, the one that marked 200 metres. So much snow had fallen it was half-buried. I panned across, picking out the route they'd take. 'Where's Sting?'

'Bringing up the rear,' said Ringo. 'As per.'

I flexed my arms and settled in again, eye to the scope. 'Time to turn?'

'Thirty seconds. Going in now.'

I flexed my hands for the final time, holding my breath. On the radio there was a scuffle, shouting, cursing as Ringo skied into Sting, taking him out while Bono and Bob skied on, oblivious. The scuffle eased, steps crunched through the snow.

'Shit,' Ringo buzzed. 'Bad news.'

'You slowed Sting?'

'Yeah, yeah, but I lost the other two in the trees. And the guy with him isn't Bono.'

I lifted my head and blinked a few times. 'What do you mean?'

'It's Midge today, Bono must have stayed in the cafe.'

'Bono always takes point. Are you sure?'

'He's not hard to miss, is he? Size of him... Bono is definitely not here.'

'Shit. The one day we needed them to stick to routine.'

'It makes no difference to the plan,' said Lennon.

'Means I can't shoot the motherfucker though.' I settled back to the scope. 'They still in formation?'

'I... I think they've switched places.' Ringo's voice had risen in pitch.

'Is Bob front or rear?' I asked.

'Ten seconds until they're on you.'

'I need to know which is Bob!'

Lennon's voice broke in. 'They always go Bob in the middle, Sting at the rear. They'll stick to that. Bob is second.'

'But that's when Bono is on point. If it's Midge...' I angled up slowly, to the left of the lone pine, finger tensing up on the trigger, thumb sliding the safety off.

Two figures shot into view, slicing through the powder.

'Three hundred metres.'

I tracked them down the slope as they slowed for the turn into the narrow pass. They wore identical gear, scarves up to their noses now the sun had dipped below the peaks. The last run of the day. The last opportunity this side of Christmas. One of the skiers tucked in behind the other.

'Ringo, I need to know which is Bob.'

The duo skied on, nearing the pole which represented the kill zone.

'Ringo?'

'I... I don't know. It's on you.'

I put the red dot on the first figure. They slowed to walking pace, skier one looking back over his shoulder to talk to skier two. I panned to skier two, who was nodding. My 200-metre stick marker flashed past behind them. Any second now they'd accelerate as the ground straightened and dipped into the trees. I controlled my breathing and tried to speak calmly to avoid the dot jumping around.

'Lennon, you ready?'

'Go. Remember, Bob always goes second.'

I was cursing Bono's decision not to ski today, did the guy have a sixth sense? Now I was faced with identical figures, impossible to differentiate height or mass as they flashed past in a crouch. I followed them both, every second an extra couple of metres closer to me, narrowing the angle, shortening the window, increasing the risk. Both skiers faced forward now, poles up, tucking in. I gently squeezed the trigger. The merest flash of neon orange as the first figure turned to look back, passing my second marker, 150 metres, I was out of time.

'Shoot the first guy,' said Lennon.

A curl of hair stuck out from under the skier's hat. They'd switched places. I swung the rifle onto the second skier, adjusting for the reduced distance. 'Lennon, heads up in five seconds, four, three...' I exhaled and held my breath.

The rifle punched into my shoulder, the heavy .450 Bushmaster round exiting the Ruger's suppressor at 1,500 mph with enough energy to put down an elephant. After a hundred metres the bullet was still travelling with nearly eight times the energy of your average handgun round over the same distance. The bodyguard was no elephant.

The bullet slammed home, burrowing and expanding through soft flesh to obliterate his chest. He kept going, delayed reaction, before slumping sideways, legs following. The skis flashed in the sun as he slipped, almost in slow motion, over the edge of the precipice.

The suppressor hadn't dampened the sound like it would a small-calibre handgun, you can't silence shit like that. I swung onto Bob. In my scope he looked up, searching for the source of the sound, confusion painted on his actions. He glanced round, couldn't see his body-guard, looked over his other shoulder, but still he kept going. His mind would be whirring now, wondering where his buddy had gone, wondering what the noise had been, slowly putting two and two together in real time in my cross hairs.

There was a loud *whump* sound in the earpiece, followed by a bout of German swearing. '*Flachwichser*,' said Lennon. 'He bounced, just missed me.'

Bob was thirty metres from me now, the penny had finally dropped.

Twenty metres from me he started to turn, pulling down his scarf.

I tugged a loop of cable tied around my wrist.

Fifteen metres from me he turned his skis, digging his poles to help him stop.

Too late.

He hit the cable sideways, folding in half. The cable which had now leapt out from being buried, to exactly knee height. He'd turned side-on, momentum carrying his body over the wire, landing on the other side in a tangle of skis, cable and confusion.

'Bob is down.'

I exploded from the hide, sliding the few metres down the snow bank, running over to the struggling figure. He heard me and turned just as the palm of my hand flattened his nose. I crouched beside him.

'Ringo, status on Sting?'

'Two minutes from the turn.'

'Stop him.'

The man on the ground gurgled behind the broken nose and reached up. I slammed a fist into the baggy jacket, into the belly behind. He went limp, gasping.

I pulled a syringe from my jacket pocket, biting the cap off, bringing it in hard against his neck. It only took seconds from depressing the plunger for the writhing to stop.

'Ringo, where's Sting?'

I pulled off my gloves and patted Bob's body down, finding his phone in a chest pocket. It lit up as I waved it. I took a guess, pulled off his right glove, and rested my thumb on it. It unlocked, a bright screen filled with apps. The phone would contain valuable information; I scrolled looking for the settings, then went in and tried to remove the phone's lock. It asked me for a passcode before it'd let me change the settings, an existing passcode I had no way of knowing.

'Fucking hell, Ringo, gimme an update. Where's Sting?'

'Sorry, he got by me.' Ringo panted. 'He'll be on you in sixty seconds.'

I flicked open a carpet knife from a leg pocket and pushed it into the man's thumb, slicing a chunk of flesh down to the bone, then pulled his glove back on. I took out a sandwich bag, scooped a fistful of snow into it, and dropped the thumbprint in. The bag and phone zipped securely into my pocket.

I pulled out the smartwatch I'd bought in the village and fastened it to his wrist, then yanked off his hat, throwing it over the cliff, and took a canvas shopper bag from my pocket. I pulled it over his head, tugging a drawstring tight under his chin.

'Ringo, fucking kill Sting, NOW!'

I unclipped the tripwire from a cam set in a boulder near the edge, threw the cable over, then removed the cam from the crack. Off my shoulder came a simple figure-of-eight climbing harness, which I looped under Bob's arms and pulled tight, dragging him to the boulders at the edge of the precipice.

'Sting's making the turn,' said Ringo. 'I'm on my way.'

I clipped another carabiner with a short rope on to Bob's harness. 'Radio silence,' I said, looking back at my snow hide, at my rifle and bag. A silhouette was growing against the darkening sky as Sting approached. Already nervous following his encounter with Ringo, he could easily screw the job, or at least make things difficult. He had a radio on him, not to mention a weapon.

I placed the cam in a crack in a boulder I'd earmarked earlier, attached the rope, and lowered Bob over the edge. The rope slipped, he dropped a few feet and jerked to a stop, the cam biting hard into the rock. I slid over after him until I was standing on his shoulders, gripping the rope with my head just above the edge.

I had to hope Sting didn't notice the blood and scuffed-up snow, hope he'd ski straight past.

We hung together, creaking in the wind, Bob's unconscious body attached to the rope, me standing on him. The cam was placed in the boulder directly in front of me, I could see the teeth jammed into a centimetre of rock, all that was stopping us from dropping. I know these things are up to it and can hold more than us, but logic went out the window the moment I looked down. One wrong move and there was nothing between my boots and the sharp rocks 120 metres below.

I screwed my eyes shut, trying to control my breathing as my heart pounded ever faster. Visions of McCartney's broken body at the bottom of the ravine played in a loop through my head. The wind rustled the pines along the edge, dropping snow across us. Then another noise, the hiss of skis on snow, approaching slowly. I crouched lower, pulling my head down, holding on to the rope. The hissing stopped.

Shuffling in the snow above: he'd seen something. The tracks, the glistening red on the fresh snow… Something had stopped him. I tentatively moved one hand to my pocket. The rope creaked, we started to spin round. My pocket was empty, my pistol wasn't there.

I gripped the rope with both hands again and slowly raised my head. A dark figure crouched below my hide, looking at the disturbed snow. My pistol was still in my bag in the hide, along with the rifle that he was sure to see if he just climbed a couple of feet up the bank.

I reached up and scooped snow in my fist, made a snowball, pulled myself up higher, and launched it at the trees further along the edge to my right. He didn't see it but his head snapped sideways as it crashed through the branches. He jumped his skis round and slowly slid towards it, reaching in his pocket, either for his radio or his pistol. *Where the fuck is Ringo?*

I hauled myself up the rope, sliding belly-first along the ground. When I was behind the boulders I pushed onto my knees, moving round them as the figure slid the other way. He'd reached the trees hanging over the ravine, and I could see now he'd gone for his pistol over the radio.

My crampons dug in as I launched towards him.

He turned as I approached, surprise switching to fear. He should have pulled his radio, called it in immediately. He scrabbled at his jacket with one hand, trying to unzip it as he brought the pistol up in the other but too late, I was on him.

I stood on his skis, with his boots locked to them his legs may as well have been encased in concrete, he tried instinctively to back away but lost his balance and almost pitched sideways without my help, throwing his gun arm out to steady himself. I helped him on his way with a fist to the head, which he blocked easily with his other hand, the trade-off putting himself further off balance. I pulled my knife, he whipped the pistol down. I adjusted and swung the knife up into his wrist, he grunted, hand springing open. The pistol dropped without a shot, bounced off a root and disappeared over the edge.

He snarled and swung a fist, I jumped to my right, off his skis, into the trees along the edge, yanking him towards me, bringing my boot up. The skis slid out from under him, he stumbled, clawing at the knife embedded in his arm. I slammed my boot down into his thigh, felt the crampons bite flesh, he roared and collapsed on the edge of the ravine. At the last minute he grabbed for my jacket, dragging me with him. The branches parted to reveal empty space, we landed side by side, heads sticking out over the long drop.

His hands went for my neck, I felt his blood hot on my cheek. I pushed out with my feet, crampons digging into the snow. Our shoulders slid over the edge. Gloved fingers clawed my face, going for my eyes. I bent my legs, extended again, digging in, pushing. He tried to counteract but his skis were tangled, boots useless, all he had to stop himself were his hands, and they were currently wrapped around me. His thumb found my right eye socket and pressed hard, fortunately his thick gloves prevented him from doing real damage. I thrust out again, hard, sliding over the edge up to my stomach, momentum doing the rest as we slid over. At the last moment I grabbed for a branch of the nearest tree.

He had a split-second choice to make, and predictably made the wrong one. He'd been focused on me, hadn't fully realised the danger, and now it was too late. He scrabbled then gripped even tighter, huge fingers now encircling my neck as we slipped all the way over. I kicked his skis away, he pressed harder but he was done and knew it. There was a flash of realisation in his eyes, fear, panic, then he was gone, all without a word.

'Lennon, look up!'

A blast of static a few seconds later followed by another bout of German swearing indicated the bodyguard had made it to Lennon waiting at the bottom.

I swung my legs back up, slid round the tree, pushed back onto the snow, giving myself a few seconds' rest. Just from that short burst of action my lungs burned, arms ached, heart raced. It raced too much these days. If I had a set number of beats in my life I was going through them far too quickly. I was overdrawn on time, past life expectancy for someone in my profession. These were reminders I should be getting out, not limping from one job to the next.

'Where's Sting?' asked Ringo, sliding to a stop beside me.

Chapter Thirty-four

Tiburon

I swung in the darkness, rope wrapped around my right wrist several times, clutching the loose end in both hands. As I slowly paid it out it slid over the railing and down to me, lowering me towards the glow from the cabin window below. Centimetre by centimetre I let out the rope, keeping it tight around my wrist, fingers burning. I realised as I dropped lower I actually got further away from the window, as the ship climbed upwards and swung me out towards the stern.

I looked down past my trainers at the churning water at the back of the ship, huge props pushing us onward, up, then we levelled off. I braced myself, holding tight. The ship groaned, every rivet strained, the screws lifted out of the sea, spinning wildly for a moment, it seemed like they were metres from my feet, I lifted my legs and gripped the rope even tighter, then the ship dropped forward, the rope swung, I bounced along the side of the ship, letting rope slip from my arms as I did, dropping lower as I swung forward.

I hit the window seam, bouncing painfully off, kicking at the glass, trainers squeaking and sliding and then I was flailing past it. I wrapped the rope tighter around both wrists, holding on as the ship hit the bottom, the crash reverberating through every girder and weld. Something moved at the window, a shadow across the light, the glass opened an inch.

'Fields!' I shouted above the roar of the waves.

The window opened further as I swung back, I turned and angled my feet first, they slid off the glass and bounced against the window frame. I braced against it, my grip on the rope slipped, I dropped a foot, grabbing tight, wrapping it round my arm some more. The window opened fully, a silhouette appeared.

'Tyler?' It was Marty. 'What the hell are you doing?' She grabbed my arm.

'What the hell does it look like?' The screws churned beneath me again, we started to level off. 'Pull me in!'

Marty had her arms out of the window, holding my wrist, Fields was next to her but there was little room for them both to help. I let go of the rope with one hand and reached up, catching hold of the porthole opening. The rope slipped off the railing and dropped into the sea, I kicked it away and reached for the window. Another hand grabbed my arm, pulling up in a last-ditch effort, this time I managed to grab the metal edge. A hand grabbed my collar, hauling me up, I pulled and got my head in, my shoulders, soon the sharp edge of the window was digging into my wound dressing as I dragged myself over it and down inside.

I fell onto the bed, Marty beside me. Fields pulled the window shut behind us and then stood looking down at me, expecting answers.

He didn't get them as the door pounded.

'Open up,' shouted Miller.

'What the *fuck* is going on,' Marty hissed.

I held a finger to my lips and slipped into the bathroom, motioning for Fields to open up as I closed the door and locked it.

I heard him opening the cabin door as I stripped off my wet jeans and socks.

'Where is he?' Miller shouted, there was a scuffle, I could picture him pushing into the room.

'Where's who?' Fields asked.

'Don't be a fucking smartass,' Miller replied. Noises, muttering, I could hear Katanga speaking to someone else. I pulled off my T-shirt.

'Tyler, where's Tyler?' Miller continued. 'He's not in his cabin. Kat, get Seb, I want this ship turned upside down. He gives you any trouble, shoot first.'

'I won't give you any trouble,' I shouted.

'Tyler?' He banged on the bathroom door. 'What the hell are you doing?'

I wrapped a towel around my waist and unlocked the door. 'What do you think?'

Katanga and Poubelle held their rifles up in the doorway.

'There's a perfectly good shower in your cabin,' said Miller as he looked me up and down.

The dressing Doc had applied had been ripped off, the stiches held but fresh blood was trickling across the towel. I put a hand over it and looked at Miller. 'There's safety in numbers.'

'You need Doc again?'

'Since when did you care? What do you want, anyway?'

'Need you on the bridge.'

'You'll forgive me if I'm not overly enthusiastic about that.'

'Situation's changed.'

'The situation changed when one of your crew...' I looked at Katanga and Poubelle, the fewer people knew about my dead prisoner the better, '...when one of your crew murdered my mate.'

Miller looked down at the floor, muttered something, and walked over to me. Marty flinched, I waved her hand away from her holster.

'The shit has hit the fan,' Miller whispered.

'Let me get dressed, I'll be ten minutes.'

Chapter Thirty-five

Château des Aigles
Two days ago

Hanging from the rope, the unconscious man swayed in the wind rushing up the vertical rock face. I lay on the snow, braced against the rocks, holding the other end of the rope. I squeezed the descender gear gently, the rope passed through as our cargo was lowered down to Lennon and the car waiting below.

Ringo strapped his skis together and picked up the rifle. 'Told you this Ruger would put him over the edge. You can keep your Heckler & Koch.'

'Didn't so much put him over the edge as vaporise him. We all clean back there?'

He nodded. 'Some spray but most of it went over with him. I've wiped down everything I could see.'

He crunched over to my hide. I'd already checked it over, packing my gear into the rucksack on my back. He paused, bending down. 'One spot of blood.' He kicked at the snow. 'Gone.'

'Package down,' said Lennon in my earpiece. 'All yours.'

The rope went slack, I pulled off my gloves and opened the descender. Ringo pulled on a climbing harness and slung the rifle over his back. I looped the end of the rope through the cam still wedged into the boulder, tying it off.

I gave Ringo a nod then crouched to remove my crampons. I grabbed my harness and pulled it on, made sure my pistol was secure in my jacket pocket, and gave the place one last look-over. The sun was down, darkness descending rapidly. In another hour the snow would cover the tracks, there'd be nothing left to say any of us were ever here. I clipped the crampons to my harness and looked back at Ringo, he'd already started, only his head now visible above the edge.

He nodded and waved. 'Don't look down.'

I ignored his advice and leaned over to watch him dropping down the face to the waiting car. The Porsche's headlights cut a path through the whirling snow in the narrow pass far below, I leaned back in, breathing heavily. I tightened the straps of my harness, slackened them off and re-tightened them as I waited.

'All yours,' Ringo finally said through the radio.

I opened my descender and threaded the rope through. I locked it, opened it, checked it again. I went through this cycle several more times before I finally snapped it onto the carabiner on my harness. Far below, the figures loaded the car. I looked back at the cam wedged securely in the boulder, breathed in, held it, trying to stop my hands shaking, finally leaning back, over the abyss, boots firmly planted on the edge. I brought one hand down to the descender but quickly grabbed the rope again, still shaking.

'FUCK,' I shouted.

I eased back and let the rope take my weight. I didn't go anywhere, the rope could have held all of us without breaking, the more weight on the descender the harder it gripped the rope. I knew all this, of course, and had relied on it umpteen times before, but it never got easier. Another glance at the lights below, I let go of the rope, squeezed the descender, and walked backwards over the edge.

I hung from my harness, boots planted against the rock face, the worst bit over. I squeezed the handle of the descender gently, slowly creeping down the rope.

A sharp crack echoed, flecks of stone hit my face. I looked at a fresh gash in the rock next to my boot, then glanced down at the car below. A flash next to it, another bang, there was a sharp tug on my jacket. He was getting closer, the bastard. I'd sighted the Ruger for 200 metres, Ringo's next shot wouldn't miss.

I jumped away from the rock face, squeezed the descender handle, dropping as the rifle flashed again, hitting rock above me. Three shots, the Ruger was out of ammo.

I counted.

One Mississippi.

Two Mississippi.

I pulled out my pistol.

Five Mississippi.

Another gunshot, he'd loaded the spare magazine, he'd not had time to chamber an extra round which meant another three shots. I kept the handle of the descender squeezed, the rocky face rushing by as I fell. The metal was heating up in my hand.

120 metres, rapid calculations flashed through my mind.

Nine Mississippi, another gunshot.

Minus ten metres for slowing.

Twelve Mississippi.

I could see a dark shape behind the SUV, the rifle flashed, I pulled the gun up and aimed at the car, squeezing the trigger three times rapidly.

Sixteen Mississippi.

Glass smashed as my bullets found their target. The descender was burning up now. I pulled the trigger another couple of times, no way could I hit them at that distance or speed, but it was giving them something to think about.

Eighteen Mississippi.

Nineteen Mississippi.

I eased off the descender, thankfully it gripped without melting straight through the rope and dropping me the remaining distance to my death.

The rocks zoomed up to meet me, I eased off again and let go as my boots hit. I rolled, sliding on the ice, one hand unclipping the descender from my harness, the other still holding the pistol outstretched. I leapt over the mangled bodies of the two bodyguards and ran for the road.

The Porsche's taillights vanished around the bend, leaving only glowing red snow piled either side. The narrow pass faded into darkness, silence except for the wind in the dark pines and the trickling stream alongside the road. Ringo and Lennon were gone, but more importantly, so was my prize.

Chapter Thirty-six

Tiburon

It took me less than five minutes to get ready to go see Miller. I pulled on my last dry pair of trousers – a faded and patched-up pair of combats – tucking my waist holster inside. A thick woollen jumper went over my favourite Nirvana T-shirt, adding an on-point fisherman vibe but, more importantly, covering the holster nicely. I left my battered shell tops jammed behind the heating pipes in my cabin and put my slightly less soggy Cons back on.

Raised voices drifted down the passage, I stumbled along, about to make my way up the stairs when I noticed the engine room door was ajar, tapping against the bulkhead with every crash of waves. I took my foot off the stairs and slid next to it.

Two people were arguing in French, they spoke so quickly and used so much of what I assumed was a mix of slang and technical jargon it was impossible to keep up. What I could make out was they were angry about something.

The door opened, I jumped but managed to style it out by leaning on the doorframe and casually looking in.

Poubelle was holding the door open, back to me, shouting at Vincent, who was crouching on the raised platform over on the far side of the room, straining with the door handle into the workshop. He jumped to his feet as he saw me.

'Trouble?' I asked.

Poubelle turned, stepping back into the engine room. 'You can't be in here,' he shouted above the engines.

Vincent picked up an old revolver from the floor as he climbed down the ladder into the engine bay. 'Get the fuck back in your room,' he screamed, waving it in my direction.

'No can do, I'm needed upstairs.'

Poubelle looked from Vincent to me. 'He's not kidding, back in your room.'

'Move,' Vincent shouted as Poubelle stepped into the doorway, blocking the shot. 'Shoot first, that is what the captain said.'

'Problem?' Miller shouted, sauntering up behind me.

'GI Joe is out of his room,' Vincent shouted, still waving the gun.

'Put that away,' Miller said. 'Did you find Seb?'

Vincent thumbed over his shoulder. 'He's sealed himself in the workshop.'

'You can't lock that door.' Miller frowned, pushing past us into the room. We watched as he dropped down the short ladder, walking between the engines, shouldering past Vincent. He climbed the ladder to the platform at the far end and gave the door handle a pull, looking back at us, confusion on his face.

'Why would he seal himself in?' He banged on the door. 'Open up. Now!'

He'd no way of knowing he was talking to a crowbar jammed down between the spokes.

'Cut through,' he shouted at Vincent and Poubelle, still banging on the door. 'Cut these hinges off.'

'With what?' said Vincent. 'All the tools are in there.'

'Neptune on a pedalo! Vincent, you stay here.' He was already dropping back down to the engine bay walkway. 'Poubelle, you and Kat go through the forward hatch, see if you can get in the other side.'

Poubelle didn't need telling twice, launching up the stairs two at a time. Miller climbed up the ladder, ushering me out into the corridor and turning to slam the door behind us. The thrum of the engines dropped to a background hum that pulsed through the floor and walls.

'If you need another pair of hands, I'll help,' I said.

'We don't need help,' Miller spat.

'So what *do* you need?'

He turned and climbed the stairs. I followed him to deck level but we didn't keep going to the bridge, instead pushing into the radio room.

Nic removed his headphones as he felt the door go, closing his laptop on the desk. I felt guilty when I saw a long bruise forming across his forehead, he looked down at his shoes.

Miller glared at me. 'Don't worry, he's sorry. Aren't you, Blofeld?' He didn't wait for an answer, fishing out his cigarettes, placing one in his mouth and offering the pack to me. I shook my head, he held them out to Nic.

Nic took one, stuck it in his mouth, taking forever as Miller first lit his own then held the lighter out to Nic.

'You made out it was urgent...' I said, leaning back against the wall.

Nic made a show of drawing the flame into the cig slowly, looked at me like he wanted to blow the smoke at my face then turned away again when he saw the look on it.

'Tell him, Nic.'

Nic took another drag on his cig. 'The HF, here.' He tapped a cracked dial. 'It was changed.'

'Changed?'

He pointed his cig at the radio, as if I had any clue what I was looking at. 'It has changed since I used it.'

'Someone's been using the radio? When?'

'I didn't notice earlier. This morning, maybe four, I listen for the weather traffic. There is always a Morse code transmitted between traffic. I had to retune. I didn't think about it.'

'So what *did* make you think about it?'

'I came again to get the latest weather just now. Same again, I had to retune. This, I thought, was strange.'

'Were they communicating?'

He pulled on the cig and blew smoke across the radio, nodding. 'Possibly in contact with someone, yes.'

'Any way to tell who's on the other end?'

'No.' He tapped the dial. 'I listen on this, this…'

'Frequency,' Miller added.

'Yes, no one responds now. But,' he shrugged, 'they could have changed the dial after, there is no way to know what frequency they were using or who they were talking to.'

'But someone's definitely been using the radio?'

He nodded.

'Nic, I want you listening out,' said Miller. 'You hear anything at all, you come straight to me. And don't tell anyone else about this.'

He nodded, slipped his earphones back on, turning the dials.

I looked at Miller. 'Well I think we know who they were speaking to.'

He frowned, holding a finger to his lips.

I pointed at the earphones. 'It's gotta be linked to that boat.'

'Seems someone on the ship took them up on their offer of killing your passenger.'

'We already knew that, or he wouldn't be dead. But this means someone's been in touch with them since. Possibly the same person that killed King.'

'I don't like it. Where's Seb? And why is the workshop sealed?'

'I think we can rule out my guys,' I said.

Seemed the wrong time to mention it was me that'd sealed the door, and that I'd thrown Seb overboard.

Chapter Thirty-seven

Tiburon

The storm had weakened, the waves now carried the crushing, nausea-inducing monotony of a lazy, over-weight clock. The rain had stopped too so I was outside in my T-shirt, gripping the railings on the port side bridge wing to let the salt spray wake me up. To my left the sky was still black, over the other side the sun had still to rise over the rollers but the sky had brightened. The sea was a mess of dark grey in every direction, I turned aft, leaning over the railings to look at the rolling waves merging with our wake, churning off into the murky distance.

A bang on the window next to my head spun me, Katanga had returned. I opened the door and stepped back into the relative warmth of the bridge. Poubelle was cradling a cup of coffee.

'Seb's missing,' said Miller simply.

I put on what I reckoned was the right amount of frown. 'How the bloody hell can he be missing on a ship this size?'

'Door was secured with this.' Katanga held up the crowbar. 'We went in through the forward hatch. No sign of him.'

'I'm sorry, Tyler,' said Miller. I looked at him, standing with one hand on the wheel. He looked at the floor. 'Looks like Seb killed King.'

Poubelle moved out of the way, something was on the table, resting on an oily towel. The wrench, bloody and sticky, which Seb had launched at me in the workshop. Katanga finished my train of thought for me.

'Found it under the workbench. It's got black hair on it.'

'Seb was bald,' Miller added.

I pictured him snarling towards me, like a bigger Vin Diesel. Then I pictured his wide eyes, the plastic bag on his head filling up with blood, blowing in and out with each laboured breath. 'Thanks, Poirot.'

'I'm sorry, Tyler,' Miller said again. 'Looks like it puts your guys in the clear.'

My fingers traced the edges of the piece of paper in my pocket. 'What did you guys do after I left you in the saloon?'

Miller shrugged. 'That was what, four? We were all in there for...' he shrugged. 'An hour or so?'

''Til five,' Poubelle agreed. 'That's when you relieved me up here.'

'So that's the last time anyone saw Seb?'

They looked at each other and nodded in turn.

'And you were together in the saloon all that time? Everyone?'

'Except me,' said Poubelle. 'I was at the wheel.' He nodded at the chair.

Unless they were all lying it put them all out of the frame for the murder in my cabin. And yet, someone killed him. Poubelle? No, apart from the fact I couldn't work out how it would have been done, he couldn't have trusted the autopilot during a ferocious storm, not with those waves and the constant corrections they'd demanded.

'I saw Mr King go outside just after six,' said Katanga. 'But I didn't see Seb.'

'Seb was already outside by then,' I said. 'In my car.'

'How do you know that?' asked Miller.

'King came up to the bridge to fetch you just after six. He saw something out there, out the windows. Maybe he saw Seb on deck, maybe the light on in my car, something drew him outside.'

'Why didn't he say anything to me?' asked Miller. 'I didn't see nuthin'.'

'You weren't looking. He's a – was – a suspicious type of guy.'

'You bastards have all got a death wish,' said Miller.

Katanga nodded enthusiastically. 'What was Seb doing on deck?'

'He put my car window through.'

'Why?' asked Miller. 'What was he lookin' to steal?'

'When I arrived in La Rochelle I came in hot, to put it mildly, with false plates on. He was looking for documents or something to get the true registration. Probably took the real reg off the VIN etched in the window. Anything to try to get some more info on me.'

'On you?'

'Well *someone* disabled the bilge pumps and gummed up the tank gauge to slow us down, *someone's* been communicating with that boat. I'm guessing whoever's tailing us wants to know who they're dealing with.'

Miller chewed it over.

'And Mr King tried to stop him…' said Katanga. 'I should have gone with him.'

'And you might have ended up dead, too, and we'd be an experienced pair of hands down,' said Poubelle.

'I buy that,' said Miller, finally having considered it. 'He killed King, maybe panicked, sealed himself in the workshop. Guy's gotta be batshit to do that. Why not just go back to work, act like nuthin' happened?'

It was my turn to shrug. 'I don't have the answers.' It was an outright lie, I did have them. The simple answer was he *had* gone back to work, then either seen or heard me and followed me into the hold, to send me the same way. But, still not a good time to tell them I'd taken matters into my own hands. I'd lied this far, better to keep it up. I nodded at the window. 'Storm seems to be on its way out, can we increase speed? How long before they overhaul us?'

Miller picked up his notepad of scrawled calculations. 'Not long enough. And meanwhile, Seb's down there somewhere doing holy shit knows what.'

'We should stick together,' said Katanga.

Miller nodded. 'Double up the crew. No one should be alone.'

'Especially Vincent.'

Miller gave me daggers. 'We don't need vigilantes.'

I held up my fingers. 'Cub's honour. Katanga, can I have a word?'

He looked round at the others. 'Sure.'

Miller and Poubelle eyed us as I put my arm round him, leading him through the door into the stairwell.

'We should hit the Channel what, late afternoon?'

He nodded. 'Should be off Cornwall by sundown. That's as long as the engines hold out.'

'And as long as we're not overtaken by then.' I looked down the stairs, the passageway was empty. 'Time for you to earn that bonus.'

He stood straighter, glancing round. 'Go on.'

'There's going to be an attempt on someone's life.'

His face dropped. 'Who…'

'Go get some rest then meet me outside my cabin at one p.m.'

'But I don't understand, Miller said…'

'You'll need to be armed.' I looked through the window in the door, into the bridge, Poubelle swaying at the wheel, Miller still watching us. Satisfied there was no way anyone on the ship could overhear us, I laid it out for him, all the details.

Chapter Thirty-eight

Tiburon

Fields, Marty, and I had used the lull in the weather to move King's body from my boot into the ship. We'd wrapped him in a blanket on the floor of the cold store, I'd mouthed a promise to get him a decent funeral back in England – one I'd no intention of attending. I had enough memories, and no interest in sharing them.

I'd started my car too while we were outside, given it a few revs before pocketing the key. Good old German engineering, strapped to the bow of a ship through a winter storm and she hadn't hesitated. How much rust I'd have to contend with when I got her back in the garage was another matter, all that seawater forced into places it should never reach couldn't be good.

I'd opened the glovebox again, checked the old CD changer. Nice and dry and untouched, either by waves or Seb when he'd broken in. I hooked a finger round the front panel and pulled, revealing a black plastic box inside the hollowed-out carcass of the CD changer. A single green LED flashing away to itself. Seb hadn't understood the significance of the equipment – not that it had anything to do with him.

Now I was sat in the corner of the saloon, feet on the table, watching Marty nursing her third cup of coffee at the starboard windows. Behind a counter, Doc and Poubelle were arguing over the hob, each trying to cook an entirely different type of breakfast. The dying back of the storm and arrival of the sun, albeit swaddled in mist, had brought a new sense of optimism to everyone on board.

My own optimism was slower to rise, because while we'd been able to speed up, our pursuers had also taken advantage of the calmer weather to increase their speed even more. And I knew what kind of people they were. If they caught up, then best case scenario, no one on the ship would be left alive. It could be worse.

Poubelle brought out a plate of seemingly random items, dubious-looking cheese interspersed with slices of cold meats, and some greasy sausages swimming in beans that Doc had insisted we wanted despite our assertions to the contrary. Marty didn't even look round from the window, putting her hand on her stomach.

'Doc,' I shouted. 'Any more scopolamine? I think someone's feeling it.'

'Yes, yes.' He looked over at me, then Marty. 'Of course, I'll fetch some more tablets.' He wiped his hands on his trousers and hurried from the room. Secretly I hoped he'd bring enough for all of us, it was making me feel sick just watching her.

'You need to eat,' I said to her.

Marty looked back at me, at the plate, then back to the window. 'I wouldn't even eat that if I felt well.' She looked over at Poubelle. 'No offence. I don't eat anything that could wear sunglasses or shoes.'

He tutted, frowning as he tried to work it out, and stamped from the room.

I pulled out the soggy, torn page from King's book with my timeline and suspects. With the time of death so unquestionably nailed on at 04:12, there was a very narrow list of candidates. The entirety of the crew had been in the saloon together, other than Poubelle, who'd been at the wheel. I just couldn't see them all lying, which put not only Seb in the clear, but everyone else as well.

So who did that leave? Marty and Fields, alibiing each other in their cabin at the time, and King with me. I put my head in my hands. I'd been in a situation like this before, what had it taught me? To look for the obvious solution. Not to trust everything my senses were telling me, and not to believe anyone. Easy with hindsight but not giving me much to go on right now.

'Who was he?' I looked up to see Fields swaying over me. 'The guy, the job, who was he? What's he done?'

'Nothing you need to worry about.'

'Did you know him?' he asked.

I shook my head. 'Not until this month, you know how it is. Why the interest?'

'Just wanna know why I'm risking my neck.'

'He was bad news, you don't need to know anything else.'

He pulled out the chair opposite and sat down, reaching for a sausage from the plate. 'But that's what I mean, how do you *know* that? Just because someone told you? A folder full of pictures taken out of cars parked across the street and the word of some government stooge?'

I held my head in my hands. 'I could do without this right now.'

He bit half the sausage and waved it, my stomach flipped.

'Bloody hell, this is gopping,' he said between chewing, dropping the rest back on the plate and wiping his hand on his shirt. 'Look, I was on a job a few years ago, when I was with Cresswell. We were ordered to...'

'I couldn't give two shits about your backstory, okay? Keep your brain on what's happening now, on this ship.'

He sat back, crossing his arms. 'The point was gonna be that you're just a tool, aren't you? Do whatever the man says, yes sir no sir no questions. Now that guy's dead, that's on you as far as I'm concerned.'

I narrowed my eyes. 'It's on all of us. We were hired to transport him back home. You think they'll throw a party when I turn up with a corpse?'

'Aye, sorry. I'm just... I dunno. I'm tired, okay?'

'Go get some rest. I'm heading down myself in a minute.'

We were interrupted by the return of Doc. 'Eat, eat, what is the point of me slaving in that galley if none of you will eat?'

I gave him a weary smile. 'The sea's rolling us around and I've not slept for three days.'

'Anyone would think it were poisoned,' he muttered to himself. 'If we wanted to kill you there are myriad easier methods, I can assure you.' He shook his head and fished out a packet of pills.

I slammed my hand on the table. 'Doc, you're a genius.'

'A stretch, my boy, but I appreciate your enthusiasm.' He handed me the seasickness tablets.

'I mean it, a genius. There are easier ways of killing someone indeed, that's the whole point, isn't it?' I shook out a capsule and swallowed it, tossing the pack across the table to Fields. 'The shit's gonna hit the fan sooner rather than later, you need to be on top form.'

'King was right, you do have a screw loose.' Fields shook his head.

'Marty!' I called.

She turned, saw Doc was dishing out the tablets again.

Thanks to Doc, if my theory was right my problems had just halved. I'd have a quiet word with him later on to confirm my idea, but for now, with one problem solved, one at the bottom of the sea, and the rest still several kilometres behind us, I felt buoyed up enough to get some shut-eye.

'Right, come on Fields, let's get some rest. Marty, you're on point until,' I looked at my watch, 'two p.m. Anyone wakes us for anything other than a life-or-death situation I'll be pissed off.'

The passageways of the ship looked entirely different by day, with the sunlight forcing itself through the greasy windows and reflected light from the waves dappled across the ceiling. On one hand finding our way around was easier without the flickering caged bulbs dotted around the walls, but on the other you could really see the filth and grime that'd worked its way into every seam, weld, corner and crevice. The seasickness tablets hadn't kicked back in yet, and Fields was sliding along the damp wall again, hand at his mouth.

'You'll be all right after a kip,' I said.

He nodded and stumbled down the stairs, sliding along the wall again at the bottom, all the way to his cabin. As soon as I got inside mine I locked the door, put the satphone on charge, and took out my pistol. I slid out the magazine, filled it full of hollow points from a box in my rucksack, then tucked it under the pillow.

Chapter Thirty-nine

Château des Aigles
Two days ago

I ran for the road, felt something on my face. I brushed away muck and flecks of stone, my fingers came away red. That bullet had been far too close. I stumbled on, towards a layby round the corner, where my Audi was parked – our backup vehicle in case the shit hit the fan.

Mercifully when I reached it the tyres were still full of air, and she fired up immediately. Lennon and Ringo hadn't messed with it, instead opting for a rapid getaway – and why wouldn't they? I had no way of catching them now – or so they thought.

I shuffled in my seat and pulled out my phone, unlocking it and putting it in a bracket on the dash. I swiped to a jogging app, and the route tracker. The icon spun on screen as it connected to the smartwatch on Bob's wrist. As it did I reloaded my pistol, cocked it, placed it handle-up in the cup holder.

The screen flashed to a map display, a little dot pulsing half a mile or so away.

I shifted into first, off the clutch, letting the snow tyres bite, sending me on my way towards the village. Up into second, then third, I drove quickly through the outskirts, one eye on my phone, on that pulsing dot.

It had slowed, navigating the one-way system through the village and the evening crowds. Château des Aigles' narrow streets would be packed. I pulled a right, down an alley parallel to the centre, slowing for the last skiers making their way back to their hotels, a quick change before tea.

A car reversed into the opposite end of the alleyway, the back end of a Rolls Royce Cullinan. I swore under my breath. Its lights cut out, I realised it was parked facing the restaurant we'd visited a few days ago; no doubt waiting for their mates to finish their ski.

The flashing dot was on the move. I beeped angrily, revving my engine. The passenger got out, Bono, speaking angrily into his phone – no doubt harassing someone into finding out why his mates hadn't made it down the mountain yet or been in touch. He slammed the door, tucked the phone in his pocket, and started walking back towards my car.

I glanced round, crowds in the main street behind, more people milling in the road ahead beyond the mouth of the alley. I could do the world a favour and get rid of Bono here and now but there'd be heat on, jeopardising the mission. I pictured my friend in the bottom of the ravine, looked at the flashing dot representing the Porsche, still stuck on the other side of town, and decided heat was a price worth paying.

I took off my seatbelt and opened the car door, beeping the horn again just to wind him up. Bono's huge head turned even redder, he sped up. I grabbed my gun from the cup holder and swung a foot out onto the cobbles.

A shout came from the driver of the Roller as a couple of cops had appeared at the end of the alley, pointing angrily at the one-way and no parking signs on the wall.

Bono turned, stormed back to the SUV and climbed in, face thunderous. I closed the car door and put my seatbelt back on, pushing the gun under the seat. Ahead the Rolls sped out of the alley and round the corner.

I pulled forward, gave a nod of thanks to the cops. One of them smiled and shrugged, holding up his hands and shaking his head, international code for *stupid tourists*. The back of the SUV disappeared up the street.

I turned in the other direction, towards the edge of town, past piles of snow heaped along the edge of the road, dark in the shadows of gingerbread buildings, carved balustrades and balconies under overhanging roofs. The Audi's Conti Viking tyres made short work of the snow-covered lanes as I took a left at a roundabout and pulled up the hill out of town. The road meandered upwards though clouds of woodsmoke rolling from chimneys level with the low wall. Beyond it, children played on the ice rink in the square below, the top of the Christmas tree rocked with the wind.

The little dot came to the edge of town and took the same road, now behind me. I smiled. *Predictable.* I ground the accelerator deep into the carpet, the dash lit up like the Christmas tree below as the traction control fired all the car's horsepower to each wheel in turn, seeking grip. I held my finger down on the button to turn it off, then hit the sport button on the steering wheel. The side bolsters on the bucket seat inflated to hug me tighter.

The Porsche hadn't stopped in the village to set the target free, which meant their motive was likely money. A ransom: send him back where he came from for a tidy fee, presumably more than I was paying them. Double-crossing bastards.

Wouldn't take someone like that long to rustle up cash, he was a multimillionaire with friends in low places. Lennon and Ringo would want rid of him as soon as possible so they could crawl under a rock. So where would they take him? Bob's place was over the other side of the valley, with our chalet above it. Neither was neutral ground, and they'd probably want to put some distance between them.

They were about a quarter of a mile behind me now, the gap was widening. I was driving faster on the snow-packed roads; they had a precious cargo, after all. I kept it up, wipers on overtime battling the snow driving straight at me, drifting sideways on each corner as all four wheels spun.

A crossroads asked me where I wanted to go. A back road north, towards Geneva, the dual carriageway south, towards Chamonix. What had Ringo said? *Shame we can't head to my place in Geneva.* I turned right, away from people and houses, further into the mountains. The snow was worse here, less traffic. The indicator poles along the side of the road said the drifts and plough piles were over a metre deep, and the way the car was handling told me the plough hadn't been through for a while. I pulled over to get the snow chains from the boot, spent a couple of minutes fitting them before I was off again. Even with them, the threat of getting stuck and stranded was very real. Beyond the poles the ground dropped away steeply, tiny lights at the bottom giving an indication of the altitude I'd reached. There'd been no houses for a while, just the twisting road and swirling snow.

On my phone screen the little pulsing dot turned right, following me up the mountain pass. *Good call.* I made the final turn, my satnav told me the road in front straightened now, a run all the way down into the next valley. I couldn't see beyond the swirling clouds of white in front of me. I flicked off the headlights as a test, couldn't see a thing. At the rate the low clouds were depositing snow it was like trying to drive with a blindfold on, even the snow markers were invisible in the darkness. *Perfect*.

I flicked the lights back on and accelerated, powering down the hill at sixty-plus in an effort to get to the bottom before any traffic appeared. Behind me, the pulsing dot climbed the winding mountain road.

I slammed the brakes, turned left, yanked the hand-brake and pressed the clutch, sliding to a halt sideways across the road with the passenger side facing uphill, in the direction I'd just come from. I turned the lights off again, driving lights and sidelights, too. Leaving the engine running I jumped out, ran round to the boot and retrieved my HK rifle.

I jumped back in, wound the passenger window down, cocked the rifle, and leaned it on the door. I kept one eye on the little dot. They were about to reach the top of the hill.

The rangefinder struggled to get a reading on the road at the top through the thick snow. The rifle was still zeroed at 400 metres, I turned on the scope and squinted through the flakes, adjusting the focus, then tried to estimate the distance and wind. Judging by the satnav the distance was easily over twice that, wind was about 20 mph from the left. I adjusted the scope, flicking the top and side turrets with my thumb a few clicks. It'd have to do, adjust as you go.

The snow lit up in the magnified image as headlights rounded the corner. The car was travelling slowly, no prizes for guessing why on the lonely mountain pass. I exhaled, rested my cheek against the stock, flicked the safety off.

The headlights drew closer. The scope sorted out most of the glare and took the brightness down, but it was still impossible to be accurate. I could pump lead directly into the windscreen and be pretty much guaranteed to nail them, but I needed them alive. Similarly, I could pump lead into the front of the car and hope to stop them mechanically, but the Porsche was a hybrid with batteries under the floor and motors in the rear, so wouldn't be stopped by the loss of its petrol engine.

I squeezed the trigger. The rifle thumped my shoulder, the crack quickly smothered by the wind, in front nothing happened, the headlights steadily advanced. I squeezed again, still nothing. I adjusted and squeezed a third time, this time the lights dimmed as flashes of broken glass spun away across the snow-covered fields. The Porsche kept advancing, they'd be wondering what the fuck just happened and why their passenger headlight had exploded, I had an extremely limited time window. I breathed, focused on the other light, adjusted for the reduced distance, squeezed again. The driver's headlight shattered.

I propped the rifle in the footwell and pulled my seat-belt on, into first, slamming the accelerator down and dropping the clutch to spin the car round on its axis, easing off and changing up into second when the car was aiming up the hill, right at the oncoming Porsche.

I glanced at the pulsing dot, it was moving much quicker now. Standard defensive driver training – if an unknown attacker is taking shots at you, don't stop to see who it is and where they are – just bug the fuck out of there. It's what I was banking on.

I checked the dash, changed up into third. My headlights still off and driving blind, the dot was closing fast, except they didn't know we were converging on each other. Looking out of the windscreen was pointless, I kept my foot down and drove purely by my satnav screen and my phone. The blue dot was heading straight for me.

I looked up, could just about see one of their dim sidelights glowing, no brighter than a torch in the blizzard. The big Porsche was close, I was playing chicken with three tons of super-SUV barrelling down on me at a combined speed of over eighty miles per hour. Problem was, they didn't know we were playing chicken. The darkness told them the road was clear, that trouble was somewhere in the snow-filled pastures behind them. That huge Porsche would tear through me like a hammer through a Kit Kat.

Time to let them know I was here. I looked down. Fifty metres. I waited a fraction of a second longer then turned on my headlights, full beam.

The Porsche was damn close, I caught a flash of Ringo's startled face directly in front of me, he threw a hand up, dazzled, less than a second to make a decision. His body automatically made it for him, self-preservation slamming on the brakes and spinning the wheel. I won the game of chicken, kept going straight, the Porsche missed me by centimetres as it slewed violently, hitting the snow piled high at the side of the road, pushing straight through.

I watched in my mirror as the brake lights disappeared, changed into second and raced up the hill. I drifted at the top, looking out of my side window down at the red lights sliding around crazily in the dark below. I turned down the twisting road, cutting back across the hillside, looking out at the snow-covered fields where the big Porsche was sliding down the hillside completely out of control, disappearing from view.

I kept going, the road criss-crossing the Porsche's toboggan run straight down. I passed cartoon-like SUV-sized holes in the snowdrifts either side where the big car had punched through, slid across the road, and kept going down the other side. I drove on, turning the corners back down the hill. Near the bottom I found my quarry, stuck in a wall, half-buried in the snow, teetering over the edge at the side of the road.

I stopped the car, watching the Porsche carefully. I noticed my hand was trembling, I held the wheel firm and reached over to the glovebox with the other. I fumbled with the latch and rummaged inside, finding the box of tablets. It felt light.

I opened it and held it by the windscreen. Empty. She'd ditched the contents.

My left hand started shaking too, I thought back, when had I last taken one? That morning I'd finished off the pack in my bag, the pack in the car had been supposed to last me on the ship home. *Fuck.*

I grabbed my pistol and climbed out, striding towards the mangled SUV. The road glowed red in the swirling haze of its rear lights, every panel was crumpled and dented. The windows were obscured by what looked like dishevelled curtains hanging limply: the airbags had all deployed. Nothing moved, the undisturbed snow told me no one had got out.

I held my pistol back, out of reach, as I ploughed through the snow round the car to the bent driver's door. Inside, Ringo looked at me blankly.

I jabbed the pistol into the window, cubes of safety glass rained down. I reached through to press the lock

248

release, a few tugs and I got the door open. Ringo went for me half-heartedly, he was still dazed. I pointed the pistol into the car, the other seats were empty. I presumed the mark was in the boot, but there was no sign of Lennon. I swatted Ringo's arms away, swung the butt of my pistol hard into his face, feeling the pop of cartilage. He made no sound, arms still flailing drunkenly. I leaned in close, the blood pouring from his broken nose steamed in the frigid air. I bit the cap off a backup syringe and plunged it into his neck, depressing it all the way. He flailed some more before his arms sagged.

I popped off his seatbelt and dragged him out, dropping him on the snow while I opened my Audi's boot, one eye on the road and mountainside, black as the sky, the other on the Porsche, at the puddle of steaming water melting through the snow beneath it.

I dashed back to the Porsche, wrenching its boot up then backing off across the road, pistol up, finger ready.

Bob hadn't fared too badly, all things considered, being unconscious as he'd been tossed around had probably done him a favour. Lennon, on the other hand, had not fared well at all – though that was nothing to do with the crash.

I shoved the pistol back in my jeans and felt Lennon's neck for a pulse, nothing, not surprising given the bloody bullet holes in her ski jacket. She hadn't double-crossed me at all, the bastard had killed her. I stepped back, held my head in my hands, my throat was dry, ears ringing.

A shout rang out, I looked over the snow bank to see several lights had come on behind a row of houses at the bottom edge of the meadow. I stepped back to the boot, rolled Lennon over, pushing her out of the way. Plenty of time to mourn, right now I needed to move fast.

I dragged Bob out of the boot, dumping him on the road then reaching back in to rip open the inner side panel. Screwed inside was a black box, about the size of an old VHS tape. Wires threaded out of the top, snaking behind the car's interior panels. Next to them a green light blinked.

More shouts from below, closer now.

I grabbed the wires, pulled them free then wrenched the box from its housing. I dragged Bob along the road to the Audi, threw the box on the back seat, and risked a glance at the shadows approaching, halfway up the meadow now. I returned to the Porsche and put five bullets through its boot floor, roughly where I reckoned the petrol tank was. A few seconds later my nostrils told me I'd been successful.

I was thankful Ringo always had a lighter on him. As I drove away I saw the silhouettes of locals flitting around the flames. The orange glow was bright in my rear-view mirror all the way down the hill. By the time the emergency services arrived there wouldn't be much left.

Chapter Forty

Tiburon

I'd been sleeping so soundly I'd momentarily forgotten where I was, then the waves rolled me in the tiny bed and it all hit at once. I reached up to the shelf and switched off the alarm on my phone. I must have really needed the sleep, no surprise since I hadn't been able to relax for days.

Nearly half one, just after midday, my body clock was all over the place. I did some stretches to try and get the full benefit of the rest but that didn't work out so well when my knee gave out on a wave and pitched me painfully into the wardrobe. I sacked it off and took a long, hot shower, then fished out a packet of biscuits from my rucksack and grabbed the satphone that I'd plugged in to charge on the desk before getting my head down. It was showing half battery, I shoved it into my pocket.

I went over the plan again in my head as I trounced half a pack of the chocolate digestives, satisfied myself that it was as solid as you get on a moving ship with so many variables, and collated some dry clothes from the various hangers on the pipes and heating vents.

A T-shirt, a pair of baggy combats, and my warm, dry, slightly stiff Adidas shell tops later and I was good to go.

I checked my pistol again, its magazine full of hollow point big-bastard-stoppers, safety on, and slid it into my holster. A couple of minutes to go.

I opened my door to find Katanga cradling an AK-47. Behind him, flashes of sunlight exploded through the porthole between crashing waves.

'Everything okay?' I asked.

'All quiet.'

'Where is everyone?'

'Doc and Miller are asleep, Vincent is in the engine room, Nic and Poubelle are on the bridge.'

'And Marty?'

A shout answered me from the cabin opposite, then a pained howl that turned to rage before it was cut off. Katanga looked at me, gripping the rifle tighter.

I stepped across to the opposite cabin door and pressed my ear to it. Two people were talking, low voices, impossible to tell what was happening.

With a glance at Katanga and a nod in return I grabbed the handle and kicked the door in, the simple bolt flew across the room. My hand was up in an instant, pistol sweeping the room. Fields tied to a chair, blood on his clothes, I barely had time to register what was happening before a fist was swinging towards the side of my head.

I ducked, spun, brought my pistol up hard. It connected with Marty's chin, she flew back onto the bed, dazed. I didn't give her time to recover, leaping across the room and swinging the gun into the side of her face. A gunshot exploded, a bullet ricocheted off the steel wall. Behind me Katanga crashed into the room with an angry shout, Fields was shouting too. For a moment, everything was a mess of confusion.

Marty was snarling. I grabbed her arm, twisted it, pressing my thumb into her wrist. She screamed, in fury rather than pain, as her pistol clattered to the floor. In my peripheral vision Katanga scooped it up. I dragged Marty off the bed, she spun and kicked out, sending me across the room onto the other bed.

Fields yelled, shouting and screaming for help. I ignored him and focused on Marty, who was coming at me again, knife in hand. I sprang from the bed, crouched, trying to weave in the shifting cabin but a boot flashed from nowhere and caught me in the ribs, doubling me over. I dropped my gun, Marty lunged, knife heading for my throat, I rolled, grabbed her arm and went with her momentum, burying the blade in the mattress. She pulled but I held on, a boot came up again and before I knew what was happening I was on the cabin floor gasping for breath.

My fingers scrabbled on the bed, I found the knife at the same time as her, dragging her down onto me. She let go of the knife and rained a flurry of blows into my face, forcing me to curl up to protect my head.

The fire alarm started up in the corridor outside, a red light pulsed on the cabin wall.

The blows stopped, I rolled over. In the flashing red light she was halfway out the door but was stopped by Katanga. He flung his rifle over her head, gripped the stock and the barrel and pulled her back, using it to pin her arms. I landed a punch into her stomach, she folded, gasping, Katanga hauled her out. I reached in my pocket and quickly pulled out a couple of cable ties, taking advantage of her temporary dazed state to bind her arms behind her back. She regained her strength quickly, anger doubled, but by that time I was already pulling them tight round her ankles.

Boots were pounding the deck, I looked up to see Poubelle racing towards us with a rifle in his hands and, running behind him, Miller, still buttoning his fly.

Katanga and I stood up, panting, looking down at Marty writhing and kicking out on the floor. She looked between us, face contorted with evil.

Poubelle skidded to a halt, barrel of his Kalashnikov centimetres from Marty's face.

'I think she's done for now, don't you?' I said. 'But thanks anyway.'

'What did I say?' Miller shouted. 'One of your team!'

'We don't know what her involvement is.'

'She was going to kill me,' shouted Fields, still tied to the chair inside the cabin.

'But why?' I asked, looking down at her.

'Working her way through everyone on the ship,' said Katanga.

'No doubt you were next,' added Miller.

Marty thrashed against the wall and got Poubelle's boot in her mouth for her trouble. She looked at me, eyes burning with rage.

'We don't know that.' I pushed Poubelle back and bent to grab her arms. 'Let's get her in my cabin and...'

Poubelle flicked the rifle at me, catching me in the side of the head. 'She's not going anywhere with you.'

I glared at him. 'She's one of my team.'

'She's a killer,' said Miller. 'Law of the sea.'

Poubelle grinned and straightened up, still pointing his rifle at me. 'Over the side.'

'What? You can't...'

Miller pulled his gun, too, as Vincent came running up behind him. 'You know the rules on my ship. You break them, you swim.'

'Don't let them do this, Tyler.' Marty looked at me, the fury had been replaced by fear.

'We can't throw someone overboard, even if she is a killer.' I edged forward, closing the distance to Poubelle.

'You've got no say in it this time. Katanga, get her up on deck.'

Marty shunted across the passageway. 'Tyler, don't let them—'

Katanga kicked her, she rolled against the wall.

Poubelle grinned. 'Save your energy, bitch. You'll need it.'

I stepped forward again, lightning fast, left hand swiping the barrel of Poubelle's AK down and towards the wall, while my right hand reached for my holster. My fingers closed around the waistband of my trousers, empty leather. Even as Poubelle started to move I glanced back inside the cabin, saw my pistol lying on the floor where I'd dropped it. I back-pedalled, trying to put distance between us but too late.

A flash of movement in the corner of my eye as Katanga lunged, butt of his rifle outstretched, a flash of light, then black.

Chapter Forty-one

Tiburon

In the distance there was a shout, laughter, a scream, all muffled through fog. I screwed my eyes shut tightly and let out a groan.

'Tyler, get up!' someone shouted, it started off far away then zoomed in close, sounds exploding behind my eyes as my brain rebooted.

'Fields?'

'Get up, man.'

'Hang on.' I opened my eyes, blinked a few times, got my arms underneath me.

'Anytime soon, mate. I'd rather not spend the rest of winter tied to this fucking chair!'

Fields was still where we'd left him, duct-taped to a chair next to the desk. I pushed up to my feet and picked up Marty's knife from the bed.

'Where are they?' I asked, running the knife up the tape holding his arms.

'Katanga and Miller took Marty. The others, I dunno.'

'What was she doing?'

'She took me by surprise, bashed me over the head in bed.' He rubbed his head and held up a bloody hand to the light. 'Before I knew what was happening she had me tied up.'

'On the plus side, your cut of the profits has just increased.'

'You really think they'll throw her overboard?'

I nodded. 'I've seen them do it before.'

'They really are pirates.'

I knelt by his legs and sliced up the tape. 'I wouldn't spare too much pity for her, she was going to kill you.'

'Aye, maybe. Fucking savages though, these fellas.'

'Careful what you say, because we're stuck on this ship with them. You don't think I'd have rather taken her back to the UK to be interrogated? But these guys are out for blood and where do you think they'll get it, if not here? Besides, I've already lost one captive, I don't fancy babysitting another in these circumstances, do you?'

He nodded, rubbing blood flow back into his ankles. 'Aye, true.'

'What did she want to know?'

'What do you mean?'

'She had you tied to a chair, that usually means inter-rogation. What did she say?'

'I dunno, I mean… I guess she hadn't got to that part yet. I'm lucky you came along when you did.'

I nodded. 'Small boat, everyone on top of each other, it's not really luck, is it?'

He sat on the bed, it creaked as he shuffled across to pick up his gun. He slid the magazine in and out, leg bouncing on the floor, eyes fixed on a point somewhere beyond the heaving window and overcast sky.

Footsteps sounded again in the passageway outside, I opened the door to find Katanga had returned.

'Sorry about the head, Mr Tyler,' he said, still gripping his gun. 'You were just in the way.'

Fields muttered something under his breath.

Katanga looked round me. 'You don't like how we operate, Mr Fields?' he said. 'Maybe you'll change your mind when you hear her story.'

'She talked?'

'People do when the end's coming up fast.'

'She's gone?' I asked.

He nodded. 'Maybe not dead yet but yeah, she's gone.' He whistled and pointed a finger down.

'Can she swim back?' Fields asked.

Katanga laughed. 'I don't think she can swim at nearly thirty knots. No, Mr Fields, she was having enough trouble keeping above the waves. Feisty one, nearly took the captain over with her!'

'Let's go to my cabin,' I steered Katanga back towards the door, Fields grabbed my arm.

'If Marty said something before she went over, I want to know.'

Katanga looked at me. 'He has a right, it was him she wanted.'

I let go of his arm, Katanga moved into the room and closed the door behind him.

'Go on then,' said Fields.

Katanga leaned on the door. 'She was an assassin.'

'Who'd want me dead?' Fields' eyes were wide.

'Probably a ton of people,' I said. 'Who hired her?'

'She didn't know. But she said she wasn't the only one.'

'On the ship? How?' I looked at the door instinctively.

'No, no. On her job. All she said was there's a bunch of them been hired to take people like him out.' He pointed at Fields. 'You wanna tell us why?'

'Did you get any more intel?' I asked.

He shook his head. 'She didn't know any more, and I believe her. All she said was there are mercs in several countries taking out all your old team,' he jabbed a finger at Fields again. 'Right now.'

Fields looked confused.

'What's this got to do with me?' I asked.

'Don't flatter yourself, Mr Tyler,' said Katanga. 'Not everything revolves around you.'

'I don't believe in coincidences. I hire a random merc for a job who turns out to be an assassin – who's been hired to kill the other team member I hired? Sounds a stretch.'

'But why me?' asked Fields. 'Did she kill King?' He looked at me. 'Probably going to kill you, too.'

'She mentioned Cresswell Security.' Katanga shrugged. 'Something about a job you were on ten years ago, in—'

The door opened, it was Miller. 'You told him?'

Katanga nodded.

Miller looked at me. 'So there *was* a rotten apple on your crew. You can apologise any time.'

'Don't push it.'

'I don't intend to. We need to get our heads together and come up with a plan.'

'For?'

'For those friends of yours on our tail. They're really moving, doesn't look like we're gonna make Poole.'

'Captain, could I use the radio?' Fields asked.

'Comms are off limits,' he replied gruffly. 'Come on, Blofeld.'

Fields shoved his Glock into his leg holster, puffed his chest out and crossed his arms. 'If there are assassins out there hunting down my old team I need to warn people.'

I reached into my pocket and pulled out my satphone, tossing it to Fields. 'Bring it upstairs when you're done.'

His face lit up.

I followed Miller into the corridor and closed the door, leaving the two of them to talk.

'I owe you,' I said to Miller.

'You owe me several. Let's talk about that bonus.'

'If I can use your sat Wi-Fi I'll transfer it now.'

He smiled. 'I like that. Now, let's talk about what else you owe me.'

'Go on.' I let him lead, following upstairs.

'An explanation. That boat's closing in and I wanna know who's on board.'

'We might have a more immediate problem.'

He threw his hands up. 'Sure, why not, it's been boring so far.' He swung round the handrail and walked backwards, wagging a finger towards me. 'Why not sink my boat and be done with it.'

'Hey, this is why you get paid the big bucks.'

'I know you've got your own shit going on but what's more important to us right now than that boat?'

'Well, it's about the boat...' I stopped at the foot of the bridge staircase and grabbed Miller's arm. 'How do we know for sure it was Seb talking to them on the radio?'

Miller closed his eyes, massaging the bridge of his nose. After a few moments he opened his eyes. 'No, Tyler. No. I know there's a lot going on, but no.' He climbed the stairs.

I followed him through into the bridge, where Poubelle was standing behind the wheel.

'I know you don't wanna hear it but...'

Miller spun and jabbed a finger into my chest. 'Damn right I don't wanna hear it. The only shit that's happened on this boat is because of you and your team.'

'And Seb?'

The deck shuddered, I fell against the table as the ship slewed to port. Poubelle leaned, spinning the wheel to correct.

Miller recovered and leapt to the helm, snatching the radio from the ceiling. 'Vincent! Vincent!'

The ship leaned over drunkenly as a wave hit, I held on to the table. 'What's going on?' I asked.

'Vincent!' Miller yelled into the radio, holding on to the doorframe.

Poubelle turned to me, feet wide as the deck shifted beneath us. 'Engines have stopped.'

I looked out of the window, the ship was being turned by the waves, thankfully the storm wasn't what it had been but the way we were rolling sideways couldn't be good.

The speaker crackled above Miller, Vincent came on, breathless. 'Engines are offline, I'm restarting port side now.'

'What's the problem?'

'I can either tell you or I can fix it,' snapped Vincent, the radio went dead.

'Get it started in the next two minutes or you'll be next over the side.' There was no reply, Miller hooked the handset back. 'Poubelle, stay at the wheel.'

He dashed from the bridge, I followed him. Halfway down the stairs the ship rolled onto its side, must have been over twenty degrees, as a bigger wave washed around us. I clung on to the rail as Miller accelerated below me. The ship righted itself, I launched down the stairs two at a time, along the passage where Nic was emerging from the radio room.

'Stay in there,' I shouted.

Round the corner, down the stairs, I held on to the handrail again as we rocked violently over to starboard.

As the ship righted itself there was a shudder and then the juddering clatter of an engine starting back up. The diesel settled back into a rhythm, vibrating throughout the stairwell, a feeling I realised I'd grown accustomed to.

I reached the foot of the stairs, Miller was holding the door to the engine room open, back to me, shouting at Vincent, who was kneeling by the starboard engine surrounded by parts. Vincent shouted back at Miller, then jumped to his feet as he saw me.

'What's happening?' I shouted above the racket.

Miller turned. 'He's just started up engine number one, we're under way again now,' he pressed the intercom on the wall to speak to Poubelle on the bridge. 'Port engine is back online, keep the power down for a while.'

The radio crackled and fizzed, there was no response. Miller slammed his hand against the intercom.

'Why did he stop the engines?' I shouted.

He pointed over at engine one. 'Timing issue, nothing major, Vincent took her offline a short while ago to check it over.'

'Isn't that bad news? Katanga told me we have to keep moving to stay head into the waves.'

'No problem. We've been running on just the starboard engine for half an hour,' Miller said.

'Until it started overheating,' Vincent shouted. He climbed the ladder and wiped his hands down his overalls. 'I think I caught it, we'll see.'

'Any ideas?' asked Miller.

He shook his head. 'She's been running hot for a while but the temperature shot up suddenly, hopefully the gaskets haven't gone.'

'It's the thermostat,' I said.

Vincent sneered. 'It could be a hundred things but yes, I'll check the thermostat.' He muttered in French, questioning how long I'd been an engineer.

I turned to Miller. 'Remember when we were leaving port? Seb said the starboard engine was taking a while to come up to temperature.'

'Yeah, but that means it was running cold.'

Vincent caught on and jumped back down into the engine bay, already grabbing a wrench.

I turned to Miller. 'If the thermostat was stuck halfway it'd let too much coolant through and warm up slowly. Then when it was hot, it wouldn't open fully to let enough coolant through and it'd start to overheat. Pushing it hard when you took the other engine down was the final straw.'

Miller nodded and leaned over the railings to shout at Vincent. 'How long to fix it?'

He shrugged. 'If it is the thermostat, then half an hour? I need to drain the system and refill but shouldn't be a big problem.'

Miller pressed the intercom again. 'Poubelle, keep the revs down for now, until we've got engine two back up.'

Static burst from the speaker, the lights flickered.

'Damn electrics!' shouted Miller, opening the door to leave. 'Quicker to walk! Vincent, I want to know the instant you know what's up.'

'Guys!' a shout echoed down the stairwell from above. 'Anyone?'

It was Fields, I'd presumed he'd been in his cabin with Katanga throughout but evidently not. I pushed past Miller and ran upstairs, could hear him thudding behind me. At the top the red lamps flickered and went out but the afternoon light was enough to navigate the gloomy passageway. The door to the radio room was open, I could hear voices inside.

Nic was sat on the floor, one hand to his head. Fields knelt beside him and pressed a cloth against his head. He took it away to look, it came away red.

'What happened?'

'I found him unconscious,' said Fields.

Nic pointed at the radio. 'Someone hit me from behind.'

'How bad is it?' I asked, stooping to grab his arm.

'It's fine,' said Nic, pushing me away and grabbing the desk to stand.

'What's happening?' asked Miller, arriving in the doorway.

'Someone's been talking to the boat again,' I said. I looked at Fields. 'Where were you? How did you find him?'

He pointed at the door. 'I was in the saloon rustling up some scran, only came out to go to the head. Saw him on the floor. Whoever it was must have split way before I came along, cos I didn't see or hear anything.'

Miller pushed me out of the way and grabbed Nic's head, pulling it down so he could get a look. 'Get Doc to glue that, it's nasty.' He turned to look at us. 'It's Seb, isn't it? He's running around the ship.'

I nodded, didn't know what else to do. I couldn't possibly tell him it wasn't, but it did confirm that someone else on the ship still wanted to slow us down.

'Where are we now?'

'About fifty miles off the Pointe Saint-Mathieu.' He looked at my blank face and added, 'Brittany. Ya know, the bit of France that sticks out?'

'All right, piss off. So how long to go?'

'If this weather holds, maybe seven hours, but that's if we get that second engine working.'

'And what if the weather improves, can we speed up?'

He laughed. 'Look outside, we're in the North Atlantic. This is as good as it gets this time of year.'

'So we're looking at hitting Poole sometime after midnight?'

He shook his head. 'If Vincent gets that second engine going we'll make up some time, should get in long before that.'

I looked out of the window at the endless rolling grey, then back at the radio someone on this ship was using to communicate with our pursuers. 'We're not going to make it in time.'

'Bingo.'

'When will they overtake?'

'It's not an exact science, Tyler. A few hours.'

Fields looked worried.

'Nic, I'll send Doc in. Keep on the radio, see if you can pick anything up.'

He nodded, turned his chair to face the door, and sat down. He put the headphones on, wincing as they rubbed his head.

'I hope you made all your phone calls,' said Miller to Fields, 'because you might not be talking to anyone for a while.'

'The satphone's back in my cabin.' He looked at me. 'Can we call in reinforcements? Gotta be close enough for some air support or...'

'We're on our own,' I said.

'But the dead guy,' said Miller, 'they still want him, right?'

I gave a wry smile. 'I don't think the Brits are gonna care about us any more.'

'But they don't know he's dead.'

'Look, it doesn't make a difference: there's no cavalry. It's just the nine of us on board, and I don't think we can count on Seb's help.'

'Eight of us against how many of them?' asked Fields.

Chapter Forty-two

Château des Aigles
Two days ago

The rope creaked. It was tied off to the sofa leg, holding a carabiner. The carabiner was clipped into one of our climbing descenders, which in turn had its teeth locked on to a second rope stretching up over a beam in the double-height lounge, and back down. Hanging from it by his feet was Ringo, still unconscious.

I stood in kitchen doorway listening to the creaking rope. The lights were off, the house was in darkness but the snow had stopped, the clouds had rolled on, and the Moon had put in an appearance. It shone through the small window in the front door and the patio doors along from it, the balustrade outside casting stripes across the wooden floorboards.

Through the windows I could see the neighbouring chalet's lights blazing in the upstairs rooms, though its curtains were drawn. At the opposite side of the room, the enormous sliding doors looked out over the rear decking and lights flickering in the valley below. I picked up my mug of tea and carried it into the lounge.

Bob had woken up while the kettle was boiling and started to scream the place down. I'd shut him up with a combination of my fist and another dose of thiopental and ketamine. This meant Ringo would be waking up soon.

I sat on the sofa, careful to stay out of the moonlight, and took a sip of tea, looking back over my shoulder at the village below. I put the mug down and picked up my smartphone. A quick glance at the fitness tracker app told me Bob's heartbeat was stable, blood pressure low. He was safely tied up, still swaddled in his ski gear, tucked away in the boot of my Audi in the garage under the house.

Ringo groaned, I looked up. He was staring at me, in the silver moonlight his face was dark from hanging upside down for over an hour. The blood flowing up had helped turn the bruises across his face from his broken nose into black patches like a highwayman.

I took another mouthful of tea.

'Tyler,' he said thickly through his bent nose. 'It's not what...'

I held up a hand for him to shut up, bending to put my mug on the floor. 'You figured you'd make more on your own, that it?'

He shook his head, reaching upwards, nails scrabbling at the rope tight around his ankles. 'Where is he?'

'Waiting in the car.' I stood, stretched, and looked out the front patio doors again, up the mountain. The chalet across the road was the only light. 'What were you going to do, ransom him back to his own people? Tell him you'd freed him, collect a fee?'

He stopped scrabbling and dropped back, exhausted. 'Don't tell me you've never done it.'

I smiled and nodded. 'Opportunism. Capitalism even, you're right. You double-crossed me, but that's the business we're in. Shooting at me? That's taking it a bit far.' I opened the patio doors at the front just a crack, snow blew in off the balcony, melting as soon as it hit the warm floor.

'It was a warning shot, to buy time!'

I pointed to the gash on my cheek.

'What do you want? Take my share.' He focused a little too long on my shaking hand, I turned away. 'We need to get out of here,' he continued. 'Cut me loose. You're the only one, take him in alone, you'll get all of it.'

I slammed my hand on the window, the glass shook. 'I'm the only one left because you *killed* her!'

'The cyclops? I warned her!'

'Her name was Katrin,' I shouted, fists tight. I breathed in, held it, sat back on the sofa. I relaxed my hands and stared into his swollen eyes. 'Say it.'

'I don't care what her name was, she was a fucking criminal, good riddance.'

'Say her name.'

'Look, it was an accident, I didn't want to do it. What time is it?'

'Put your arms down.'

'Katrin, you happy?'

'Put your arms above your head, like you're diving.'

He frowned and did what I asked. I reached down and squeezed the descender, the rope hissed through the cam, he dropped like a stone, bouncing off the wooden floorboards with a sickening thump. There was a moment of silence before an anguished cry, like an animal. I pulled the rope, hoisting him up. Blood ran from his nose again, black in the moonlight, up into his screwed-up eyes.

He steadied his breathing and looked at me through tears and blood. 'You could have killed me.'

'You killed Katrin in cold blood.'

'Don't tell me you *care*…' He saw the look on my face. 'I'm sorry, I swear, I told her to get out of the car, she pulled a gun…'

I felt a tear just nudge the corner of my eye. 'It's not what I wanna talk about.'

'What, then?' He reached up and tried to pull at the ropes but he'd no strength left. He dropped, chest heaving. 'What time is it?' he asked again, more urgently this time.

'You know what happens if you're left upside down?'

'We need to get out!'

'There was a caver a few years back, fell and got trapped upside down. Twenty-eight hours before he died. Your body isn't designed for it you see, your heavy organs fall onto your lungs. Over time you'll suffocate. It's nasty.'

'Come on, Tyler!'

'That's if the blood pooling in your head doesn't cause a haemorrhage or stroke. Or maybe the increased pressure on your heart will make it give out.'

'What do you want?'

'Answers.' I picked up my mug and stood. 'Didn't David Blaine do sixty hours? But he's in better shape than you. With those injuries, and your system full of ket, you shouldn't be hanging like that.' I took a mouthful of tea.

'So what, you're just gonna bounce me off the floor all night?'

I shook my head. 'As cathartic as that might be I realised I don't need to. Why do you keep saying we need to leave?'

He stared, chest heaving as he tried to fill his lungs. He was starting to panic, his hands worked at the rope with renewed enthusiasm, but it wouldn't help.

'You told them about this safehouse, didn't you? Get those Nazis to take me out, tie up your loose ends for you. Out of the way so you're in the clear.'

He dropped back down, swinging around the hallway. 'Just business, Tyler.'

'Do you know the kind of people you chose to do business with? They're animals, they can't be reasoned with.'

His eyes were darting between me and the big window behind me.

'Well, you can give it a go when they get here.'

His eyes went wide. 'We need to get out.'

'You read the intel, you know what they're like. Did you know the French got to someone inside their organisation last year? Turned them. Unfortunately they found out. It was the big guy that did it, Branko – the one we call Bono. Sadistic bastard, took his dick off with a belt sander and left him outside a Starbucks. It took him a while to die. Must have been painful.'

I could see Ringo was worried. He knew the sort of people these were – they were not to be fucked with.

'You know, Branko got stopped for speeding once, in Germany. The copper was dumped outside a police station three days later. They'd used the sander on him, too. Something about him not being proud enough of his white skin. He lived for a week without a face.'

'I've told you everything you wanted to know.'

'I've not asked my question yet.'

'*Ask it!*'

'I was going to do this the easy way, on the ship. But you fucked that right up, didn't you? So now we do it the hard way.'

'I've got nothing to hide.'

'I should clarify, I mean hard for you. Not me. You wonder why you were picked for this job?'

'Because I could ski.'

'That's what I told you. It's not the real reason, though.'

'I'd never met any of you before this job!' he hissed. 'We don't even know each other's names.'

'Let me take you back, just over a decade. To Zurmat.'

'What's in Zurmat?'

'District in eastern Afghanistan, not too far from the Pakistani border.'

'Yeah, I know it, we've all worked in Afghanistan.'

'You worked for Cresswell at the time?'

'You know I did.'

'There was another team operating in the area.'

'Every man and his dog was within a fifty-mile radius.'

'Their vehicle was taken out by an IED on a route they were specifically told to take. Word is the IED was planted by a rival team. A team working for Cresswell.'

Ringo had somehow managed to blanch despite hanging upside down.

'A few weeks ago I finally managed to catch a break. I was in Scotland. Fella called Mason, a spook, he gave me the name of the person responsible for that bomb.' I pulled a crumpled piece of paper from my pocket and held it out. 'It's your name, David.'

Chapter Forty-three

Tiburon

They were all worried about Seb stalking the ship, picking people off; I knew better but couldn't explain as we split into three groups. I left Fields on guard in the radio room, with Nic scanning every frequency while Doc bandaged his head. Katanga and Poubelle stood guard in the engine room while Vincent laboured with the coolant system on the starboard engine.

Miller and I held the bridge, him at the wheel while I pored over his charts and land maps, my HK pistol never far from my hand.

'How far are we from Cornwall?' I asked.

He turned to look over his shoulder. 'Couple hours or so?'

'Let's run there instead.'

'Could still be a close thing.'

'A close thing's better than a sure thing.'

He checked the autopilot and eyed the waves, then left the wheel to stand looking over my shoulder. 'We'd need wicked deep water.' He flicked over the charts. 'Falmouth?'

'Deepest port in Europe but crawling with coastguard. Besides, it's a decent-sized town, lots of police.'

'Well that's the problem, ain't it? Anywhere big enough for us is gonna be a sizeable port, sizeable ports tend to have cops.'

I traced the rocky coastline and beaches of south-west Cornwall. 'The other problem is I need a quick exit once we hit land, and Cornwall's all country lanes. Won't last too long if we come in hot and get bottled up behind a tractor.'

'Wait a minute – you're expecting me to put you off in the car? That's a serious operation, I mean waiting for a berth then getting the car unloaded – you're talking hours. Better we sit offshore, you take a dinghy in.'

I looked up, giving him a face that invited no arguments. 'We're taking the car.'

'Docking and unloading the car means coastguard, customs and cops, man. Probably a search.' He shrugged. 'Your choice.'

'We need to find a way.'

He glanced at the waves again, satisfied nothing too ugly was incoming, then sighed and looked back down at the charts. 'You want my opinion?'

'Go on.'

'We need an estuary. We're coming in at high tide. We time it right, with the wind behind us and Lady Luck on our shoulder, I might be able to land you somewhere further inland.' He leaned in close to the map. 'A sheltered tidal river would mean no waves to contend with, I might be able to put your car down. Might.'

'I like it.'

Miller's stubby finger travelled over the inlets and bays. 'Somewhere near Plymouth would be the quickest landing.'

'Navy.'

'*Your* Navy.'

'Besides, it's further north and that yacht's to port. Wouldn't that be a quicker intercept for them?'

Miller nodded and stroked his beard, I scanned the map, eyes resting on an estuary further down the coast, a deep gash into a headland jutting out from south Devon. 'I know this place.' I tapped my finger on a small village.

'Combe Wyndham?' Miller cross-checked the map with his charts and shook his head. 'Mouth full of sand-bars.'

'Nothing you can't handle.'

He looked up and gave me a thin smile.

'It's perfect,' I continued. 'It's a bit further but I've been there a few times, tiny place. Small roads but we'd be on Dartmoor in minutes. How long?'

He checked his satnav, scribbled a few calculations. 'Three hours, give or take. If this weather holds.'

'And how long until they catch us?'

He raised his eyebrows. 'Three hours, give or take.'

I stood and stretched. 'That's the one then. If you can get us in and get that car off quickly there'll be another bonus in it.'

He grinned, folding the map. 'Nothin' like a little incentive. We'll get there.'

The speaker crackled. 'Captain, you might want to come to the engine room.'

Miller walked back to the wheel, grabbed the radio handset and flicked a switch. 'Katanga, I need you to take over the helm.' He hung the handset back on the ceiling and pushed his hat up on his head. 'Let's go see what fresh shit we've got to contend with.'

Chapter Forty-four

Château des Aigles
Two days ago

I unhooked Ringo's climbing harness from the rope and dragged him across the floor, dropping him in the hall by a door down to the garage. He huddled into a ball, flexing his fingers to try to get the blood flowing through his tightly bound wrists. His face was still beetroot, an effect of being hung upside down for too long but also his smashed nose, still trickling.

'Hurry,' he said.

I looked back at the big windows, at the torch beams cutting across the snow, and shook my head. 'Sorry mate, out of time.'

'That's the only name I have, I swear!'

'I had it all worked out, you know. Keep your enemies close, I wanted you on the ship with me.' I opened the door, grabbed Ringo's harness, pulling him to the top of the dark stairs. 'It would have been so much better without all this,' I waved my hand back at the loop of rope hanging over the beam in the hallway, 'all this unpleasant-ness.'

'I'm sorry, all right? What do you want?'

'You've a history of doing owt for money.' I looked out of the window again, we had a few minutes at best. 'Hope this time it was worth it.'

I could see he was worried. He knew what sort of people were coming – they were not to be fucked with.

'So we killed a few mercs. It was a decade ago, why do you even care?'

'Someone has to.'

'Wrong place wrong time, man. Probably deserved it!'

'I suppose she was in the wrong place at the wrong time too?'

'Lennon knew the risks when she took the job, just like me.'

'Risks? The only risk was you, you bastard.' I kicked him, he rolled down the stairs, bouncing off the wall at the bottom. Silence for a moment, then a long moan as he writhed on the floor. I stamped down the stairs after him, he shrank back, trying to shuffle away. I grabbed his harness, dragging him across the dusty garage floor, dropping him at the rear of my car. 'You say we signed up for the risks, so you won't mind what comes next.'

'Please,' he whimpered. 'I told you everything.'

'Keep quiet.' I took out my phone, debating whether to ring Holderness now to get the ball rolling, or wait until the shooting had ended.

'I swear, that's who you need to talk to!' His voice rose again. 'I was only hired to make the device, I didn't have any contact with the others. The whole team, all of them, talk to…'

I kicked him in the stomach to stop him moving then opened the boot. I grabbed a pair of handcuffs from next to Bob's sleeping body, snapped one end around his right wrist. I fastened the other round one of the spokes of the rear wheel.

He coughed and spat on the floor, blood and phlegm bubbling on the dust.

'We're surrounded,' I said. 'I really need to start shooting soon, so keep quiet.'

He spat another mouthful of blood. 'You can't take them all by yourself,' he said, eyes pleading. He knew that despite everything, he was still better off with me than the people he'd made a deal with.

'You'd best hope I can, or neither of us are getting out of here alive.'

I closed the garage door and made my way back to the lounge. Outside, the snow had started again, I could see it whirling in the beams of the various torches converging on the house through three different windows, to the side, from the meadow below the rear of the house, and up the road past the patio doors to the front.

I took out my pistol and laid it on the floor next to the big window, picked up one of the HK MP5s from next to the sofa, cocked it, checked the safety was on. I laid it next to the pistol, stacked loaded magazines for both next to them then went into the kitchen, returning with my HK rifle and its night optics.

I sat three magazines for the rifle on the floor in the middle of the room. The magazine in my hand contained a round with an orange tip at the top, I inserted it into the rifle then laid on my belly, squinting through the night-vision scope, out the crack in the patio doors. In the black and white image four figures were creeping slowly towards the house, hunched over in the deep snow, I panned across to see more advancing up the road, another group in the pines to the east.

I cocked the rifle, steadied myself. They were so close I could hear the murmurs of the team advancing up the road below the open patio door, thankfully I was deep in shadow. The trembling in my hand had calmed, I used the breathing space to click the scope, put my eye back to the thermal imager. One of the figures outside was crouched on the driveway next to Katrin/Lennon's BMW, an old 850 coupe with the pop-up headlights. It'd been a crying shame to leave it on the drive but I needed the extra bait.

I watched through the top night-vision scope as a masked man pushed a knife into the tyres of the BMW, blocking the garage door. I shuffled and rested my cheek against the rifle stock, looking through the normal scope, watching a shadow crouching beside the front door. Didn't matter how a job started, I always ended up in the same position: alone, outnumbered, looking down the barrel of a gun.

Chapter Forty-five

Tiburon

Vincent held out the innocuous-looking component and nodded at me. 'He was right, it was the thermostat.' He sparked up a cig and blew smoke across the top of the engine. 'Welded.'

Miller took it from him and turned it over in his hands. 'When?'

'Must have been before we left port – can't remove it with the engine running.'

'Can you replace it?'

'Already have, I'm about to restart the engine.'

'Get to it, man.'

Vincent hopped back down the ladder, I grabbed Miller's arm and ushered him out of the door. I looked back in at the others down in the engine bay, all more interested in the engines, though Vincent had one wary eye on us.

I led him down the passage and leaned in. 'Someone on your crew wanted to slow us down.'

He nodded, running a hand through his greasy beard.

'We already knew that,' I continued, 'but this means they planned it before I arrived on board. This, the pumps, the ballast tank…'

'Seb,' he said.

'Yes, but who else? You took Vincent on at the same time.' I let the implication hang there for a while before whispering, 'He only fixed the engines because he was forced to.'

Miller shook his head. 'He could have left it to over-heat.'

'He wanted to slow us, not sink us.'

'Then why would he tamper with the ballast valve, and disable the bilge pumps? Must have wanted to sink us then.'

'Maybe so, a quarter of a mile from shore. Not out here, in the middle of the ocean.'

Miller frowned. 'We need to find Seb. He's loose somewhere on this ship; he's behind all this, I swear.'

Chapter Forty-six

Château des Aigles
Two days ago

The thing about these rental chalets is they all look the same, the reason the one over the road from ours had been empty is I'd rented both. Or I should say, a mining company based in Johannesburg had rented both for a Christmas employee getaway. A company with no past, no future, and nothing tying it to me. God knows how Holderness had pulled it on short notice, but pulled it he had. I'd rented them both partly to ensure we weren't disturbed, but partly to give me this; a fallback defensive position should we need it.

I lay on the floor of the second chalet, watching through the scope as four figures paused at the top of the steps outside the other place's front door. The house was built into the hillside, garage underneath and above it, on the first floor, those huge picture windows from which we'd gazed down at the target property. Another two figures had already scaled the walls to the raised decking outside, no doubt others were doing the same round the back. The old BMW sat blocking the garage door on four flat tyres.

Movement on the steps as one of the figures brought up a bosher, a handheld police battering ram. At a signal he swung at the lock, the door flew inward.

The figures swept into the house, there was a blast from the balcony at the side as a second group blew the locks on the patio doors and charged in. Shadows moved behind curtains, dashing between the rooms, searching and finding them empty.

I took my face away from the scope, counted in my head, visualising their room-to-room search. Figures entering through the front door would have emerged straight into the lounge, while those going in via the windows would have stormed straight for the stairs. They'd be in the bedrooms by now, overturning beds, opening wardrobes, checking bathrooms.

Curtains waved in an upstairs window, the crack of gunfire echoed down the hillside as the trigger-happy assault team swept room to room.

I put my eye back to the scope, swinging the rifle across to the kitchen window. Off with the safety, I settled the sights on the bright red gas bottle I'd stood in the kitchen sink, and wondered how many of the intruders would have smelled the gas I'd left on.

I squeezed the trigger. The tracer round sparked towards the other chalet, I closed my eyes, saw the flash through my eyelids. It was followed by a loud whump, I felt the heat in my cheeks even down here. A moment after that, a delayed reaction secondary explosion as the other cannisters I'd placed around the house went up in rapid succession, rocking the foundations as the whole lot went up. The glass in my chalet blew in, shards speckling my face. *There go two deposits.*

The blast hadn't died down before the screaming started. I panned the rifle across the flaming timbers, the top floor of the huge open-plan house all but gone. Shadows flitted in the flames, I swept hair, glass, and splinters from my eyes and looked through the scope, already squeezing the trigger. Figures danced into the fire, I saw two of them drop but others took cover behind pieces of debris. I pulled the trigger faster, emptying the magazine into burning beams and chunks of masonry.

I swung over onto the pines on the left at the edge of the garden and squeezed again at the shadows darting across the snow. More screams and flashes replied, something buzzed through the shattered window and buried itself in the wall, a puff of plaster indicating someone had got a bead on me. I shuffled backwards, ejecting the empty magazine and grabbing another, snapping it in place and cocking as I stood, back pressed against the wall. Another bullet zinged through the door, followed by another shattering the deer skull above the fireplace, cracking it in half. The antlers dropped onto the hearth and shattered across the floor. I looked at the angle, the shooter was above and to the right, so somewhere along the side of the burning chalet.

I swung round, aiming at the corner of the house and squeezing the trigger rapidly to get their head down then put my eye to the scope, quickly checking. There, laid on the snow by the bin store, a flash. I aimed and squeezed, pulling the trigger several times, watching puffs of snow erupt. I paused, red dot on the shadow, no flashes replied this time.

The wood panelling behind me exploded, I dropped to the floor as bullet holes stitched a jagged line up the staircase, someone out there had come equipped with serious hardware. I rolled away from the window, kicking the spare magazines across the room and scooping them up as I dashed into the kitchen. I put the rifle to my shoulder and squeezed off a couple of shots at figures running down the hillside towards me then ducked and ran back into the lounge as the kitchen exploded in showers of wood and lead.

I dropped the empty magazine from the rifle, pushed my pistol into the waistband of my jeans, and bundled the spare magazines into my rucksack. I slid the last one into the rifle itself, then swung round onto my back.

The door flew inward, I grabbed the MP5, it coughed rapidly three times. The man stumbled back onto the steps, dead before he landed. I pulled on the rucksack, pushed the submachine gun into my shoulder and swept into the kitchen, risking a glance through the smashed windows. More dark figures were sprinting towards the house, I ducked as another torrent of lead tracked across the ceiling.

There was a noise from the lounge, the crunch of combat boots on broken glass, I crept backwards, away from the door, pulling out my phone. I dialled Ringo's phone and held my breath. A moment later his phone started ringing upstairs, I waited a couple of heartbeats then cancelled the call. There was a whisper then boots crunched again, creaking on the bottom step as they made their way up to what they assumed was me.

I slid onto the kitchen worktop, waited another couple of beats for them to get halfway up then peered around the corner into the lounge – my head up high near the ceiling, not where they'd be expecting a head to be, in case they were waiting for it.

They weren't – combat trousers tucked into heavy work boots crept up the top of the stairs, the man's body unseen as he scanned the landing above, trying to decide which room the ringtone had come from.

I fired a burst into the legs, a scream, he dropped, another burst into his head stopped the screaming. I dashed across the room, crouched, pulled out the man's bloody earpiece and pushed it into my own ear. It was quiet, no frantic gabbling, no tactical instructions, just panting as whoever was left was charging around looking for a target.

With another glance out the front door to confirm there were no more bounding up behind him, I ran for the window at the other side of the room, dropping the submachine gun, letting it hang from the strap. Out the rear patio doors, onto the balcony looking down the village, I spun the big rifle round into my hands and brought it up. The meadow below glowed in the firelight, my chalet cast a long dark shadow down the orange snow.

'Moving to the rear,' a voice hissed in my ear.

I swung the rifle round, aiming at movement, squeezed off a group of three shots, there was a grunt in my earpiece as the figure dropped. I could hear him panting and groaning in my earpiece, I looked through the scope and found him, a dark shape writhing in the snow. I put the red dot on his head and squeezed again, the writhing stopped.

I swung the rifle round onto my back and slid over the railings, dropping the short distance into the deep snow, staying low. In the shadows beneath the balcony was my snowboard, to which I'd already duct-taped a torch. I kicked it across the snow, sending it skimming away down the fields.

'He's getting away!' said a voice on the radio.

I backed in against the house and brought the rifle up. A man ran from behind the wall to my left, charging after the torch which by now was a good fifty metres away, the light bouncing away down the hill.

'He's skiing down.' The man raised a weapon and fired, the torch continued. 'Get back here!' he shouted to his comrades. He chased after the board, pausing every few seconds to take another shot at what he thought was me trying to make my escape. 'He's gonna get away.' I watched him through the sights and waited for whoever he was talking to. Didn't take long, another man charged across the fields from behind the house, following in his mate's footsteps. I held my breath and moved the sights onto him, at his back leaping through the knee-deep snow.

Any more? How long should I wait? My decision was made for me as the torch beam below suddenly lurched and shone directly up into the whirling snow like a Bat-Signal. The board had crashed into something.

'Got him, he's down.'

'He wants him alive!' a second voice said.

In a few seconds, those pursuers would be on the board and find not me, but a little torch taped to the bindings, and when that happened they'd be back up here. A bullet in the spine felled the guy at the rear immediately, howling into the radio, I swung onto the lead guy, hitting him in the chest as he turned to see what'd happened. I followed his progress to the ground, put another three into him, then moved the cross hairs back to the first and did the same. Neither would be back up here now.

I lowered the rifle and paused to listen. How many was that, six or seven? And the explosion must have taken care of everyone in the house. The information was pointless as I didn't know how many had come up here.

I waited, hunched over in the snow for a full two minutes. Nothing moved, no sound, either on the mountainside or on their radios. I slowly stood, stretching out my cold legs, and stepped towards the corner, rifle at my shoulder. I edged towards it then brought the rifle down and risked a peek.

The black mass came up fast, I pulled the rifle up and squeezed the trigger but it was too heavy, too long, he was too close. He grabbed the suppressor with his left hand while bringing up a pistol with his right. I dropped to my knees as a shot sliced above my head, rolling onto my back, dragging the rifle away and kicking out with both feet. He flew backwards, flailing, putting some much-needed distance between us. I pulled the trigger rapidly, emptying the magazine in his direction before he could get off a shot.

I slung the empty rifle onto my back and pulled round the MP5. No voices left on the radio now, not even any breathing. Good.

Chapter Forty-seven

Tiburon

I had a perfect view along both directions of the central passageway of the ship, seated half in the radio room, chair wedged into the doorway. Through the window overlooking the stern, the oppressive sky was pushing the sun into the sea. We were in the dead of winter: it'd be pitch black again soon. The darkening sky had brought with it a return of the waves crashing over the bow, so far not as severe as the previous night's storm, but a far cry from the fat, rolling seas of the morning.

From my spot in the doorway I could see the door to the saloon, also wedged open, inside the adjoining galley Doc was cooking a stew that I certainly wouldn't be eating. If he stepped foot outside, I'd know about it. Next to the door I could see the foot of the stairs up to the bridge, where Katanga was keeping us on a direct course to south Devon. Behind me in the radio room, Nic monitored traffic, weather, and anything from the authorities, while also scanning news articles to give me the latest from La Rochelle.

'Divers have brought a car up,' he said, holding his laptop out to the side to show me a picture of a mangled BMW M5 hanging from a crane, dripping onto the similarly mangled wreckage of a yacht. 'What actually happened?'

I turned the page of an old, dogeared magazine on my lap. 'Probably driving too fast.'

'It says the car has bullet holes in it.'

I tutted, shook my head. 'Road rage.'

He put his headphones on and went back to the radio. I rested my pistol on the magazine and looked at my watch, 5:30 p.m. Since getting both engines online Vincent had managed to increase our speed to thirty knots, forging through the swell towards the narrow, deepwater inlet that would take us to the village of Combe Wyndham, and hopefully our route inland.

Unfortunately, our pursuers had also increased speed and were now within spitting distance.

Voices drifted up from below, Miller leading the crew plus Fields back up. He appeared round the corner shaking his head at me, his confirmation that Seb was nowhere to be found.

'Nothing,' he said. 'Hours, we've checked every single space, even 'tween decks and the spaces down in the bilges, the tanks, under the engine room floor… He's not on this ship.'

Fields stepped round him, holding his hand out. 'Found these in the workshop though.'

Brass cartridges glinted in the light. Mine, from when Seb had tried to kill me.

I picked one up. 'Nine-millimetre. Marty used a nine-mil Walther PDP.'

Miller grimaced. 'That's what we figured, though if she did for him I can't say I'm overly distraught. I'd throw the bastard over myself just for messing with my engines.'

Poubelle clapped Fields on the back. 'Looks like maybe your assassin wasn't just here for you.'

Fields grunted. 'That's comforting.'

Miller looked past me. 'Any noise on the radio?'

Nic lifted the headphones from his ear and shook his head. 'Whoever they are, they're running silent now.'

'How's the weather looking?' he asked.

'It'll be rough but we've had worse. Tide's on our side at least; it's high now, it'll still be deep enough.'

Miller nodded. 'At least that's something.'

'Gentlemen, dinner is served,' Doc announced from the saloon doorway.

I poured the cartridges back into Miller's rough paw and stood, stretching, as Poubelle, Vincent, and Fields followed their stomachs into the saloon. Nic got up from the desk and pushed round me.

'You coming?' Miller asked.

I looked up and down the passageway. 'I can wait until we get to a Maccy Ds on the mainland, thanks.'

'Suit yerself.' He glanced round at the swinging saloon door and leaned in close. 'Did Marty kill Seb?'

'No.' I left it there.

He pointed down at my pistol on the chair, at the lettering etched into the slide. 'That says nine-millimetre.' His eyebrows lifted.

I slid it into my holster. 'You better go get some tea.'

He continued to watch me through narrowed eyes for a moment then walked away to join the others.

Pulling the chair into the radio room, I closed the door, got down on my hands and knees, wincing as the dressing on my side split, and crawled to the radio sets. Leads ran from them under the desk, where everything was plugged into an extension. I pulled it from the wall, took out my knife, and unscrewed the plug. I pulled the fuse out, screwed it together, and pushed it back into the wall.

I scrawled some calculations on a pad of paper and left it in the middle of the desk along with a note at the bottom of the page. *Arrive Devon 6:30 p.m. At thirty knots they can't overtake us now. Full power, easy.*

I left the door open and walked to the lounge. The TV was on, picking up the BBC now we were off Cornwall, a pointless Christmas gameshow with a celeb panel. The crew and Fields were all seated round the two tables; the only man missing was Katanga on the bridge.

I leaned in the doorway, hanging on to the frame. 'Miller, I'm gonna wait 'til we hit land to eat.'

'Yeah, okay,' he looked puzzled at my repetition, waving his fork, 'suit yourself.'

I nodded, started to leave, then swung back in again. 'And I've been exercising my maths, we're home free.'

The others looked up.

'How so?'

'We're not making much less speed than the boat that's following us. We'll make it to Devon comfortably, no problem.'

Miller cocked his head, forehead furrowed, but the other faces lit up at the prospect of not having to deal with a boatload of armed bastards. I watched Vincent carefully, but if anything other than food was on his mind he was hiding it well. He glanced up at me, I turned away.

'Good times,' said Fields.

I smiled at him. 'I'm gonna go wait up on the bridge until we dock.'

Chapter Forty-eight

Tiburon

'So how far's the dot?' I asked, squinting at the radar screen.

'Just over the horizon,' said Katanga, flicking a thumb over his shoulder.

'And Devon?'

'Over the other horizon.' He nodded ahead out of the black window.

'What are our chances?'

'Non-existent.' He grimaced. 'We're at full speed.'

'At least the engines are holding. So far so good.'

'That is what the man said as he fell off the roof.' He smiled. 'Give it time.'

'At least the weather's better.'

'She's on the change, Mr Tyler. Another storm coming in.'

He pointed out of the port window, where the sky roiled black. I couldn't see the difference myself, but the look on Katanga's face said it was about to get hairy again. I opened the outside door, feeling the blast of frigid winter air, the rain and salt spray stinging my skin.

'What you doing, man?'

'Take this.' I dug around in my pocket and held out my hand.

'A fuse?' He held it up to the light. 'What…'

'Keep hold of it for now. I didn't fancy anyone talking to that yacht on the radio, not yet. You'll need to put it back in after.'

'After what?'

'I'm going outside.'

'I just told you, weather's coming!'

I gave him a wink. 'I may be some time.'

I stepped out onto the wing and closed the door, leaving him wondering. I waited for the ship to right itself then launched down the slippy metal steps to the deck. The sea was black again now we were nearing the end of our journey. At the bottom I slid sideways, grabbing the railing, out of the main glare of the spotlights attached to the front of the superstructure. I clung to the railings as I made my way forward. Above me, Katanga watched, I could see the confusion on his face. In the saloon below shapes moved past the windows, I had to be quick. Katanga switched on the powerful work lamps on the cranes to help me as I neared my car, I turned and waved, making a cutting motion across my neck, they flicked off.

My knuckles ached on the cold metal as we dropped down a wave, I gave my eyes a few seconds to adjust, looking out across the charcoal sky. In the distance, a dim glow reflected off the clouds, visible only because the rest of the sky was so dark. The mainland. The glow disappeared as we hit the bottom, I gripped tighter as white water engulfed the foredeck, spray shooting up and soaking me. As the ship groaned and started its ascent I lurched for my car, grabbing the door handle to steady myself. I gave the roof a tap and headed for the forward hatch down into the hold.

I knew neither Seb nor Marty had clocked Nic over the head. And I was willing to bet that now that person thought we were home free and there'd be no payday, and they couldn't use the radio to contact our pursuers, they'd resort to less subtle methods.

Chapter Forty-nine

Château des Aigles
Two days ago

It had taken me nearly ten minutes to check the bodies. I was slowing down, reflexes dulling, yet I'd just bested at least twelve men – probably more, I didn't check all the remains in the burning chalet. No use kidding myself, though, they had definitely not sent their A-team. There was that complacency again.

None carried any ID, which was to be expected. The runic 88s, Sonnenrads, Wolfsangels, and other far-right tats adorning the bloodstained necks and faces told me enough. Unlikely to be military or professional mercs employed by the group, these were thuggish incels drawn to the cause, probably handy in a fight but evidently not a gunfight, and not when they came up against someone who'd spent their adult life hopping between war zones from South America to East Asia.

The only one I recognised was a German guy we'd nicknamed Simon Le Bon, a former KSK operative who'd been discharged for far-right extremism. I reckoned he'd led the assault team – more fool him, as most of him was still steaming, spread as he was across the decking out back. Seemed he'd taken a fair amount of the blast from the gas explosion and been blown out the bedroom window.

Bono was not among them, which told me two things – that their best was yet to come, and that it was likely in the form of a team in reserve somewhere nearby, waiting. For what, I couldn't know, but I suspected I'd find out the hard way as I tried to get off the mountain.

A shame, because no way could I lug two people off the mountain on foot. I'd crammed Ringo into the boot with the target, laid my HK rifle on the rear seat and the MP5 in the passenger footwell.

Now I was shivering in a layby, engine off, letting the fat flakes settle on the windscreen and bonnet that hadn't been running long enough to have warmed up. Sat waiting for the sirens.

I'd called the police before I'd left, swept the second chalet clean of anything – not difficult since I'd hardly used it. No evidence of my occupation left, but I'd set it burning anyway. Now, despite the carnage, several bodies, and a hundred or so shell casings scattered around, it was doubtful anything would be traced back to me – plus Holderness would have me covered. As soon as the cops figured out who these guys were, French intelligence would be all over it to suppress it with fake news stories. Behind the scenes they'd be livid, but that wasn't my problem.

The sirens were closing. I looked through the narrow gap where I'd opened my window, squinting through the blizzard at the blue lights pulsing off the drifts. If my theory was correct, there'd be a team waiting at the bottom of the road to intercept me, should I make it past their hit squad. That team – having no doubt seen the explosion, heard those first accounts of the firefight, and then been out of radio contact for nearly ten minutes – would be extremely wary and extremely trigger-happy.

But the police would clear the way for me.

The flashing lights swept past with an accompanying wail, two four-wheel drives on their way to investigate my frantic call about an explosion and possible gunfire. I waited until the lights had rounded the corner then put her in gear, turned the key, and – keeping the lights off for now – pulled out from the layby. The wipers kept the blizzard at bay as I turned down the hillside, flashing lights and orange glow now far above in my rear-view mirror. I floored it, sliding the corner, flicked the headlights on. I raced down the hill before the path in front was blocked. If I was that second team I'd have had spikes or a van across the road. They'd have moved them for the police but I now had to get through before they closed the door again.

The lights of the main road shone bright up ahead, I changed up, not braking for the junction, flying out into the road sideways, engine screaming, all wheels spinning. No gunshots, no cars, no tail. I slowed for an upcoming corner; headlights in front revealed upcoming traffic, lights flared, it was a fire engine following the gendarmes. I dropped my speed, not wanting to give them anything to tell the gendarmes about when they reached the burning chalet.

As I watched the flashing lights in my mirror something else caught my eye. A car had pulled out of a side street and was accelerating behind me, headlights off. I changed down, burying the loud pedal and feeling the tyres seeking out the best route across the hard-packed snow.

The headlights turned on in my mirror. A big BMW, possibly a 5 Series.

Round the corner I planted it to the floor and used a straight to put as much distance between us as possible. Several seconds later, and way behind me, the lights came round the corner, the angle of the beams slicing through the falling snow telling me they'd taken it sideways. The headlights slewed one way then the other as the driver fought the ice to accelerate. I flicked my eyes back to the road.

I wove through the meandering alpine roads as fast as the tyres allowed, clawing miles from them, using every advantage my four-wheel drive could bring to bear. I glanced at the fuel gauge, half a tank left. A fair bit in most cars but in this you can practically see the needle dropping, especially with the revs constantly soaring on the ice.

I roared past the garden centre where we'd acquired the Porsche the week before. The light behind was a pinprick in the mirror, only visible on long straights before disappearing round rocky walls in the tight mountain passes.

The road widened as it wound lower, the snow thinned as the altitude dropped until, after a few minutes, I was firmly on tarmac and able to double my speed while they still had to negotiate the iced corners. No lights behind now.

Drivers on the right always turn right when evading a tail: it's an easier, quicker turn – just like left turns are easier in the UK. That's what police are taught, and it's the logic I used on the outskirts of a town when I took a left instead, cutting through a Super U car park onto a main road through a light industrial area, business parks and garages and DIY stores. Still no lights. I swung right at a traffic lights and immediately left again, snow piled at the side of the road against factories and warehouses. The road turned, I followed around the edge of town until I exited to the west onto a dual carriageway where I could dial up the speed even more.

Geneva 50 km, the sign flashed past quickly, I followed it onto the autoroute. The revs climbed in time with the speedo, 100, 120, 130, 135 miles per hour, I eased off and watched the mirror. Nothing. I gave the road my full attention, dialled it up to 150 miles per hour, held it there as long as I dared, until a mental image of me wrapped round a bridge support climbed to the front of my mind. The road was wide and clear, no cars and no snow, but that didn't mean no ice. I had four-wheel drive and the best snow tyres on, the rubber compound gave fantastic grip in low temperatures – none of that matters on ice. On ice, four-wheel drive can just mean twice the number of spinning wheels.

I eased down to 115 miles per hour, which still seemed like overkill given my pursuers were probably way back still navigating at a crossroads somewhere in the town. The miles passed by, almost one every thirty seconds, the fuel needle dropped lower and lower.

It was a dicey strategy: bored gendarmes had a notorious distaste for British numberplates, and could be lurking anywhere – not to mention I was burning through petrol I couldn't afford to waste. I waited another minute then eased it down to eighty and checked the fuel gauge again. I had thirty miles or so if I held at this speed, just enough to get to Geneva.

Chapter Fifty

Tiburon, off the south Devon coast

I dropped quickly down the pitching ladder at the front of the hold. The lights still flickered ominously, the neon characters and deck-spinning DJ dripping down the rusty walls still scowled down at me, the ghosts still whispered from every rivet and weld. I ignored them all as I crossed the heaving tread plates in worsening waves, the rolling motion juddering through the keel, the laboured groans and shrieks of the old ship desperate to make it to port. Murky water splashed up across my trainers, the stink of saltwater, oil, the constant racking cough of the bilge pumps.

I climbed the ladder up to the platform as quickly as possible then stopped to pull out my pistol. I cocked it, held it down low, remembering how easily Seb had knocked it over the railings into the hold. Not gonna happen again.

I stepped silently through the doorway into the gloomy red access corridor, pausing outside the door into the workshop. A Russian warning sign was painted in red, the German sticker which had been stuck over it peeled and cracked. Damn right there was danger, but not the kind they'd been worried about.

I pulled my gun in close, easing open the door, ready. The room was empty and just as I'd last seen it. Even the plug for the circular saw still sat on the workbench where Seb had pulled it from the wall with that smug grin on his face. If only I'd managed to get some information out of him first, I might have been able to find out who his partner in crime was, and wouldn't be scurrying around the ship like a rat. I was fairly sure Vincent was my man, but it pays to keep an open mind; I needed to catch him red-handed, and planned to do just that.

I closed the door behind me and jogged across to the other side of the room. The engines vibrated through the door as I placed my hand on the wheel. It turned easily, the sound of the engines rose in volume. Again I held my pistol ready, swinging it across the engines and walkway between, but again the room was empty. I stepped forward and looked over the low railing down into the engine bay, both engines were happily chugging away on their own.

I ran to the wall, grabbed a rope, and tied it to the wheel on the workshop side of the door, tying the other end round the pillar drill inside to hold it open. The heavy door pulled the rope taut as the waves pitched us forward and backward, less rolling now as we adjusted our path: on the final run through the Channel now.

I backed away from the bulkhead, across the other side of the room, crouching behind a battered wooden workbench. From here, I was fairly well hidden but could see into the engine room, and if anyone came in the other way, through the hold, I'd know about it.

I pulled in my feet, pushed back as far as I could, cold steel wall pressing my spine, eyes on the walkway in the engine room.

I didn't have to wait long, no more than a couple of minutes before I heard the loud clunk above the constant thrum of the engines, the metallic thunk of the locks sliding off the engine room door. It creaked as it swung open then grated shut. I pushed back further, pulling my head in and my gun up.

Above the clatter of the diesel engines, I thought I heard someone jump down onto the walkway, I glanced out to see a shadow, the figure was just out of sight. I eased out, pausing as a sweater bobbed into view, then the back of someone's head, the low-pulled hat obscuring their features. He looked up briefly then knelt, pulling out a knife from his pocket.

I was across the room in an instant, into the doorway before he turned, gun up and on his back.

'Don't move, Poubelle,' I shouted from the doorway.

He froze, hands out.

'Stand up – slowly – and drop that knife.' I walked out onto the platform above the engine bay, holding the higher ground.

Poubelle turned slowly, face set in stone as he decided whether to bluff his way out of it or straight out try to kill me. I waved my gun, he dropped the knife with a clatter.

'Which one of you killed King?' I shouted.

He narrowed his eyes.

'Was it you or Sébastien?'

He just stood there, chest rising and falling as he breathed in deeply, clearly furious but refusing to speak, to move, anything.

'I think it was Seb, but still.' I smiled. 'How do you think the rest of the crew will react to you selling them out?'

He twitched, as if he was thinking of making a move, I squeezed the trigger. He ducked, throwing his hands up as the bullet ricocheted off the wall behind him.

'And when Miller realises you killed my cargo, that you've cost the crew thousands.' I made the same hand motion he and Miller had made. *Over the side you go*.

'No, no,' he spoke for the first time, 'I didn't do that, or kill your friend.'

I noticed his pocket was weighed down with something. 'Take out your gun, slowly, and drop it on the floor.'

The door at the far end opened, I glanced round to see Vincent enter, AK-47 in hand, looking back over his shoulder talking to someone.

'Check the engine temperature and...' His eyes went wide as he turned to the room, cig dangling from his mouth.

'Vincent!' Poubelle screamed, '*Il va me tuer*.' *He's going to kill me!*

Vincent spun, rifle raised, I kept my pistol on Poubelle.

Nic shuffled into the room, closing the door behind him, then turned. His eyes ballooned as he took in the standoff in front of him.

'Put it down,' shouted Vincent, cig hanging from the corner of his mouth.

'Can't do that, Vincent,' I said. 'This is our saboteur. He was about to kill the engines.'

'I found him in here!' shouted Poubelle. 'He's going to kill us all.'

Nic finally found his voice, but unfortunately used it for the wrong purpose, face breaking into a smile as he realised he could get his revenge for the earlier kicking. 'Shoot the bastard, we'll throw him overboard.'

Vincent jabbed the rifle forward. 'Gun down or I blow your head all over the wall.'

I'd no doubt he would, he already didn't like or trust me.

'Do it, do it now,' Poubelle said. 'He was going to shoot me, he killed Seb!'

Nic nodded. 'Do it.'

'Three,' said Vincent.

I breathed in deeply, not taking my eyes off Poubelle.

'Two,' Vincent steadied the rifle in my peripheral vision, I briefly wondered how quickly I could spin my gun onto him. Not quickly enough, he was itching to shoot.

'One,' I could hear the intake of breath as he finished counting.

I dropped, his rifle erupted, a bullet hit the wall behind me.

'All right, all right,' I dropped my gun and held my hands up.

Vincent kept the rifle straight at me. 'Don't move,' he said.

'Shoot him!' screamed Poubelle. 'You know he wants to kill us all.'

'Listen to me, Vincent,' I spoke slowly. 'I know you're looking for a reason to shoot, but...'

'Shut up.'

'Get the captain down here,' I nodded at the intercom on the wall to the side of the door. 'He'll tell you it's this traitorous bastard you wanna throw over the side.'

'Shoot him,' hissed Nic.

Vincent crept his hand towards the intercom but Nic was in his way. He couldn't call the captain without taking his eyes off me and he knew it.

Finally he worked out a compromise and waved his rifle. 'Kick your gun over the edge,' he said, shuffling forward. 'Now!'

It was that or Nic and Poubelle would have their way. I gave the gun a tap with my toe, it dropped off the platform onto the walkway. 'Now get the captain down here.'

He nodded slowly, leaning the rifle on the railing, still pointed at me, other hand crawling along the wall until it found the intercom. Nic looked disappointed as Vincent crept his fingers around the switch, eyes not wavering from me, rifle rock-steady. In my peripheral vision, Poubelle twitched.

The door opened again, knocking Nic forward, Vincent glanced round as Fields stepped onto the platform.

'Look out!' I shouted.

A gunshot echoed around the room, smothered by the engines. Too late, Vincent's eyes went wide as the white painted steel wall behind him was redecorated red. Fields scrabbled at his holster, pulling his Glock. Before he could raise it another two gunshots cracked, Fields jerked, dropping the pistol and staggering back against the door, slamming it shut. Vincent's rifle clattered down to the walkway between the engines, his body finally slumped over the railings and dropped after it. Fields left a trail of red down the door as he slid, eyes on me, asking me what was going on.

Poubelle was already turning to me, revolver in hand. I leapt backwards before Vincent's body even hit the floor, diving back through the open doorway into the workshop.

Bullets smacked the bulkhead, bouncing around the walls like angry hornets as I ducked and rolled across the workshop floor. I glanced back, saw Poubelle had now picked up Vincent's rifle and was lined up in the middle of the engine bay, just his face and the gun barrel visible. Behind him, Nic cowered behind Fields, pressing himself against the door.

Poubelle turned his back to me, bringing the rifle to his shoulder, levelling it at Nic, the only remaining witness to his treachery. I leapt to my feet, grabbing for the tools, launching a spanner through the doorway at the back of Poubelle's head. It struck as he squeezed the trigger. The bullets went wide, Nic screamed and ducked as they ricocheted around him.

'Get the gun,' I yelled to Nic, pointing at Fields' Glock.

Poubelle ducked and spun, squeezing the trigger again as I dived sideways. I rolled to one side of the door, the bullet smacked harmlessly into the wooden tool board across the far wall, sending tools flying across the floor.

Boots clanged on the walkway then the ladder on the other side of the bulkhead, I looked round frantically for anything within reach. The crowbar I'd used earlier to lock the door shut. I reached for it just as the gun appeared in the doorway.

I ducked, swinging my arm through a wide arc to get plenty behind it. Poubelle fired, the bullet missed my head by a centimetre as the crowbar found its target, catching him across the knees. He grunted, stumbled backwards, I leapt forward, closing the distance, reaching for his gun. He snarled, whipping a fist round. It caught me on the shoulder, I turned into it as I pushed his arm up with both hands, putting the barrel of that rifle out of my way.

Poubelle brought his fist round again but it never made it as I brought up a knee into his stomach, still pushing, forcing him back through the doorway. He tripped over the high threshold. I followed him through, pushing him over. He started to drop back but swept out a foot, catching my knee, slamming my leg sideways into the frame. I stumbled, still gripping his gun with both hands, pushing forward, and let my weight drop against him, toppling his already unbalanced stance.

Poubelle fell back against the railing, I dropped onto him, face inches from his. Before he could recover I pulled my head down sharply, feeling the cartilage of his nose pop against my forehead. He grunted and went limp. I let go of his arm, moving back and lashing out rapidly, *one two*, both blows thumping into his chest. His arm came down, the rifle swung, but I was too close for him to bring it to bear. I took a heartbeat to steady myself then landed a perfect right-hander under his already outstretched chin, sending him flying backwards over the railing.

He didn't have far to fall, there was a dull thud and another grunt of pain as he bounced off the top of the starboard engine. He somehow landed on his feet and brought his arm round, still holding the rifle, waving it in my general direction. I put two hands on the railing and vaulted over, feet outstretched, landing them in his chest. He flew backwards, dropping the rifle. I hit the walkway and rolled across into the port side engine, springing up onto my feet and looking for my gun, his gun, any weapon.

Over on the other side of the room, Poubelle groaned and got his hands beneath him. On the platform behind him Nic still hid under Fields' body, making no attempt to intervene. Poubelle scrabbled for the rifle, I grabbed the rungs of the ladder and hauled myself up just as a bullet hit the wall. I scrambled over the platform, jumping through the doorway with gunshots chasing me back into the workshop.

Bullets punched the paintwork across the ceiling, bouncing around the workshop as I crouched, running for the door at the far side.

I gripped the wheel and turned, the levers groaned off their stops, I heaved the door open.

The clatter of the AK-47 stopped, I turned to see Poubelle stood in the middle of the walkway, still squinting down the rifle, then looking up as he realised the gun was dry. I paused, about to rush back to finish him, then looked at the platform just behind him, at Fields' pistol still sat next to the railing. Poubelle looked round at the same time, dropping the rifle and reaching for the Glock.

A bullet hit the door as I sprinted through the forward corridor towards the hold, grabbing the handle to the next door. Another bullet hit the bulkhead next to me, I pressed in hard against the door as I fought with the stiff mechanism.

There was a bang from the engine room, not a gunshot, it'd come from the engines themselves. The vibrations underfoot changed, the ship rocked over to one side. He'd taken out one of the engines. The handle finally gave, I launched through onto the platform overlooking the hold, fighting to close the door behind me.

Another bang came from the engine room. The ship groaned and shuddered, suddenly pitching forward then rolling sharply over to the side again, throwing me off my feet and across the platform. My head bounced off the railings, forcing my eyes shut. I wrapped my hands over my head and let out a groan of pain into my arms. My hands were wet, warm and sticky.

Only the crashing of the waves now, slamming the empty hold and echoing around the metal walls but, crucially, no other sound. He'd achieved his goal, killing both engines.

I grabbed the railing and climbed to my feet, shaking the bright lights from behind my eyes. I had to shut that door.

Too late, I could hear boots as Poubelle stormed along the passageway towards me. He saw me and fired.

I ducked to the side, trying to swing the door shut but a bullet buzzed through the gap, tearing through my trousers. Poubelle slammed against the other side of the door, jamming a heavy steel toe-capped boot into the gap. The pistol stuck round the frame, he squeezed the trigger, waving it around. The ship shuddered from bow to stern, rolling to starboard, shrieking like a wounded fox, I heard the rush of water behind me as waves cascaded through the forward hatch.

I stumbled back against the railings, the door in front of me flew open.

Poubelle brought the gun up, level with my head. His face contorted into a grin as his finger twitched on the trigger. 'You know, I should leave you for them to deal with when they get here.'

Gunshots exploded in rapid succession, I ducked as crimson flowers bloomed across Poubelle's shirt. His eyes narrowed in confusion then glazed over as he stumbled back into the passageway, dropping the Glock and slumping down the wall. He stopped twitching and came to rest in a heap in the doorway.

I turned to see Marty in the waterfall of the forward hatch, clinging to the top of the ladder. One arm was wrapped through the rungs, the other held her Walther pistol outstretched into space.

'You took your bloody time,' I said.

Chapter Fifty-one

Tiburon

I ran back through the workshop, dropping down into the engine bay, sprinting for the platform at the other side. Fields' breathing was shallow, eyes rolled back, chest moving only slightly, but he was alive.

I climbed up onto the platform and knelt to unzip his fleece. One of the holes was immediately visible, straight through his right side and through his lung by the sound of it. The other hole was further up, near the middle of his chest, and the way it was pumping out blood told me there wasn't much could be done.

I put a hand over each anyway but could feel his pulse weakening. He opened his mouth to talk but only blood trickled out, sucked into his lung and then spat down his cheek as he spluttered dying breaths.

I glanced round to Marty, running her hand over the dead engines.

'Get help,' I said. 'Get the others.'

The door flew open, Miller and Katanga pushed into the room.

'What the fuck is going on?' shouted Miller when he saw the carnage. 'Kat, get the engines restarted, quickly.'

Nic lurked in the doorway as Katanga leapt down the ladder.

Miller followed him down. 'Didn't think we'd be seeing the mermaid so soon,' he said to Marty as he crouched by Vincent's body, holding his fingers to his throat.

Doc pushed past Nic and bent down, placing a hand on my shoulder.

I looked up at him. 'Get your gear, Doc, fast!'

He shook his head. 'He's dead, Tyler.'

I looked down and saw Fields' chest was no longer moving under my hands. I moved them away, no more blood flowed from the wounds, he'd all but run out.

I leaned forward, head in my hands.

Marty crouched to look at him impassively. 'I thought you wanted him dead?'

'Not like this, not...'

Truth is, I *had* wanted Fields dead, the only reason I'd hired him was to ensure the bastard never reached England.

I stood and wiped my hands on my trousers, sighing, shaking my head. It was meant to feel good, wasn't it, revenge? After all this time?

Why didn't it?

Chapter Fifty-two

Daylight had been creeping through the pines behind
Ringo's house as I'd pulled into his garage. Now shadows
were creeping the other way as the orange sky darkened.
I'd left the two captives in the car as I'd slept late, then
woke to eat him out of biscuits. Now, as the sun dropped
again over the distant peaks, I stood in the garage, sipping
my tea and looking at the two unconscious bodies in the
open boot of my car. The fitness app on my phone still
showed a steady heartbeat, and since I'd sedated the two
of them at the same time, that was good news.

Business was clearly booming for the mercenary we'd
called Ringo. His place in Céligny was small but nice
and private, with a view of Lake Geneva if you squinted
between rooftops and trees below. It wasn't to my taste,
all concrete and glass, but kudos to him for being able
to afford anything round here. That an ex-Marine like
Ringo could, told me he was into some seriously bad shit
somewhere.

I was still thinking of him as Ringo even though I'd
known his real identity all along. David Fraser had been
contracted to a Belgian-based private security firm, but
often took freelance work if the money was right. On this

job I'd made sure the money was right – even offering up half my fee to get him to join the team. He seemed both capable and willing enough. We'd established he was an explosives expert, which had been of no use on this job, and sadly that seemed to be the extent of his skills. His skiing ability had been an unexpected bonus, but otherwise he was no more than an extra pair of hands – or an extra gun – for the right sort of jobs.

I hadn't *needed* him at all. I'd *wanted* him.

I took a mouthful of tea as the last of the red faded from the sky, turning deep blue. No more snow forecast, an easy run to La Rochelle. I put the tea down on the workbench and looked at my watch: five p.m. The rendezvous at the port was scheduled for 2:30 a.m. and it was an eight-hour drive. I'd already changed onto my third set of fake numberplates. Piles of screwed-up black self-adhesive vinyl sat in the corner of the garage where I'd peeled it from every panel of my car, revealing its original shining metallic grey colour underneath. Didn't want to make things *too* easy for any pursuers, who were out there somewhere, watching and waiting.

I used a burner phone to send two texts. The first was to the captain of the *Tiburon* waiting in La Rochelle, a simple message. *We're on.* The second was to Colonel Holderness and just as simple, a prompt for him to call me.

I picked up a black box from the workbench, the piece of kit I'd removed from the boot of the Porsche. Thanks to Ringo's well-stocked garage it had only taken me minutes to remove the CD changer from the Audi's glovebox, and this fitted inside perfectly.

I was halfway through connecting its power up to the Audi's wiring harness when Holderness called.

'Halifax Couriers,' I answered. 'What can I do for you?'

'Enough nonsense, this is a secure line. This is a mess, Tyler, twelve on the Beaufort scale.'

I switched the phone onto loudspeaker and put it on the garage floor. 'You knew he had a small army around him, what did you think would happen?'

'As subtle as a brick and almost as sharp. Surgical extraction, I specified, not an invasion.'

I bent down into the passenger footwell of my car and twisted the exposed power wires together, wrapping tape around them. 'I'm fine, by the way.'

'Then I fail to see why it's taken you this long to check in. I take it you're holed up in a secure location?'

'A safehouse near Geneva, it'll need a sanitising team to give it a once-over. I still have a tail.'

'Law enforcement?'

'No. Did you secure the replacement team member? I know Fields is at home for Christmas, hopefully he'll be up for a last-minute job.'

'Hiring an unknown didn't work particularly well this time, what makes you think he'll be any better? You should have let me send…'

I tucked the wires under the carpet. 'No, I want Fields.' I picked up a screwdriver and started attaching the black box into the glovebox. 'Offer him the German's fees, she doesn't need the money any more.'

'Christ, Tyler. What have you done?'

I flicked a switch, a green light winked on in the glovebox. 'Nothing you need to worry about.' I had the missing link to the team that had killed my brother and tried to kill me, now I needed to look him in the eye. I needed him on the ship. 'Offer my share as a late bonus.'

He sighed. 'That's not necessary, twenty thousand pounds for two days' work is enough to lure anyone away from their Christmas dinner. Fields is already en route to La Rochelle, but don't forget whose operation this is.'

I stood and picked up my mug of tea. 'Don't forget I'm an independent contractor, and right now I have what you want in my boot.' I walked round to the rear of my car and looked at the two unconscious figures curled up.

'Is that a threat?' He laughed mockingly. 'Let's not talk about hiding things in the boot of your car, Tyler. Not after what happened last time.'

'Yeah, been thinking about that.' I gulped the last mouthful of tea and looked out of the window at the lights on the far side of the lake. 'I reckon we're even, after what I've been through.'

'After what you've been through? This mess is entirely your creation. After what you've been through, give me strength.' His Doric Scots accent crept in at the edges, he was angrier that I'd thought. 'You've left a trail of destruction that is both extremely unlike you and extremely undesirable. I can't stress to you enough the importance of this operation.'

'I've risked my life several times to get you this guy.'

'You're usually tidier than this. You're either slipping, or there's something else going on entirely.'

He paused, the line was quiet. I watched a solitary boat cruising across the lake. Didn't care who it was or where it was going, I'd trade lives with them right now.

Holderness finally spoke again, barely above a whisper. 'That's it, isn't it? There's something else going on.'

I coughed. 'What do you mean?'

'If I find out you're using this job as a means to any ends other than mine, I will be displeased. So displeased you needn't think of returning to these shores. In fact I'd keep going as far as you can, and then keep going some more.'

'Are you threatening me now?' I frowned. He was right, of course, about everything. About my motives and about the fact that this job had gone south quicker than Amundsen. Not so much surgical precision as carpet bombing.

'This mission is important to lots of people, and if reports from France are anything to go by, feathers will be extremely ruffled.'

I crouched back by the passenger footwell and picked up the screwdriver again. 'Please tell anyone nursing ruffled feathers in their centrally heated office in Whitehall or Westminster that I've just finished dressing my wounds after being caught in a firefight with an entire SS mountain division.'

'Don't exaggerate, Tyler. Listen, I've been getting more requests for information on you and this op than ever before.'

'I thought I was a deniable asset? So deny.'

'I mean it, if you're using this mission to pursue some personal vendetta you'll be out in the cold.'

'Don't kid yourself, Colonel, that's where I've always been.'

He paused again as I finished screwing the box into place, I could hear an intake of breath, then silence as he checked his temper. I rarely used his rank, but since what happened in Scotland I'd been reconsidering our working arrangements.

Finally he let out his breath. 'The team are already in the air, give me a location.'

I threw the screwdriver onto the bench and closed the glovebox. 'Céligny, near Geneva. I'm emailing the details through.' I picked up the phone, walked round to the boot, looked at Ringo lying sedated, bruised and bloodied. I grabbed a handful of his jacket and pulled him out, dragging him across the floor. 'Tell the cleaners to check in the garage first, I'll be gone by the time they arrive.'

'Half your fee has been deposited. If there are any more incidents on French soil – or Swiss soil for that matter – it'll be your last job. Do *not* contact me again until the transport is under way.'

I hit the red button and rested my hand on the raised boot lid, staring at the orange jacket moving with each shallow breath.

Chapter Fifty-three

Tiburon

Poubelle had used his knife to slice through the wiring harnesses of both engines, an easy fix but a time-consuming one. Marty and I had stayed to help at first but there was only so much several pairs of hands could do at a time in the confined space, so we'd trusted the others to get everything soldered and spliced back together. Now Nic and Katanga laboured below while Miller and Doc held the bridge. I'd gone to my room to get cleaned up, holding my shaking hands under the scalding tap for nearly ten minutes. Didn't matter how much I cleaned them, they were still drenched in blood.

'Do you think you got everything you needed?' Marty asked.

I poked my head round the doorframe. 'I bloody hope so, now he's dead. Were Miller and Katanga easy on you? They should be on the stage.'

'Yeah. That bastard Poubelle wanted to help throw me overboard, sadistic motherfucker, Miller had a hard time getting rid of him. I feel carsick, being cooped up in that Audi all this time. Did Fields suspect anything?'

I dried my hands and stepped into the cabin, throwing the towel on the bed. 'No, he took it in. Thanks for the new black eye by the way. You think you could have pulled your punches a bit better?'

'Likewise.' She scowled. 'I thought you'd broken my ribs.'

'Sorry. Would have been easier with King to help.'

'Hey listen, are you okay?' She shuffled into the cabin, throwing a kitbag on the bed. 'We didn't get a chance to talk, but if you need to…'

'You have a local?'

'Local what?'

'Where everybody knows your name. A pub. A bar. I'm not a regular anywhere. I watch these TV shows sometimes, on planes and in hotel rooms and stuff, you know? No one anywhere knows my order when I walk in, no one knows what I'm having. No one knows my name, anyone that did is dead.'

'*I* know it.'

'Well don't stick around, for your sake. They're taking it all from me, everything that means anything.'

'Who's they?'

'The world.'

'Ah, so that's why you hate it.'

I grabbed the shelf as a powerful wave rocked us. 'I've nowt left to love about it.'

'Seems to me you're the common denominator here.'

'Great, thanks. That makes me feel a lot better.'

'It wasn't supposed to. Stop feeling sorry for yourself, take some responsibility or do something about it.'

'King was different. He's… was… he was my brother.'

'I know, I've lost people like that, too.'

'No, I mean literally, if Justin had still been alive they'd be married by now. Or maybe killed each other, I dunno.' I shook my head, pointed to a kitbag. 'Is that Fields' gear?'

She nodded. 'Everything apart from the weapons, I left those in the cabin. A small bonus for me, I thought.'

I raised an eyebrow as I threw last night's shirt on, stale and grimy but not awash with blood. 'I hired you specifically to play your part, don't be getting greedy or I really will feed you to the sharks.'

She gave me a lopsided smile. 'Played it well though, didn't I?'

'And I always promised you his share. That not enough? Fine, take the weapons, but mind who you sell them to.'

'I'm not stupid, Tyler. Anyway, I was thinking, now there's only the two of us, do we split King's share?'

'Don't even think about it.' I shook my head. 'He has parents and a sister who could do with it. Come on.'

We stumbled through the swaying passageways, up the stairs, diverting across the tilting deck to launch Fields' kitbag over the side, then climbing the stairs to the bridge.

I opened the door. Doc stood from the table but I waved him away. Beyond the windows daylight had surrendered entirely. Waves hammered, each tipping us further over than the last as the ship twisted at the mercy of the sea.

Miller gave me a nod and spoke into the radio. 'Kat, gimme an update.'

It crackled, Katanga's breathless voice coming back a moment later. 'There's no manual for this, Skip. Slow going.'

'How slow?'

'Another… Twenty minutes, maybe?'

'We've got no chance,' said Marty, walking to the radar, eyes flicking between the glowing blip on the screen and the black horizon.

'No shit, it was fifty-fifty when we were making good speed.' Miller pressed the handset again. 'Kat, I want those screws spinning in ten.'

Miller hooked the handset up above him, the hanging wire leaned over towards the door, indicating the crazy angle of the ship. We hung on as he spun the wheel; I thought it was more to make himself feel better than to have much of an effect on our direction, given the lack of propulsion. He looked at me, brow creased. 'We've been at the mercy of the waves for too long now.'

Doc held a hand up. 'Did you hear that?'

We all stopped. Nothing above the crashing waves. Then it came, a burst of static and a voice, barely audible.

Doc made for the stairs first but Miller called him back. 'Stay at the wheel, I'll go.'

I didn't wait for Miller, charging down the stairs with Marty two steps behind. As we approached the radio room we could hear it more clearly. A voice dripping with malice, speaking English but thick and accented. Branko.

'Freighter *Tiburon*, this is the yacht *Zuben*. Come in *Tiburon*.'

We stared at the radio.

'I know you are listening, *Tiburon*.'

'What do we do?' asked Miller.

Marty looked at me, eyes narrowing to hard points. 'How many rounds you got for that 417 in your trunk out there?'

'Zero.'

'We've got fifty nine-mil rounds.' She turned to Miller. 'Round up all the weapons and ammo.'

Miller nodded frantically. 'We have a couple of AKs and a few revolvers.'

'*Tiburon*, it will be worse for you if you ignore me.'

Marty moved towards the door, I grabbed her arm. 'We can't win a firefight with these guys, they're faster and likely better armed.'

'We've got the Kalashnikovs,' said Miller. 'And we've got plenty of ammo for...'

'They're as bad as some of the counterfeit Darra AKs I saw in Afghanistan, and probably not even as well maintained as those.'

'They've never let us down,' said Miller.

'And how many naval battles have you won with them? Regardless, those and a few handguns aren't gonna be much use until that yacht gets close enough to spit at, and I guarantee we'll already be sinking by then.' I thought back to the night before, when they'd assaulted the chalet. They may have been untrained hired thugs, but they'd been well tooled.

'So what do you suggest?' asked Miller.

'Our only chance is to run. We need to buy ourselves some time to get the engines turning.'

'And then? We can't outrun them.'

I picked up the handset and held it out to Miller. 'Speak to them.'

His eyes went wide, he looked as if the handset was going to bite him, I'd rarely seen him this worried. I nodded at him and waved the handset.

He took it and flicked the transmit button. '*Tiburon* here, what can I do you for, *Zuben*?'

There was a pause, I could picture some Nazi underling on the yacht scurrying away to bring Branko back. Finally, the voice came through.

'Who am I speaking to?'

'This is Captain...' he paused. I nodded, whispering for him to continue. 'Captain Miller. Who's this?'

'I am, at this moment, your worst nightmare. You have taken something from me. I am coming to reclaim it.'

I scribbled on Nic's pad and held it up to Miller, gesturing him to read from it.

'We found your spy.'

'My spy?'

'Sébastien.'

Branko chuckled. 'That is too bad for Sébastien, but he knew the risks. But you did not find him, I think, in time, since your engines are stopped.'

'Unfortunately for me one of my crew decided to take you up on your generous offer. So what now?'

'I am coming aboard to take back what is mine.'

Miller covered the handset even though they couldn't hear us, he'd let go of the transmit switch. 'Dead or alive, they said. Well let's just let him take the body and be done with them.'

'You think they'll pick up his body and leave? They'll kill everyone on this ship and then sink her.'

Miller flicked the radio switch. 'Can't let you come aboard my ship.' He added a bit of swagger that I could tell he instantly regretted.

'I can see you now, we will be alongside in ten minutes. We will take what we want and then blow your ship from water.'

I looked at my watch then scribbled another note for Miller, he read it out.

'Look, your friend is dead. Sébastien killed him.'

There was a pause on the other end, when Branko spoke again it was a deeper growl. 'Then I'm coming aboard to collect the body.'

'A trade. I'll send it across.'

I shook my head frantically.

'And what do you get in return?'

'We get to sail in the other direction and forget this happened.'

Another pause.

'This is not good deal for me, I am only getting dead body, you are getting your lives.'

'Listen, half my crew's dead because of your plant.'

There was a pause and then, 'You send across body and I might let you sail away.'

I gestured to Miller, drawing my hand across my throat to kill the call.

Miller looked at us and smiled. 'Deal.'

'You will also send John Tyler with the body.'

I clenched my jaw. Marty and Miller looked at me.

Miller let go of the transmit button and covered the handset again. 'What's the play?'

'Seb must have filled them in on the radio. He gave them my name.'

'Are you there, Captain Miller?' crackled the radio.

'I'm here.'

I scribbled one last note and held it up.

'Tyler is dead,' continued Miller. 'I killed him. He was of no use to us.'

'Then send across his body also.'

There was nothing more from the radio. I leaned on the table to look out of the window. Beyond the white foam spraying the glass, rising on the distant waves, were the lights of a boat.

'So what the hell now?' asked Miller.

'Believe me, as soon as they get in range they'll kill everyone on board. If we allow them to get in close we die, all of us.'

'I believe you, okay? So what's the plan?'

'We need to buy those guys below some time, get the engines running, put enough distance between us and that boat,' I jabbed a finger at the window, 'to build up a head start so we can hit Devon and not look back.'

'We need a distraction.' He looked out of the window at the lights, closer now. 'We've got less than ten minutes to come up with something.'

'We need to stop them and we can't do it from here, we gotta take the fight right to them.' I inhaled deeply and looked at Miller. 'I'm gonna need some tape, two bin bags, and a razor.'

Chapter Fifty-four

Tiburon

I shivered in the sodden jumper, lying in a pool of freezing seawater, looking down at the bodies by my feet. My hands were bound behind my back, but I gripped a rope tightly to avoid being pitched out of the dinghy and into the swell. From down here, laid in the bottom of one of *Tiburon*'s two tiny inflatable lifeboats, the waves were enormous. Black walls towered above, plucking the little boat up, throwing it skywards again and again. Though the waves weren't breaking – the boat was buoyant enough and wouldn't be swamped – my concern was being capsized or thrown clean out of it.

The sound of an engine gradually rose above the waves, powerful marine diesels but more refined than those of the *Tiburon*. They'd be homing in on the bright lamps strapped to the sides of the dinghy or the even brighter pulsing strobe sticking up at the top of the pole. The flares fired from the *Tiburon* had long since died but they'd put the yacht right on top of me.

I strained at the ropes, managing to crane my neck around far enough to see a sleek white hull towering above me, a jolt as the inflatable sidewall bumped against the yacht. Shouts from above, my neck ached, I dropped back into the freezing water and waited.

I felt something hit my leg, more shouting, a boat-hook scratched for the cleat on the side of the dinghy. It pulled, I managed to roll sideways to see a silhouette leaning over the railings, pulling the dinghy down the side of the yacht. More silhouettes shouted along the railings, figures moving in the bright lights of the flybridge. The dinghy banged against the low stern of the yacht, someone muttered close by. A hand shoved me roughly, I felt them tying off a rope.

The dinghy bobbed and rocked violently, I realised someone had jumped down in with me. They shouted up to the people above in a language I didn't understand, almost sounded like Russian but as I tuned in I could tell it wasn't. Wasn't Branko Serbian?

The hand grabbed my leg again, turning me over, I yelled in pain as the rope bit my wrists, threatening to dislocate my shoulders. Hands pulled at the rope, suddenly I was free.

'Who are you?' the man asked.

I rolled over, blinking in the lights, rubbing my wrists. 'The crew call me Poubelle,' I said quietly, English with my best Marseillais accent.

'You are the one who stopped the engines?'

I nodded.

The man in the boat was young, shaved head, ugly scars on his face. Tattoos ran up from the neck of his T-shirt. He picked up a rope, pulling a knot tight, I realised he'd tied the bodies. Strong hands hauled them up into the light.

'Who is he?' came a shout from above.

'Frog crew. He was tied up.'

I shielded my eyes from the bright lights and tried to see the man.

'Throw him overboard,' said the silhouette on deck.

The man grabbed my shoulders, I twisted and shouted out, he dragged my legs.

A gunshot cracked, torn off by the wind, a rush of air as one of the dinghy's inflatable cells collapsed. The man in the boat stumbled back.

'Leave him, get back up here,' the voice above shouted. The dinghy shifted as the man jumped out, onto the rear deck of the yacht.

'Wait,' I shouted. 'I helped you.'

'And?' The dark figure above didn't move.

'I disabled their engines. I…'

The gun flashed, another cell exploded, the dinghy leaned over in the swell. I climbed unsteadily to my feet as seawater rushed around my ankles.

The man above laughed. 'Are you strong swimmer?'

'I can help you!' I shouted, trying to balance as water reached my knees, the inflatable boat was rapidly becoming a misnomer.

'We don't need any help.' He took aim again. Before he could fire someone else shouted, the man turned and looked behind him. He barked instructions to his unseen team, voice rising until he was shouting rapidly, slipping into his native language.

He looked down at me and pointed the gun at the steps. 'Get up here.'

I jumped onto the slippy swim platform, easier said than done, up the rear stairs of the rolling yacht as the engines spooled up beneath me. By the time I hauled myself through the gate in the railings and up onto the polished teak main deck it was empty. Figures moved behind blinds in the full-length windows in front of me, more on the flybridge above. I leaned out, looked down the graceful hull, all the way to the waves slicing cleanly across the bow, as if the yacht was meant to be here, unlike the ungainly *Tiburon*, trespassing in these waters.

I looked back across the stern as we turned, caught a flash of *Tiburon*'s running lights in the distance as she rose on a wave. I couldn't tell if she was still floundering or under way.

'You!' I turned. Branko's huge frame filled a glass doorway a couple of metres away, still waving his gun. 'In here!'

I swayed around an outdoor dining table and followed him through the door into a plush, polished lounge, straight into a punch that sent me staggering sideways. As I blinked, hands moved up and down, into pockets, grabbing everywhere. I pushed them away and steadied myself.

'He's clean.' It was the young guy that'd climbed down to the dinghy.

Behind him, Branko lowered himself onto a puffy white leather sofa, huge arms folded, glaring at me. Several other men were positioned around the room, each sad twat bigger and uglier than the last. Five of them in total, dodgy tattoos, muscles filling out black T-shirts, leg holsters and knives in sheaths, big boots. I looked round each of them, weighing them up. One was holding his gun all wrong, no problem there. Another was standing like he thought he was tough but had never been in more than street fights, a slap or two and he'd be out of the running. I recognised a couple of the security guys from their chalet, the better ex-military ones. I'd wiped out a good chunk of the security team the night before last. How many more on the bridge or belowdecks though?

One of them was uglier than the others, his face a mess of tiny cuts. His arm was held in a sling. He looked strangely familiar, I realised the last time I'd seen him he'd been hanging out of the rear window of that BMW M5 in La Rochelle.

The main focus in the room was no longer the huge TV on the wall behind Branko, or the large, well-stocked bar in the corner. Next to a polished wood and glass coffee table, ruining an otherwise spotless cream rug, lay the two corpses I'd come across in the dinghy with.

Branko leaned forward, hands on the table. 'You are the one they call Poubelle?'

I nodded.

'The crew member Sébastien told us about?'

I nodded again. 'He needed my help to sabotage the ship. He said you'd pay…'

'Who is this man?' Branko leaned to the side, grabbed a handful of Fields' top and pulled him up into a sitting position with one hand. His lifeless head lolled forward.

'That's John Tyler,' I replied. 'Some British merc who hired us to…'

'I know all about his mission. Who killed him?'

'The captain. Tyler tried to double-cross us, wasn't going to pay.'

Branko dropped Fields with a thud, I winced as his head bounced off the teak. He stood, eyes burning through mine. He crouched by the second body, the man I'd bundled into my boot in the Alps and driven to La Rochelle, one tiny step ahead of these guys all the way.

Branko moved the orange ski jacket, grasped the handle of the knife and slowly pulled it from the man's chest, it made a sucking sound as it slid free. He turned the knife over, looking down at the corpse, and took a breath through gritted teeth.

'And who...' he held the dripping knife out towards my face, turning redder even as I watched, and pointed his other hand down at the body. 'Who the FUCK is this?'

I tried to look puzzled. 'This is the man Tyler brought aboard in La Rochelle.'

Branko roared, threw the knife in my general direction, I stepped out of the way and saw it miss one of his crew behind me by inches before thunking into the wall. There was a smash of glass, I turned back to see Branko had put a bottle of whisky through the TV and was now holding one of this team by the neck. Everyone in the room tensed and took a step back, I took several, using the distraction to reverse right up to the wall.

Branko's face was by now almost the colour of a para's beret. 'Take the bodies below,' he screamed in the man's face, shoving him backwards. He stumbled and fell, Branko kicked him, and turned on me, eyes on fire, chest heaving with huge panting breaths. He looked round at his team, all shuffling nervously and looking at the deck. He kicked the coffee table with a huge boot. The leg splintered, the table toppled, the glass top cracked. 'NOW!'

The crew sprang into action. Most of the men started picking up the bodies, another held the door. Branko watched them disappear into a passageway, door swinging shut behind them. His shoulders dropped, chest deflating, he ran a huge hand over his stubbly head and turned back to look at me. His breathing had almost returned to normal. I shuffled half a step closer to the knife embedded in the wood panelling.

A woman opened a door to my left, which I guessed led to the bridge. She walked straight to Branko. She looked familiar, her hair was pulled up in a ponytail that showed off a shaved patch that'd been glued back together, and a large dressing had been applied to a bloody-looking wound on her cheek.

I looked down at my shoes, rubbing my eyes to cover my face as I remembered who she was. The driver of that BMW in La Rochelle. She'd seen me – only briefly, speeding through those narrow streets, but if I'd recognised her then she could recognise me. I shuffled sideways again, could see the black blade sticking from the wood in the corner of my eye. Branko was clearly unstable. A knife was better than nothing.

'The freighter's moving away again,' the woman said in a Brummie accent.

Branko grunted. 'Are they holding course?'

'Yes, running for Plymouth.'

I wondered how quickly I could reach up and pull the knife. I'd have to be fast.

'We follow,' Branko said. 'Keep me updated.'

I heard the door slam and looked up to see the driver had gone, leaving just me and Branko. He was gazing down at the bloodstained rug. *This is it, this is my opportunity.* I pictured pulling the knife from the wall, spinning round, launching it at Branko. One fluid movement, I'd be across the room and on him in a second, he'd be dead before he hit the deck. I edged closer again, tensed my right arm, ready to grab the knife.

'You!' Branko shouted. 'What did you do to their engines?'

I paused. Branko was looking at me, I flexed my fingers. 'I removed the electrics.' Everything depended on how quickly I could rip the knife from the wood and bury it deep into his throat before he could shout, move, or realise what was happening.

'Your sabotage obviously didn't work.'

'I just wanted to slow them down so you could catch up. It worked fine.'

'Who is on board? How many?'

'Four left. Captain, the doctor, the radio operator, and the first mate.'

'And the others?'

Branko turned away, grinding bits of coffee table into the bloody rug with his boot. This was my chance. I kept talking normally as I reached for the knife. 'Tyler killed some of the crew. We killed him and his mercenaries.'

The far door opened, I dropped my hand as three of Branko's team entered the room. Branko walked towards me, reached up and pulled the knife from the wall. He wiped it on his trousers and put a meaty arm around my shoulders. 'Come below, we'll get a drink, and then you can tell me more about the crew while we chase down that ship. It's going to be a long night, I think.'

Chapter Fifty-five

Outskirts of Poitiers
Early hours of this morning

The balaclava was itchy but I didn't want to get complacent; I hadn't seen any CCTV cameras in the rest stop but that didn't mean there weren't any. I heard Ringo's zip in the darkness, he muttered something.

'You can piss with the bag on your head,' I whispered.

I was in no rush to get back in the car. After so long in the bucket seat, the stiff suspension and droning exhaust was taking its toll. I savoured the cold night air and sound of the wind in the branches. Ringo was handcuffed to a tree while I stood silently to one side in the bushes, one eye on him and the other on the path back to the layby. The bag on his head twitched at every sound: an owl deep in the woods; the occasional rush of tyres as lights sped through the trees, whistling along the autoroute beyond. Whispers flitted past my ears, shapes behind the bushes in the darkness, gone every time I turned my head. I stopped, screwed my eyes shut, breathed deeply.

The voices were getting louder, the shadows closing in. I needed my tablets. I reminded myself this was merely a patch of wasteland next to the motorway, a pocket of that strange hinterland separating industrial units and business parks, verges between motorways and the undergrowth behind superstores. Or in this case behind a toilet block and a few picnic benches. A pocket humans had allowed nature to reclaim. It was not the cursed woods of horror films, no matter how much a mind marinated in adrenaline and starved of sleep wanted it to be.

I'd hit the outskirts of Poitiers without incident, my satnav told me there were several petrol stations in easy reach. Just over an hour out from La Rochelle and bang on target, time-wise – not a bad job, all things considered. I'd had to stop for petrol twice on the run from Geneva but I hadn't seen a tail.

Although thirty seconds ago a car had pulled in to the rest stop.

I hadn't noticed at first. Stupid of me, negligent. Potentially deadly. Holderness had been right on both counts, I was slipping, though I'd never agree aloud.

The car's lights blinked back on, it reversed, beams briefly sweeping the trees in front of me as it turned. At the end of the car park it accelerated, red lights disappearing as it rejoined the autoroute.

I pulled my balaclava up, scratched my nose, pulled it back down again.

'Lock your hands again.'

Ringo followed the instructions without a second thought, I unlocked him from the tree. Another push and he was shuffling back through the undergrowth and along the path as I hung back, pistol in hand, eyes scanning the car park for any more visitors.

As we approached the edge of the trees something indistinct crept along the wall of the toilet block, a huge demon, limbs all splayed across the brickwork. Over twenty-four hours since I'd had a tablet, it didn't even phase me. I knew it was a hallucination, they were more frequent now, especially in the dark. I carried on walking, tried to focus on the now, on the journey I still had to make to reach the ship, before hot food and a bed.

I rushed forward, grabbing a handful of Ringo's ski jacket and bringing my pistol up quickly as the shape by the toilets suddenly took form, a man hiding in the shadows, watching, waiting for us.

'You move and he dies,' I said, holding the pistol up under my captive's ribs.

The man froze, then slowly stood upright as we emerged from the trees, gun held firmly in one hand.

He stepped forward into the moonlight. It was Branko, the big Serbian, and he did not look happy. I realised he'd been looking the other way, watching my car. The car I'd just seen leaving must have dropped him off.

Branko smiled. 'Where do you think you can go?'

Ringo flinched in my grasp, twitching, I held firm, pistol out slightly so he could get a good look at it. It didn't seem to bother him a great deal, he just kept that big Desert Eagle on us. Thankfully, since I'd switched their clothes, he didn't realise the man under the hood was not the same man I'd kidnapped from him.

'Back away,' I said. 'Slowly.'

His smile glowed in the moonlight. 'You need him alive, I think.' He didn't move.

I squeezed the trigger, just enough to take up some pressure, angling myself behind Ringo, using him as a shield though knowing full well that big .50 calibre bullet would rip through both of us.

'One less white supremacist in the world, the only difference to me is the valeting bill for my car. Back away or I perforate his lungs.'

Branko took a step backwards, still holding the gun rock-steady. I ground the barrel of my HK deeper into the ribs under the stupid orange ski jacket so he couldn't see my hand shaking.

He continued to back away, I sidestepped, edging across the grass towards my car.

I reached the kerb and risked a glance behind, nothing, we were alone. Not for long; the car that'd dropped him off couldn't be far, I looked up the slip road onto the autoroute. Nothing there.

I turned back to see Branko had his head tilted, whispering into a mic. Radio or hands-free phone. Either way, I had to move. I put my left hand in my pocket, holding down the button to unlock the car. Amber light flashed across the car park. I'd made it halfway, Branko still watching me with an amused look on his face.

'We will find you,' he said. 'And when we do, we will *not* kill you.'

I reached my car, held down the unlock button, all the windows lowered. I felt behind me and opened the boot. Now was the tricky part.

I edged round the far side of the car, holding my captive at arm's length as I extended back as far as I could, putting the car between us and Branko. Eyes on the big man, right hand gripping the pistol in my captive's ribs. I pushed him sideways into the boot.

Branko's gun flashed, something pulled on my hoody. I jumped behind my car, thrusting my left hand through the open rear window and grabbing the MP5 from the back seat. I pulled the trigger inside the car, a burst of automatic fire ripped into the toilet building. Branko ducked as chips of stone and plaster exploded across the grass. I pulled the submachine gun out of the car, another burst with it plus five rapid shots with the pistol saw Branko retreating behind the building. I slammed the boot lid shut. Lights flashed in the trees from the approach road. His ride was coming up, fast.

I stumbled as I ran to my door, pain flared through my side, dropping me to my knees. I put a hand on my ribs and winced. Branko appeared and fired again, I squeezed the trigger continuously as I yanked the door open, the MP5 ran dry. I threw it into the car and turned, firing my pistol five times in the direction of the approaching car. It skidded to a halt.

I jumped into the driver's seat, turned the key with one hand while still firing at the toilets with the other, the engine roared.

'Run, pig!' Branko shouted behind me. 'Run!'

Into first, I mashed the accelerator as the pistol clicked empty, I threw it on the passenger seat and changed into second, then put a hand under my hoody. I gritted my teeth, my hand came away hot and very wet.

Chapter Fifty-six

Yacht *Zuben*

I looked around the superyacht's expensively decked-out cabin, all polished wood and cream leather. The guest berth wasn't to my taste, and the décor was not enhanced by the two corpses on the huge bed in the centre of the room. Four more were piled next to a wardrobe, naked. Owners or crew, either way now regretting spending Christmas moored up in La Rochelle marina.

'Come in, then.' Branko leaned back in a shiny steel and leather chair, propped his feet on the desk and held up a glass. '*Živeli.*'

'*A la tienne.*'

He took a sip and gestured at the naked bodies on the floor. 'This upsets you?'

I looked at the poor bastards. 'The rich float around in their palaces while we slave away in the engine rooms. No, it doesn't upset me.'

'A socialist?' He smiled, baring his teeth.

'I'll be anything you want for a price, which reminds me.' I gulped the burning liquid down and supressed the urge to cough. 'We didn't discuss my fee.'

'*If* we overtake that ship, and *when* you lead my team in killing everyone on board, *then* we can discuss your fee.'

I raised the empty glass. 'With pleasure. I have no loyalty to them.'

'As you've already shown.' He took his feet off the desk and reached for the vodka bottle. 'Tell me about this John Tyler.'

I shrugged, holding out my glass. 'I don't know anything about him. He chartered the boat, him plus passengers to England.'

Branko filled the glass to the brim and set the Stoli bottle back down on the floor. 'Where did he contact you? And when?'

'A week or so ago, in Santander.'

There was a knock at the door, one of the guards from upstairs entered with a carrier bag, shuffling to the wardrobe, eying me warily. Another man followed him in, a huge muscle-bound goon that I recognised as Boy George, one of the chalet security detail. The guy clearly thought he was Jack the Biscuit but from the way his eyes flitted and arms fidgeted he was out of his depth. He held the door open behind him.

I looked at Branko. He'd put his glass on the desk and had both huge hands on his knees, leaning forward. 'Sit down, sit down.' He nodded towards the bed.

I sat on the edge next to the bodies, watching the two goons in my peripheral vision, sizing up each and noting the positions of those holsters.

'I am a fan of watches.' Branko pulled up his right sleeve. 'This is a Rolex Double Red Sea-Dweller from 1968. It is expensive watch, but it is functional. Good watches are better investment than gold, but only if you choose carefully. I have a few Breitling Superoceans and an Omega Seamaster. I would lose money on some, gain on others. I even have a 1967 orange-faced Doxa Sub

300T, pre-sychron.' He shrugged. 'I was a diver, you see. I trained Russian commandos. You wear your watch on your right, I wonder if you are a diver also?'

I smiled. 'Only in warm water.' I took a sip, wondering if he had a point.

'We will fix that soon enough.' His smile had been as fake as a shark's to begin with, but now it dropped completely. 'That is a Bremont Supermarine on a NATO strap, is it not?' He pointed at my wrist, where my jumper had ridden up as I'd taken a drink. He got to his feet with a sigh. 'Not, I think, the watch of a French mechanic.'

I threw the glass at the guy on the right's face and sprang forward. He put his hands up to ward off the glass as I drove my right fist deep into his gut, a muted scream as he doubled over. In the doorway Boy George finally made a move. I grabbed the first guy's head, brought it down against my knee, grabbing his pistol from the holster as I spun him into his mate. They both stumbled and fell to the floor, I finished with a stamp to his head as I backed through the open doorway, bringing the gun up at Branko, squeezing the trigger.

My head exploded with light, everything stopped for a moment, no sound, no vision. I felt myself falling, my body wouldn't respond. Hands were all over me, sound came back with Branko barking orders. When I opened my eyes I had one guy on each arm, dragging me backwards. A woman stepped into the room – their driver – smirking, still holding up the M4 carbine she'd clubbed me with.

'This is him?' asked Branko.

The woman nodded. 'He was driving the Audi in La Rochelle.'

'I've never seen her before in my life!' I shouted.

Branko walked closer.

'I stole this watch from Tyler's body,' I said, straining at the hands pinning me.

Branko lashed out, lightning fast, pain shot through every nerve, every muscle seized. The goons either side let go as I dropped to the floor, gasping. Branko loomed above me, swinging his boot into my ribs several times in quick succession. Lights exploded behind my eyes, again I couldn't see or hear, couldn't move, wasn't sure if I was even breathing. Eventually the pain receded enough for me to cough and blink the tears from my eyes.

Branko stood over me, panting, rubbing a hand over his stubbled head. His knuckles were coated with blood. He grinned, reached down, pulled up my jumper. Doc's dressing had flapped open, the wound was welling up with dark blood, smearing on the shiny floor.

'That is a gunshot wound,' Branko said, eyes shining. The goons grabbed my arms, dragging me backwards, into the chair. 'And it looks infected.'

I was still stunned, his fist hit my face before I knew what'd happened. My eyes shut again, something popped, heat spilled down my front. I tried to breathe, blood filled my mouth. I spat, gasping for air through a crushed nose and mouthfuls of blood.

Strong hands pulled my arms behind the back of the chair, I strained but no good, I felt something bite into my wrists then the goons grabbed my legs. I threw my weight side to side but it was no use, the chair was big and heavy and my energy had left me, pouring out from various wounds. By the time I'd opened my eyes and blinked away more tears, they'd cable-tied my ankles to the chair legs.

Branko sat on the bed next to the bodies. The woman stepped forward, swinging the rifle around and driving it into my stomach. I gasped in pain but no sound came, I strained against the ties, gritting my teeth. She made to swing again but Branko put an arm out, holding her off.

He pointed to the bandage on the shaved patch of her head then gestured to the carrier bag on the floor. 'Don't worry, you can take payment from him soon. Go, see if we are in phone reception yet. You need to call our friends and have them meet us.'

She glared at me, slung the rifle and nodded, taking the goons with her, leaving us alone.

Branko picked up the carrier bag and placed it on the desk. 'So, John Tyler. This was not such a clever idea, was it? You thought you could come over here and kill us?'

'It crossed my mind.'

'You have a death wish?'

I could see my reflection in the mirror on the wardrobe. When I smiled my teeth looked yellow through blood still streaming from my nose. 'It's been noted several times.'

'You took something that does not belong to you.' He opened the carrier bag and reached inside, eyes on mine. He took out an extension lead and walked round the bed to plug it in behind the chair, placed the socket on the floor between my trainers. 'Where is the man you kidnapped in the Alps?'

'Somewhere you'll never find him.'

He reached back into the bag and lifted out a heavy belt sander, placing it on the desk, smiling as he saw the look in my eyes. 'We are closing in on your ship. We will board it, and yes, we *will* find him.' He took time to fold the carrier bag up and pushed it into a drawer in the desk.

My right arm trembled, my hand shook against the chair arm, Branko grinned, obviously mistaking it for fear.

He carried the sander over, narrowed his eyes, bending to plug it in. He stood, pulled the trigger, the noise made me jump. The sandpaper belt became a blur, a whirr of colour. He brought the spinning tip close to my face, I leaned away as much as I could. He touched the sandpaper to my ear, it burned, I gritted my teeth.

He let go of the trigger, the noise died down as the belt slowed. He dropped it in my lap. It jolted as the fly caught on the rough sandpaper.

'The first time you give me wrong answer,' he grabbed my ear in a huge paw, 'you will not be able to wear glasses again. The second wrong answer...' he looked down, 'you will not be able to do lots of things.' He looked back into my eyes. 'My man is still alive, yes?'

I looked down at the sander then up into Branko's smug face. 'Very much alive. By now he'll be spilling his guts to save himself.' Branko's smugness turned to confusion, I smiled with satisfaction. 'Your man never got on the ship.'

'Impossible. We followed you from Geneva. We watched you all the way. We saw your car loaded onto the ship.'

'You fucking idiot.' I chuckled, spat blood. The flow was stopping. 'He never left Geneva.'

'No... no...' The penny was dropping, slowly, beads of sweat broke out across his head as he pieced it together in real time. 'You couldn't have predicted...'

'Who do you think tipped off your organisation to the *Tiburon*? Who told your informants that something was about to go down and you'd be wise to keep the ship under surveillance?'

Now he was confused. 'But that was a week ago.'

'I'm the rat, you bellend. Kudos for getting someone aboard as part of the crew: I'll be honest, I hadn't counted on that. All for nothing though.'

'No!' Branko's face was practically burning. 'Where is he?' he shouted, resting a hand on the sander.

'Long gone!' I needed him to lose his temper and hit me. 'Don't you get it yet, you stupid bastard? I'm just a bloody rabbit.'

He picked up the sander, the other hand was flexing at his side, making a fist.

'I tipped you off myself, I gave you all the information. I'm a rabbit running round the racing track just in front of you, this whole operation was a lure.'

'But you kidnapped him from Château des Aigles, we followed you to Geneva.'

'Yeah, and I left him in Geneva, you thick fucking bag of steroids.' *Come on you bastard, punch me!* 'I left him for another team to pick up while I drove off with that dickhead in the boot,' I nodded at Ringo's body on the bed. 'You've been following us on that stinking ship, while your guy was being whisked back to England on a helicopter.'

'If what you're saying is true, you could have got on the helicopter with him and been back in England now.' He put the sander on the dressing table, his other hand stopped flexing, face turning into a smug grin as if he thought he'd uncovered a plot hole. 'Why did you need a diversion?'

'Tell you the truth, I'm scared of flying.' I smiled. 'But the real reason was to draw you out. To draw all of you out here into the middle of the sea where no one can save you.'

Chapter Fifty-seven

Yacht *Zuben*

Branko's expression flipped several times in seconds as we went from disbelief, through anger, to realisation. He strode to the door and flung it open, grabbing steroids Boy George, the goon on guard. 'Get upstairs. Tell them to stop – no – tell them to turn around. Is there anything on the radar?' Boy George turned to leave, Branko dragged him back into the room. 'Watch him, I'll go.'

His huge boots pounded away, the goon closed the door and leaned against it, eying me coldly.

'You know why he's running, don't you?'

He continued to stare but said nothing.

'He's shitting it. You're all about to die.'

His face was impassive.

'You stupid fascist pricks. You've just followed me all the way from your nice safe enclave in the Alps, where you were untouchable, to the largest naval base in Western Europe.'

His face changed then. 'Shut up, you little wanker,' he spat in Danny Dyer. 'You think the snowflake Navy gives a shit?'

The deck shifted beneath our feet as the engines changed pitch.

'Your boss thinks so. I'll tell you what's happening right now upstairs. They've just picked up a low-flying helicopter out of Plymouth on the marine radar.'

'Shut the fuck up.'

'And right now that helicopter is on its way to blow us out of the water.'

The deck shifted again as the yacht slewed broadside to a wave then picked up speed. Boy George grabbed the desk to stop himself going arse over tit, eyes darting to the window.

'Don't worry,' I said. 'That chopper's gonna have a wasted journey.'

'Shut *up*,' he hissed through his teeth, eyes flitting between the door and the window.

'Because before it gets here, I'm gonna kill everyone on this posh little boat. Every single scrote, but you should feel proud, cos I'm gonna start with you.'

The deck steadied, he regained some bravado and took a step forward, face glowing. 'I'd like to see you try.'

'Well I already sent two of your mates off a cliff.'

The punch landed square on my cheekbone, the chair rocked but didn't tip. *Not hard enough, matey.*

I spat blood onto the cream rug. 'You're much uglier close up. You do Boy George a disservice.'

'The fuck you on about?'

'I've had my cross hairs on you loads of times. Should have pulled the trigger, put you out of your misery.'

'Bollocks.'

'You're their little skivvy arse-licker, I watched you putting logs on the fire and getting the big boys drinks.' I grinned. 'You were doing their washing the other night.'

The second punch landed in the same place again, rocking me backwards, he grabbed a fistful of T-shirt and pulled me back to him, face right up in mine. 'One more word and you'll be shitting teeth tomorrow.'

I seriously doubted it given his efforts so far.

'Playing tough guys in your nice warm cabin, you overestimate yourselves. It's been your downfall.'

His third punch was better: it still didn't measure up to Branko's sledgehammer fists but at least it knocked me sideways onto the floor. I winced as my arm hit, crushed under the weight of the chair and me tied to it.

I spat more blood. 'Yeah, for sure I'll kill you first.'

His boot hit my ribs, I turned away and held the pain down while I concentrated on what I had to do. I worked my tongue around my teeth, a fresh cut inside my cheek, yet more blood filling my mouth. I pushed my tongue out and spat again, rolling around in pain as Boy George looked down at me with a big stupid grin on his shiny red face.

I jumped the chair up off the floor and crashed back down, he leapt back then laughed at me flailing around. My fingers crept across the floor until I found what I'd been searching for in the puddle of blood, one of the razor blades I'd pushed up next to my gums, the only thing small enough to bring aboard when I knew I'd be well searched, but more than enough to turn the tables in most situations. I felt the edge, jammed my thumb against the back, and steadied it between my fingers.

Boy George grabbed me, lifting the chair and standing it back up.

'You think you're hard, don't you?' he said. 'Fuckin' mercs.'

I worked the blade against the cable ties on my wrists. 'Harder than a pretend soldier.'

'Who's pretending?'

I coughed again and wheezed, trying to draw breath. 'Says the man who buys his gear from Millets.' I looked at him, tried to speak again, descending into a coughing fit. He leaned in closer. The cable tie around my wrist snapped open.

'Complacent,' I whispered. I grabbed his ear in my left fist, yanked his head down towards my face, brought my other hand round. I plunged the razor blade into the side of his neck, he pulled his arms up, trying to fend me off, but too late. I pushed him off me, the blade flicked through the flesh, he staggered back. A spurt of blood decorated the wardrobe, he pressed a hand to his neck as more bubbled up around his fingers, his eyes were wide. I flicked the blade across the cable ties on my ankles, jumped to my feet, grabbed his stupidly tight T-shirt, pulled him towards me, sticking my foot out, dropping him off balance. He stumbled, still silent, hands about his own neck as his life spilled away.

I ran to the door, locked it.

The man's face had paled as the blood pooled beneath him. His arms sagged, a feeble pulse of blood spurted onto the mirrored wardrobe door, and he was gone.

I dragged Ringo's body to the edge of the bed, ripped open his shirt, exposing pale skin beneath.

A wide patch of duct tape covered his belly, I ran the razor blade across it and dropped it on the bed. I reached into the void and pulled out a small, tightly bound plastic package, dropped it on the bed, pulled another out.

The first contained my satphone, which was waterproof anyway but at least wasn't covered in Ringo's insides. I pushed it into the leg pocket of my combats. I sliced open the second bin bag, took out my HK pistol and screwed the suppressor into place, cocking it, pushing the safety off.

I dashed to the window, pulled the blinds open. Outside was pitch black but the waves were clearly washing the glass from left to right, which gave me the orientation of the boat. I opened the drawers of the desk, nothing interesting. In the bedside table I found a pack of prescription painkillers, I necked a couple, washed them down with a generous mouthful of Stoli from the bottle rolling around on the floor. It wasn't a lot but that plus the adrenaline I could feel surging in my guts, shaking my hands, would have to do for now.

Crossing to the door, pistol down low, I slid off the lock and opened it. The passageway was a far cry from those of the *Tiburon*, with its pipes crawling the ceiling, condensation-damp rusting walls, and grime-infused tread plates. Here the polished wooden floor shone in the glow from recessed LEDs along the skirting and ceiling, framed artwork took up the spaces between the doors stretching in both directions.

Footsteps echoed, I ducked back into the room, pressing myself against the wall alongside the door.

The steps came closer, pausing outside the cabin. An arm appeared, a man stepped into the room, taking in the scene, the arterial spray, the body of his mate sprawled next to the bed. His mouth opened to shout just as his head completed its circuit of the room, landing on me and the business end of my gun. He hesitated, sneered, hand going for the holster at his thigh.

It only made it halfway when the barrel of my gun whipped across his temple, he stumbled, bringing his arms up, I kicked him backwards, into the wardrobe. The door cracked in half and dropped from the frame as he landed in a heap of designer clothes. He scrabbled at his holster again, I'd given him plenty of chances so stopped fucking around and put two bullets into his chest. His fingers twitched, I put a third through his forehead.

I pushed the splintered wardrobe door away and grabbed a fire extinguisher from a bracket inside, laid it in the passageway outside the door, and wedged it against the wall with a folded-up dress to hold it. With a glance back at the window to orientate myself, I set off aft.

A door opened ahead. One of Branko's goons stepped out and immediately retreated back into the room as I accelerated, shoulder-barging the door before he could close it. Another was halfway out of an en-suite, already reaching for a gun on the bed. I squeezed the trigger three times rapidly, the crisp white sheets speckled red as the man dropped to the floor. I punched sideways, catching the first man under the chin, swung the pistol round, bringing it down on the nape of his neck. He crumpled to the floor. I pulled his pistol from his holster, took out the magazine and pushed it into my pocket, grabbed the other off the bed and did the same, then grabbed the man's knife from the sheath on his thigh.

I opened the window above the bed as wide as possible, held there on the bracket. Salt hit my nostrils, sea spray misted the pillows. I grabbed one then went for the wardrobe. It contained another full-size fire extinguisher, I backed into the passageway and placed it on the pillow outside the door to stop it rolling around.

The heavy door at the end opened onto a more functional-looking staircase than the areas I'd seen so far: less polished veneer, more bare steel and pipework. No prizes for guessing this led down to the guts of the super-yacht. With one last glance along the passage, I closed the door softly and made my way down to the lowest level. The vibrations rose as I stepped off the bottom step, grabbing the handle I presumed would take me through the aft bulkhead into the engine room.

I was right, and it was beautiful. I closed the door behind me, jumped the few short steps down to the spotless floor. Three enormous, sixteen-cylinder Rolls Royce engines stood at attention across the room, each as tall as me. I scanned the one immediately in front of me, the control screen and data dials, the leads and wiring harnesses, the air intakes, exhaust manifolds, turbochargers. Ironic, since I'd come aboard masquerading as Poubelle, that our places had been switched. I needed to disable the engines, and fast, to buy the others some time.

He'd cut the *Tiburon*'s wiring, but that had been easily repairable. Had Branko kept any of the crew alive? Did he have his own mechanics who'd be able to make repairs? Best to assume so. I looked across the pipework. Destroy the air intakes? Jam the turbos? There were a million and one ways to hobble the engines, but nothing seemed permanent enough.

The door opened, I looked up as a man walked in. I fired twice and ducked behind the engine as bullets replied. His gun wasn't silenced, the sound was sure to bring others running. I'd just lost the element of surprise.

I chanced a look and fired a couple of times as his legs disappeared behind the far engine. I paused, then fired several more times to keep his head down, before moving around the side. I needed to control that door, that choke point. If more of them got in here it'd be over.

I leaned round the engine and fired again, over the top of the far engine so the bullets would ricochet around and give him something to think about. I slid out the empty magazine and took one of the Glock ones from my pocket, fingers a blur as I flicked rounds from the latter and loaded the former.

The door opened again just as I'd slid it back into place, I waited until the figure crept into the room then fired twice. He dropped, screaming, writhing on the floor. I took a more careful aim and fired into his head. The racket stopped.

The other guy was still in here somewhere, but I daren't move away from the corner with my vantage point of the door. I noticed a couple of fire extinguishers were stood in brackets at the end of each engine, one foam and one water. I grabbed the water one.

I pulled the knife, holding it in my left hand, backed slowly to the far starboard engine. Above my head was the air intake. Slowly standing, eyes flicking between either side of the engine in front of me, alert for that thug, I stuck the knife up into the pipe leading to the air filter. I ragged it around, then reached behind me and pulled. The cover popped off, pieces of torn air filter rained down. I tore the safety tab from the water extinguisher and sprayed it down the air intake. The effect was instantaneous – first the engine spluttered and struggled, not getting enough oxygen, each stroke failing to combust the damp fuel mixture. I kept spraying until something went bang and the engine juddered to a halt. That bang was one of the cylinders fighting physics as it filled with water, its piston cycling up, trying to compress it, and finding that water is not compressible. The pressure was forced down, bending the connecting rod and probably fatally knackering the crank too. One engine down, two to go.

A gunshot echoed around the room, I ducked and rolled back towards the middle engine as I caught a glimpse of the guy crawling over the top of the furthest one. I peered up and watched as he slid belly-first along the top, working himself down among the pipes where I couldn't shoot him, but he could see the whole room. He was hidden behind the cylinder heads. From where I crouched I couldn't get the angle to shoot him without revealing myself.

I threw the knife over the engine in front of me, sending it sailing towards the far side of the room. I saw him jerk as his head turned to follow the noise.

I stood, firing several times at the oil cooler above him. He shouted in anger, then when he realised the entire engine was pissing scalding oil onto his legs he shouted in pain, shuffling forward, dropping his gun to scrabble at the engine, pulling himself away as his legs began to cook. He turned, face contorted in agony, I only had to fire once this time. He slumped forward, body sliding off the engine and thudding to the floor.

I ran round to the other side of the middle engine, grabbing its extinguisher on the way, used it to smash the air filter clean off. I stuck the nozzle in, jamming it against the top of the engine so it kept spraying. The engine juddered, the whole boat shook as the cylinders drowned. Already I was at the far end of the room, smashing the air filter from the third engine. The boat rolled more as it slowed, limping on one engine. The revs increased as someone on the bridge tried to compensate for the drop in propulsion.

Feet echoed on the steps to my left, I dropped and turned to the door. No one entered.

I moved to the wall, sliding along it until I was hidden behind the door. A gun entered first: this was a cautious one. It was followed by an arm, then a head, face obscured by long dark hair. Their driver.

I grabbed her arm, spinning her into the room, bringing my gun up. A gunshot cracked, not mine or hers. I twisted, pulling her round in front of me as a shield as the guy who'd been behind her in the doorway struggled to get a decent aim, I brought my own gun up with my free hand, she rammed an elbow into my stomach. I dropped my gun but managed to keep hold of her arm as I doubled over, pulling her to the floor with me. As we hit I grabbed her gun, sliding my finger over hers, pulling the trigger over and over again at the doorway as we lay on the floor. Bullet holes punched through the brilliant white wall cladding, the man in the doorway's mouth flapped open as perfect red circles appeared in his T-shirt then proceeded to spill down his belly.

The woman snarled, reaching for her boot, pulling an evil-looking knife. I managed to get my arm up to block her forearm, the knife stopped centimetres from my face. I twisted my head, she whipped her knife round again, glancing the side of my arm, still gripping her pistol.

Instinctively I let go, rolling away across the floor and springing to my feet. As I turned, I saw her bring the pistol up, she pulled the trigger. It clicked, fortunately we'd emptied the magazine into her friend in the doorway. She hissed and threw it at me. I ducked as it bounced off the engine behind. I was just steadying myself when she came at me again, knife up. I feinted left then went right as she struggled to adjust her momentum, I turned with her, grabbing her arm as she passed, sticking out my leg and pushing her onward into the engine. She tripped, spun, kicking out as she fell, catching me in my ribs. I stumbled, dropping to my knees, momentarily stunned.

She somehow turned her fall into a graceful roll, coming back up onto her feet like a cat.

As I tried to get my breath her arm whipped round, the knife flashed, I dropped to the floor again just as the knife cut the air above me. In the corner of my eye I saw her bending down, I dived away to the far end of the engine as she swept up my pistol and brought it round towards me.

Chapter Fifty-eight

Yacht *Zuben*

My silenced pistol coughed once in her hands, I rolled over, fingers scrabbling across the floor. The bullet tore through the pipework above the engine, a second gunshot echoed, this one deafening in the confined space, her eyes went wide. My pistol wavered in her hand, I pulled my arm from under me and fired again, her eyes glazed over, she slid to the floor, revealing a spray of blood on the engine behind her.

I dropped the oily Glock, wiping my hands on my legs, slick from where I'd picked the gun up off the floor, out of the puddle of hot oil beneath the body of her shipmate. I walked to her, gave her a tap with my trainers, retrieved my own gun, pushed it into my trousers, jogged to the door.

The stairwell was empty but I could hear voices somewhere above. Behind me, an alarm started barking for attention. I looked at the control screen on the first engine, flashing red. Oil pressure warning. It was about to shut itself down thanks to spilling its lubricant all over the floor. That'd put all three engines out of action, two of them couldn't be fixed without a shipyard and these idiots wouldn't get the third fixed this side of Christmas.

The third engine shuddered and finally went silent, just the noise of the warning alarm blaring in the engine room and the crash of water against the fibreglass hull. Almost immediately the room tipped up, I held on to the bulkhead as the waves spun the dead boat round. I waited until she righted herself then bent to pick up the pistol the dead guy had dropped in the doorway. A Sig Sauer with a full magazine. I pressed into the wall alongside the door, looking up the stairs. The voices were calling to each other, Branko shouting orders at someone else, I wondered how many minions he had left. Two in the bedroom, two in the other bedroom, three in the engine room. I'd counted eight thugs plus the driver. God knows how many more had been on the bridge. I was still grossly outnumbered.

'He has nowhere to go,' Branko shouted above. 'Get him up here.'

I ducked back as someone appeared at the top of the stairs, raised my gun ready. A small object bounced off the wall above me and thudded down the stairs, rolling into the doorway. A flashbang.

I kicked it backwards into the engine room as I launched through the doorway, up the stairs two at a time. The stun grenade exploded behind me. The walls muffled the blast, my ears rang sharply, I took another breath and stepped up, firing into the passageway. Shapes flashed, screams as figures ducked or fell into cabins either side, gunfire erupted. I pressed myself into the wall, aiming low, at the fire extinguisher I'd placed by the far door, and fired. A white cloud instantly filled the passageway, blocking their view of me. Coughing and spluttering accompanied a hail of fresh bullets as the dense cloud rolled towards me. A shadow moved in a doorway to my left, I aimed at the closer extinguisher and fired. The fog grew thicker. I fired again to keep their heads in, held my breath and dived through a doorway into the nearest cabin.

On the far side of the room the window was sprayed with blood from the guy I'd tagged coming out of the en-suite but, crucially, it was still wide open on the bracket, just as I'd left it. Water sloshed over the ledge onto the bed as another wave slammed the side, I shifted my balance, pushed the Sig into my pocket, kicked the door closed behind me.

I saw the movement from behind the closing door too late. Branko hit me like a train, driving me across the room and into the desk with a crunch that bent me sideways, driving the wind from my lungs and smashing my head through the cladding on the wall. My eyes dimmed as I was vaguely aware of Branko dragging me by the lapels, then an odd sensation of weightlessness which ended with a smash of glass as I hit the mirror on the far wall. I landed on the floor, still winded.

I let the room stop spinning, pushed up onto my hands and knees, blinking away tears to see my hands were bloody. I was pressing down onto shards of mirror, I rocked back onto my knees and plucked a small piece of glass from my arm, before I flew backwards as Branko's boot connected with my stomach. I rolled over, reaching out, grabbing a shard in my right hand, swiping it at his leg. He backed away, I sprang to my feet, gripping the glass in a bloody fist, watching him carefully. He weaved side to side then darted forward, one arm ready to parry my inevitable strike, the other poised to follow up. Instead, I stepped forward and turned inside him, into his arms, bringing my hand down hard as he encircled me in a bear hug.

The shard sank into flesh, at the expense of my hand. He shouted in anger and released me, clawing at the glass sticking out of his thigh. Blood spilled between the fingers of my right hand, I crouched, spun to face him, reaching across for the Sig with my left. It was an awkward angle, the gun jammed on my pocket. He went for the Desert Eagle under his arm. I kicked high, he blocked it but in doing so couldn't draw his weapon. He tried with the other hand and I kicked again, forcing him to defend himself. He turned side-on, hunched over, finally managed to pull the gun, drawing it round onto me in one fluid movement. I grabbed a pillow from the bed and flicked it at his head, not the best weapon but it made him flinch, meaning the bullet ejected from the barrel punched through the ceiling instead of me. I grabbed a corner of the duvet and ran, throwing it over him.

More gunshots erupted, punching holes through the fabric and into the walls. I managed to pull out the Sig with my injured right hand, fumbled it, then fired into the mass. Five, six, seven times, the slide stuck back as the gun ran dry. No idea how many times I'd hit him, or where, but he toppled backwards and that was good enough for me.

I dropped the bloody Sig, wiped my hand on my trousers. The door opened, faces crammed the corridor outside, the cavalry had arrived too late for their boss.

I jumped on the bed just as the mass started moving. Branko pushed the duvet out of the way and stood up. One of the goons lifted a rifle, I fumbled with my jumper, trying to get to my own HK pistol. Branko pushed the man's hand down, smiling. He looked at me as he slowly unzipped his fleece, revealing body armour. Only a couple had actually hit him, trickles of blood on his neck said one

had done some damage but clearly he didn't seem to think
so.

He raised his gun, grinning.

I leapt backwards, straight through the open window,
out into the cold night and the colder sea.

Chapter Fifty-nine

English Channel

The window wasn't high. As far as bullet-avoiding leaps into the sea went it didn't rank up there with my worst. I dove straight down, ignoring the stinging saltwater in fresh wounds, striking out underwater into the black. These yachts have a fairly shallow draft, no more than a couple of metres, and being a streamlined, high-speed superyacht, she had a relatively narrow beam. Bullets sliced the water around me as I pulled hard under the hull, easily clearing the keel. When my lungs burned and I couldn't swim any further I came up on the other side, forcing myself to break the water slowly.

The waves lifted me almost as high as the boat's deck, I'd come up a few metres off the port side. She was being rolled around in the swell, dead in the water. The glow from her lights lit the crests all around me. A shout from the flybridge, I ducked back under and swam further away. When I surfaced again I'd only gained another few metres, but at least it was a few metres in the right direction. I treaded water, watching figures running around on the deck and flybridge, leaning over the railings. Occasionally a flash of torchlight on the waves, the crack of a pistol as they fired blindly into the sea.

Lights came on at the rear of the deck, the steps I'd climbed up were brightly illuminated and the sea beneath the stern glowed a deep green. The rear of the yacht opened up like a boot lid, more shouting as people ran down the steps to the low swim platform, on level with the sea.

Something moved. I realised they were launching the yacht's tender. An outboard barked into life, revving and grumbling as a couple of dark figures climbed on board. More movement, more noise as a jet ski started up, immediately setting off in the opposite direction. Another jet ski shot aft, moving in ever-increasing circles behind the stricken yacht.

The launch revved and set off on my side of the yacht, a powerful spotlamp flared across the waves. They moved slowly along the yacht's low, pointed hull, lamp scanning the sea in long sweeping arcs. The boat turned, looping back towards the stern of the yacht, the beam of its lamp moving ever closer. I kicked hard, rising out of the water, shouted, then dropped back under. The beam played over the sea nearby, the boat adjusted its course and buzzed towards me.

I could see the two people on board, their eyes searching the dark waves. One guy hanging over the side, gun in hand, another at the wheel, one hand on the spotlamp. I pulled my pistol from my waistband with my injured hand, holding the barrel above the water, and waited for them to draw closer.

Thanks to the suppressor I'd fired three times before the guy at the wheel realised anything was happening. As the man hanging over the side collapsed backwards the skipper pushed the throttle to the stops, and the boat shot forward. Unfortunately for him it was too late.

I grabbed the handle at the front of the boat as it accelerated, bringing my right hand up and firing point-blank into the guy behind the wheel. He screamed, falling backwards out of sight. The boat was skimming now, jumping on the waves, crashing against my head. I threw my pistol into the boat and grabbed the ropes along the rigid inflatable sidewall, wincing as they bit into the cut on my palm, swinging myself up and over.

I rolled into the boat, onto my hands and knees, found the throttle and pulled it back. The boat slowed, still rolling heavily but not crashing through sheets of water now. The guy that'd been at the wheel was groaning in the back of the boat, I grabbed his tactical webbing vest, picked him up, dragged him over the side. The other guy was already dead, I threw him overboard too and looked at the lights of the yacht receding into the distance. I flexed my injured fingers, still bleeding, and picked up my gun from the water washing around in the bottom of the boat, its grip resting against the open wound on my palm. The boat's previous occupants knew only too well that I could hold and fire it, but it was a toss-up whether I'd be more accurate with my injured right hand or working left.

The dashboard exploded in a shower of glass and plastic, the crack of a gunshot chased the bullet across the waves, followed by the sound of a jet ski approaching rapidly. I pushed the throttle forward and grabbed the wheel, swinging into the seat.

The jet ski was approaching from my left. I turned left, into him, narrowing the angle. A burst of light, he was firing at me. I turned the spotlamp onto the jet ski, it was Branko, one hand on the handlebars, the other gripping his Desert Eagle. It jumped in his hand again, I ducked as a bullet tore into the front of the boat.

I threw myself behind the console, letting the little boat surge forward on its own as I lay in the bloody water washing around. We flashed past each other, he swooped round to follow as I reached up, throttled back to slow down, turning to aim at the noise buzzing behind me. The jet ski jumped over the waves in my wake, racing towards me in a zigzag. I fired several times, but he was too far away and moving too erratically to get a decent shot. Gunshots replied as he flew past again, the side of the dinghy exploded in a rush of air. I was a much bigger, brighter, slower target. I shoved my gun into my pocket as water rushed around me.

The boat dug into the waves, petrol stung my eyes. Something had ruptured, either the engine or the tank, didn't matter which because neither was good news. I climbed back into the seat behind the wheel. The prow of the little boat was dipping beneath the oncoming waves. The jet ski was turning for another pass. I pushed the throttle to its stop again, the prow picked up temporarily but was soon swamped. Behind me the outboard spluttered.

I pulled back the throttle and ducked off the seat just in time as the jet ski flashed past again, several more bullets punching into the rubber sides. The outboard coughed again, the boat lurched. It stank now, awash with petrol and steadily slipping beneath the waves.

As the jet ski started a wide turn, I jumped around the seat and opened the panel in its base. The second jet ski flashed across the beam of the spotlight in front, heading towards me. I spotted one of the goon's pistols in the water in the bottom of the boat, grabbed it, racking the slide. I aimed forward, emptied the mag towards the approaching sound and threw it over the side. The jet ski accelerated, engine rising in pitch as it swooshed away into darkness, temporarily warded off. I crouched back down to the storage compartment, pulling everything out until I found what I was looking for in a waterproof box at the bottom. Flares.

I pushed the throttle forward again to coax the last dregs from the engine, popped the top off a flare and struck it. I waited for the buzz of the two jet skis to approach then grabbed a lifejacket from the compartment, dropping the flare as I jumped over the side.

I held myself under the water, felt the crump of the explosion above as the petrol ignited. I kicked away, staying under as long as possible before breaking the surface. The boat had carried on droning away from me, finally coming to a stop a good hundred metres away, flaming wreckage flapping about on the waves.

The jet skis buzzed around it, shining torches across the waves, floating in ever-widening circles as I kicked away into the night. After a couple of minutes, the flames died away as the wreckage slipped beneath the surface. Soon after, the jet skis retreated back towards their stricken mothership, itself now a dim, distant dot.

I slid my arms into the lifejacket and inflated it, lying back, thinking about the last time I'd been adrift alone at sea. There I'd not been far from land, caught in the pull of the currents. Here I was still miles out to sea, in December, with only a lifejacket. Worse, I was barely in the Channel – more like the North Atlantic. I was exhausted, could feel warm blood still seeping from wounds as my skin numbed. I reckoned I had maybe fifteen, twenty minutes until hypothermia claimed me. I couldn't have swum back to the yacht even if I'd wanted to.

Chapter Sixty

English Channel

The *Tiburon* should at that precise moment have been circling back round in a wide arc. They'd have seen on the radar that the yacht was drifting, and thus my sabotage mission had been successful. Now it was time to complete their mission and pick me up.

Miller, Katanga, Doc, Nic and Marty. I trusted them to varying degrees, but I did know each of them would pull out the stops to get me back so I could transfer their bonuses – particularly now the yacht was no threat, and we were free to continue to Devon unmolested.

I reached into my leg pocket and pulled out the rugged little waterproof satphone. The screen lit up, I was glad I'd stuck it on charge earlier that afternoon. Two bars of signal out here on the open sea, thank God for technology. I cycled to a saved number and pressed call. Now I just hoped it'd be answered.

It was. Miller's voice was music to my ears.

'Wasn't sure I'd be hearing from you.'

'You doubted me?' I said in between mouthfuls of seawater.

'I never will again. What are your co-ordinates?'

I took the phone away from my ear and read the GPS numbers off the screen.

'We're five miles north-east of you.' The line crackled, he mumbled in the background, I could picture him turning to Kat at the wheel to give him a bearing. 'We're putting on power now, maybe ten minutes or so.'

'Less of the "or so", or I'll be dead when you get here.'

'You'd better not be, you're paying for the extra fuel.'

I ended the call to preserve the batteries, should I need it. I was reassured they were holding up their end of the bargain, for now at least, though I was acutely aware there was always the possibility of them double-crossing me.

Particularly the person who'd murdered Ringo in the hold of the ship.

Chapter Sixty-one

Tiburon

Nine minutes later I was back in my cabin, under a hot shower, with a pair of jeans begged from Nic and my last dry T-shirt laid on the bed, and my now hot and dry Converse still jammed up behind the heating pipes. Miller had put all speed on for Devon, which we'd decided was still a better option than the original destination of Poole, given the distinct possibility of an unfriendly welcoming committee in Dorset. As I dressed, I heard the speaker crackle in the passageway outside the door.

'If you're finished preening yourself, Blofeld, we're less than thirty minutes out. That yacht hasn't moved. You fucked them wicked good.'

I caught myself in the mirror on the way out, two black eyes coming up nicely, though weirdly my nose looked straighter than it had yesterday. I grabbed my grubby hoody from the heating pipes and thought about small victories.

I looked out of the porthole in the passageway outside the cabin and dialled Holderness on the satphone. It was a brief conversation, all business. My abduction and subsequent diversion mission had been successful, if bloodier than originally anticipated. The big fish had landed at a British airbase nearly twenty-four hours ago, and apparently he hadn't stopped singing. Arrests had already been made in the Netherlands, Belgium, and England. By next week, their paramilitary group would be extinct thanks to our altercation in the Alps a couple of nights ago and the activities of the last few hours. I gave Holderness the rough co-ordinates of the yacht for the Royal Navy coastal patrol that had been standing by to mop up. Branko in particular would make a nice prize. Holderness started ranting again about collateral damage. Apparently the French were upset – can't think why – about what they perceived to be an MI6 operation on their soil without their knowledge. Sounded like the phrase 'deniable asset', which Holderness often used in reference to me, was doing some heavy lifting.

I red-buttoned his moaning and pushed the phone into my pocket. Not my problem, politics and aftermath was why he got paid the big bucks.

My hand stung, wounds leaving sticky marks on the handrail as I made my way upstairs to my second appointment with Doc in a day.

He tutted when I entered, he already had his gear laid out on the table. 'Top off, Tyler.' He nodded towards the bed. 'I imagine as well as those new scrapes you've also undone the good work I did this morning?'

I threw my hoody on a chair and placed my phone and pistol on the desk. 'When you say "I've" undone it…' I winced as I pulled off my T-shirt, dropping it on the bed, then sat next to it.

'Yes, never you, is it? If I remember correctly, you are almost forty years old. You really ought to take some responsibility for your actions.'

'Responsibility! Remind me again why you were discharged from the Navy.'

He knelt in front of me and jabbed the wound with the handle of his scalpel. 'This is infected.'

I gritted my teeth. 'I followed the aftercare instructions.'

'The significant contusions developing across ninety per cent of your torso suggest otherwise.'

'I'm serious, Doc. Tell me again why you were discharged. Dishonourably.'

'You know why, lie back.' He poured something on the wound and proceeded to stitch me again.

'Killed someone in a bar fight on shore leave in South Africa, right?'

His eyes twinkled. 'Three people, not that there was any evidence.'

'Members of the FZAA?' He'd told me the story before, I knew they'd been heavies for a local white nationalist movement.

His frowned, eyes narrowing as the twinkling faded. 'Stop talking, you're pulling the wound.'

He worked in silence, I screwed my eyes shut as he jabbed the needle through me with vigour. When he'd finished, I sat up with a wince and held my right hand out.

'I was thinking this might need a stitch?'

He exhaled loudly and reached for the iodine again, probing the slices on my palm and fingers. When he'd finished applying a dressing he held up my left hand.

'This finger really should be rebroken and set,' he said, flexing it painfully. 'I can do it now if you…'

'No thanks,' I snatched my hand back.

He stood and walked over to his desk, pulling open a drawer. 'Take two of these.' He threw a box at me.

'Morphine? Where was this earlier?'

'I have a limited supply, and assumed – correctly as it now happens – that you'd be in greater need by the end of the day. Take two now and another couple later tonight.'

I tossed the box back to him. 'You won't blame me if I don't take tablets from you.'

He caught the box, cocked his head, frowning.

I shuffled on the bed. 'I know why you did it, and I know how. I just want to hear you say it.'

He moved quicker than his years suggested, snatching up my pistol and turning it on me in a flash.

'You're cleverer than you look, Tyler. Too clever.'

I shrugged. 'Been told that before. Put the gun down, you're not going to shoot me.'

'Don't count on it. When did you know it was me?'

'In the dining room earlier. You said yourself there are far easier ways of killing someone.'

'Then why didn't you say anything? You could have avoided this.' He waved the gun.

'I thought we could keep it between ourselves.' I shuffled to the edge of the bed, he flinched.

'What gave me away?' he asked.

'It could only have been you. I got the exact time of death from the fitness tracker. No one could possibly have got down that hatch at that time without me knowing. So how was a knife pushed into his chest? It could only have been you when you went in to check the body, you're the only other person that went in there.'

'But he'd been dead for a couple of hours by the time we arrived, you said yourself, you have the time of death.'

'Yeah, you stabbed a corpse that'd been cold since just after four a.m. A crime to cover up the real crime. What was it, cyanide?'

'You smelled it?'

'No, but his lips were flushed. I've seen it before on captured Tamil fighters in Sri Lanka. I didn't think anything of it at the time, but once I put two and two together and figured out it was the seasickness pill, it all followed. Clever, using that – knowing I'd happily see him alive when I sealed him in, tied to that chair, and the capsule would rupture in his stomach half an hour or so later when the gelatine broke down. Simple time-delayed poison. The knife was to throw me off, confuse the cause of death, make me think someone had broken in at any other time. In reality I'd been going to sleep in my bed while he was below me, tied to that chair suffering a heart attack.'

'Yes, those three men in South Africa were FZAA.' Doc took a step back, levelling the pistol. 'I have spent my life fighting racism, nationalism, fascism, every -ism you can shake a stick at. We may be a band of pirates, as you so eloquently put it, but we do not tolerate the likes of these people. They are animals. Worse, rabid animals. They need to be put down.'

I nodded. 'I didn't exactly go over to that yacht to have drinks with them.'

'Your friend from the Alps, if I hadn't done what I did, I suppose he'd have cut a deal with the government? Nice and cosy, amnesty for information. All sins forgiven, a new name on his passport and a bag full of money. It makes me sick.'

'Again, preaching to the vicar here, Doc.'

'Then why? Why transport him back to Britain?'

'I know it's a cliché, but the greater good. His inform-ation could have brought the whole group down, and others. And believe me, once that information was used up, he'd have had an accident anyway.' I didn't have the heart to tell him he'd murdered a treacherous mercenary, and that the real target was right now being interrogated in a secluded location outside London.

'Greater good,' Doc muttered. 'Well, I dare say the whole group has been brought down anyway now.'

'Does Miller know?'

He shook his head. 'No one. And I intend to keep it that way.' He waved the gun again.

'Like I said, you're not going to shoot. And I'm good at keeping secrets.'

He stared at me for a few heartbeats. I thought he was about to pull the trigger. Instead he smiled and released the grip, letting the pistol spin round his finger.

I stood, wincing, and held my bandaged hand out for it.

'I could have shot you.'

I pointed the gun towards the bed and squeezed the trigger. It clicked, I winked. 'Might have even killed me if it'd been loaded.'

He smiled again and sighed.

A knock came from the door, it opened. Marty poked her head in. 'Combe Wyndham ahoy, they're getting the crane ready.' Her eyes dropped to the pistol in my hand. 'Everything okay?'

'Peachy.' I slid out the empty magazine, replaced it with the half-full one in my pocket, pushed it into my waistband. 'Let's get off this stinking tub.'

Chapter Sixty-two

Combe Wyndham, South Devon

My car lurched as the straps pulled tight around it, buckling the aluminium front wings.

'So, you gonna tell me why the car's so special?' asked Miller.

I shook my head, stepping out of the bridge onto the wing to look at the slipways of the boatyard at the head of the small inlet. The secluded tidal creek offered the twin benefits of shelter and deep water, but a third benefit was the north bank, a mostly empty car park that ran right up to a harbour wall which, thanks to the tide, was only a metre or so above the deck.

Combe Wyndham was clearly a summer village. A warehouse across the water had been converted into a restaurant but its windows were all dark, there was no one to watch us. The terraces of houses climbing the hill behind were all in darkness too, likely second homes and holiday lets. I could see most of the old boathouses flanking the creek had been converted into boutique shops, though for every couple of shiny units there was one with a worn wooden door that still housed or repaired boats – though probably mostly pleasure craft these days. In summer, the tiny street would vibrate with middle-class holidaymakers from first thing in the morning until well into the night, but the Breton stripes had long since departed, the incessant drag and slap of Havaianas on cobbles replaced by howling gales and fat rain. I doubted anyone visited Combe Wyndham in winter.

The crane whirred with Katanga at the controls, water cascading from the car as it rose above the deck. Below it stood Nic, directing with his arms.

Miller stepped out onto the bridge wing. 'So I hate to keep asking, but…'

I leaned back on the railings. 'I've transferred the rest of the fee, including that bonus. Sorry about Vincent. Not Seb or Poubelle, but…' I shrugged.

'Wasn't you that killed him,' he said matter-of-factly.

Something caught my eye, I instantly went for my pistol but I was jumpy, it was just a dinghy bobbing in the water.

'Don't forget these,' said Doc with a sad smile as he pushed outside, holding out a pack of diamorphine.

I took it, looking past him as the dinghy floated through the glow from the work lamps on the deck. I was slow to realise it wasn't a dinghy, it was a jet ski.

Doc pushed me out of the way as gunfire tore the night air, I slammed against the railings and dropped. Bullets bounced against steel, glass shattered, everyone started shouting at once.

I rolled over, reaching underneath me, pulling out my pistol with my left hand, then quickly crawled backwards as bullets ripped through the steel mesh walkway, sparks flew, more glass rained down from the shattered bridge windows.

A shadow flashed behind the lifeboat davits at the stern, I fired several times then jumped up. Gunfire opened up again, I pocketed my gun and vaulted the railings, pushing off the top and leaping for the lifeboat.

I landed heavily, rolling across the tarp stretched across it, grabbing the edge with both hands and swinging off the other side, down under it. Both feet collided with Branko's huge back.

He grunted, stumbled forward, dropping his pistol. I pulled out mine, fumbling it in my bandaged hand and switching to my left. A gunshot exploded from somewhere above, I ducked, another crack and a second bullet ricocheted off the deck next to me. I turned to Branko in time to see a boot coming at my face. I took it across my back as I turned into him, using my momentum to knock him off balance. I brought my arm around to fire, a third gunshot cracked, I dropped to the deck and rolled away beneath the davits, looking up at a shadow sprinting along the harbour wall.

'Marty!' I yelled. 'It's me, for fuck's sake!'

She paused, crouched down behind the wall. 'Where is he?' she shouted.

I looked back, Branko had disappeared. 'He's gone forward, get round the other side!'

She ran away along the harbour wall. I jumped up, running forward. Above me, Miller was shouting instructions to his crew, Doc had disappeared.

I slammed against the superstructure, panting, switching my pistol back into my damaged hand and pressing the magazine release. It slid out, dropping to the deck while I fished out my last loaded mag with my good hand. Wrong one, I'd pulled out the empty mag I'd used on Doc. I reached back into my pocket as something flitted in the corner of my eye, I turned in time to see Branko launching from the shadows.

I ducked as a boathook smashed against the wall. I rolled, fumbling the pistol, still trying to pull out the last magazine. Branko chased me across the deck, swiping the big spiked pole after me, I rolled again, jumping to my feet just as he kicked out, it missed but his follow-up with the boathook didn't, he was lightning fast for a big fella. I stumbled, gritting my teeth and nursing my hand as my pistol spun away into the darkness. Branko grinned, raising the pole above his head, swinging round again. I dodged, letting the pole swoosh past then grabbing for it, using his momentum against him, trying to snatch it from his hands. I failed to get it off him, but as he yanked me forward I held on then jumped, kicking the pole sideways with both feet and letting go. I crashed to the deck, satisfied as I saw the boathook wrenched from his hands, sailing over the stern into space.

I crawled backwards, beneath the empty lifeboat davit. He was powering towards me, arms up. Unfortunate for him, since he hadn't seen what I had.

My fingers closed around a rope. It was tied off to a cleat welded into the deck, up into the davits, and back down to a heavy-looking hook bigger than Branko's head, suspended a few metres above the deck. That'd cave in anyone's skull, giant or not. I unhooked a loop of rope from the cleat and held on to it as Branko charged.

The deck shifted as a heavy vibration thundered through the ship, Miller was preparing to cut and run. I let go of the rope, it hissed through the pulley, the hook dropped towards Branko's head. He staggered with the sudden motion of the ship, the hook slammed to the deck harmlessly in front of him. He smiled and placed a massive boot on it, kicking out, sliding it towards me as if it were a football. It skittered across the slippery steel, hitting the gunwale next to my head.

Branko towered above me, silhouetted in the lights from the superstructure. Above him I could see people moving around on the bridge wing, I willed one of them to turn, to shoot the bastard in the back, but down here we were all but invisible to them.

I grabbed the rope and rolled away, leaping to my feet. The end was still tied in a heavy loop, I spun it round and flicked it towards him, stopping him in his tracks. He weaved side to side as I whipped the rope round to keep him at bay, scanning the deck for a better weapon, preferably one of our pistols.

We circled, every muscle tensed and ready, trying to anticipate each other's next move, all the while I could hear sirens growing in the distance. Behind him lights had come on in several buildings over the other side of the creek. The deck was shuddering as the engines reached full power, the creek churned below as the ship began to chew itself backwards. Branko bobbed and swayed with the motion of the ship, like a viper looking for an opportunity to strike.

Shadows tracked across us as the ship moved through the amber beam of a streetlight in the car park and there, not a metre from Branko's boot, was the instant game-stopper I was looking for: his glinting Desert Eagle. A poker player I am not: he saw my eyes drawn to it, looked down, lips curling up in a cross between a snarl and a grin.

He moved sideways, I whipped the rope round at his head. He paused, forced to duck and dodge the heavy rope, then spun, leg up, another kick to push me back. I blocked it easily, left forearm slamming his shin and flicking round behind it to grab his calf, trying to get him off balance. It worked, briefly, preventing him reaching down for the pistol, but with twice my mass and power there wasn't much more I could do. With my right hand I punched his outstretched thigh, the spot I'd stabbed him earlier, but he didn't seem to notice or care. For a split second I thought about going for a kick of my own between his legs, but by this stage I wasn't even sure he was human, and it would have put me within range of those huge paws. Instead I let go, slipping the loop of rope around his boot like a noose, pulling it tight as I let myself fall to the deck.

I rolled backwards and sprang back onto my feet, pulling the rope tighter. No chance, he laughed as his massive foot slid no more than an inch across the deck.

He bent to untangle himself from the rope. I took the opportunity to run for the stern of the ship, sliding onto my knees and grabbing the big iron hook. He saw what I was doing and lurched towards me but too late, I heaved the huge lump of metal onto the gunwale, then dropped it over the back of the ship.

The rope slithered across the deck, he watched with delayed reactions, eyes growing wider as the rope writhed. He panicked, bending down again, fingers scrabbling at the knot, but too late, the rope snapped taut. His boot was plucked from the deck as the rope stretched over the railings and down to the heavy iron hook under the surface.

He slid slowly sideways as the rope pulled on him, leg outstretched like a pose from a martial arts film. I was about to go in for the attack when he grinned and pulled his leg down, standing it firmly on the deck.

Of course the hook wasn't heavy enough to pull him overboard. It weighed only slightly more than a person, and the guy was a mountain.

He took a step sideways, dragging his boot across the steel, pulling the rope up from the sea.

I glanced round behind me. We'd moved away from the wall, I could just about see my car in the car park, Marty leaning on the railings at the top of the wall, shouting something to Miller on the bridge. Fight or flight? I turned back to Branko, weighed down by the rope tied to his leg but still shuffling across the deck. I needed to attack now, but getting too close would be lethal.

I spotted the range I needed in the shadow of the lifeboat davits, my HK pistol. My fingers closed around the magazine in my pocket. Unfortunately between the gun and me stood Branko, who was now bending over to untie the rope from around his ankle. He saw his own pistol just in front of him, and switched to pick that up instead as I backed away.

There was a grinding noise somewhere below, the deck shuddered. Branko brought the pistol up, still smiling, and squeezed the trigger.

His eyes went wide as he felt the sharp pull on his leg, lifting his foot into the air again. He didn't get a chance to fire the pistol as the tightening rope forced him to hop to the railings at the back of the ship. He reached the gunwale, his foot was yanked over the top, he screamed as he was forced to do the splits standing up, dropping the gun, nails tearing at his boot. His other leg was pulled tighter against the railings. He looked at me, eyes wide as the implication hit him. The moment stretched on, I couldn't pull my eyes away: there's something eerily beautiful about the look on a bastard's face when they realise they're dead. Their life, a million questions about what happens next, you can see it in their eyes even as they themselves can't comprehend it all. His mouth flapped but no sound came.

The rope pulled tighter, something cracked, his leg folded over the railings unnaturally. A deep rumble shook the deck as the propellers churned the sea below, tangled up in the rope, a crunching sound as Branko's leg was almost wrenched from its socket before he was dragged over the gunwale, out of sight.

I leaned over in time to see him thrashing in the water below. He looked up at me, finally making a sound, it started as a low moan and turned into a horrible scream that was abruptly choked off as he was yanked under the surface. Moments later a series of thuds from the prop jolted the ship.

'Tyler!' I looked up to see Miller stood on the bridge wing. 'I thought you'd split!'

I scooped up my gun and hobbled out from under the second lifeboat. 'Very much here.'

'Unless you wanna come back to France with us you better start swimming!'

Blue lights were flashing on the hillside, winding their way down into the village. I looked across at the car park, at the Audi's headlights. The ship began to turn, sliding sideways as it reached the entrance to the creek.

'Go!' shouted Miller.

With one last glance at the bridge I grabbed the railings and leapt over the side, into the sea.

I kicked away from the ship underwater, feeling the pull of its screws as it turned. When I broke the surface the harbour wall was only a few metres away, a ladder descended into the sea further along to my left. I swam for it, looking back at the *Tiburon* as she completed the 180-degree turn and poured on full power, slipping forward into the estuary that'd lead her back out to the Atlantic. Blue lights pulsed across the superstructure as police converged on the marina.

I climbed the rusty ladder, looking up at Marty as she hung down to help me. We tumbled over the top of the wall together, she ran for the driver's side of my car. The engine was running, passenger door already open.

'I drive!' I said.

'Don't be stupid. Get in.'

I looked down at the sodden bandages flapping off my hand, and limped for the passenger side.

Marty accelerated as I fastened my seatbelt. Thanks to the smashed passenger-side window I could just about hear the sirens above the snarling V8. I turned to look over my shoulder as the *Tiburon*'s lights blinked out. I could picture Miller on the bridge, tapping his foot to Led Zep as he pushed the throttles forward into the night.

Chapter Sixty-three

North Yorkshire

I took out my earphones and unplugged my iPhone from a cable snaking out of the glovebox.

'Well?' Marty asked, changing down into third for a roundabout. She looked the wrong way and accelerated, prompting a beep from a van coming up on our right.

'I think I should drive for a while,' I said.

'Relax, it's only roundabouts I can't get right.'

'There are a hell of a lot between here and home.' It was probably wise she continued to drive: my head was going. The pain had given way to a fuzzy pillowy feeling thanks to the three diamorphine tablets I'd necked half an hour back. I popped another two tablets from the packet and swallowed them.

'Take it easy on those, they're not aspirins.'

I tossed the box over my shoulder onto the back seat.

'So, did you get what you needed?' she asked.

I nodded. 'When Fields thought assassins had been sent to kill his old team he made four calls to warn them.' I threw the wires into the glovebox. 'I've got them all on here, the whole team responsible for my brother's death. Worked a charm.' I unplugged the USB cable from the box occupying the CD changer's usual place, the box I'd pulled out of the Porsche and installed in the Audi while hiding out in Ringo's garage near Geneva. A nifty piece of kit that was synced up to the satphone, it recorded both the audio and call information for every call into and out of the phone, storing it all on the hard drive for me to download at my leisure.

'And? Enough to track them down?'

'More than enough.' I smiled.

'You going after them straight away?'

I shook my head. 'I've got all the time in the world. What's next for you?'

'I'm gonna take a wild guess and say I'll be back in Afghanistan soon.'

The clock said eight a.m. I pointed to a retail park coming up on the left. 'Pull in here.'

The satphone buzzed in my pocket. I shuffled in my seat, took it out and looked at the screen. Holderness, for the fifth time. I waved the phone at a space next to a supermarket at the back.

I took off my seatbelt, waited for Marty to reverse into the spot, then climbed out and stretched. The birds were waking up in the trees, in front of us a steady stream of commuters were queuing at the bright lights of a Maccy's drive-thru. Drizzle hung in the headlights. I pulled up my hood and took out the phone to call Holderness back.

'Tyler! I've been trying to get hold of you for hours.'

'Takes a long time to drive to Yorkshire. Besides, it's Christmas Eve, I'm off work.'

'Don't get bloody smart with me, boy! I suppose that shoot-out in Combe Wyndham was nothing to do with you?'

'Not been down Devon for a while. Don't know anything about a shoot-out.'

'Or about the severed arm they found floating in the marina? Bloody cake and arse party.'

'Maybe I'm due one, seems to me I'm usually cleaning up your mess.'

'I can't help you this time, it's reached the wrong people. Consider this a warning.'

'A warning? The world's short of a few Nazis and you've got your top prize. I'd say that's a job well done, what's different this time?'

'Oh yes, all well and good, and I'm well versed in papering over your methods, Tyler.'

Marty frowned at me from behind the streaked windscreen. I rolled my eyes at her and sat on the bonnet to keep warm. 'So what's the problem?'

'I suppose it's a coincidence that this David Fraser, the fella you hired to be on your team in the Alps, worked for Cresswell?'

'Probably, they're one of the biggest defence contractors in Europe. A lot of people work for them.'

'Yes. Strange, though, that he worked for them in Afghanistan in 2011. In the same area where your brother...'

'Lot of contractors were working around there at the time he died.'

'Hmmm. And then a coincidence that nobody has heard from him for several days, and now this ex-Marine chap you requested as a replacement,' I could hear him shuffling paper, 'here he is, Fields. Worked at Cresswell at exactly the same time.'

I didn't say anything, could just hear Holderness on the other end getting more exasperated.

'Tyler, I'll be blunt. You specifically requested him for your Alps team, despite never crossing his path before. Well, God knows what you did to him, and frankly I don't care, but you then requested Fields, at short notice, to replace him. Doesn't take a genius to work it out, Tyler. You engineered this whole job into an opportunity to pursue a personal vendetta.'

I massaged my nose, rubbed my eyes. No point – he was spot-on, as usual.

'Well you've gone too far this time,' he continued.

'What does that mean? No more jobs? I've told you I was out after this one anyway.'

'No, Tyler. You've pissed off the wrong people. If I were you, I'd take some leave. Far away.'

I slid off the bonnet. 'Don't call me next time you have shit to clean up.'

I dropped the phone and stamped on it.

Marty wound the window down. 'Who was that?'

'Do you have to shoot straight off? It's Christmas Eve, you know.' I smiled and held up my bandaged hand. 'And I can't really cook a turkey on my own.'

She settled back into the seat. 'Well I guess I don't have to head off just yet.'

'In the meantime, can I interest you in a Sausage McMuffin and substandard tea?'

'Nothing that could wear sunglasses or shoes.' She turned the stereo back up and drummed on the steering wheel. 'And it's coffee. Black, like my metal.'

Something moved in my peripheral vision, my hand went straight for the pistol in my waistband before remembering it was in the passenger footwell. I turned, it was just a Vauxhall pulling up in a bay further over.

I smiled as I hobbled towards the golden arches. This was it, I was done, no rushing off to the next job, nothing to stop me from finding those four people Fields had called. *So this is how it feels to get all your debts paid.* I floated across to the takeaway rather than walked. Admittedly all that morphine may have had something to do with it.

Too slowly I noticed the commotion, the birds flapping out of the bushes – the window on the Vauxhall, a black space where it should have been. A faint outline inside, eyes watching. The grim circle of a gun barrel. I turned back to Marty. *They're taking it all from me…*

Marty was still drumming on the steering wheel, she hadn't seen, had no way to know what was coming. Perhaps that was best, I thought, as I started to run back towards her. The gun spat, it was supressed, the commuters queuing for their hash browns didn't hear it. Another *phut* of a supressed gunshot. I sprinted, desperate to outrun those bullets, to reach Marty before they did. The gun coughed again.

I tripped, rolling across the tarmac. Another gunshot, the Audi's V8 howled into life, a screech of tyres. Someone had stuffed cotton wool into my ears, my eyes faded in and out of focus. A wheel appeared next to my head. Louder gunfire exploded, close by, people started shouting, screaming, cars revving. A crash somewhere, horns blaring.

I got my senses back, climbed to my knees and pulled open the passenger door, slid inside.

'Use this!' Marty threw her pistol into my lap, turned the wheel and nailed the accelerator.

The Audi leapt forward, threading around two cars that had collided in an effort to get out of the car park. The Vauxhall accelerated behind us. Out onto the main road, I closed my eyes, panting, an alarm was going off somewhere. I opened my eyes to see a roundabout and cars screeching to a halt.

'Put your seatbelt on!' shouted Marty as she threw the car into a four-wheel drift the wrong way round the roundabout. She straightened up, weaving onto the wrong side of the road to overtake a stream of people heading for the dual carriageway.

'Are you hit?' I asked.

'What? No. Which way?'

I pointed up to the right. 'Outpace him on the ring road.'

My head was heavy, full of lead, I leaned it against the headrest.

Marty smacked me across the face. 'Put pressure on it!'

I didn't understand what she meant. I looked down, saw black blood pooling in my lap. I pulled up my T-shirt, saw a neat round hole oozing blood down onto my waist.

'Use both hands!' she shouted, dropping a gear to over-take someone. I watched a sixty road sign flash past.

'I don't have enough hands,' I mumbled, looking back down at three holes, dark on my pale skin.

I leaned back in the chair, closed my eyes, listened to the revving engine. Marty was shouting. Whispers crept in, slowly drowning both of them. Faces joined them, flashing through my mind, fading, darker and darker until everything was black.

Acknowledgements

A huge number of people have supported me with this book, but there are a few in particular I'd like to thank.

Jules, my first reader as always, who took his time to pull his helpful comments together and then we flew through them quickly so we could watch *The Mechanic*. Thanks in particular for the climbing stuff! Bob, who shared his early thoughts and helped lift it up, not least through abundant WhatsApping of typos in real time. Fordy, who constantly takes the piss and manages to somehow make it feel like he's supporting me. Burt for the boarding deets!

My elusive advisor on all things military, codenamed Jaz Carpet, for the little but important details. Just like *Anthrax Island*, anything I got wrong here was my error rather than his. The watch scene is a big tip of the hat to you, my friend!

Mari, always a cheerleader, and always incredibly supportive of others. Thank you so much for everything!

Phil, my agent, the best there is and always guaranteed to spot a reference. Forever on hand for stupid questions, and with an old or obscure film suggestion for every occasion.

My editor, Craig, whose help turned a rough manuscript into a book. It really saddens me that the editing comments are never seen by anyone else, because there were some real belters in there. Everyone else at Canelo that worked on my book, including Francesca, Nicola and Elinor. Thanks to Elodie and Miranda for some great catches, and Mark for a fantastic cover.

Vic Watson and Simon Bewick, masterminds of Virtual Noir at the Bar and Bay Tales. Thank you for giving people a platform and an opportunity to meet like-minded geeks. The first time anyone heard anything about *Black Run* is when Vic asked me to read an early extract at Virtual Noir at the Bar.

Rob Scragg, the first author to read *Black Run*. Thank you for the incredible support, look forward to meeting up again soon! Rob Parker, thanks for all the inspiration and kind words! And my circle of trust for keeping me sane through the year and for keeping me overweight.

Bloody Scotland, Theakston's Crime Fest in Harrogate, Newcastle Noir, and Hull Noir for providing opportunities for writers in the early stages of their careers. All the writers who've supported me and the bloggers, booksellers, and others who championed *Anthrax Island*, including Roxie, Russ, Effie, Chris, Mik, Dr Noir, Nick, Anna, Jonathan, Helen at Forum Books and The Bound, New Writing North, The Blood Brothers, the Northern Crime Syndicate, Barry, Tim, Gordon, Louise, Susi, Ian, Matthew, Shona, and many others.

As always, the best is last. Louby; the most supportive person I could possibly have on this ship with me, who is fortunately far better with words than I will ever be. XXX